ADVANCE PRAISE FOR

Broken Promises

"Very well-written and a pleasure to read, and presents an aspect of the Civil War saga that is out of the ordinary."
—DAVID J. LANGUM, SR., director of the Langum Prize

"Charles Francis Adams is an unlikely subject, best known as the son of John Quincy and father of Henry Adams. But he does have a story of his own to tell. . . . Hoffman recovers it with conspicuous grace and style in a work of historical fiction that brings the man and era to life with considerable sophistication and narrative flair."
—JOSEPH J. ELLIS, Pulitzer Prize–winning author of *First Family: Abigail and John*

"Writing with a novelist's panache and a historian's command of both context and detail, Elizabeth Cobbs Hoffman has written a stirring tale of diplomacy and intrigue in America's most precarious hour. . . . A compelling read and masterly history as well."
—DAVID M. KENNEDY, Pulitzer Prize–winning author of *Freedom from Fear*

"Full of life, with a little history on the side . . . refreshingly honest."   —Kirkus Discoveries

"*Broken Promises* delivers the best that historical fiction has to offer. . . . Hoffman navigates fictional waters 'as choppy and deep as those between England and America,' with an engaging and fluid styl[...]ng on facts and sch[...]

[...]*ling Emilie,*
...Daughter

BROKEN
PROMISES

BROKEN PROMISES

A NOVEL OF THE CIVIL WAR

ELIZABETH COBBS HOFFMAN

ORIGINALLY PUBLISHED AS
In the Lion's Den

BALLANTINE BOOKS TRADE PAPERBACKS

NEW YORK

2011 Ballantine Books Trade Paperback Edition

Copyright © 2009 by Elizabeth Cobbs Hoffman

Published in the United States by Ballantine Books, an imprint of The Random House Publishing Group, a division of Random House, Inc., New York.

BALLANTINE and colophon are registered trademarks of Random House, Inc.

Originally published in trade paperback as *In the Lion's Den* in the United States by iUniverse in 2009

Library of Congress Cataloging-in-Publication Data
Cobbs Hoffman, Elizabeth.
[In the lion's den]
Broken promises: a novel of the Civil War / Elizabeth Cobbs Hoffman.—
Ballantine Books trade pbk. ed.
p.   cm.
Originally published in 2009 as: In the lion's den.
ISBN 978-0-345-52455-3
eBook ISBN 978-0-345-52456-0
1. Adams, Charles Francis, 1807–1886—Fiction. 2. United States—History—
Civil War, 1861–1865—Fiction. I. Title.
PS3603.02315 2011
813'.6—dc22   2010041877

Printed in the United States of America

www.ballantinebooks.com

2 4 6 8 9 7 5 3 1

Book design by Victoria Wong

BROKEN PROMISES

ONE

MARCH 1861

Then came the outbreak which had been so often foretold,
so often menaced; and the ground reeled
under the nation.

—John Bright, member of Parliament and friend of the Union,
Speeches of John Bright, on the American Question

Charles Francis Adams curled his fingers around the armrest of the ancient mahogany chair, feeling for the familiar groove on the underside. Wearing a finely stitched suit from London, he sat erect and still, as his mother had taught him during dark, snowy afternoons in Russia, when winter's cocoon confined them to the solemn embassy for months. But his fingertips betrayed the anxiety beneath his exterior calm. The chair had been at the White House since his father was president. Generations of politicians and other favor-seekers had camped on the Regency velvet until the brown backing showed through like the fallow field in Quincy, mowed close to the sod. The emerald plush of the armrest was dry stubble now. The president's living allowance must be as puny as ever.

Charles silently traced the deep scratch he had worried countless times as a student, waiting for his father to invite him into the book-lined office and deepening the crack as only a bored child would. He was hardly that disheveled youngster anymore. Charles was nearly as old as his father, John Quincy, had been when he labored in the White House. At fifty-three,

Charles was two years older than the man who kept him waiting like a boy now.

He hoped, more intensely than he would have acknowledged even to Abby, who knew him better than anyone but his father, long dead, that the time would be well spent. He had anticipated this moment his entire life. Year after year, dreading the catastrophe, he still ached for the opportunity to prove himself. At last, the summons to history had arrived. It had been delayed so long that he almost ceased expecting it. Now, to distract himself, he concentrated on the flaw that meandered under his fingertips like the Charles River winding through cobblestoned Boston.

The door to the office opened abruptly.

"President Lincoln will see you, Mr. Adams," William Seward announced, poking his head through. Seward's words were as formal as his black wool suit, but he angled one eyebrow and flashed Charles a quick smile as he opened the door wide. "Charles," he added sotto voce, gesturing toward the inner office.

Seward's bushy white hair struggled against the pomade he used to press it flat. The thick tufts reminded Charles of the pompadour crest on the barnyard rooster back home. His old friend was only secretary of state, not president as the abolitionists had expected, yet he was still cock of the walk. Seward had let Lincoln stew in Washington's cook pot three long weeks before finally accepting the public offer of secretary. The brash New Yorker had enough nerve to equip two presidents. Charles knew no one else in politics with as much self-assurance, and he envied him.

"Good afternoon, Mr. Adams," the president said, barely glancing up from a stack of letters as Charles entered the room. A sheaf of telegrams spilled across the opposite corner of the desk. Lincoln waved a long hand at a chair across from him. "Take a seat, please. I'll be with you in a moment." He continued stabbing at the letters, signing his name in jerky bursts.

Charles studied the obscure Westerner whom fate had

elevated to the republic's highest office. It was the first time he had seen Lincoln up close, aside from shaking hands in the inaugural reception line, and he marveled anew, with no conscious disrespect, at the strange debris kicked up by the wheels of the American political process.

Lincoln's nomination had been a surprise. He had served one forgettable term in Congress a decade earlier and was just as homely as the newspaper artists sketched him, with a plain, plowed face. His beard softened the angular jaw, but it couldn't hide the deep furrows running under his prominent Indian cheekbones or the dark bruises around his sunken eyes. The man was as raw as the frontier. Lincoln made weather-beaten Andrew Jackson look like a Broadway dandy. Of all the presidents Charles had known—and he had known most of them—none seemed so unfinished.

God help us, Charles thought. If appearances meant anything, the man was as fit to be president as the Quincy blacksmith—though probably less inured to the heat.

Lincoln finally pushed aside the last letter with the tip of his index finger. He wore a black broadcloth coat, tight across the shoulders, and his wrists stuck out from the cuffs. He sat at the Louis XVI table as he would a school desk, angled sideways to fit his knees. The spacious office shrank around the gangly Kentuckian, who now looked expectantly at Charles.

"Mr. Adams. Secretary Seward tells me the Senate has accepted your appointment as minister to England. It looks like Congress has seen fit to give us our way—for once."

Clasping his hands behind his head, the president leaned backward in a long, slow stretch. His cuffs hoisted themselves higher on the bony wrists, and the buttons quivered against the strain, ready to pop. Charles noticed that one was sewed on with white thread, the other with brown. Lincoln's gray eyes bore down on him. He wondered what plan Lincoln had devised for handling Great Britain. It would have to be ingenious.

Charles leaned forward, deferent but poised. He knew he looked every bit the Boston Brahmin for which most people took him, the elegant embodiment of America's only aristocracy and its severe, Puritan rectitude.

"So it seems, sir. Even the opposition hardly objected. It was most gratifying, especially in light of our present circumstances." Charles paused, but Lincoln remained silent, watching. "I would like to thank you for your confidence, Mr. President, and for the appointment," he continued. "I've studied the issues closely. It will be tough to bring St. James's to our side, but I believe we can do it. As you know, my father and grandfather occupied the same position."

Charles stopped himself from saying more. The chronicler in him wanted to add that they, too, served in desperate times. Grandfather had bearded the British lion after the Revolution and toasted the king who had earlier threatened to hang him from a yardarm in Boston Harbor. Thirty years later, Charles's father signed the peace treaty that ended the War of 1812—the second time that mighty paw had knocked America sprawling. Charles was third in his line to act as minister to the Court of St. James's. A direct descendant of the American Revolution.

But he held his tongue. To anyone outside the family, it was ancient history. The worn tale would reveal only vanity. "Beware of pride, Charlie," Grandfather had cautioned. "Strive to be useful. God alone is our witness." Besides, Lincoln would be well aware of his family's long association with these matters.

With his hands still clasped behind his head, the president now swiveled to look at Seward, causing the chair's iron mechanism to bray in protest. The secretary of state was studying a patch on the ceiling as if looking far into the future, where no one else could see. Lincoln glanced from Seward to Adams, taking the measure of one man against the other. He then placed his hands on the table with a deliberate air, and responded, "Very kind of you to say so, Mr. Adams. But there's no need to thank me. You're not my choice. You're Seward's man. I've no claim on you a'tall."

Lincoln pursed his full lips, perhaps aware that this statement was hardly a compliment, and then smiled. "I reckon you'll do just fine, though," he added. "England can't have much interest in our affairs. When can you sail?"

Years of training repaid Charles in an instant. Dismay might have shown on a less controlled man, but he had governed the display of his emotions since the age of six. All the ladies in St. Petersburg had commented upon it: a miniature diplomat. Old before he was out of short pants. The more intensely Charles felt, the more unemotional he appeared, as drum-tight as a Chinese cabinet.

"I'll be ready for London in two weeks, sir," Charles answered, his level tone unchanged. "I've already turned the family farm in Quincy over to my eldest son."

"That'll do, then," the president said, a faint twang in his tone. "Mr. Seward will send your instructions presently."

"He will *send* my instructions?" Charles spoke with more emphasis than he intended. Despite his low-tide opinion of Lincoln, it simply hadn't occurred to him that the president wouldn't want to discuss the looming dangers. If not now, when? Once the Royal Navy turned its lethal broadsides on America's paper fleet? Was Lincoln aware that Europe crouched in the shadows while the country careened toward war? He couldn't imagine why else Lincoln would have requested a meeting. "That is, surely you wish to discuss my instructions before I leave?" Charles said.

"This is not an opportune moment, Mr. Adams," the president said, waving his hand at the stacks of documents. One slipped sideways in the breeze and drifted to the carpet, but the president appeared not to notice. Seward bent over, then put the paper back on the desk.

"With respect, sir, don't you wish to apprise me of your plan? The queen's ministers will surely demand an explanation of our blockade. Blockades are permissible only against a foreign enemy, and yet we assert that the Confederacy remains part of the United States. It's a contradiction. Perhaps even illegal."

Charles pressed his lips together, damming the other arguments that threatened to flood forth. He mustn't appear to be instructing the president—a member of the bar, dear God—on the finer points of maritime law. Massachusetts had best be careful lecturing Kentucky. Charles knew that more than a few Westerners—whose ancestors had braved the Appalachians for the wilds of the Ohio Valley—were tired unto death of pontificating New Englanders and the fiery rhetoric that had brought the country to the brink of destruction on which it now trembled.

"I wish I had something to tell you, Mr. Adams, but there are any number of matters that require attention at the moment. Washington is in a perpetual hurry. Appointments to be made. The army to organize. I must skip to catch up. Mr. Seward will send your instructions as soon as possible." Lincoln's expression was mild but unyielding.

Seward redirected his gaze from the ceiling to Charles. "Indeed," he confirmed with half-hooded eyes. The secretary of state stood topmast straight, his expression enigmatic.

Charles knew what Seward thought. No instructions meant no plan. The president was incapable of subtle strategy or decisive action, and he had all the savoir faire of the Mississippi River boatman he had been a few decades earlier. Seward had implied as much over breakfast a few days earlier at Willard's Hotel, around the corner from the White House. The secretary wasn't explicit, but he shook his head as he diced his sausage and eggs, reluctant to report all the gaffes from which he had had to rescue his unsophisticated superior.

Lincoln unfolded a lanky arm and handed Seward a letter from the sloping pile on his desk. "Now here's something. I do believe I have solved the vexatious problem of the Chicago Post Office," he said with a satisfied air. "We'll give it to the fellow from Peoria who lost his seat last November. A perfect spot for him to land. Like a bullfrog on a lily pad."

"Excellent, sir," Seward said. He glanced at Charles and gave a quick nod of dismissal. Apparently the interview was over.

Charles excused himself, though Lincoln hardly looked at him again. The president and Seward had moved on to other matters. Charles walked out with a dazed feeling, blinded by memories. In what was once the family office, someone neither familiar nor familial now occupied the seat of power.

Seward's man. The short phrase cut to the bone. He was no one's man, Charles thought, stunned at the implication. Appointed to the Court of St. James's—America's slyest enemy—and then dismissed as casually as a two-bit party hack. Like an office-seeker. An Adams. In the same breath as the Chicago Post Office. It was mortifying. And what about his instructions? How could he sail without them?

His own concentrated, intense father had toiled over every detail of strategy, every line of his correspondence, every crinkle in the boundary lines that he wrested from Spanish negotiator Don Luis de Onís. The Adams-Onís treaty of 1821 took the United States clear to the Pacific Ocean. Did Lincoln have any idea what it was like to deal with a great power? Did he understand what they were up against, as he allowed the country to drift rudderless into war? If Great Britain lent her warships to the South, as France had aided the colonies in 1776, they would cleave the country into kindling. And how could Charles possibly implement Lincoln's strategy when the man did not have one? Seward was right. The Kentuckian was unequal to the hour, leaving so much to chance.

Charles stopped at the old mahogany chair in the hushed anteroom and looked up at the oil portrait of his grandfather that hung above it. His grandfather's face looked down as dignified as ever, but Charles thought he caught a glint of amused irony playing around the familiar blue eyes. John Adams had endured a whole cabinet of men handpicked by the rival who wanted his job. Like Seward, the imperious Alexander Hamilton couldn't let go of the idea that he was the one who really ought to have been president, and Grandfather never knew whom to trust.

A small sigh escaped Charles's lips. His shoulders drooped like an abandoned Punch doll. Perhaps the "prairie statesman," as Seward had branded Lincoln when they were both vying for the Republican ticket, was reticent for a reason. Lincoln couldn't have traveled this far without being something more than he appeared.

Was the president keeping a safe distance in case Charles fell flat on his face? In all truth, Charles thought, forcing himself to look at the situation from another's point of view, he was an office-seeker. And with the appointment to St. James's, Lincoln had given him the opportunity, at long last, to be useful—the one thing he coveted.

Charles's mouth tightened. But he would never, not ever, be *Seward's man.* He was an Adams. If he couldn't speak on Lincoln's authority, then vanity be damned. He would speak for the two ancestors who had bequeathed him a nation to defend. He wouldn't let them down.

He squared his shoulders. Steadied by the sermon, the new minister to Great Britain gave his grandfather a curt nod, drew up every inch of his average frame, and strode purposefully from the White House.

TWO

JUNE 1861

The South fight for independence;
but what do the North fight for, except to
gratify passion or pride?

—Sir George Cornewall Lewis, Secretary of War,
to Viscount Palmerston, Prime Minister

A flapping of yellow outside the window caught Julia's eye. The broad-shouldered poultrymonger wore an old dun greatcoat and a tattered but very bright woolen muffler whose ends danced together in the wind. The kitchen girl was shaking her head dubiously at the pale chicken that he held up by its sorry drumsticks. A gust kicked up the canary scarf again, and the merchant shoved it between the tarnished buttons of his coat. He leaned closer to the flustered servant, obscuring her slight figure while he gestured with his blunt free hand toward the plucked bird.

Julia draped her book over the brocade arm of the sofa to save her place and took up a paisley-patterned shawl that had slipped to the carpet. Cook must have left Nettie in charge of ordering provisions for the dinner that Father was giving the Confederate emissary. But the girl couldn't be expected to pick the best birds, and Sir Walter Birch was anxious for the soirée to go well. There was business to be had.

She stepped out into the chill, bluish light of an unseasonably frigid morning and walked briskly down the stoop. She was tall, with an unconscious aura of command. A cushiony softness to the cut of her chin revealed that she wasn't far from her teens, but she ran Belfield Manor as if she slept with *Mrs. Beeton's Household Guide* under her pillow, determined to get every detail just so. Julia now pulled her wrap close against the frost that pierced the thin fabric.

"Good morning, Mr. Penfield. What have you brought us today?" she asked. Her breath blew back at her like smoke in the cold air.

"Ah, Miss Birch," the husky man said, drawing back on his heels. "I was showing your girl here some fine, fresh birds we just got in from the countryside. She said you'd be wanting four today. I have just the ones: four beauties."

Julia glanced at the slat-sided poultry cart. A canvas tarp covered the wares to protect them from London's sooty skies. The merchant's daughter Mary sat on an upturned crate in the back, minding the merchandise. It made Julia sad to see her there. The girl used to lead the horse herself. She had earned respect among the housekeepers on Pembroke Lane for refusing to discount her prices yet selling quality birds in return. "Quite the lady, that one," Cook had sniffed. "Thinks she's the queen of Bond Street."

But Julia rather liked the saucy, freckle-faced girl who drove her own cart and pitted her wits against the Praetorian matrons of Mayfair. Mary and she were about the same age. When the girl expertly wheedled an extra sixpence from Cook for a particularly fine brace of partridges, ones that wouldn't look bad on a table in Buckingham Palace, Julia hadn't bothered to smother a smile at the girl's triumph. Cook was ferocious with a penny. And then Mary was gone without explanation, replaced for most of the winter by her father, whose set face and short answers gave everyone to understand that questions about his daughter's absence were neither welcome nor necessary. Today she was back with a bundle on her lap.

"That's right, we need at least four," Julia said. She turned her back to Penfield. "Nettie, could you please show me the ones you've picked?"

"Yes, miss. Mr. Penfield thought these would be good."

Julia looked at the plucked birds that the merchant had arranged on a clean plank. They were meaty, but the pocked skin under the wings looked wrinkled and papery, and the yellowing breast had lost its sheen. She pressed a practiced thumb into the thigh of the nearest bird, leaving behind a sad dimple. The color blanched not at all.

"Mr. Penfield, these are a good size, but they don't look as fresh as I would like."

Julia lifted her eyes and caught Mary's gaze. The girl was silent. "Mary," Julia asked, "don't you have something better we could look at?"

Before the young woman could answer, her father cut in.

"Don't be minding Mary, Miss Birch. The stupid girl has a brat to look after now. These birds were butchered before dawn. You can't get anything fresher than that." The merchant lifted a carcass. "Feel the heft of this," he offered, wrapping a piece of clean linen around the bird. "Near the size of a goose, with meat as tender as a gosling. Practically still warm."

Julia's eyes narrowed. A provident, conscientious God would have given liars red hair or a third eye. "No, thank you, Mr. Penfield," she said. "I believe we'll just wait until tomorrow. Cook can serve fish tonight before the beef."

"Oh. Wait now." Penfield turned toward his daughter, as if he had just thought of something. "Mary. Where did you put those other birds, the ones from Murphy's farm?"

Her arm crooked securely around the baby, Mary bent over to lift the rear of the tarp. "They're back here, Father," she said.

"Ach, you haven't a brain in your head! Didn't I tell you to put them up front? You're plain worthless, you are."

Penfield shook his head with exasperation and climbed up onto the wagon. He leaned over, deftly scooped up the chickens, and plumped them on the raw board. The new birds were far superior to the ones he had shown Nettie, as any fool could see.

"These will do nicely, Mr. Penfield. We'll take them. At the usual price," Julia said.

"Well now, sorry about that, Miss Birch. I wish I could. But these ones are considerably more."

Julia raised her eyebrows as if perplexed. "Why is that, Mr. Penfield? They are the same size as the others. I assume they were also butchered this morning—practically still warm and all."

She knew she had him in a corner and was pleased that he had walked into it so readily. His petty swindling rubbed like a cocklebur between stocking and shoe—as did the way he spoke to Mary.

"Well, it's just that old Murphy charges such a dear price," Penfield protested. "He's close to town. Knows he can drive up the cost. A real Jew."

"Then you'll have to strike a better bargain with Murphy, Mr. Penfield. We won't accept anything less than the best quality, and we won't part with more than a fair price—as in the past."

That should set him straight on which member of the Penfield family it was whose marketing she preferred.

Julia turned to Nettie, who was observing the exchange with round-eyed attention. "Please pay Mr. Penfield, Nettie," she instructed. "Good day," Julia said with a nod.

Penfield frowned, but reached into the back of the cart for a piece of sacking to wrap the birds. Julia looked over his bent shoulders at Mary.

The girl didn't speak, but shot a rapid glance at her father and then at Julia. The shadow of a conspiratorial smile flickered across her face. Julia crooked one eyebrow discreetly.

The merchant grumbled something under his breath that Julia couldn't hear and didn't want to. She turned to let Nettie complete the purchase. The kitchen girl took the shillings out of the pantry coin purse and counted them on the plank one at a time.

Once indoors, Julia picked up her book, slipped off her shoes, and settled back into the deep sofa. But instead of reading she gazed out at the beech tree scratching cobwebs in the hoarfrost on the windowpanes. It was the first time Julia had seen Mary since the baby came—no husband in view, no ring to make it right. Mary would get nothing but abuse from her father for her mistake.

No one else would be any more charitable, Julia reminded herself, trying to be fair. Penfield must have been humiliated beyond endurance—a respectable merchant with a hussy for a daughter. Mary was irretrievably ruined. Most people would consider her lucky to be allowed to help from the back of the wagon; at least her father hadn't turned her out onto the street to starve.

Goose bumps climbed Julia's arms and she shivered. She couldn't imagine emotions so compelling that they would tempt one to such a wild, unguarded act, at odds with family and fortune. French novelists called it *la passion*—feelings that led a girl to hurl the future into the fire with both hands. Julia couldn't envision any young women of her acquaintance taking that risk; yet, despite the terrible consequences, some obviously did.

Julia wondered if she would ever have to struggle against such a head-turning, judgment-defying infatuation. It seemed there was little fear of that happening. Unfortunately.

Just then the door to the morning room swung open with a soft push, and her father strode in with a newspaper under his arm. Sir Walter Birch wore an impeccable frock coat of fine Scottish wool that suited his silver hair and dark eyes.

"Ah, you're alone. I thought you would be instructing Mr. Thomas about the seating arrangements," Walter said. His voice resonated with the elevated, rounded tone of an Eton education, acquired in youth. "It's an important occasion, don't forget."

"Good morning, Father," Julia said with a smile, rising to her feet. She put her book down again and crossed the room to kiss his lined cheek. "I took care of that yesterday. We went over everything. I gave Mr. Thomas strict instructions not to sit any Tory near a Whig lest they skewer each other's livers before the second course."

"Very amusing, my dear. Just be sure that you seat Captain Bulloch near my end of the table, and your uncle somewhere in the vicinity of Wales."

"Yes, Father," Julia said. Her smile faded. She didn't want to engage him on the subject of her mother's brother, whom her father cordially disdained, partly for the liberal causes in which he was active and that Sir Walter thought ludicrous—from granting the vote to working men to reforming the laws that deprived married women of property to abolishing the poorhouses. A committed bachelor, Randolph Barclay doted upon Julia as the very image of his sister Constance, and his niece adored him in return. Unfortunately, neither her father nor her uncle was inclined toward compromise on their differences. Points of argument were like cue balls, meant to send the colored ivories caroming across the cloth to sink a point.

"Who is Captain Bulloch?" she asked instead, as she took her seat on the sofa. Her father sat down on the divan opposite and crossed his long legs comfortably. "Is he part of the Confederate delegation?"

"He's not an official representative," Walter said, already unfolding his newspaper, "but he's in charge of building their fleet on the quiet. I'm hoping he'll take a look at the Laird shipyards. Counting on it, in fact."

"What do you mean, on the quiet?"

"Everything has to be confidential. Private merchants are not allowed to sell warships to the Southerners. The neutrality law, you know."

Julia cocked her head in query, and he explained, "Merchants aren't supposed to supply belligerents who are fighting a country with whom the queen is at peace."

A small frown collected between Julia's eyebrows. "But then how can you sell him ships? Isn't it against the law?"

Walter set aside the paper. "There are ways around, my dear—but make sure you don't ask such sticky questions at dinner. Everyone in London is vying for the Confederates' business. Lincoln's blockade off the American coastline means that prices will go through the roof. Mind you, just last week Sir Geoffrey sold a hundred thousand brass buttons for a profit of five hundred percent. He says the brass on gray is quite handsome."

Warming to his subject, he leaned forward. "But even prettier is the profit on steamships. My only worry is that we'll get the keels down for merely a handful of vessels before the whole unpleasantness blows over."

He gave a short laugh, but then sighed and looked far away for a moment, as if contemplating a fond, distant dream, and the hush of the well-insulated house fell upon the room. "Too bad it won't be a long war."

Julia knew only a little about her father's financial affairs, but she was aware that his portfolio was enviable. Profits from shipbuilding, cotton textiles, and the rent of country tenants meant that she need spare little expense on her father's frequent entertainments. He replenished the household account without comment.

"Do you think the United States will split apart, then?" she asked, curious.

"Undoubtedly. The Federals can't hold half the country hostage. The South is bigger than all of Europe." Walter dismissed the American nation with a wave of his hand. "It's *kaput*, as the queen's German cousins say."

Her father suddenly smiled, revealing deep dimples, and his black eyes sparkled with a boyish mischief that belied his sixty-plus years. "Oh, how I wish your grandfather were here," he said.

"America's position is absurd. Half of her citizens have voted to secede in defense of their inalienable rights, and the other half are trying to rob them of the privilege. It's democracy at its finest—mad as ever!" He boomed with laughter.

Julia nodded. The United States' position did seem ridiculous, like so much about the country that her father considered an unbearable upstart. But she couldn't help recalling her uncle's position on slavery, with which she agreed.

"But won't that mean slavery will go on?" she asked.

"I suppose so, but that's not really our business. We can't reform the world, my dear, and it's utter folly to try. Parliament ended slavery in all of England's colonies thirty years ago. We've cleaned our house; let others clean theirs."

They both looked up at a soft knock as Mrs. Worthy entered the room, gave a deferential bob in Sir Walter's direction, and turned expectantly to Julia. Her round face was pink and shining. The heavyset housekeeper was a loyal, pleasant woman upon whom Julia had depended since her mother died many years before, leaving behind not only a husband and a seven-year-old daughter but an infant son as well, Julia's brother, Edmund. Mrs. Worthy and the efficient Mr. Thomas were as reliable as clocks.

"Excuse me, miss," Mrs. Worthy said in her comforting West Country accent. "At what time would you like your tea this morning?"

Julia looked inquiringly at her father.

"I'm on my way to the club in just a few minutes," he said. "Don't bother."

"Only a cup for me, then, Mrs. Worthy, when Nettie can be spared. And only the tea, please. I'm not hungry right now."

"Yes, miss," Mrs. Worthy said, and exited with another short curtsy to the master of the house.

Julia had wanted to keep her uncle out of the conversation, but she was uneasy at the thought of her father's new business partners. It hadn't occurred to her that Englishmen would undertake to supply the slaveholders whose rebellion had made all the London papers. "Uncle Randolph says that if Lincoln holds the country together, he might just abolish slavery. Do you really think that we, I mean, Britain, should supply the South? The Rebels traffic in human souls, after all."

Walter's eyebrows shot to his hairline and he snorted. "Hah! No one believes the fight is about slavery except Randolph and a few misty old maids. Really, that's terribly naïve. Randolph has it all wrong—as usual. The war is about wounded pride, like most wars, and both sides will empty out their treasuries to make the other side heel. Of course, British merchants will have to be careful not to get snagged in the blockade. But I believe our ships would sail into hell at the risk of singeing their sails if they could make a profit."

"What happens to those who are caught? Surely they can't be arrested for a barrel of brass buttons?"

Walter leaned forward again, picked up a Dresden shepherdess that was on the tea table, and set her down at a distance from a flock of ceramic lambs. "You see, the American president has announced a blockade. In essence, any ship, no matter what it is carrying, is expressly forbidden to enter a Southern port." He traced a line between the figurines. "The blockade runs like this down America's Atlantic coastline. Any British captain who crosses that line risks his entire cargo if the U.S. Navy catches him. They'll confiscate it immediately."

"But won't you lose money?" Julia asked. "And won't the blockade put our sailors at risk?"

"No. The cargoes that get through make up for those that we lose. And losses are only financial so long as the merchant is foreign. The Americans won't dare imprison a British citizen. Rebels are a different matter, of course. They might be strung up for treason, for all I know—but that's not my concern. And I am

placing most of my investment in ships. They're harder to confiscate than cargo, so my money should be safe. I don't plan to lose
one more farthing to the bloody Yanks."

Walter patted one coat pocket, and then the other, as if the
talk of money reminded him of something in them. Finding
what he wanted, he drew out a small velvet box. "Enough about
business. You really shouldn't concern yourself with these matters, Julia. Make sure the soup is hot at supper and your father
will be a happy man." He opened the box. "Here, now. I had it
resized. You must wear your present tonight."

Julia smiled with delight and reached forward to take the old-
fashioned signet ring, set with an oval ruby surrounded by diamonds. It was the one her mother wore in the portrait that hung
in the staircase. "Thank you, Father," she said. "I was wondering
if you had forgotten." She placed the heavy ring on her right
hand.

"Of course not. Twenty-one is an important milestone. Your
grandmother brought that ring back from America—the only
piece of jewelry she managed to keep. Now that you're old
enough to be mistress of this house, it's yours. May you wear it in
health for many years."

Julia lifted her hand to catch the morning light with the polished gems. Sparks of blue light jetted off the small diamonds.

The ring was all she had left of her mother and grandmother,
and she had looked forward to placing it on her hand. But her
father's comment now made her uneasy, like an unexplained
squeak of a floorboard in the night, and it took her mind off the
war across the sea and the plight of the slaves whose future was
still undecided. She was twenty-one, a delicate age in a world
where marriageable women far outnumbered eligible men. For
how many more years would she be mistress of Belfield Manor?
Would she ever have a life beyond it? Her father's words weren't
the first to make her wonder.

THREE

*European rulers for the most part fought and treated as members
of one family, and rarely had in view the possibility
of total extinction; but the Governments and society of Europe,
for a year at least, regarded the Washington Government
as dead, and its Ministers as nullities.*

—Henry Adams, *The Education of Henry Adams*

Charles Francis Adams looked up blindly, searching for the right word. A return to monarchy at this stage would be . . . inauspicious? Inappropriate? Asinine? How to tell yet another ill-informed bystander that America's form of government was none of his goddamn business?

He sighed. A mountain of mail had greeted him when he arrived in London a few weeks earlier with his wife and children. There were only a few pieces left, but he had put off the silliest to the end. Even these must be addressed with flawless courtesy. Charles had devoted the entire rainy afternoon to them. It was a taste of purgatory.

He glanced over at the opposite desk. His son Henry was tackling the legation's accounts, sorting through the backlog of receipts from the fishmonger, victualler, baker, and landlord. Henry's older brother was drilling with the Massachusetts militia in Boston while Henry was stuck tallying pounds and pence as Charles's private secretary. It couldn't be any twenty-three-year-old's idea of adventure, but the good boy hadn't complained once. The two younger children, Mary and Brooks, had also settled dutifully to their books and foreign tutors. They were Adamses.

"Henry," Charles asked, "how do I tell this man that a resumption of monarchy in the United States would be utterly ridiculous without implying that *he* is?"

Henry looked up, eyes bright, evidently pleased to be solicited for his opinion. "How about 'incongruous,' Father? Monarchy is incongruous with our constitution?"

"Yes, that's good. Incongruous," Charles repeated. "Thank you." He turned back to his letter.

After a long moment, Henry cleared his throat and Charles looked up again.

His son hesitated, but then said in a clear voice, "Father, I meant to tell you that I overheard yesterday that the Confederate envoys were invited to nearly every party this season. It was all the talk at the opera. The merchants are actively wooing them."

"That's hardly surprising. They arrived in London before we did," Charles observed.

Henry shook his head. "No. It's more than that. They enjoy genuine popularity. Several people said that the foreign secretary plans to extend diplomatic recognition by the end of the week."

"Well, son, that would be but a short step from the position Lord Russell took when he proclaimed the queen's neutrality a month ago," Charles said calmly, as if discussing a change in conductor at the symphony, or the newest plantings from Australia at Kew Gardens. "But Russell is much too clever to go further than neutrality at the moment. He knows that any explicit indication of partiality to the South would provoke a hostile response from Lincoln. Seward might break off relations. And the British want eager customers on both sides. Wars are good business, after all."

"But what will we *do* if Lord Russell does recognize the independence of the Confederate States?"

Henry looked at his father as if the elder Adams ought to have the answer. Charles recognized the expression. He himself used to wear it long ago, before he knew better. "As you are aware from the account books, I've engaged the house only month-to-month," Charles replied. "If the British choose sides—and we will have to take it as an expression of extreme hostility to our country if they bless the Confederacy—then we'll be forced to leave. Fortunately, we won't have to make good on a year's lease. The Adams fortune could hardly withstand it."

He gave a half smile, since there was no Adams family fortune, as Henry well knew. Charles's wife, Abigail, heiress to the Brooks empire, had brought considerable wealth into their marriage, but it wasn't the Adams legacy, which was a heap of unpaid bills, the outdated homestead in Quincy, and an overdeveloped sense of duty embellished with Puritan self-doubt. Charles had taught his children to watch expenses with a farmer's cautious eye.

Of course, he understood what Henry meant. Everywhere they went—to the theater, private clubs, or even for a stroll on the green—they overheard confident predictions of the stunning breakup of the United States. There hadn't been any new fighting since April, when South Carolina troops forced the federal government to surrender Fort Sumter, but both sides had been drilling and provisioning furiously. Hardly a single member of high society failed to assume that President Jefferson Davis had launched a new nation and that the northern United States deserved to lose to his rebel army.

British matrons clucked over the news like the long-awaited birth of a first grandchild. Businessmen snapped up Confederate bonds as a sharp buy. Aristocrats pointed to the folly of democracy and laughed up their gold lace sleeves at the spectacle of the United States putting down, yes, a war of independence. Even the House of Commons, the voice of the people, had entertained a motion—tabled, thank God—to recognize the Confederacy and the bursting of "the great Republican bubble." They were all so very glad to see the United States brought low, and their own government confirmed by contrast.

England, France, Spain—all Europe stood watching the

brawl unfolding across the Atlantic, decrying the bloodletting while placing their bets on the Confederacy to make old Sam cry Uncle. It was stated as fact each and every day in the British newspapers: The South was too big and too determined to restrain. By saying so, they might soon make it so.

Lincoln and Seward hadn't helped, either. After sending Charles and his family halfway across the world, the State Department had finally deigned to send explicit instructions to its new minister. In them, William Seward directed Charles to tell Foreign Secretary John Russell that America would break off all diplomatic relations if the Brits spoke again with the Confederate representatives, whom they had already received twice, albeit unofficially. President Lincoln apparently toned down Seward's text before forwarding it, allowing the American minister to use his discretion in communicating the ultimatum. Charles had expressed said discretion by pocketing the damned note. If he had delivered the reckless threat, Her Majesty Queen Victoria's proud ministers would have invited the Confederate diplomats to tea and crumpets within the day.

The United States could have war with England in five minutes flat if they wanted it. All the Federals had to do was twist the Lion's tail hard enough. The British were punctilious about defending their honor.

Sometimes Charles hardly knew what to think. Perhaps Seward did want war. Rumors were flying about that he was urging Lincoln to start a foreign war to divert attention from the civil conflict. An external threat might derail secession. It might even bring quarreling brothers back together in a fight against their common enemy, the eternal redcoats. Charles wondered if the secretary of state could really be that Machiavellian. He wouldn't put it past him.

"You see, the British are confident we will fail, and so are content to wait," Charles said, picking up the thread again, aware that he hadn't really responded to Henry's concern. "They see no point in tying the noose if we are going to hang ourselves anyway. So we must wait, too. Let's hope for an early Federal victory."

"I wish I had your aplomb, Father," Henry said. "I feel rather like chucking an inkpot at the next man who tells me the Union is a dead letter. I don't see how we can win with the whole world against us. I suppose I'm upset because I felt sure that in a fight against slavery the British would have to take our side."

"Why should they take our side?" Charles asked. "They never have before."

"But they've led this crusade. How can they turn their backs on us now?"

Charles put down his pen and interlaced his fingers. "Henry, our family has been trying to teach the English aristocracy its larger interests for virtually a hundred years. It cannot be done. They have opposed slavery since 1807. But Lincoln has said the war is not about slavery, so they agree, despite every stitch of evidence to the contrary. The British mind is the slowest of all minds. One might as well read Dante to a mule."

Henry's worried expression evaporated and he laughed out-right. The change lightened Charles's spirit. He loved to see his son happy. It was a tonic.

"Father," Henry asked, "would you mind very much if I fin-ished these accounts tomorrow? The rain seems to be stopping; I think a walk would do me good."

"Not at all. Take the grand tour. Enjoy yourself."

Charles watched his son gather the ledger books and hustle from the room. When the clock's ticking became the only sound once more, the minister allowed himself to ruminate over the worst possibilities suggested by Henry's observations, the ones he hesitated to tell the boy. The loss of a year's rent was the least of them.

Britain's colonies dotted two-thirds of the globe. At the ring of a silver bell she could command the resources of the world, brought in by ships that vied for space at docks from Glasgow to

Liverpool to Southampton, loaded to their gunwales with tea, ceramics, silk, and cotton from India, China, and America. Masts filled the harbors with a swaying forest of varnished Swedish pine. Foundries cast cannons, muskets, and swords in the hardest iron and steel. Entrepreneurs had transformed London from the dirty city of his itinerant childhood into a paved, efficient metropolis with trains and telegraphs. Britain was the most modern nation in the world, and by far the most frightening.

He inhaled sharply and pressed his eyelids closed. He dreaded what would happen if Great Britain succeeded in arming the Confederacy, or went so far as to launch her invincible fleet against the Union. America would be pulverized. Ground to rags. A beaten United States, her potential halved, would suit the British Empire just fine. America's third conflict with the greatest power in the world, in the midst of a ruinous civil war, would be her last as one nation.

It must not happen, Charles thought, flexing his hands into fists before composing them again in the diplomat's habitual posture of calm. He must make sure that it didn't, or at least postpone the clash until the Union was better prepared. The nation hadn't one friend, and only one ally: delay. There was little that the Chief, as Henry called his father, could actually *do* other than wait to douse the fires that broke out, as they inevitably would. There were plenty of hotheads on both sides of the water. The challenge would be to extinguish each blaze before it joined with the general conflagration, burned out of control, and consumed the house his fathers had built.

The minister opened his eyes and looked down at his hands, folded now as if posed for a portrait. It seemed as if they had been folded all his life, passive and ineffectual. His own political career was hardly more impressive than that of Abraham Lincoln—a failed run for the vice presidency in 1848, a few stumbling years in the Massachusetts legislature, most recently a two-year term in his father's old seat in Congress, where men younger than he still recalled John Quincy Adams's incendiary rhetoric. Nothing to suggest that Charles was uniquely qualified for the challenge ahead, beyond his surname and the friendship of William Seward. If his father were still alive, John Quincy would have known what to do. The sixth president always had an opinion, usually correct.

But Charles wanted to be needed by his country. He himself. Not his father. He had yearned to make his mark in politics as long as he could remember, just as other men dreamed about pretty women or piles of gold. It was an odd, inherited trait, like bushy eyebrows or a turned-up nose. He had grown up with the Greek and Roman classics, haunted the galleries of Congress during school vacations, debated politics late into the night with his father and his grandfather, and read for the bar. He had studied the family business. He had waited patiently as the decades advanced, passing him by.

The venom of slavery had, meanwhile, worked its way through the veins of the republic—turning friend against friend, fueling hatred between perfect strangers, reducing rational men to beasts. His father and grandfather had known that abolition was the only cure, and that it would probably kill the patient. Now the crisis was upon them like a fever. Duty called, luring his generation and his sons' to the rocks. All that he had ever wanted and feared had come to pass. How would he know what to do? What if he failed?

Unaccountably, the room brightened. Charles looked up from his desk. Rain and fog had given way to a weak, vaporous sunshine. He could now see the legation's reflection in the windows of the building across the street. The star-spangled flag hung limply in the reflection, like a washerwoman's cloth slung on a peg. "That old striped rag," a Charleston paper had said, deriding the banner when secessionists stripped it from Fort Sumter in April and trampled it in the mud. It was as if they had walked upon his heart.

The minister reached automatically for a fresh piece of paper. He would instruct the legation's staff to make sure that the flag was laundered and freshly ironed before being hoisted each morning outside the residence. If torn, it should be mended immediately. In a rain, it should be lowered and taken indoors. Self-respect was fundamental to international respect. Act like a nation and others will treat you as one. Grandfather had bluffed his way through France and Holland during the Revolution in just that manner.

Charles paused, his pen suspended. A single, small gesture had such fragility and potency. The tiniest of symbols might make or save an entire nation. He merely had to persist, despite the assumption on every side that the Union was no longer real. Being in London, keeping the legation open day in and day out, made it real.

A fierce, reckless gladness gripped him and Charles signed his name to the note with a decisive flourish of the pen. The dogmatic, brilliant John Quincy wasn't at his side to quote maxims and make recommendations. Win or lose, it was Charles's turn, at last, to play high-stakes poker with John Bull.

FOUR

~~~~~~~

*To him, the Legation was social ostracism, terrible beyond
anything he had known. Entire solitude in
the great society of London.*

—Henry Adams, *The Education of Henry Adams*

The young Virginian rounded the corner into Mayfair, London's most fashionable neighborhood. Elegant clubs and houses faced the street proudly. Their white façades gleamed like bank vaults, and graceful columns flanked the covered entrances that protected guests from even a drop of rain. Gas lamps burned brightly day and night on either side of the porticoes, keeping London's famous fogs at bay. Just then the door to an impressive stone mansion opened and a man clutching a folded umbrella stepped lightly down the stairs and into the promenade. He moved so quickly, with his hat pulled down against the damp, that he nearly collided with the Virginian.

"I do beg your pardon," the man apologized in a tenor that betrayed a Yankee upbringing. He reached for the ivory-headed cane that the Virginian had dropped.

"Henry Adams, you old dog!" the young Southerner exclaimed. "I thought I might have the pleasure of running into you." H. Baxter Sams, Harvard class of '58, looked with delight into the familiar face of his former college friend. "I read in the papers that your father has been appointed to St. James's."

"Baxter Sams! 'Run into me' you did. You nearly brought me down, steaming along full bore like a sailor on leave. What are you doing here?" Henry's face beamed with pleased surprise.

"I've been attending lectures at the Royal College of Surgeons. Father has decided to waste his money on educating a physician. I suppose he thinks we have enough merchants in the family."

"Come now," Henry said. "You were one of the three best students at Harvard—and the only Virginian who actually wanted to be there. The rest of your compatriots looked as comfortable at a desk as a Sioux on a sidewalk. Both belong on horseback."

Baxter Sams grasped the cane that Henry handed back to him. "True. Remember the time Rooney Lee rode his gelding into Harvard Yard, whiskey in one hand, saber in the other, demanding an apology from the physiology lecturer for insulting Southern womanhood? 'How dare he discuss the sections under a lady's bustle?' Wasn't it you who talked him off the horse?"

"I admit to the deed. It was accomplished by appealing to his native hospitality. I pointed out that on such a blustery day the least he could do was offer me a drink, and he dismounted immediately. I knew then that I was born to be a diplomat."

"I heard that you later helped get him a commission in the army."

Henry shook his head. "No, I merely helped him compose the letter of acceptance. Rooney knew that he could grant me no greater compliment than to ask for the assistance of my pen, poor as it is. But he liked you much more."

"He just liked my first name. It reminded him of his grandfather, Light Horse Harry Lee. 'Let's show the Yanks how it's done, Harry,' he'd say. Rooney never would call me Baxter, like everybody else." The Virginian folded his arms, frowned as if puzzled, and added, "Now, Rooney actually respected *you* as a brain. Of course, that's a common enough assumption Southerners make about the old Bostonian elite. Though I can't say why, in the face of all the evidence." It was a time-honored Harvard tradition, folding the insult into the compliment.

Henry laughed heartily. "You're on a fool's errand if you think you can provoke me, Baxter Sams. I'm perfectly aware that my faculties are sodden. It comes from too many generations of introspection and education. At least your family isn't similarly encumbered," Henry said, turning the tables. Both men smiled.

"Any idea where Rooney is now?" Henry asked.

"I heard he's married, lucky fellow," Baxter replied. "But I expect he's spending more time with his father than with his bride. No one could accuse Robert E. Lee of promoting his son unfairly. Rooney's a natural. He could nip a bird on the wing with one of those old muskets that the rest of us couldn't hit a cow with."

As if on cue, a goldfinch chirped overhead and bolted out of the tree, which in turn triggered the flight of half a dozen other songbirds. The flock scattered rapidly, silhouettes winging toward the last pink clouds in the west. The yolk of the sun was now only a smear of yellow on the horizon, though it would linger there for another hour in the long twilight of early summer.

Carriages rolled past, wheels crunching against gravel as the men started walking up the street. The rain had cleared completely. A fine evening was unfolding.

Baxter wondered when his old friend would broach the subject that had forever divided the one hundred members of the class of 1858. He knew the Puritan streak wouldn't allow Henry to leave a subject alone merely because it was uncomfortable. In fact, conscience might force Henry to bring it up precisely for that reason.

"So tell me, why haven't you been to see us at the legation?" Henry asked, fulfilling Baxter's expectation. "You must know that we're nearly outcasts here. We're invited to parties only to fill the furniture. I'm certain someone's going to mistake me for a lamp some evening and pop a shade on my head. It's damn depressing. A friendly face, even your mug, is most welcome."

"I thought it might be awkward to receive me. Our families are at odds now."

"We never judged each other according to family connections before," Henry replied. "Why start now?"

"How can we avoid it?" Baxter's blue eyes darkened. "My brother Robert has been called to the Virginia militia. Jacob is an aide to General Beauregard. Everyone is choosing sides. Whether I like it or not, I belong to the Tidewater."

"I know what you mean. My older brother Charles has joined the Massachusetts militia and is threatening to enlist in the Federal army. But you're a Unionist, aren't you? You used to quote Jefferson: 'I tremble for my country when I reflect that God is just, and that his justice will not sleep forever.' Remember that?"

"It was one thing to oppose slavery over oysters and beer in Boston. I'm still opposed, but my home is under attack. Everything has changed."

"What's changed? I haven't changed. I'm still your friend, slavery is still unjust, and America is still man's best hope. Surely you don't wish to see the country torn apart? All our enemies gloat at the prospect of democracy discredited."

"I know," Baxter answered, his eyes trained on the path ahead.

"So?" Henry pressed him.

Baxter stopped and stared Henry full in the face. "Look, Henry, I'm a Virginian. Of course I don't want to turn my back, but I also can't forsake my family. If I sail for the States, I have to take the oath or risk being imprisoned for treason. And if I take the oath, I renounce publicly all those I hold dearest, at their moment of greatest peril. Whatever else you may say about Southerners, we are loyal."

Having lived in Cambridge, just across the river from Boston, Baxter knew all the smug prejudices that New Englanders entertained with regard to Southerners, whom they dismissed as uneducated, volatile, lazy men with hair triggers. But Henry Adams didn't believe that, Baxter thought—or, at least, hoped.

"Can't you simply stay on here?" Henry asked. "The rebellion is bound to be short. Perhaps you won't have to make the choice."

"Hiding hardly seems honorable," Baxter said.

"My father says there's little honor in any war. You could finish your studies instead."

"I would like to finish my courses at the Royal College of Surgeons. In fact, my father is insisting on it. Frankly, I don't think he wants three sons at the front. He feels as your father does—there's little glory in the awful mess. If the war is as brief as everyone says it will be, I suppose I might miss it altogether."

"Then let's not talk about it again tonight," Henry proposed.

"I'd like that," Baxter said, glad of the opportunity to forget there was a war on.

"Let me take you to supper at Rules. I saw Dickens there last week, and enough pretty girls to give any man hope. We can raise a glass to old Rooney, wherever he is."

"All right," Baxter agreed. "To Rooney."

Neither man said, although both knew, that they would avoid discussing which side might win the short war back home.

FIVE

AUGUST 1861

As a mere question of independence I believe the thing
to be settled. We cannot bring the South back.

—Henry Adams to his brother Charles,
A Cycle of Adams Letters

By tradition, London's fashionable season began in December and ended in July, when the privileged classes retired to their summer homes. Hunting and fishing replaced theater, concerts, and royal receptions. Leisurely visits between the great houses became commonplace, and guests—who expected to stay a fortnight or longer—brought large, iron-strapped wardrobe trunks for changing clothes the four or five times a day that social convention required. Breakfast, tea, walks in the countryside, foxhunting and fishing, formal suppers, and dances each called for different attire. Sometimes Julia Birch got so sick of buttoning and unbuttoning that she almost wished herself back at Belfield counting silver teaspoons. But not tonight.

The Forsythes had organized a ball, and Julia looked forward to the possibility of dancing. She now cheerfully lifted her arms to allow the lady's maid to slip a tiered ball gown over the cage crinoline that gave her skirt the shape of a wide bell. A tight corset, laced from the back by the maid, made the emerald velvet fit her waist without a wrinkle. Julia had been at Foxwood nearly a week while her father took care of business in the city. Lady

Catherine Forsythe, her hostess and chaperone, had urged Julia to pay special attention to her choice of dress, as there were certain to be a number of eligible suitors from surrounding estates at the ball.

Julia looked critically at her reflection in the gilt-edged armoire. The cut velvet brought out the green in her eyes and accentuated her waistline. Her square shoulders did not meet the sloping fashion set by Queen Victoria, but at least her neck was long and smooth. The armoire cut off the top of her reflection, so she turned around, dipped her knees, and held up a hand mirror to check that her coiffure was secure. A generous brunette chignon sat neatly on her crown. Only a small tendril, a bare curly wisp, escaped at the nape of the neck.

Julia smiled back into the mirror, trying to gauge her prettiness, which seemed to vary day by day. She wasn't a beauty, at least she didn't think so, for even now the mirror showed a forehead that was too broad, cheekbones that were too high, and brows that were too straight and assertive for a Fragonard nymph or any other depiction of womanhood as delicate, fair, and yielding. Nonetheless, tonight her dark eyes revealed a sparkling, inner intensity, and her skin was luminous against the rich emerald gown. It would do, she decided. She felt prettier than usual, and that gave her confidence.

Julia's height precluded her from being the belle of the ball, but gentlemen who might not ask for a waltz still looked at her with interest. Their covert glances were some consolation for failing to measure up to Queen Victoria, whose short, plump figure set the standard for beauty. One would have to be shaped like a partridge to be fully in style.

Descending the stairs to the ballroom, Julia swept her gaze around the room, hoping to make an unobtrusive entrance. She spied an empty chair next to Louise and Flora Bentley, twin sisters from a neighboring manor. The Bentleys were an entertaining duo, full of cheerful gossip about events in the countryside, including the latest victories and defeats of the sorority of young women in search of beaus.

"Do sit with us, Julia." Louise smiled and patted the seat when she approached. "You are our only friend who will not treat this evening as one more battle on the march to Waterloo. It's war out there."

"Rescue us from ourselves," Flora echoed. "Louise has danced with half the bachelors here, and I have danced with the other half. No British regiment ever endured such a pace." Flora sighed over the burden, but her cheeks were flushed rosy and her china-blue eyes sparkled. She looked the picture of an English coquette—creamy, pink, and blond.

"Robert Cartwright has insisted upon any dance not claimed by another," Louise told her sister. "Do your feet ache as much as mine?" she asked, stretching and pointing her toes in the tight satin heels.

"Of course not. I told you to wear the sensible slippers," Flora reminded her twin. "Those make you too tall anyway."

Louise flashed a meaningful look at her petite sister, whose color deepened.

Julia gave an easy smile that belied the awkward self-awareness that sometimes stole upon her at a ball, where she usually found herself talking into the airspace above her partners' heads, if she danced at all. The complacent expressions of London's dowagers had told her since age eighteen that they did not fear for their daughters' prospects when she was in the room. Julia stood a hand's breadth above the average Englishman. Most suitors wanted a pretty penny to make up for being looked down upon.

"Not to worry," Julia said, conscious of Flora's embarrassment and hoping to ease it. "I have the first distinction in that regard, and so first call on any gentleman who's in danger of hitting his head on the lintel. Though there don't seem to be many tonight."

She glanced round the assembly with an unconcerned air, but

she felt the familiar pang of disappointment. Pride kept her from admitting that she wouldn't mind waltzing until her feet fell off and walked away without her.

"Then you haven't seen the gentlemen from America," Flora said.

Julia looked in the direction that Flora indicated, with a slight nod over her fan. Two men whom she didn't know stood near the punch bowl talking with Lady Catherine's husband, Sir William Forsythe, and John Bentley, the twins' older brother. One of the Americans was a young man of middle height with a serious expression and a receding hairline that hinted at a bald future. The other was tall, with well-cut clothes and the erect bearing of a man who rides a fine horse. He was gesturing with his hands and appeared to be telling John Bentley and Lord Forsythe a story.

"I see what you mean," Julia said. "Who are they?"

"My brother told me that one of them, the shorter one, is the son of the American minister. I think the family name is Adams. The taller gentleman is apparently his acquaintance from Virginia," Flora said.

"The family name would indeed be Adams," Julia agreed, recalling that her father had mentioned the arrival of the new representative from the United States—or, rather, "the North," as he emphasized. "It's a famous one, too, if you've followed colonial history."

"History is so dreadful. Nothing but wars and beheadings. Blood and gore and whatnot. And as for the colonies . . ." Flora wrinkled her nose in dislike and gave her ringlets a small shake.

"At least history has more drama than needlepoint," Louise retorted, not hesitating to contradict her sister.

Louise was an avid reader. In this she had more in common with Julia than did Flora, who was talented at embroidery, screen-making, and the ornamental arts. It was as if the twins had determined early to be opposites, making two halves of one well-rounded personality. Flora had long ago conceded the intellectual role to her sister. "Louise is literary and all that," she had told Julia with an airy wave of her hand.

"The case of the Adamses proves your point," Julia said, concurring with Louise. "They certainly have a dramatic history. Some consider the first Adams responsible for the War of Independence."

Glancing across the room at the mild-looking young man clutching his glass, she added, "Of course, the drama might have skipped a generation or two."

"The *Times* said the same thing—about his relations, that is," Louise said. "When the elder Mr. Adams was appointed, they called him the representative of one of America's few historic families. Amusing, isn't it, to think a whole country could have only a few historic families? What a small world it must seem."

In England, famous lineages filled whole books. At Queen Victoria's levees, as many as a thousand nobles might kiss her hand, from dukes and marquises down to barons and baronets. And that did not even include the gentry, who were also entitled to coats of arms.

"Perhaps it's not so surprising when one considers America's origins," Julia said. "After all, many began as indentured servants. The best families were driven out."

She didn't elaborate. It was well known that the Birch family had been on the losing side of the rebellion.

Flora shook out her lace fan. Glancing across the room again, she observed, "The Virginian looks much more interesting than the historical specimen. He's unusually tall, Julia, and very good-looking."

Taking care not to be obvious, Julia considered the foreign visitor. Unlike young Mr. Adams, the Virginian appeared quite at ease. He had a high, intelligent forehead, brushed with dark locks, and even from a distance she could see that his eyes brimmed with good humor. He was smiling broadly now, showing lovely, straight teeth.

"I'm compelled to agree with you, if only to show my objectivity when it comes to specimens," Julia said. "But don't you think they look surprisingly civilized? One expects barbarians. Remember Mr. Dickens's description of his travels in America?"

"You mean where he described the men 'chawin' tobaccy' and spitting that disgusting brown juice all over the place? I thought that was only on the floor of Congress. Surely they can't all be like that—at least not out in society."

"True. Still, they appear more refined than I expected."

"I think it's rather queer that they're together, one from the South and one from the North," Louise said with a glance across the room. "One reads continually in the *Times* about the awful war and how they positively long to bludgeon one another, yet here they are sipping punch."

"Perhaps they'll get to it later in the evening," Julia suggested with a smile.

Flora ruffled her fan and with a carefree shrug declared, "I don't give a fig for wars, but I do want to know more about any man as handsome as that one," she said. "He's the perfect height for you, Julia. I've already asked John to introduce him. Brothers can be quite useful, on the odd occasion."

As if he sensed that he was being talked about, John Bentley looked in his sisters' direction, and then guided the two Americans around the circumference of the full ballroom.

Flora whispered, "Now don't shake hands, Julia. He'll think you're fast."

The three gentlemen approached before Julia could ask why. Flora had an instinctive, sophisticated grasp—rivaling that of a Byzantine theologian, really—for the complex rules of flirting, though Julia sometimes wondered if she just made them up.

"Ladies, may I present Mr. Henry Adams and Mr. H. Baxter Sams?" John Bentley said. He turned to the two foreigners and added, "Mr. Adams, Mr. Sams, these are my sisters, Louise and Flora Bentley, and our good friend Miss Julia Birch."

Flora lowered her pretty chin a smidgeon and looked up through her black lashes. She held her fan close, declining to offer her hand.

"Welcome to Lancashire, gentlemen. Have you been in England long?" she asked in a musical voice.

"My friend Mr. Adams is only recently arrived, but I have been here for the past year, at the Royal College of Surgeons," Baxter Sams answered for the two of them.

"How admirable," Louise chimed in warmly. "Physicians are in such urgent need. London's growth outpaces the supply of doctors. What branch of medicine are you studying?"

"I'm interested in the treatment of traumatic wounds. It's advanced tremendously since Napoleon's wars. There have been a number of discoveries here and in Germany that I hope to learn from."

"If you take an interest in wars, you must chat with Miss Birch," Flora said, her wide eyes innocent. "She knows much more about history than either my sister or I do."

Julia cringed inwardly at Flora's attempt to steer Mr. Sams in her direction. She enjoyed the twins' liveliness, but sometimes their pursuit of eligible gentlemen did feel like a forced march.

Baxter met her eyes with an expression of pleasure, however. "Would you honor me with this dance, Miss Birch, so that you can tell me how you came by such serious interests?"

As Julia rose, she shot Louise and Flora a chastising look, but the twins blithely ignored her. They now had poor Mr. Adams under their wing. The quiet New Englander held his punch glass stiffly, like a talisman.

Julia looked up into the Virginian's face as he extended his arm for the waltz. He was taller than her father and most other men with whom she had danced. He hadn't appeared so from across the room because he didn't suffer from the odd elongation one sometimes saw in the faces or limbs of very tall men. Hands, feet, face were all proportionate. It was unexpectedly unnerving to be looking up, rather than across or down, at her partner. She felt a sudden shyness, but was determined to make a clean breast of Flora's battlefield maneuvers regardless.

"You must forgive Miss Bentley for her boldness, Mr. Sams. I'm afraid she was determined to get me on the dance floor."

"Quite the contrary. I'm indebted to her." Baxter smiled as he guided her to an open spot on the polished marble. "Mr. Adams and I have been positively shackled to each other."

"I hope this dance is not merely an opportunity to remove the shackles."

"Not at all. I assure you that the company of a young lady is far superior to that of my old friend. It's just that it sometimes seems we Americans are resident curiosities. English society hardly recognizes us as individuals. We are types."

"I promise to look upon you as an individual if you will extend me the same courtesy," Julia said with a smile that took the sting out of the rejoinder. "Young ladies also differ considerably." The orchestra launched into a Strauss waltz and Julia offered her hand.

"I'm finding that out at this minute," Baxter Sams said as he took her hand with a confident grip, placed his arm around her waist, and swung Julia into the swirl of dancers.

"Please tell me what you mean by types," she said. "What types do you and Mr. Adams represent?" Unlike quadrilles, lancers, and older dances, the waltz allowed for a sustained conversation between two people, and Julia found his comment curious.

"Before last spring I venture we would have both been dismissed as *Rusticus americanus,* boors from the former colonies. Now we find that society casts Mr. Adams as a dastardly Northern aggressor and me as a cavalier defending Southern honor. Neither of us is anything of the sort. I think we were better off when society merely expected us to be bumpkins, fresh from the country with snatches of hay in our hair."

Julia's eyes crinkled. "I have to admit that we do find Americans strange at times," she said. "Your previous ministers to the Court made a show of dressing in simple black, as if to reprove our frivolity. My father enjoyed pretending to mistake them for the butler at the queen's receptions. He liked to hand them his empty glasses."

Baxter laughed. "I can't say that I blame your father. I myself sometimes find the Puritan severity of New Englanders hard to take. Even the sinners sound like preachers."

"Your new minister appears to have made a better impression. He was presented at court in a silk and lace suit, sporting a cocked hat and a ceremonial sword. Gossip has it that Victoria received him with the observation 'I am thankful we shall have no more American funerals.'"

"Indeed?" Baxter replied. He knit his brow in concentration, considering the information. "Well, the Adamses are a breed apart. Our second president, the minister's grandfather, suffered biting criticism for his aristocratic tendencies. When he was George Washington's vice president, Adams proposed that the general be referred to as 'His Highness the President,' or something of the sort. Opponents sneered and booed until the term 'Mr. President' won out. No one forgot it, though. And when he later refused to take the side of the Jacobins who beheaded Louis XVI, many Americans felt it spelled an unhealthy preference for monarchy. Thomas Jefferson said as much."

"Surely an Adams couldn't be taken for a monarchist? Upon my word, no one in Georgian England would make that mistake."

"I see your point. I suppose the Revolutionary generation tended to be rather zealous that way."

"So tell me how this scurrilous reputation passed into the next generation," Julia said, her awkwardness forgotten. She found herself enjoying the story of the American rebellion from an unfamiliar angle, as well as the firm arms that encircled her. She gave herself over to her partner's interesting observations and the broad, sweeping pattern of the dance.

"Well, then the minister's father—who was our sixth president—made quite an unfortunate contrast with *his* successor, Andrew Jackson—a Westerner who didn't hesitate to welcome rough crowds with muddy boots into the White House. Or so they said. The public turned poor Mr. Adams out of the White House after one term, just as they did his father. It's ironic, since despite their formality the Adamses were plain farmers. Plainer, certainly, than the spokesmen for democracy like Jefferson and Jackson, with their mansions and plantations."

Americans were such a bundle of contradictions, Julia thought. It seemed their Southern aristocrats were admired as democrats, while their Northern democrats were scorned as aristocrats. It was a marvel that anyone could keep it straight. She wondered how Mr. Sams and Mr. Adams had become friends.

"Miss Bentley told me that you are a Virginian. How did you meet Mr. Adams? I understand he is from Massachusetts," Julia said as the waltz glided them past the French doors, where they started another circuit of the ballroom.

"I passed four very cold winters as a student at Harvard College. Henry and I lived at the same rooming house. We're both rather dull collegians, I'm afraid to say—hardly warmongers."

"You don't define yourselves as Southerners or Northerners, then?" Julia refrained from using the terms she had seen bandied about in the press, "Confederates and Federals," uncertain whether it would give offense.

Baxter paused an instant before steering Julia into the next backward loop of the waltz. Failing to anticipate his hesitation, she stepped on the toe of his gleaming black shoe.

"Oh, I'm sorry. Please pardon me!" She flushed with embarrassment and came to a confused halt in the midst of the packed ballroom. He must think her as nimble as a giraffe. Her dancing skills were like those of a rusty old maid.

"My mistake," Baxter apologized in a light tone. "You can see for yourself that I fall short of the fabled Southern cavalier. I was thinking how to explain the situation. I'm afraid the effort taxed my brain to its limits."

Julia smiled at his effort to take the blame. He made her feel that she wasn't merely Cinderella's oversized stepsister, for whom she had always harbored a perverse sympathy. She laid her palm in her partner's upturned hand once again and stepped back into the waltz.

"I was going to say," he continued, "that Mr. Adams and I both consider ourselves Americans, and we wish this war had never started. Neither of us sees that any good can come of it."

"But I understand that some believe it may result in abolition—long overdue, our Whigs would say. Does your family own slaves?"

As soon as the words popped out of her mouth, Julia regretted the question. It was terribly impertinent. "Own" sounded especially wrong, though she didn't know what other word one might employ. Britain had outlawed slavery well before she was born, and she had never met anyone who owned a slave. Even the idea of it seemed exotic, like something out of a geography book with color plates of Chinese foot-binding or the Turkish sultan's one thousand concubines.

"My parents keep two servants: the nursemaid who cared for me and my brothers as children, and a woman who tends their house," Baxter replied. "We are a mercantile family, not planters."

Julia noted that he had substituted the word "servants" for "slaves." Was it cowardice? Sophistry?

"Then surely you would consider the war worthwhile if it brought slavery to an end? It's such a blight."

"Perhaps—but it won't," he said, a small frown growing between his well-defined black brows. "Even Mr. Lincoln says the war is about reunion, not abolition, and I see little glory or gain in the bloodshed that's sure to follow. There's no telling where it will end. Good men will die."

The waltz swelled to an end, concluding on the triumphant,

romantic note that the popular dance invariably did. Baxter bowed, thanked Julia, and led her back to the chairs by the French doors. Flora and Louise had disappeared into the festive crowd. Mr. Sams excused himself to go in search of Mr. Adams, who was surely holding up a wall somewhere. He thanked Julia again, meeting her eyes only briefly as he bowed.

From her seat on the sidelines, Julia watched the tall Virginian retreat across the ballroom. Their conversation had not ended as smoothly as the music, but there seemed little chance of repairing it. She wondered if she had put her foot in her mouth after she stepped on his toe. Did it matter? He might be tall and seriously handsome, as well as the best dance partner she had had in ages, but he was also an American and a slaveholder. Neither attribute would excite admiration at Belfield Manor in Mayfair.

SIX

⁓⁓⁓⁓⁓⁓

It is idle to talk of putting down the rebellion whilst our power is resisted successfully within a dozen miles of the capital.

—Charles Francis Adams to Charles, Jr.,
A Cycle of Adams Letters

C harles sat down to breakfast with the appetite of a man who has slept soundly next to the woman he loves. The Adamses typically married late, but they had an enviable knack for choosing well. Grandfather's romance with his wife, Abigail, was legend. Charles had published a collection of his grandmother's letters, vibrant with longing for her mate during the years of their wartime separation. He could still feel the start of a youthful blush when he recalled the portly, white-haired John Adams saying to his granddaughter's betrothed, "You'll soon discover the real joys of domestic life—peace, nourishment, copulation, and society." As a gawky thirteen-year-old, Charles had felt that he would sink right through the floorboards. Certainly he would have welcomed it. Leave it to the gentleman farmer to mention copulation, as if humans were horses. But forty years later he concurred with his grandfather as he looked across the table at his own alluring Abby. She made this London post bearable. It had been nearly four months since they had left home and said goodbye to the three oldest children, now occupied with their own adult affairs, but with Abby at his side the time had flown by.

Summer sunshine poured through the broad windows of the legation's family dining room. At his wife's insistence it was furnished in the finest style—a mahogany sideboard under the indispensable silver tea service, a wide oval table covered in patterned green damask, and a high mantelpiece topped by a looking glass. The buttery scent of baking filled the air. Charles had stayed in bed later than usual, and he observed with pleasure that the children had left the table already. Breakfast would not be interrupted by the babble or bickering of fifteen-year-old Mary and twelve-year-old Brooks. Their morning chatter jangled his nerves like a banging screen.

"Dear, didn't we receive today's newspaper?" Charles asked as he shook out the white Irish linen beside the plate and placed it on his lap.

Abigail Brooks Adams had a long, shapely nose, full lips, and warm brown eyes. Never quite beautiful but always expressive, she now radiated gentle calm at her husband of more than thirty years. "Yes, Charles, but I thought you might like to enjoy your breakfast first. Emma has prepared her Scotch scones and a fresh ham. We've also gotten in some fruit from the country. The raspberries look almost as good as those at home."

"Abby, you know very well that I like to read the paper with breakfast," Charles said with mild severity. Experience told him the delay of the newspaper and the offer of a bountiful breakfast did not bode well. Abby was trying to manage him. Come to think of it, where *were* the children? Banished?

Abigail sighed with a hint of exasperation. "Well, after watching Henry choke on his toast and bolt his coffee I simply thought I would spare your digestion. It's not a good day for the news. You know English journalists—pen, paper, and prejudices."

"Henry is a young man still learning to govern his temper, my dear. The good scones may improve the bad news. I'll take the risk."

Abigail shrugged one shoulder and sighed again. "I'm afraid Scotch scones won't be enough this morning," she said, but she rang a small bell and asked the maid to bring in the paper.

Charles slowly read the long report from the *Times* correspondent in Virginia, taking care not to choke on a crumb and prove Abby right.

The situation was worse than bad. A fortnight earlier, in a small Virginia town called Manassas, Northern troops had broken and run in their first major engagement against the Rebels. Despite their superior numbers, they had gotten in hardly a shot. Within just a few leagues of Washington, D.C., Federal soldiers had turned tail. There was no kinder description for it. The war had begun at last—disastrously so.

"A cowardly rout . . . such scandalous behavior on the part of soldiers . . . I have never seen the like of it . . ."

Charles forced himself to take in each awful word. Every phrase sliced a little deeper: "Miserable, causeless panic . . . Sheer cowardice."

In view of the entire world, America's green troops had scattered like quail at the boom of a few cannons. Charles's humiliation and impotent anger could not be more profound. He was grateful that only Abby was in the room, and that she was applying orange marmalade to her scone, eyes downcast. Even Henry would have been hard to face. Charles felt the embarrassment of a commander who suddenly realizes that he is alone with his raised sword at the bridgehead, the troops having taken to the hills a full league back.

The inexperienced Federals had lost all their artillery and eight thousand muskets. They abandoned the wounded where they fell. Soldiers had tripped and spilled over one another, clogging the lanes in their haste to make it back to the capital and hide.

"Seventy-five thousand American patriots fled twenty miles in an agony of fear, although no one was pursuing them," the *Times* special correspondent wrote. "It was no use trying to outstrip the runaways." Charles suspected the reporter had exaggerated the number of troops, but that didn't excuse their undisciplined behavior.

He could just envision Lord Palmerston, the British prime minister, roaring with laughter. Even the preternaturally dignified queen might manage a giggle at the absurd scene. Better than comic opera. Unable to take any more of the caustic report, Charles flipped to the editorial page.

"We do not like to laugh, but the sense of the ridiculous comes too strong over us when we would be serious," the *Times* editors mused.

Hardly, Charles thought with bitterness. But he had a grudging feeling that the smug British had reason to snicker. His spirits sank even lower. He had been taught to admit when the English were right. It was sour medicine, but it strengthened the backbone.

The editors went straight to the point: "America's empty, provocative boasts . . ." The London editorial quoted liberally from New York newspapers that had outdone one another with their windy bombast in the weeks leading up to the start of the fighting. They were so ridiculous that it really was hard not to laugh, unless one was an American with an iota of shame.

The United States would snatch Canada in retaliation for the Crown's tolerance of Confederate envoys, one New York journal threatened. "We have, first, to put down the rebellion at home, but every hour proves that the war that has begun will be a short one, and that, ere the lapse of another half-year, armies will exist on the American continent of over half a million men thirsting for a foreign foe upon whom to expend their strength. . . . Let Great Britain beware!"

Charles could feel the start of a throbbing headache. He pressed a thumb against his left temple and kept reading, but with a squint. His coffee grew cold. Across the table, Abby fiddled with the jam jar, matching up the roses on the Wedgwood lid with those on the base. Apparently, it was a task that took all her attention.

The editors summed up their opinion with the exquisite dignity of which the English were such consummate masters: "If this is what we are to receive from the supremacy of the North, the North can scarcely expect that we should put up very ardent vows for their conquest of the South. If the conquest of the Southern States also means the conquest of Canada . . ."

Charles could not go on. He looked up to find Abby's grave eyes on him. The morning light illuminated his wife's face, erasing the fine lines that testified to years of generous laughter and lively conversation.

"Amazing, isn't it?" she said, putting Charles's thoughts into words, as they often did for each other. "That they can boast of punishing England when the president's generals cannot even hold a straight line in Virginia." She had obviously seen the paper. Abby's voice shook slightly. Her hand trembled and the Wedgwood lid tinkled against the jar.

"Now, Abby. We mustn't get riled. Not at the British, not at our own people."

"Charles! There is no one in this room but you and me. You needn't lecture me on diplomacy."

"We are entitled to our private feelings, my dear—and I wouldn't for a moment wish you to keep yours from me. But we must restrain ourselves. We can't afford to become overwrought. We just can't."

The declaration made Charles feel better. Speaking the words to Abby was like saying them to himself, only more calming. Watching her emotions spill over drew off his own. He was the diplomat, back in control. The pain in his temple eased.

Abigail's eyes filled with tears. "I just feel so helpless. This war isn't going to be short at all, is it? Charles, Jr., will undoubtedly insist on signing up. Henry may, too. If we pick a fight with England on top of everything else—" Abby broke off, looking down at the napkin in her lap.

"But we won't. We won't let it happen," Charles said with finality. He picked up the *Times* and quoted the editorial aloud:

"These people do all in their power to alienate our sympathy. . . . Nothing civilizes them."

Charles gazed at Abby directly, willing her to look deep into his eyes, into the soul of his conviction. "We shall show them civilized behavior, Abby. You and I. You and I, and Henry, and Mary, and Brooks. Ours will be the faces that British society comes to see as the face of America."

Abby looked across the table at her husband, the American minister to Great Britain. The queen did not even deign to extend him the rank of ambassador. The United States was not considered important enough, not one of the great nations like France, Sweden, or Prussia. England exchanged ambassadors only with countries she considered to be her equal. The United States was not in this category.

"Yes, of course, Charles," Abby replied, taking up his tone of confidence with a steely note in her voice. "I cannot believe that the war will be short, and I pray to God above that our sons will be safe. But I can be brave if you can, or at least . . . how did you put it? Civilized."

SEVEN

OCTOBER 1861

Mr. [Jefferson] Davis believes that we will do all that can be done by pluck and muscle . . . [but] either way he thinks it will be a long war. That floored me at once. It has been too long for me already. . . . He said only fools doubted the courage of the Yankees, or their willingness to fight when they saw fit.

—Mary Boykin Chesnut, *A Diary from Dixie*

B axter Sams washed his hands, turning one over the other with assiduous care, scrubbing his nails with a boar-bristle brush. He had returned by train from the west of Scotland the night before. One of the professors he most respected at the Royal College of Surgeons suggested that he tour the infirmary at Glasgow. The new head of the hospital, Joseph Lister, had begun experiments with what some called "clean healing." Like many doctors, Lister thought there must be a way to diminish the rate of sepsis in patients undergoing amputation. Infection carried so many of them away.

The energetic chief surgeon had little time for visitors, but he granted a brief interview when informed that the young doctor was from Virginia. "'Tis a great pity, but war is often the best school for doctors," Lister told Baxter, gesturing toward a chair in his cluttered office.

"I hope not to attend that school," Baxter admitted. "My family prefers me to stay in London."

"Are they pacifists, then?" Lister inquired. He had an alert, kind face. "My wife and I belong to the Scottish Episcopal Church, but my parents were in the Society of Friends. Quakers. I know many who would refuse to fight in any war."

"No. My older brothers are in the Confederate army. I'm still in London because my father wants me to complete my studies."

"That must be what brings you here, then. How may I help?" Lister asked.

Baxter explained his interest in clean healing. Lister grew animated and related his belief that wounds festered because some kind of foreign body entered them. "It's not just bad air, I'm convinced of that," the eminent surgeon said, dismissing one popular theory with an impatient shake of his head. "It may be a dust or a pollen. I'm not sure which, but it seems we must devise ways of keeping the wound free of these particles. Do you know that half the men in our ward die following amputation? If the enemy doesn't kill them, the surgeon does."

Lister's goal was to discover what caused sepsis, and then something to prevent it. An anti-sepsis of sorts. Baxter listened intently while the English doctor outlined his clinical procedures and research under the microscope. The spirit of scientific inquiry took Baxter's breath away. Brilliant doctors like Joseph Lister were whisking away centuries—no, millennia—of ignorance. It was stunning. Baxter could stay in Britain for a lifetime and never learn all they had to teach.

Back at his lodgings in London, Baxter thought bleakly about what the Confederate surgeries must look like as he washed his hands after the long train ride. Mere dusty tents staked at the edges of smoky battlefields. What if Robert or Jacob came under the knife? His mind went blank, unwilling to accommodate the repellent thought of a surgeon taking a crude saw to the snowy flesh of their young limbs. What good was all his learning if he couldn't use it to help his brothers and the other boys with whom they had grown up? It seemed inconceivable that he might lose Robert or Jacob, yet all it took was one bullet, or a quick thrust from a bayonet, or—worse—a lingering infection from an amputation, to still the heart forever.

He dried his hands thoroughly with a fresh towel. Lister said that a surgeon must be careful not to pollute the wound with his own hands or instruments. They look clean, Baxter thought, examining his short fingernails with a frown, but what might be revealed under a microscope? Too bad there wasn't one in the room. He suddenly laughed out loud at the image, breaking the stillness. How many of the lodgers at this Mayfair club desired a microscope in their rooms? Most would be content with a willing maiden in the closet.

He sat down on the bed, reached for the letter that had come up with tea, and tore open the envelope from Virginia.

My dear son, I hoped not to ask you home . . .

The letter began, his father plunging directly forward.

As you know, my feelings about this war are mixed. Your mother and I are determined to manumit Jesmina and Clara—despite the difficulties. They'll be forced to leave the state within twelve months, but your uncle in Philadelphia has promised to take them in. We don't want it to be said that our sons are fighting for slavery. Robert and Jacob are too dear to us to enlist their lives in such a benighted cause. But we understand their desire to defend Virginia and our country. Lincoln's war gives them little choice. . . .

The onionskin parchment felt flimsy under the weight of the message. Baxter's hand fell to his lap. Would his father really ask him to come home? Things must be more desperate than he realized. No one had expected the war to last even the summer. He lifted the page again and read on.

From Jacob comes the news that General Beauregard's troops are in severe need of medical supplies, most particularly opium and morphine to aid in surgery. England has the best supplies of the poppy compound from her colony in India. I have made arrangements through our factor in London to purchase a substantial quantity—enough to see our local militia through the end of the year. I believe it is the least that we can do.

I regret that this requires me to ask for your help. The cargo must run the blockade. This means evading not only Lincoln's warships but also the bounders who profit from the high prices that are attached to everything coming through the gauntlet. Your mother paid twenty-five dollars for six spools of English thread last week. Every cargo is so valuable that corruption inevitably results. Opium is worth a king's ransom.

This assignment is perilous. I must ask you to go with the shipment to make sure it is delivered as intended. If the Federals stop your ship, you should try to pass for an Englishman. Don't forget your mother was born within hearing of the bells of St. Paul's, the truest definition of a Londoner—and your years there will have acquainted you with their manners. Yet there is no gainsaying the risk of capture. A great many ships have run the blockade successfully, but not all.

Our London representative tells me that Sir Walter Birch of Pembroke Lane in Mayfair has been of great assistance to others in arranging for transport of goods out of Liverpool to the Confederate States. Please, son, contact him as soon as you can. For your mother and me, be brave, but be careful.

Baxter laid the letter on his night table. His father had written "Confederate States" as naturally as he would once have written "United States." Baxter had not been home since 1858, when he first sailed for England, and it didn't seem real now that two nations had come into existence. How could Virginia, the home of Washington and Jefferson, be outside the United States? Would the Confederates reject John Adams, champion of independence? Was the Union supposed to forswear George Washington, the hero of Valley Forge?

The surreal questions swirled in Baxter's consciousness and combined luridly with the images of surgery and dirty, bloody battlefields. He wished he could pick up the scrub brush and wash his hands of all of it, but temperament and training would not allow him. A doctor did not walk away from a crisis. His vocation commanded him to respond to human need. It was what Baxter loved about medicine—the urgency and the commitment.

He pulled back his shoulders and straightened with resolve. Enough questions. Of course he would help his family. And he would get the wounded the medicine they required. There was no other honorable, meaningful choice. Everything else was politics.

He closed his eyes against the brightness of the morning, and suddenly felt less anxious than he had in months. Relieved. For better or worse, he was going home, and the only question now was, where was Pembroke Lane?

SIR WALTER BIRCH grasped the Virginian's hand firmly. "It's a pleasure to make your acquaintance, Mr. Sams. I thought I had met all of the Confederate purchasing agents in London."

"Thank you, sir, but I don't represent the Confederacy. I am here on behalf of my father's firm, Sams and Sons. He has asked me to accompany this shipment," Baxter said, taking a proffered chair.

Walter lifted one eyebrow. "I see. You are not a Confederate buyer, then, but a private party. Isn't that splitting hairs? Surely you aren't a Unionist. All the Southerners I've met seem to feel that the American president has made quite an ass of himself. Or is it an ape? I've heard the Confederates call him Ape Lincoln."

Baxter was taken aback at this bluntness. He had heard the expression, too, but not from a foreigner, which somehow made it more offensive. "My business is a family matter," Baxter replied simply.

"Well, whatever the case my associates and I are certainly willing to help you," Walter said. "I believe that common decency requires us to do what we can to bring the war to an end. You must know that voices in Parliament are advocating mediation between the two countries. The Northern attack is pure aggression."

Baxter was aware of Walter Birch's sympathies. The Englishman was part of an influential circle that importuned Her Majesty's ministers day and night to recognize the Confederacy as a legitimate member of the community of nations. They argued that a British fait accompli—the forthright acceptance of credentialed Southern diplomats—would force the Union to accept the inevitable and the senseless bloodshed would stop.

"We agree on the need to prevent more suffering," Baxter answered. "The wounded require this medicine as soon as possible."

"Yes, well, I'm afraid that you've just missed the latest sailings," Walter said. "Three vessels left for the Confederacy last week. I don't think there are any more going out until next month."

"As it so happens, I'm still awaiting the clipper *Amelia*, coming in from Calcutta. She is due to land in a fortnight, so we're delayed in any case. Once the opium has arrived, my father's business associate in Liverpool will arrange to transfer the cargo and we can sail."

"I hope you're aware of the hazards. Hundreds of ships have

made it through safely, but some are captured. The Federals confiscated one of our cargoes just last month. A Confederate purchasing agent on board was taken to New York in irons—a nasty business."

"Yes, I understand the risks. We intend to minimize them by going through the port of Nassau," Baxter replied.

The London representative of Sams and Sons had suggested routing the cargo first to the capital of the Bahamas, a group of British islands only sixty miles off the Florida coast. Blockade-runners used Nassau as a way station. British captains could claim they were simply conveying legal products from one royal port to another, which was sometimes even true. Once the goods were safely unloaded, any portion destined for the Confederacy was placed onto a smaller sloop designed for speed, and with a good wind a daring crew could slip right under the nose of the overburdened, underequipped U.S. Navy.

"So how can I help?" Walter asked.

"I understand that you can advise me which merchants are best for expediting this kind of cargo."

"That's true. Not every shipper is willing to take the risk. Any suspicious cargo can expose him to interception, and no one wants the inconvenience of a bad reputation with the Union navy if he can help it. My company helps put interested parties together in a quiet way. I can refer you to an excellent captain who will find space. He'll reimburse our fee. Have you made arrangements for the leg from Nassau to the Confederacy?"

"My father has engaged a captain out of Nassau who will make the run to the coast. Apparently, he hasn't lost a shipment yet," Baxter said. "I understand he considers outfoxing the Federals a form of sport."

Walter's eyes brightened with amusement. "Ah, yes, some of us consider it sport as well. Shipbuilders in Liverpool actually have a running wager on which vessels will make it through. I have a friend who recently won a hundred guineas. Of course, if a ship gets caught the players lose their bets—and the English captains their cargoes. It stings, but not for long. You do realize, however, that you may lose your freedom if apprehended."

Baxter looked directly at his host. Walter's repeated query betrayed an unusual degree of curiosity about a mere business transaction. His expression was not quite readable, as if what he was imagining gave him some satisfaction. Did the man wish him well or ill?

"I am fully aware of the risk I take, Sir Walter. To be candid, I take no pleasure in the division of the Union. My family didn't support secession, but my brothers feel called upon to defend Virginia since it's under attack, and I feel called upon to defend my brothers. I can think of no better way than to make sure the army has the medical supplies it needs."

"Questions of treason and loyalty in America intrigue me," Walter said vaguely. "They are always so complicated."

Baxter could not recall any particular complications before the election of 1860, though life had certainly become interesting since then. He felt discomfited at the inexplicable allusion, guessing that if either of them probed deeper, he would find a man with whom he might not agree on any number of matters. Baxter decided that he would be glad when his business with Sir Walter was done.

The door to the drawing room opened at that moment and a dark-haired young woman walked in, her head in a book. She looked up at the sound of voices, lowered the volume, and slipped a finger between the pages.

"Oh, please excuse me, Father. I didn't realize you were receiving callers this morning."

"Julia, my dear, come in. Allow me to introduce our guest. He's one of the few Southerners who have managed to avoid our net. Mr. Sams, my daughter, Julia."

Baxter rose to his feet, startled. It was the girl he had met at the country ball. He remembered how tall and poised she seemed then, like a queen, or at least like he imagined a queen ought to be, since the real British monarch was short and dumpy. Julia's hair was fixed more loosely than it had been at the dance. Errant curls escaped the twisted bun at her neck.

Julia smiled. "Mr. Sams and I have already met, Father. We were introduced at Lord Forsythe's ball at Foxwood."

Baxter noticed that she didn't mention Henry Adams, whom she met at the same time. He wondered if she was avoiding the name in front of her father. A Confederate sympathizer, Sir Walter wouldn't find an Adams to his liking.

"It's good to see you again," she said, proffering her hand. At almost the same moment, she seemed to hesitate, as if to draw back, but then put her hand forth again.

Baxter had not forgotten Julia's pleasant directness. She seemed less artificial than many women he had met since coming to England. Perhaps it was her height, which she carried with unabashed grace, or her expressive eyes, which met his with confidence. The light of day made hazel an inadequate description of their remarkable color. Green, gold, and gray flecks reflected the morning warmth, like sunlight filtering through a glen in the Blue Ridge. He held her outstretched hand a heartbeat longer than was customary.

"I'm pleased to see you again, too. You and the Bentley sisters were very gracious to me at Foxwood," Baxter said casually to cover the sudden interest he felt in Julia Birch. The voyage ahead had heightened his sense of the significance of every moment. Each day brought him a step closer to the approaching risks— interception, exposure, imprisonment—and enhanced his emotions. Julia Birch was extremely pretty and seemed intensely alive in the light of the drawing room. She reminded him of someone, though he couldn't pinpoint whom.

"I expect that the Bentley sisters were gracious to all the

gentlemen," Walter observed with wry levity. "I predict that one, if not both of them, will be betrothed before Christmas."

Julia's eyes flashed with good humor, but she said nothing. Apparently she refused to give her father the satisfaction of agreeing that the Bentleys were determined flirts.

"If you wish, you may read at the window seat, Julia. Mr. Sams and I are nearly finished."

"Thank you, Father. It's such a gloomy day and the light is better here." Julia took her book to a cushioned bench under a bow window and settled in among the pillows.

It was the loveliest section of the room, Baxter noticed. Overlooking the garden, the window was framed on the outside by climbing red roses that had not yet been touched by the frosts of autumn. Drapes of Chinese silk hung at either side, puddling in deep-blue folds on the floor. An upper fringe of diamond-paned windows filtered the light and cast diaphanous rainbows on the walls. Julia's intent expression registered instant absorption in the book. Baxter wondered how many hours she had spent there, watching her father work, retreating into literature when bored. She was a reader, he saw, like himself.

Baxter turned back to Walter. It would be all right if the meeting didn't end quickly after all.

"Shall we examine the sailing schedules, then?" Walter asked, taking a large folio from the drawer of his writing desk, an expensive inlaid piece that looked Italian. It matched a smaller table across the room under a heroic, full-length portrait of a man in the style of wig that had gone out with George III.

The two pored over the intricate timetables. Ships arrived and departed from Liverpool almost daily, destined for the four corners of the globe.

Baxter kept losing his place, aware of Julia sitting close by. He finally sneaked a peek across the room. She was looking down, deep into the book. The soft light caught the rounded edge of her jaw, highlighting a delicate but determined chin.

"The *Lady Luck* is leaving for Nassau at the end of the month," Walter pointed out. "That should be about when your shipment is ready."

"Do you know if it will have room for more cargo?" Baxter asked, his attention drawn back to the problem at hand.

"There is always room for supplies to the Confederacy. Captains can charge twice the normal carrying rate. The *Lady Luck* will make space if she doesn't have it already."

Walter scrutinized the timetable, and added, "It would be good to have an alternative, however, in case your cargo isn't ready to go when the ship is." He grimaced over the crowded schedule, looking for other sailings.

Baxter glanced at the window seat again. It must be a very good book. Julia frowned slightly, unconsciously mimicking her father's expression. She possessed an arresting combination of femininity and seriousness. Her deportment was as refined as any Southern belle's, but she showed little of the flirtatiousness that most women relied upon to attract attention. She managed to look as desirable concentrating on a book as she did gliding across a dance floor in a formal gown. He wondered what the book was.

"This should suffice. The *Will-o'-the-Wisp* leaves in late November," Walter said. He reached for his fountain pen to circle the two sailings.

"May I borrow this copy?" Baxter asked, looking down at the schedule. "In case the cargo is delayed past November."

"I'm afraid that I cannot part with it, but please allow me to order you another." Walter wrote a brief note to his clerk and, excusing himself, left the room to give it over for delivery. A clock chime sounded from somewhere in the house.

Baxter's eyes wandered back to the window seat, illuminated in the soft morning light. He recalled what Julia reminded him of: his father's description of his mother, whom he had met in London decades earlier. They became acquainted on his father's first business trip to Europe. The two fell in love almost immediately. William Sams had been charmed and enchanted by Muriel Livingston's gentle manners. "She held herself like a princess," he'd recounted with admiration more than once.

Baxter worried for his parents. Their last letter was particularly strained, despite his father's matter-of-fact business news and his mother's postscript giving cheerful reports of home. With constant food shortages and two sons at the front, the war must be an ordeal. He sensed that they hadn't committed their worst trials to paper.

Julia suddenly glanced up. She met his meditative gaze with a bold stare, as if to catch him looking. Surprised, Baxter quickly glanced back at the schedule, pretending to study it. Then he looked up again.

"Pardon my impertinence, Miss Birch. But may I ask what you're reading? It appears quite engrossing."

"It's *Jane Eyre.* Louise Bentley recommended it as wonderfully dramatic. But then Louise loves a good cry."

"I've not yet read the Brontës," Baxter said. "I suppose I should."

Julia wrinkled her nose. "I haven't yet decided whether I like the characters or not. It seems that their every emotion is so *fraught,* if you know what I mean."

Baxter considered her word choice. It was a curious one, but he knew just what she meant. "No sensible women, then, like Jane Austen's heroines?"

She smiled in recognition and took up her book again. "Not so far."

Baxter reexamined the schedule, distracted as much by the departure choices as by Julia. He could hardly think about fiction at the moment. The U.S. Navy might well stop one of these ships. He wished he knew which.

"Will you stay for tea, Mr. Sams?" Julia asked.

Baxter looked up at her again, mildly surprised. She had a quizzical but welcoming expression that made her dark-lashed hazel eyes even more intense. "That's very kind of you, Miss Birch. I would be delighted. That is, if Sir Walter does not have other business to attend to."

"My father never schedules more than one appointment each morning. Isn't that true, Father?" Julia asked as he strode back into the parlor.

He retook his seat with the erect posture of a man who had completed one task and was ready to move on to the next. "Pardon me, my dear?"

"Mr. Sams has agreed to stay to tea. I assured him that he would not be upsetting our plans."

Walter paused imperceptibly and then said, "We would be pleased to have you join us, Mr. Sams. You can share what news you have of the war."

"I'm afraid that I know only what I read in the *Times*."

"Then you've read the accounts of Bull Run. You must feel very heartened by the Yanks' cowardly performance. Not much to fear there."

While he spoke, an Irish maid rolled in a silver cart, set with a pot of tea and a plate of shortbread and seed cake. Julia rose from the window bench and took her seat in a tufted lady's chair that dispensed with armrests to accommodate wide skirts.

"You mean the fighting at Manassas? I did follow it. Rather closely, in fact. My brother is serving under Pierre Beauregard. General Beauregard commanded the Confederate forces at Bull Run."

"Excellent. Then you can clear up a point of confusion that arose at the Carlton Club last night. We've heard both terms, 'Manassas' and 'Bull Run.' Are they the same place?"

"Manassas is a town, and Bull Run is a stream nearby," Baxter explained. "In Virginia, a 'run' is a creek."

"Some papers have called it the Battle of Bull Run. Considering how abbreviated the engagement was, the title hardly seems fitting—except that the Yanks ran."

"Yes, they did, but with two brothers in the army I don't find the Federal defeat as comforting as do our London supporters. I know from four years in Massachusetts that Northerners are made of stern stuff. I'm afraid we underestimate them to our peril."

"And so the laying in of supplies?" Sir Walter asked, in oblique reference to the anticipated opium shipment.

"Exactly," Baxter answered.

Julia lifted the full pot. She held the lid down with one hand and poured the steeped tea with the other. "Please tell me what you mean by supplies, Father," she said.

"Mr. Sams is arranging for a shipment of opium to the Confederacy, Julia. Medical supplies for the troops."

"I thought you were here in the pursuit of learning, Mr. Sams," Julia commented, the tiny furrow of concentration reappearing. "I didn't realize that you are engaged in commerce as well."

"It's good of you to remember, Miss Birch. I am indeed studying at the Royal College of Surgeons, but I'm also obliged to help my father. He's trying to get supplies for surgeries at the battlefront."

"Mr. Sams will be accompanying the shipment, Julia. I am afraid he won't be here to invite to the Christmas ball," Sir Walter added lightly.

"Then you have no opinion on the war yourself?" Julia asked, ignoring her father's comment.

Baxter looked down at his tea. It was a pure, coppery brown, like the curls that nestled at the back of Julia's luminous neck. All the colors of the room seemed brighter than usual. He felt an urge to touch the soft ringlet that brushed her collar, to see how many times it would wrap round his finger. It was a preposterous thought. He hardly knew her.

"My opinion on the war is that I hope it is over soon," Baxter replied. "May I ask about yours?"

"I'll admit that I don't understand the passion for preserving the Union," she said. "It seems foolish. So little gained for such a great price. But I also believe slavery is a true evil. My uncle, Randolph Barclay, thinks that if Mr. Lincoln prevails, the institution will be abolished entirely."

"Nonsense," Sir Walter retorted. "Randolph has an incurable case of wishful thinking. He always has."

"The president has indeed said that the war is not about abolition," Baxter added, at the same time wondering if she thought him a mercenary. Everyone in London knew that the gains on cargoes to the Confederacy could be extraordinary.

Julia twisted a ring on her right hand. "Why accompany the shipment?" she persisted. "Isn't it enough to hire a competent captain? Surely you will make the same commission either way."

Baxter wanted to tell her that he wasn't making a commission. He wanted to say that his parents planned to manumit their servants and that he wished all plantation owners had followed George Washington's example and freed their slaves two generations ago. But he refrained. He wouldn't criticize the cause for which his brothers might die, and it also wasn't wise to defend his actions in front of Sir Walter, who clearly had no qualms either about the war or about making good money from it. The Englishman's help was more important than his daughter's favorable opinion.

"Opium comes at such a high price that it presents an extraordinary temptation for smugglers—men not much troubled by scruples at any time," he explained instead. "We have to be certain that the cargo gets through to its rightful owners."

"Accompanying the shipment is a sound idea," Walter concurred, as if that settled the matter. "In fact, you must have quite a bit to do to get ready."

"I do indeed," Baxter said, and set down his cup. "Please allow me to thank you for your hospitality and your help with arranging the shipment."

"You're quite welcome," Walter replied. "Once you receive the schedule, you can settle on the voyages by speaking directly with the captains sailing out of Liverpool. You may say that I sent you. They all know me."

Baxter stood to go. He looked Julia fully in the face in order to capture her image in his mind. Such an extraordinary image.

"Miss Birch, it was a pleasure meeting you again. I hope you will give the Bentley sisters my warm regards when you see them."

"I shall. But perhaps you'll have the opportunity to do so yourself when you return. I'm certain they enjoyed your company."

"Oh, but Mr. Sams is not likely to be back, my dear, at least not until the war is over," Walter said. "Blockade-running is rather like roulette." Turning to Baxter he added, "And perhaps you will decide to stay and serve your country, if you get past the Federals. Either way, best of luck."

Baxter left Belfield Manor with mixed feelings. He would take care not to be in the vicinity of Pembroke Lane during the next month. A man with a risky mission had no business dwelling on a young woman, he thought as he hailed an empty hansom cab. Any prudent father would certainly agree, and Walter Birch was one man whom he could not afford to offend. Julia had no place in his plans, at least until he finished his task, and he determined to put her out of mind.

ALONE AFTER HER father departed for his club, Julia Birch spent the rest of the day fruitlessly trying to read *Jane Eyre*. Every few pages, she realized that she had read the same paragraph twice. The melancholy gothic style didn't hold her interest. She preferred happier stories in which people who defied convention for love didn't have to die in a snowdrift or go blind and wind up in the madhouse.

She also kept recalling her father's warning that Baxter Sams might be caught in the blockade. Flora Bentley was right that he was good-looking. And he had lovely manners, like an Englishman, or possibly even a Frenchman. But he was a slaveholder and a blockade-runner. How could any man, especially a well-educated one, justify such a vile practice? It galled her to think of him running supplies past the blockade, aiding a war to keep Africans in chains. He hadn't seemed the mercenary type—a doctor, after all—but everyone knew that the profits were extraordinary. He was an American, too. Her father's grudge against the United States was lifelong, going back to her great-grandfather's misfortunes. Someone like Baxter Sams would never be invited to a Christmas ball at Belfield Manor, despite her father's little joke.

Julia finally closed the book, realizing that it was best to give up. It was then that she remembered, quite vividly and unexpectedly, how warmly the Virginian had grasped her hand when she offered it to him. She could picture him treating a patient, his touch gentle but authoritative, and yet he certainly had not looked at her with professional detachment. Was it her imagination, or had he hesitated before letting go? Perhaps that was why it wasn't considered proper to shake hands, at least according to Flora Bentley. Too much feeling might pass between a woman and a man—feelings that could lead into waters as choppy and deep as those between England and America.

EIGHT

*A true democracy is a pretty hard thing to whip and I cannot
help thinking that, in a war forced upon us . . . England would
find us as ugly a customer as she had often dealt with. Still it is a
conclusion terrible to think of. As great a cause as ever men
struggled for ruined forever by so needless a side issue!*

—Charles Francis, Jr., to his brother Henry in London,
A Cycle of Adams Letters

"Damn!" Henry interjected passionately. "Do you think that Secretary Seward could possibly have authorized Captain Wilkes's capture of those men? If he did, he will have started a war with England!"

"I have no idea, Henry," his father answered. "And what's worse is that I will have to tell Lord Russell I have no idea."

Charles and Henry retreated to the study the minute the minister arrived home from the long train ride. They were at their desks now. It was the first chance they had had to discuss the telegram that Charles received while he and Abby were visiting the country home of Richard Monckton Milnes. Milnes was a noted Yorkshire poet and member of Parliament, a fashionable combination in Victorian society. He was also sympathetic to the Union and thus one of the legation's few friends. Renowned for holding independent views that regularly contradicted those of conceited Londoners, Milnes was, in short, exceptionally entertaining.

The Yorkshire man had brought together a small, congenial group to visit the Roman ruins on his country estate. It was a lovely day for late November, with a watery blue sky and a bracing chill that cleared the air. Charles and Abby had looked forward to the diversion, especially since their children were staying behind in London. She had bought a new walking dress for the occasion, and the party was clambering among tumbled columns and mossy stones when a rider dismounted with a telegram from the legation in London.

There had been an incident in the Bahamas Channel. The USS *San Jacinto* had boarded a British mail ship over the protests of her captain and taken two Confederate emissaries into custody, James Mason and John Slidell, on their way to Europe. Mr. Adams was needed urgently at the U.S. Legation. The British foreign secretary, Lord Russell, was demanding an explanation for this extraordinary breach of protocol. Abby had immediately insisted that they leave for London, refusing to let Charles think that he was the one to spoil their small holiday.

"What I don't understand is why John Russell learned of this before I did," Charles said to Henry with exasperation. "Seward should have sent a telegram. Instead, we find out from the British foreign secretary that our navy has violated the rules of engagement. It's embarrassing. It's intolerable."

"Are we necessarily in the wrong? Might the law sustain Wilkes's action?" Henry asked. "He arrested the emissaries off Havana. They had to have run our blockade to get there."

Henry reached out to a tray that the housekeeper had left on the writing table. He poured two glasses of water and walked one across the room to his father.

"Thank you, Henry," Charles said, though he put the glass down without taking a drink. It had already been a long, wearying day, though it had barely begun.

"It's not entirely certain that this Captain Wilkes was in error, but if I had to render a legal opinion, it would be that Wilkes had no authority whatsoever to remove the Confederate emissaries. So either he took the authority upon himself—and deserves to be court-martialed—or, worse, our government condoned his action."

Charles spoke with assurance. He had handled cases in maritime law in Boston for three decades. What was more, his own grandfather and father had negotiated most of the country's maritime disputes with England. They had practically written the laws.

"Our informant said that Wilkes seized the Southerners and their documents as 'contraband.' Why wouldn't that definition apply?" Henry asked. "This is war, after all. There has to be some way to yank traitors off a British ship. Mason and Slidell were on their way to persuade England and France to side with the Confederacy. Napoleon III has made clear his sympathies for the South."

"That's irrelevant, Henry. Maritime law is quite clear. Even if a court were to rule that the emissaries and their documents were contraband, Wilkes seized them illegally. He fired a shot across the bow of the British ship, forced her to stop, boarded with pistols and cutlasses, and seized two of her passengers. International law requires that a captain steer a neutral vessel into port for trial by a prize court. Only a court may rule on what is contraband, and thus forfeited, and what is not. If Wilkes had escorted the *Trent* to Boston, instead of simply taking Mason and Slidell off the ship, we might have a leg to stand on."

Charles spoke precisely, as if dictating a legal brief. His emotions were on ice as he prepared himself to face Russell. He couldn't concede his government's error without authorization, but it also would not do to pretend that the facts were any less compromising than they were. Lord Russell, recently elevated to Earl, would spot an empty excuse faster than the palace guard could mark a pickpocket. Charles now lifted the glass Henry had given him and drained it, grateful for the water but wishing it were whiskey.

"I should think the British ought to be relieved that Wilkes didn't waylay the *Trent* itself," Henry observed.

"Waylay the *Trent?*"

"Yes, press it into port. I should think it would have been more galling to have the ship commandeered by Wilkes. Imagine the uproar in London if he had forced the *Trent* into Boston Harbor at gunpoint."

"That's where you fail to appreciate the British mentality, Henry. They stand by their rules. Wilkes did not show good form. The English would be much less offended if the United States had at least insulted her ship properly. He ought to have taken the *Trent* straight to Boston or New York for adjudication by the prize court, or not removed even a thumbtack. Just let her sail away. Now it's a matter of honor for Whitehall—and for the British, honor is a matter of war."

Charles resisted saying the rest of what he was thinking. If Lincoln and Seward condoned Wilkes's provocation in any way, they were simply not fit to govern. Absolute incompetents. It would not take much to tip England into open hostility toward the Union; after all, many Brits still instinctively resented America for its defiance in 1776. The legation balanced on the knife-edge of British opinion. His countrymen deceived themselves if they thought tweaking Great Britain was a sport they could afford.

At the same time, Charles understood the impulse to goad the British. Henry had initially greeted his return from the countryside with the shining face of a schoolboy whose team had come from behind. Damn the Brits and score one for the Union! Henry appeared chastened now, but his broad smile when Charles first arrived showed how badly he and most other Americans would misjudge events. *Fools rush in,* Charles thought.

"When do you expect to hear from Washington?" Henry asked.

"I don't know. I've cabled our consul in Southampton, but it will take well more than a week for a steamship to relay the message to Boston. Once it's telegraphed from there to Washington, I can only hope Seward will reply immediately. If he doesn't, we may be home in time for Christmas," Charles stated grimly. "The English government is quite likely to ask us to leave. They'll break off relations—and that will leave the field open to the Confederates."

A knock at the door of the study announced the legation's housekeeper. "I have the rest of today's mail, Mr. Adams. Would you like to see it now?"

"Yes, Kathleen, thank you. Is there anything from Washington?"

"I'm afraid not, sir, but there are some newspapers, and a letter from your son Charles, it appears." She set the bundle on the desk and left.

The minister divided the stack, giving the newspapers to Henry. "You look over these, while I see what Charles has to say. Maybe he can enlighten us. Or at least make us laugh."

Charles, Jr., often embellished his letters with amusing anecdotes of the Massachusetts militia. After perusing his other correspondence, the minister opened his son's letter, hoping for diversion. But he soon looked over at Henry with a face even paler than before.

"Well, it's done," Charles said, holding the letter written by his namesake. "I don't know how I am going to tell your mother."

Henry looked up from the gray newsprint spread around him. "Tell Mother what?" he asked.

"That Charles has enlisted with the Army of the Potomac." He cleared his throat and read aloud: *"You say there is neither glory nor honor to be won in civil strife. I answer that it cannot be otherwise than right for me to fight to maintain that which my ancestors passed their whole lives in establishing."*

Charles stopped, unable to go on. The words were exactly what he hoped any of his sons would say—that they embraced the family legacy—but the thought of Charles, Jr., in mortal danger made them now seem the height of folly.

"You expected it, didn't you? Last spring he said the same thing," Henry reminded his father.

Charles sighed deeply. Reaching into his rolltop desk, he pulled out a letter that occupied an otherwise empty pigeonhole. He unfolded the creased missive that he had read more than once:

> In the Civil War in England or in the Revolution here, what should we now think of a man who, in the hour of greatest danger, sat at home reading the papers? . . . It is not as if I were an only son, though many such have gone; but your family is large and it seems to me almost disgraceful that in afteryears we should have it to say that, of them all, not one at this day stood in arms for that government with which our family history is so closely connected.

His strong-willed son had written as formally and eloquently as if composing another Declaration of Independence, which, in a way, he was. Charles tried and failed to imagine his third child and namesake at the front in Virginia. All he could call up was the daylong pilgrimage they had made years before to Mount Vernon, when Henry and Charles, Jr., were still small. He had wanted to show the boys where the great man had lived and died. It wasn't an easy trip, though the distance from the District of Columbia wasn't far. The wheels kept getting stuck in the muck. He got down at least twice, rolling up his sleeves and urging the pair of horses to pull free. Even the color of the mud was disquieting—a lurid terra-cotta, more like blood than dirt, that left a red stain on the hem of his trousers. Charles hadn't said a word, but the boys were old enough to understand what bad roads meant. To the New England mind, a good road was like a clean face and a fresh collar. One couldn't get into school or heaven without one. A bad road meant bad morals. Now his older son was headed back to those treacherous, boggy roads. Rangy, mountainous, mysterious Virginia might be his burying ground.

Charles lined the new letter up with the old one, folded the sheets of paper into each other, and placed them back in the slot. The Adamses did not shrink from duty—it was their polestar. He and Abby would support Charles's decision, whispering their fears only under the bedcovers at night. It was a simple fact that when they gave their children life, they gave them mortality, too. It was a hard bequest.

"What have you found in the newspapers, Henry?" he asked in a calm, controlled voice, signaling an end to the discussion about Henry's older brother.

"Well, at first glance it appears that Captain Wilkes was greeted with universal acclaim when he sailed into Boston with the two envoys," Henry said, holding up a Massachusetts paper. "The governor gave him a public banquet, and the secretary of the navy wrote a personal letter of congratulations. Congress voted him a gold medal. In other words, if an Englishman read this newspaper—and some will—he wouldn't believe for a minute that the United States is not squarely behind Wilkes."

Henry laid down the New England daily and picked up two New York papers. "Meanwhile, it seems that lunatics inhabit the rest of the country. One editor swears to take Canada. Another blames our losses on Britain for supplying the Confederacy through the blockade. Both gloat over the insult to England in snatching the Rebels off the *Trent*. If I were reading them over the breakfast table in Quincy, they might sound perfectly righteous. In London, each sounds a bit more ridiculous than the last."

"Damn!" It was the minister's turn to swear. He slapped a hand on his desk, temper flaring. "They just don't get it! Europe from end to end will be arrayed against us on this matter, yet people back home don't entertain a shade of suspicion that they are not absolutely right. The simpletons fail to understand that passions and pride are not to be trifled with. England can crush us. Good God, my son is turning his life over to a government of fools."

Charles rarely spoke in such strong terms. He normally measured displeasure with a teaspoon, keeping the rest bottled inside. Now he abruptly shook his head, pushed roughly away from the desk, and stood up. He straightened his jacket and rolled down the top of the oak secretary, quieting his emotions.

"If you'll excuse me, Henry, I am going to find your mother. If you have time, please make me a summary of the news. I wish to be prepared for Lord Russell. He's already better informed than I am."

"What will you tell Charles?" Henry asked.

"I will not tell him anything. He is a grown man."

Charles, Sr., walked to the door, placed his hand on the brass doorknob, and then turned to face Henry. He hesitated. He felt that he had to know. "More to the point, what will you do?"

"Me? What do you mean?"

"You're also your own man. You must share your brother's feelings. Will you enlist as well?"

Henry averted his eyes, stood, and walked to the window that overlooked the gray street. Outside, a chill November wind battled the last stubborn leaves clinging to the trees. The street was a rust-colored mosaic of the fallen. Charles waited.

"What can I say?" Henry asked finally, his back to the room. Charles couldn't see his son's face, but Henry's words were edged with bitterness.

"It was bad enough when he wrote about training with the militia," Henry continued. "Up at reveille, drilling five hours a day, slopping in the mess hall, sharing a tiny room with eleven other men. Having the time of his life! Now my brother has joined the greatest, most important crusade of our generation and I'm stuck in London, copying letters and being chided to keep my handwriting neat."

Henry turned on his heel to face Charles. His face showed an inner struggle. "The honest truth is that I feel like a coward. Everyone I know except Baxter Sams is at the front. What will they say about *me* in afteryears?"

"They will say that you helped keep England out of the war. There is heroism in that, too," Charles replied.

Henry looked intently at his father, as if considering the answer.

"I can't say what I may decide in coming months," he replied, "but for now I won't enlist. Lincoln and Seward have left you to dangle on a string, and there are, obviously, many people here who would take great pleasure in snipping it. I can't leave. But I wish our government would make emancipation the battle cry. I would like to think we're fighting for something nobler than pride. It would make being chained to these desks worth it."

"We *are* fighting for something important, Henry. I promise you we are."

Henry's face registered doubt, but Charles had to believe that, ultimately, his son would understand. He couldn't face the possibility of telling Abby they would have two sons at the front.

NINE

A thousand lives seemed to be concentrated in that one moment
to Eliza. Her room opened by a side door to the river. She caught
her child, and sprang down the steps towards it. The trader
caught a full glimpse of her, just as she was disappearing down
the bank; . . . he was after her like a hound after a deer.

—Harriet Beecher Stowe, *Uncle Tom's Cabin*

The packed audience listened spellbound to the dramatic
reading of *Uncle Tom's Cabin*. The soft light of the gas lamps
threw shadows into the far corners of the great hall. When the
performer for the British Anti-Slavery Society came to the part
where Eliza jumped in panic from ice floe to ice floe, clutching
her baby against her bosom to save him from the slave hunters,
mothers in the audience pressed handkerchiefs to their faces and
wept.

Julia listened dry-eyed, but with a gloved hand at her throat.
At a previous meeting of the society, she and her uncle Randolph
had heard a former slave sing "Sometimes I Feel Like a Motherless Child." The voice of the Negro woman soared to the rafters
in eerie sorrow, the notes ascending in a slow, sad wake.

The last elusive bars of the song reverberated in Julia's imagination as she pictured Eliza's desperate flight across the melting
river, cracks in the ice shooting outward under the feet, racing
her to the nether shore. Julia felt as though a part of her were the
runaway mother, while another part wished she were the closely
held child for whom someone would brave the perilous water.

Constance Birch had bled to death bringing a son into the

world when Julia was only seven. Since then, Julia had watched over her brother Edmund, now away at boarding school. She would do anything for him. He was her pride and joy. Yet she also was a motherless child. She couldn't remember when anyone had loved her with the ferocity of Eliza. The clearest memory she had of her mother was of fingers pinching slightly as she pulled up Julia's sagging stockings, tugging at the ankles, edging past the knees, fastening them to a lace garter on which her mother had sewn a small silk bow. Julia loved that pretty garter. "Don't wiggle," her mother had said, bending over her daughter's legs. Julia treasured the fading impression of a sweet-smelling, dark-haired woman who cared if her seamed stockings were straight.

"We're taking up a collection for the arming of colored troops," the society's chairman announced after the actor reading the novel had retaken his seat on the dais. "I have here a letter from the former slave Frederick Douglass, whom some of you heard speak in this very chamber a number of years ago. He is now acting as a consultant to President Abraham Lincoln."

A flurry of thrilled whispers broke out across the large hall. Randolph Barclay turned to Julia and gave her forearm a quick squeeze in excitement. "I was here when he spoke. I doubt a greater man ever lived," he told his niece. The audience quieted again as the speaker waved a scrap of paper in his right hand.

"Mr. Douglass calls upon the British Anti-Slavery Society to donate whatever funds it can spare for the formation of a colored regiment to fight on behalf of the Union. He says that President Lincoln believes the Union can never survive half slave, half free. It's only a matter of time before the war becomes a fight for abolition. When that happens, colored troops need to be ready to take up arms for their brothers, sisters, mothers, and fathers still in chains."

The speaker paused for dramatic emphasis. He glared into the crowd. "Will you help them?"

Julia and Randolph rose to their feet in the same spontaneous wave that swept the rest of the audience from their seats, clapping wildly and reaching for billfolds and handbags.

"Uncle, you *will* give something, won't you?" Julia asked, looking up at him. The thought of mothers and children in need, at the mercy of vicious hunters, tore at her heart.

"Of course, my dear," Randolph said. "Abolition is England's greatest moral achievement. Not one Negro slave lives under British rule. With God's grace, this war will eliminate it in America as well. We introduced slavery there—and we must take some responsibility for bringing it to an end." He drew a billfold from his waistcoat. "I'll be right back."

Randolph weaved his way to the front of the auditorium, and Julia walked to the rear of the hall, where a ladies' committee was setting out tea and sweet biscuits. "May I assist you?" she asked the plump matron in charge.

"Thank you, miss. We do have our hands full. If you'd pour these cups, we'll get a head start on the crowd." The older woman straightened her flowery cap and turned the handle of the teapot toward Julia. "There you go. You take this, and I'll fetch more biscuits."

Julia slipped off her gloves, grateful for the chance to be of help. She removed the quilted tea cozy from the full pot and began filling the row of white porcelain cups, each just short of the brim, with room for cream. The prosaic task soothed her spirit, made pensive by the dramatic speeches of the evening. Her emotions felt close to the surface, almost on her skin, and she felt a yearning for something, though she wasn't sure what. When the pot was empty, she placed it on a trolley by the table. Members of the audience began filtering back to the tea table.

"May I have one of these?" an American voice asked. "Or are they spoken for?"

Startled, Julia turned to look into the smiling blue eyes of H. Baxter Sams. She no more expected to see him at an anti-slavery meeting than she did Santa Claus or her father.

"What are you doing here?" she asked a split second before she thought to bite her tongue. Julia turned pink at her own rudeness and could feel her cheeks glow in the soft gas lighting.

Baxter apparently refused to be offended. "I'm here for the same reason you are. To save my immortal soul," he said with a half smile that shaded into seriousness. "Slavery is a crime against the heart. When they admit it to themselves, Southerners know that better than anyone."

"How in the world can you go back to the Confederacy, then? How can you help the wrong side?"

Julia knew that she shouldn't speak so bluntly. Such directness was provocative and ill-mannered. But the occasion demanded plain speaking, and something about Baxter Sams undid her normal reserve. Perhaps it was because he was an American, whose social conventions she little understood. Perhaps it was because he was on the brink of a voyage from which he might never return. A lock of dark hair fell across Baxter's forehead, lounging just above his left eye, and Julia smothered the temptation to push it back, as she would have for Edmund.

"Will you allow me to explain? I believe I owe you that. This is the third time you've asked." Baxter gestured toward a nearly empty row of seats.

The audience was dispersing for tea and conversation. Glancing toward the front, Julia noted that her uncle appeared to be engaged in a dialogue with the chairman of the society. The didactic impulse seemed to have taken possession of both of them. Handing a teacup and saucer to Baxter, Julia took a chair in a long row of emptied seats at the shadowy rear of the hall.

Baxter sat beside her and looked into her eyes with a sober expression.

"My parents own two slaves," he started, speaking slowly, "though that's a word we rarely use. It doesn't feel polite or, somehow, loyal. I've known Jesmina and Clara all my life. Yet calling them slaves seems to demean them, even though they would use the word themselves. That must seem terribly hypo-critical to you. To spare their feelings while denying their reality. But for us it's inborn."

Baxter paused and frowned down at the tea.

"Jesmina raised me from an infant. She's like a second mother. In fact, I think I'm more afraid of her than I am of my real mother." He looked up with a slight smile. "She scolded me more times than I care to remember—but she also never told on me to a soul. No matter how many times she found me with my hand in the proverbial cookie jar. I didn't really think about slavery, or consider it wrong, you see, until I read Thomas Jefferson's *Notes on the State of Virginia* when I went North to school. He wrote that slavery degraded both whites and blacks. That it robbed masters and slaves alike of their humanity." Baxter spoke now with hushed heat. "And yet he never freed his own people. Jefferson is like a god to us in Virginia. Our hero, my hero, didn't live up to his own ideals! He didn't do what was right."

Julia could see that the admission cost him something. It must be hard to bare Virginia's dirty linen to a foreigner.

"Because of this war, my parents have decided to free their servants. They say they hate slavery, they always have. But only the war would have led them to take this step. My own parents. Lincoln says the fight isn't about slavery, and the Confederates say it isn't about slavery. But every man, woman, and child, North and South, knows that slavery is exactly what divides us. You asked me what I thought of the conflict. I tell you that it is horrible—and absolutely necessary."

"Then why in heaven's name are you running the blockade? How can you possibly justify it?" Julia asked. She flushed again at her own temerity, but added, "Actions speak louder than words."

"As I explained to your father, my family has asked me to help. I won't turn my back on them."

"Can't you aid them without sending supplies to the Confederacy? Won't that just help the slaveholders win? People just like Simon Legree?"

"I have to help the wounded, regardless of consequences. I'm a doctor," Baxter added with the finality with which most people would have said, "I'm a Christian."

Julia was struck silent. She had met many gentlemen with a birthright, but none with a calling that involved personal risk or self-sacrifice. It impressed her, though the idea of aiding the South was still repugnant.

"They're asking for a drug to ease the agony of men whose arms and legs will be amputated in dirty field hospitals," Baxter continued. "The soldiers on both sides fire minié balls. The newer muskets are more accurate than ever before and the bullets leave huge wounds filled with dirt and debris, bits of clothing. Their bodies are chewed up and infection is rampant. Surgeons have no choice but to just remove destroyed limbs. Amputate them. As a doctor—as a human being—I must do what I can to alleviate that suffering. I can't refuse to help. I *won't* refuse to help."

The graphic description was indelicate, unfit for a gentlewoman, but the rawness of his words touched her. Julia looked carefully into Baxter's face. Her chair was edge to edge with his. She could just make out the beard under his pale skin—a bluish shadow that seemed like masculinity itself. She wondered if his closely shaved cheek would feel smooth if she put her hand to it. The hall suddenly felt too warm. She looked down at her hands and twisted her signet ring.

For all its earlier urgency, the problem of slavery now seemed far away. Julia realized that she simply wanted to know Baxter better. He wasn't an unredeemable slaveholder, she now understood. He wasn't a mercenary or a coward. Far from it, he was willing to risk his freedom for the safety of others. But the war wasn't the only thing in his life. What made him laugh? Did he like England? Was his family large, or small like hers?

And what right did she have to judge him? Her own father was invested in ships that everyone knew were meant for foreign buyers, probably Confederates. She had seen the letters from Laird Brothers on his desk. She had planned parties, decorated their home, and entertained slaveholders with the money that her father gave her for the household. Who knew what suffering paid for Belfield Manor?

The young Southerner reached over to still her nervous fiddling. "You do understand, don't you?" His hand was warm over hers.

Julia sat very still, looking down. The image of him turning over her palm and kissing it flashed unbidden through her mind. She could feel her heart beating high in her chest, and wondered with alarm if he could hear it. Baxter removed his hand, but remained close. Her hand tingled where he had touched it. She glanced up, eyes wide. "Will you come to see me when you get back?" she asked in a low voice.

Struck speechless for a moment, Baxter then broke into a brilliant smile. "Yes, I'll call on you when I get back! The minute I do, if you'll allow me."

Julia stood up. Her woolen dress fell in blue folds to the floor. She guessed that her father would not want her to see Baxter Sams, or any American for that matter, but she pushed the thought to the back of her mind. She simply wanted to find out if the soldiers received the medicine they needed. Or at least that's what she would say if her father asked. It's what she told herself now.

"My uncle and you—and I," she added, "share a common outlook. Perhaps you could visit us at his home in the country. I spend a month there every spring. He has wonderful gardens."

"I shall make a point of it. Thank you for the invitation."

Julia held out her hand to say goodbye, despite Flora's admonition, expecting an American handshake. But Baxter raised her hand to his lips in the manner of the French. Though fleeting, his kiss was soft and expressive. It seemed that time slowed, and that her heart skipped a beat.

"Good luck to you, Mr. Sams. Please let us know when you've arrived safely," Julia said, withdrawing her hand and speaking in as normal a tone as she could manage despite her racing pulse. She gave him a nod and turned to look for her uncle, acutely aware that the Southerner's kiss was more than mere continental courtesy, though she could not have said why. The moment his lips touched her stood out in high contrast from all those before—brighter, sharper, more colorful. For reasons she didn't understand, it was hard to keep from crossing the lines of propriety with this man.

At the front of the hall, Randolph Barclay had not moved an inch. He still stood nose to nose with the society chairman, engaged in the spirited dialogue that was emblematic of his dizzying political enthusiasms.

As she approached them, feeling strangely elated, Julia saw Randolph draw back, reach for his billfold, and take out a bank draft. She hoped her uncle, who was normally pleased to grant her wishes, would not mind that she had invited a Confederate to tea in the country. Southerners had been the villains of the evening's drama.

Julia stopped in the aisle. Randolph might never know, she realized. Baxter Sams might not return from across the ominous Atlantic. She turned at the thought to take one last look at him, but he was gone.

TEN

December 1861

These people speak our language, use our prayers, read our books,
are ruled by our laws, dress themselves in our image, are warm
with our blood. They have all our virtues; and their vices are our
own too, loudly as we call out against them. They are our sons
and our daughters, the source of our greatest pride, and as
we grow old they should be the staff of our age. Such a war as we
should now wage with the States would be an unloosing
of hell upon all that is best upon the world's surface.

—Anthony Trollope, *North America*

A stiff gust pushed hard against Charles as he struggled up
the street to the offices of the British foreign secretary,
clinging to his top hat. He leaned into the wind to stay upright.
The leaves were gone from the trees now and the muddy December sky threatened rain. Folded safely inside his breast
pocket, protected from the blustery London weather, was the
dispatch he had received from Secretary of State William Seward.

Once inside Whitehall, Charles paused to straighten his coat
and cravat. He checked his sleeves to make sure the proper mar-
gin of white cuff peeked out from under the dark suit, and
glanced briefly at his brilliantly polished shoes. Stooping, he
wiped away a speck of mud before the butler could return. Lord
Russell was fastidious. It would not do to have a bit of grass
clinging to the boot, as if the Yankee minister were a country

cousin come to call. The English instinctively viewed the former colonials as yokels. They were as ready to underestimate Americans as Americans were to overestimate themselves.

"The earl will see you now," the butler announced, showing him into John Russell's office.

The Right Honorable John Russell, also known as the 1st Earl Russell, the Viscount Amberley of Amberley, the Viscount of Ardsalla and third son of His Grace the 6th Duke of Bedford, rose from his desk to greet plain Charles Francis Adams of Quincy, Massachusetts.

"Good morning, Mr. Adams. How are you today?"

With an elegant gesture toward intricately carved chairs that framed a sitting area, Lord Russell invited Charles to sit. The British foreign secretary was a short, exceedingly spare man in his late sixties with neat muttonchop whiskers, an aquiline nose, and a square, decisive chin. His eyes were intelligent and piercing, but gave no hint of his attitude toward his guest. Indeed, his cool manner was neither friendly nor unfriendly, neither welcoming nor indifferent. The queen's neutrality, personified. Utterly correct, dangerously uncommitted.

"I'm very well, thank you, although my family and I are deeply grieved by the death of the prince consort. Please accept our very sincere condolences, Lord Russell."

Charles had sent cards to the queen and the prime minister, but he had not seen anyone in government since the terrible event of the week before. England had held its collective breath while doctors rushed in and out of Buckingham Palace. But none were able to save the queen's beloved German husband, tragically and unexpectedly overwhelmed by typhoid fever at the age of forty-two.

Now that the outspoken prince was gone, ministers who might have liked to quiet him in the past feared the effect of death's more enduring silence. In the years since Victoria proposed marriage to her dashing first cousin, the flighty girl had steadied into a hardworking, dutiful monarch. The shock might unhinge the royal mind. If so, Prince Albert would be deeply missed by more than his adoring wife and their nine children.

The American Legation had special reason to mourn the death of the enterprising, opinionated consort. It was well known in club circles that he had counseled the queen to soften her ministers' dispatches to President Lincoln about the *Trent* mishap. The prince did not think that a breach of conduct by a brash American sea captain should be allowed to escalate into a war best avoided by diplomacy. Patience is a virtue, he commented, propping himself in his sickbed to look at the cables. Her Majesty's ministers quietly resented the meddling prince consort, but they had little choice except to tolerate the man who shared the queen's bedchamber.

"I thank you for your sympathies, Mr. Adams. We feel the loss quite keenly."

Lord Russell spoke as formally as he did on every occasion, appearing to quote directly from the pertinent page in *Debrett's Etiquette,* the indispensable guide to proper form since 1769, but Charles sensed that the earl was genuine. His lined face, fine as parchment, blanched at the mention of the young prince so rudely snatched from life. Perhaps the reticent earl did have a heart somewhere under his marble façade.

"Your letter said that you had received further news from your government," Lord Russell continued, after a brief pause in which the butler poured the two diplomats a splash of Spanish sherry. The facets of the crystal glasses now glimmered with color, as if imprisoning rainbows from the misty Irish coast where they were made.

"Yes, I received a dispatch from Mr. Seward yesterday. I'm very pleased to confirm that Captain Wilkes had no prior authorization whatsoever to remove James Mason or John Slidell from the *Trent,*" Charles said. "My government has no wish to provoke war with Her Majesty."

"That's most welcome news, Mr. Adams. I can assure you that my government shares your sentiment, especially in this time of bereavement."

John Russell took a tiny sip from his glass. "I assume that means we can expect a formal apology and the immediate release of the prisoners," he added.

Charles stilled the impulse to shift in his chair. The foreign secretary clearly did not intend to let up on Britain's demand for full satisfaction. Without the slightest alteration in expression, Charles replied, "Unfortunately, Mr. Seward has not yet communicated what action my government will take at this point. The matter is under consideration by Mr. Lincoln's cabinet. I can assure you that the problem has their full attention."

Lord Russell accepted this with an air of mild unconcern, much as if Mr. Adams had commented on a change in the weather. A diplomat, especially a British one, never conveyed emotion.

"I see. Then we shall expect a further response from President Lincoln in the near future. Of course, I must reiterate that my government shall await his decision with interest."

Lord Russell did not have to tell Charles the catastrophic consequences that might follow, depending on what Lincoln decided. The London government had already ordered ten thousand well-drilled redcoats to Canada to reinforce defenses against the United States and stop any attack across the border. They were mustering in Halifax even now. The admiralty had also dispatched three ships of the line and two frigates to patrol the North Atlantic. Confederate newspapers hailed the momentous news as Britain's first step toward open war with the Union.

But as time passed without a specific battle cry the American minister had begun to hope that the worst would be a temporary rupture. Prince Albert's death seemed to dampen the general enthusiasm for bloodshed, and the London dailies had drawn back from their hysterical calls for punishing the impertinent, impossible Americans. At the least, Lord Russell would probably hand Charles his passport and request the recall of the American minister to assuage British public opinion. The government needed to take out its displeasure on someone, and Charles Francis Adams was as good a candidate as any. In fact, it would be far better for him to be disgraced than for the two countries to go to war, Charles thought. Then Lincoln could send some other fool to wait on the Court of St. James's.

All's well that ends well, Charles thought grimly. Too bad it wouldn't be in time for Christmas. He missed Quincy more each day. There would be thick carpets of snow on the roofs by now. From the window of his library at home, Charles could rest his eyes upon the red barn and sleeping pastures that were as pretty as any Currier and Ives print. There, in beloved Quincy, only a barking watchdog might disturb his peace, instead of the hounds of the British Empire. He could hardly remember why he had wanted the job of minister, except when he wrote his last name.

Lord Russell stood. Charles followed his lead, expecting to be dismissed.

The English earl hesitated and then said, "I understand that the abolitionist leader Frederick Douglass is a friend of your president."

The American minister considered quickly the reasons for John Russell's question. It was well known that the foreign secretary harbored abolitionist sympathies, but he had never revealed them directly. Indeed, Russell's liberalism was a subject of droll amusement around London. In his youth, he had acquired a reputation for eccentricity by traveling around Ireland. No one visited Ireland. He hadn't even been *sent*. It was like Japan or Mars, beyond the pale of civilization. Indeed, the very term "the pale" had been coined to describe the part of the island that was outside British control. Many considered John Russell a queer bird, despite his successful career in government.

"They are indeed friends," Charles confirmed. "Mr. Douglass is consulting with the White House even now on the disposition of slaves in captured territories. As you know, the president has decreed the slaves as contraband, and intends to free anyone confiscated."

"I heard Mr. Douglass speak in London a number of years ago," Lord Russell offered. "He was most impressive."

"Yes, he is. I consider him one of the greatest speakers of our generation. I made his acquaintance in Boston. He now lives in New York," Charles added, grasping for ways to extend the conversation. "He's quite a powerful writer, too. Have you seen his autobiography?"

"My brother and I read it together a few years ago. The story of his close escape affected us deeply. It had never occurred to us that a slave might deter a beating by sheer force of personality. Douglass is a remarkable person. I hope he will be able to help Mr. Lincoln resolve the problem of slavery."

"Thank you for your concern, Lord Russell," Charles said with sincere appreciation. "I shall convey it to the president."

John Russell nodded to indicate that the interview was at an end, and Charles took his leave with a polite bow.

Against challenges from both radical abolitionists and die-hard slaveholders, Lincoln had maintained that the Federal government sought only reunion. Charles originally thought the policy prudent. They had lived with slavery for two generations under the Constitution and could stand it a while longer if it meant keeping the border states loyal. The minister could certainly go no further than his president in statements to John Russell, but he hoped that Russell would take Lincoln's relationship with Douglass as a sign that the goals of the war might yet change. If they did, it would help the Union's international position immensely. Perhaps Russell could even be drawn in as an ally against those who favored the Union's destruction.

Charles was not at liberty to put any of this into words with Lord Russell, any more than Lord Russell could give hints about British policy. But in Victorian England the things that were not said were often more important than those that were. Charles stepped back into the blustery London street, now dark in the wintry night, cupping a spark of hope.

ELEVEN

I never quite appreciated the "moral influence" of American
democracy, nor the cause that the privileged classes in
Europe have to fear us, until I saw how directly it works. . . .
You can find millions of people who look up to our institutions
as their model and who talk with utter contempt
of their own system of Government.

—Henry Adams to his brother Charles,
A Cycle of Adams Letters

Baxter handed his card to a diminutive Irish housekeeper of indeterminate age who wore a full-length white apron. She had red hair, a square Celtic face that looked as if it would color easily when she was in a temper, and a sharp, determined chin. Now her eyebrows flew upward like crows off a branch. One crooked diagonally. She held his card by a corner.

"He's in the parlor, sir. But all the other afternoon callers have come and gone. I doubt that he's still receiving."

"Would you mind asking, please?" Baxter gave her what he thought was his most winning smile.

The housekeeper did not return it. "Please wait here," she replied with obvious reluctance.

Within moments, Henry Adams strode into the entry hall. "Baxter! How splendid of you to drop by. I was perishing from boredom. Do come in."

Henry turned to the housekeeper, whose stern expression showed disapproval at the breach of protocol. Callers normally left cards if they missed the usual visiting hours. But Baxter needed to speak to Henry.

"Kathleen. Could you please send in some tea—no, make that brandy, it's late in the day—for Mr. Sams and me?"

"'Tis a chill evening, Mr. Adams. I'll have Emma fix you a hot whiskey," the housekeeper said, apparently determined to set him right on matters of refreshment at least. She placed Baxter's card in the silver salver, which she then repositioned on the mantel in what seemed an unspoken rebuke.

Henry started to reply, but checked himself. He shot Baxter a confidential smile, and then asked, "Incidentally, can you tell me where the minister went, Kathleen? I haven't seen him since I arrived home more than two hours ago."

"Mr. Adams is over to the Foreign Ministry. He asked me to tell you he is meeting with that man, and not to expect him until suppertime."

"I see. Thank you, then," Henry said. He opened the parlor door for Baxter. "Please, come in."

"My God, she's a fright!" Baxter commented once they were inside with the door safely shut. "Her apron is so starched it could walk. I thought I had left her type behind in Boston."

"Oh no, they follow the Adamses everywhere. We need minding. Any Englishman who calls the Irish shiftless never met Kathleen. I sass her only when it seems I must otherwise forfeit manhood altogether."

"You mean like Mrs. Hellmann?"

Henry wagged one finger in the air. "Exactly like Mrs. Hellmann!"

The two old friends laughed, remembering the other housekeeper they used to dodge. The boardinghouse at Harvard was kept in a semblance of order only by terror. The German hausfrau was known to grab a rolling pin whenever a student heaved an evening of drink in the entry hall. No Cambridge resident made that mistake twice.

"What did she mean by 'that man'?" Baxter asked. "Whom was she talking about?"

"Oh. That would be Earl John Russell, the foreign secretary. Kathleen holds him personally responsible for her failure to achieve five feet. She was a child during the Potato Famine of '46, and he was prime minister at the time. It makes not a whit of difference that he advocated freedom of religion for Catholics, like herself, and Jews. Bread for starving children would have been more helpful, she has told me more than once, and I have to agree with her. But she won't say his name, which is damned inconvenient in a household where the Chief—my father—is over at Whitehall at least twice a week. She keeps us all in thrall— except my mother, who could turn a tiger into a tabby."

"She implied that I would be disturbing you. I hope I'm not. Are you busy?" Baxter asked.

"Me? Not especially. In fact, you seem to be the busy one. I should be interrogating you about the last two months; you've been so scarce. But you'll probably mumble some weak excuse about needing to attend lectures or take exams. As if that were any way to get an education." Henry appeared to be in great good humor. "Before you launch into your feeble explanations, though," he continued, "let me fill you in on my morning with John Bright, since you asked—who is deservedly the most luminous star in the British firmament."

"You mean the chap from Birmingham, the leader of the Radicals?"

"Yes. The very one. He's renowned for his scathing backbench oratory toward both the Whigs and the Tories, and he's won a special place in our esteem for his dismissal of the British diplomatic corps as 'a gigantic system of outdoor relief for the aristocracy.' As if the silk-trimmed bastards needed the dole. Foreign policy is a game to them. It's all great fun, at our and others' expense."

"Bright is quite the character, isn't he?" Baxter said. "I saw him at Oxford once. He looked like Moses come down from the Mount."

"Yes, he has the great bushy beard and all. But it's his words that terrify. They boil over like lava from Vesuvius."

"What was he going on about today?"

"He was giving a speech to the trade unionist society. My father asked me to attend. You know how Bright hates the unions, having made his money in cotton manufacture. Though that's not quite fair to him," Henry interrupted his own story to add, "since I believe he would feel that way even if it went against his economic interests. Old John is a true ideologue."

"Why in the world did the unionists invite him to speak?" Baxter asked. "I have no idea how you manage to sort through British politics. I can't keep the players and their positions straight."

"Well, you see, one of Bright's favorite soap boxes is the extension of the franchise. He's pushing Parliament to give the ballot to skilled workers. Proposals for universal suffrage and the secret ballot are considered scandalous over here. On banking legislation, as one horrified lord recently put it, two day laborers might actually outvote a Rothschild. Apparently he forgot that Parliament barred Rothschild until only three years ago, when they finally dropped the law against Jews. So anyway, this morning Bright managed both to insult and please the workers, thundering against unionism and in favor of the franchise. Of course, that's how he likes it. John Bright's only real fear in life is that someone, somewhere, will think it's his aim to flatter the electorate."

"So how did he get on?"

"Brilliantly, of course. Once John Bright's done with an audience, they'll walk across coals for him."

"I take it he is a friend of the legation."

"Oh yes, he's a great friend of ours. In his speech, he also took on all the aristocrats who regularly denounce us. Spoke directly in favor of the Union as an example to workingmen everywhere."

Henry fished in his pocket until he pulled out a bit of rumpled paper. "Here. It was so good, I wrote it down. I had to give up my seat in deference to some ladies—routed as usual by the overpowering claims of the weaker sex—but I managed to get the gist. I knew Father would want to hear it."

Lowering his voice in imitation of Bright's booming, deliberate tones and waving a fist in the air, Henry declaimed crustily, "Privilege thinks it has a great interest in the American contest, and every morning with blatant voice it comes into our street and curses the American republic. Privilege has beheld an afflicting spectacle for many years past. It has beheld thirty million men happy and prosperous, without emperors, without kings, without a court, without nobles."

Henry looked up enthusiastically from his notes, eyes alight. "That's us, of course. And here is where the audience began to cheer. It was fabulous. My ears are still ringing."

Lowering his voice, he concluded, "Privilege has shuddered at what might happen to old Europe if this great experiment should succeed. Let us pray that it does. God . . . speed . . . Abraham Lincoln!"

"Bravo!" Baxter said, clapping at Henry's performance. "If you give up diplomacy, you can go into the theater."

"You may laugh, but Bright's stood by us marvelously in the *Trent* affair, you know. Wags in Parliament have taken to calling him 'the member for the United States.'"

"Has the *Trent* matter been resolved?" Baxter asked. "The papers don't seem to be calling for Lincoln's head anymore."

"My father thinks they would be content with his own instead."

"Wrapped in newsprint like fish?"

"Wrapped in the Declaration of Independence, I think."

"Do you think it will come to that?" Baxter asked. "Will they hand him back his credentials?"

Henry shrugged. "No, I'm a pessimist by nature. I fear we will be doomed to exile in England for a while longer. I think Lincoln and Seward really have no choice but to release the rats. They've already issued an apology. We'll probably be seated next to Mason and Slidell at supper parties once the season gets under way again. I'll have to perfect my technique for not choking on my food while I hold my tongue. I swear London would sate a glutton of gloom."

Baxter laughed. "Henry Adams, I do believe you are the only soul in Christendom who would consider it a blow to be confined to London, the most interesting city in the world outside Paris. Of course, if you are, it will be a great victory for your father. He's ridden out the squall with a remarkably cool head. His boat never rocks."

"I thank you for the compliment on his behalf. I'll admit he has an unerring knack for maintaining his poise—a quality I failed miserably to inherit, but one much admired by the English. If Lincoln hands Mason and Slidell back to the Royal Navy, the American legation might be in for a good long stay after all."

Baxter wondered how long Henry would be able to stomach the situation if they did stay. He had a kind heart, made for friendship, but he hadn't the knack for patching over social differences. He took them personally and clammed up. As Henry himself admitted, he wasn't unflappable like his father, for whom "sangfroid" might have been coined. And Henry lacked guile. His comments made clear that, for him, the Harvard bond was as secure as ever; that he trusted Baxter's loyalty as a friend and fellow American in the face of Europe's enmity—forgetting the pull of the Virginia Tidewater on his old roommate. Baxter wished it were all that simple.

A single knock sounded on the parlor door, followed immediately by Kathleen bearing a silver tray with two steaming hot whiskeys and a bowl of shelled walnuts. "Now. There you go. That's grand. A hot whiskey is just the thing to keep away what ails you, so 'tis." The housekeeper set the refreshments down with a sound thump, but her fearsome aspect seemed to have softened. Perhaps food and drink made her forget the famine.

Their eyes met conspiratorially. Henry shook his head, warning Baxter not to laugh. The fire crackled in the quiet room. "Do you remember how she used to press mulled wine on us at Sunday dinners?" Henry burst out after Kathleen had left.

"Frau Hellmann? Of course! 'It vill cure ze headache! It vill cure ze stomach! It vill cure ze liver.' Why do you think I became interested in medicine?"

"I should have known. You always did lap up more than your share."

"Research, my friend."

Henry grinned and raised his glass. "To research!"

The two men allowed a comfortable pause to elapse while they enjoyed their drinks. Henry got up and used the coal tongs to grab another lump from the bin and place it on the glowing fire.

"Seriously, you can't come often enough," Henry said with a smile as he sat back down. "London makes me feel like a shadow. I'm beneath notice to most of the people I meet. Their eyes glide right over me. The city isn't nearly so bad with a friend or two in it."

Baxter's expression changed at Henry's words, and he set his drink on the table with an inadvertent knock that to his own ears sounded like a judge's gavel.

"Henry, there is something I have to tell you. That's why I'm here this afternoon," he said. "I'm going back."

"Going back? What do you mean?"

"I'm going back. Soon."

Henry stared. "Back where?"

"Back home."

"You don't mean the Confederacy," Henry said disbelievingly. "You can't."

"I mean Virginia. I can't help it that some fools have declared it another country."

"You . . . you can certainly help *not* helping them," Henry spluttered, at a loss for words for once. "You don't have to give aid to the enemy," he added more succinctly.

Baxter's mouth tightened. "My *father* has asked for my aid. I cannot refuse him. You of all people should understand that."

"What can *you* possibly do? You're a physician, for Christ's sake." The instant the words had left his mouth Henry's face took on a look of shocked understanding. "You're going to the battlefield."

"No. You know I don't want to be part of the war. But Father has asked me to help him get medical supplies across the blockade."

"Then you might as well go to the battlefield. It's pretty much the same thing."

Baxter felt the comradeship between them slipping away, damaged by the hatreds misshaping all their lives. "Henry, you have to understand," he entreated. "I've watched surgery. I've conducted surgeries. Men shouldn't have to endure that pain without anesthesia. No matter what side they're on."

"I'm not a brute, Baxter, but war is brutal. Slavery is brutal, too, damn it, as you know better than I."

"And if Charles, Jr., were lying in a hospital tent? Or Robert? Or Jacob?"

"Brothers are hostages," Henry replied curtly. "All America has hostages on the front lines. What can you accomplish anyway, other than to get yourself thrown into jail or killed?"

Baxter hesitated, not sure what he could reveal without jeopardizing either his position or Henry's, and then said, "I can make sure that things get through to the right people."

"What kind of answer is that?" demanded Henry, who

seemed torn between hurt and scorn. "One designed to avoid implicating the minister's son in a violation of the blockade? 'Things to the right people'? I don't need your protection, Baxter. I need your loyalty. So does the Union. We deserve it. You were certainly vocal about your disapproval of slavery over drinks in Cambridge." Henry's jaw tensed and his lips thinned. But instead of saying more he turned to stare into the fire.

Baxter looked into his unfinished glass of whiskey. The slip of orange peel that Kathleen had put into it for flavor had sunk to the bottom. He stood up, wondering which emotion Henry felt more keenly: anger at his friend for aiding the Confederacy or disappointment at being left behind in London, which held nothing for Henry but lonely, anxious waiting. A slow flush of anger showed on his cheeks for the first time.

"Listen, Henry," Baxter said, his voice hardening. "I'd like the convenience of having my family stacked up neatly behind some plain moral line. I'd like nothing more than to say—clear back to the Revolution or maybe even the *Mayflower*—that we were on the right side of every cause. The Adamses can make that claim, and my hat's off to you. But you know what that also breeds, Henry? It breeds self-righteousness. Rather a Northern propensity, I might add. And that can get mighty thick. Even between friends." Baxter picked up his hat and walking cane. "I believe I have overstayed my welcome."

"Yes, well, perhaps you had better leave," Henry agreed. "My father will be home soon, and his interest in your plans will be of a different order from mine."

"Goodbye, then," Baxter said formally. But even as he turned toward the door, he felt more sick at heart than angry. Henry had reason to be upset. It was true that the medical supplies Baxter hoped to run past the blockade might well save a man who would later shoot at Charles, Jr. It seemed that no matter what Baxter did he would betray someone. Henry was an old friend whom he might never meet again, and this would be how they parted. As

Baxter reached for the door, he heard Henry stand up from his armchair.

"Wait," his friend called out abruptly.

Baxter turned back.

"Here, finish your whiskey," Henry said, holding out the glass. "You'll need it." The two men raised their glasses and downed the contents. Silently then, Baxter placed the glass back on the table and, with a short nod, left the room.

TWELVE

I saw that the bride within the bridal dress had withered like the dress and like the flowers, and had no brightness left but the brightness of her sunken eyes. . . . It was then I began to understand that everything in the room had stopped, like the watch and the clock, a long time ago.

—Charles Dickens, *Great Expectations*

"Over here," Julia whispered to herself, her eyes trained on a blond head that stuck out of the railway-car window along with three other eager faces. She waved her handkerchief high above her head. "Here I am!" she wanted to call out, but convention restrained her. Instead, she focused intently on the group of excited boys in high Eton collars and held up her lace square like a military banner.

"Julia!" Edmund called, leaning out the window. His voice carried across the platform. Julia smiled at her younger brother over the heads of the crowd as the train puffed slowly to a halt. One of the other lads at the window stared at her with what seemed a particularly eager expression. He turned to Edmund and said something at which they both laughed.

The crowd swelled forward at the train's last jerk, and a host of students released for Christmas break spilled out onto the platform. Families warmly embraced the sons whom they had not seen in months. Boxes, trunks, and wrapped parcels piled up quickly. Footmen gathered belongings into coaches brought out for the occasion.

"Welcome home!" Julia said when her brother was finally

close enough to clasp hands. Edmund had grown five inches between last Christmas and the summer. He had equaled her in height when he left in the fall, but now he gazed down at her. "Look at you!" she exclaimed. "All grown up!"

Edmund rolled his eyes and leaned forward to kiss her cheek, reddened from the cold. "Julia, you have to stop talking like that. Someone will mistake you for my mother. How the deuce will we ever marry you off?"

Julia laughed. Her fifteen-year-old brother had become so delightfully mature. Here he was worrying about her future. It couldn't be more amusing than if he offered to tie her shoe, as she used to do for him.

"Come, the coach is waiting," she said, taking the brown-paper parcel he gave her to hold while he shouldered a bulging satchel. Julia looked askance at the lumpy bag as they made their way through the dispersing throng. "Is *anything* in there clean and folded?"

"It was once," Edmund answered. "I had to bring it back dirty or Martha would feel I had deprived her of the chance to spoil me."

"Oh, I'm sure she would find an opportunity. The heir of Belfield Manor walks on water as far as the house staff is concerned. Of course, once the maids see your clothes they may conclude that you also swim in dirt. I'd be reluctant to open that satchel for fear of what might crawl out!"

Edmund raised his eyebrows and gave Julia a lopsided smile. He took her gloved hand to guide her up the high step into the carriage. The coachman had tied Edmund's largest trunk on the top and now waited while his passengers climbed in. A cast-iron brazier on the floor warmed the cab. Once they were settled, Edmund rapped his stick on the ceiling of the coach. The driver shook his reins and gave a silvery whistle to the matched roan mares, which pulled the carriage smoothly onto the thoroughfare.

"Tell me everything! Your letters give the scores for every cricket match and polo game, but I want to hear about your life outside sports. Is it going better this year?"

Edmund shrugged. "It's okay. Sports are the best part."

"What about your classes? Do you have any good teachers?"

"They're all right."

"How are the other students? Have you made any new friends?"

"A few."

"Were those the boys you were riding with on the train?" Julia persevered. She had grown used to Edmund's short answers about school, but she missed the long, voluble tales he used to tell her as a youngster. Since leaving for Eton three years ago, he had become increasingly conservative with the information he imparted.

"Pretty much."

"Who was the short one with curly hair? He gave me rather a *look* from the window."

Edmund seemed pleased at her perspicacity. "Jonathan Spencer? Oh, he's a rake of the first order. An absolute cad. Makes eyes at anything in skirts within twenty yards. You had better watch your step."

"I think I'm pretty safe around a fifteen-year-old." Julia laughed, secretly glad that she had got him to open up a crack. "So, is he a friend?"

Edmund pondered the question. "I'm not sure," he answered at length. "One doesn't really have friends at Eton. They're more like allies. Allies against the older students and against the teachers. One can't afford to look weak."

Julia absorbed Edmund's answer, not wanting to pry but hoping he would tell her more. At the end of his first year away, Edmund had insisted that he would never go back. He was almost hysterically adamant, much as he used to balk at going into dark rooms alone. But Sir Walter overruled his son's objections.

Edmund must do as he was told. That meant following in his father's footsteps at England's most prestigious school. When Julia asked Edmund privately what was wrong, he told her about an upperclassman who forced his face into the mud and paddled him with a cricket bat because he cried when a ball struck him on the cheekbone. Edmund refused to say more, but Julia guessed it was but one of several humiliating incidents. And, in the end, she was as powerless to sway their father as he was. Edmund went back to Eton.

"Well, you seemed to be having a good time on the train. At least you were making proper spectacles of yourselves, hanging out the window. I'm surprised the conductor didn't reel you in by your collars. Perhaps you'd like to invite some of the lads over after Christmas."

Edmund's eyes crinkled with amusement. "Julia, no need to get our nannies together. I've already arranged to meet Spencer and Beresford-Hope at the Carlton Club. Their fathers are members, too."

"Well then, pardon me. I guess I've outlived my usefulness," Julia said with pretend hurt. She made her eyes big and puffed out her bottom lip, as she did only with Edmund.

He smiled. "You may climb down off your high horse now. You know we can't do without you. You're the mainspring. Tell me about life in London. Any news, or is it just the usual round of parties?"

"The season has actually been rather solemn. Quiet as a churchyard. There have been almost no parties since the death of Prince Albert. Father asked me to cancel the annual Christmas ball out of respect."

"Fabulous! I won't have to stand around like a toy soldier. We can eat a quiet supper, get the obligatory presents out of the way—Father will give me a book on Admiral Nelson or some other stuffed hero—and I can be off to the club after he beats me at chess."

Julia looked down. The look of pretend disappointment was replaced by a pensive expression. As if sensing her regret at his lack of family feeling, Edmund added, "Of course, since you're already holding your gift you may as well open it now. Father wouldn't understand it anyway."

With a happy gasp, Julia shook the brown parcel she had carried from the train platform. "Why, Edmund, thank you!"

"Don't shake the parcel, silly! You'll break what's inside." Edmund now smiled freely. "I've been hanging on to it for two months."

Julia unwrapped the gift carefully, taking care not to tear the paper. Nestled inside the box was a petite but heavy object wrapped in red velvet. She unwound the cloth and pulled out a small, ornate silver hand mirror, enameled with blue posies and white lilies. It would fit perfectly in her handbag.

"Oh," she said, "it's lovely." Julia held up the mirror to catch the fading light of the day. "I won't have to duck anymore to see my bonnet!"

"The bonnet is not nearly as pretty as the face underneath it," Edmund said, flushing slightly. He cleared his throat and added, "It's about time that you see yourself as others do."

"Well, haven't you become quite the gallant? To what do I owe such chivalry?" Julia laughed and bobbed an abbreviated curtsy in the cramped space of the cab.

"Someone ought to tell you. You know Father won't. He certainly will never push you out of the nest, like he did me."

"That's silly. Papa would be perfectly happy to give me away if he could find someone Lincoln's height to take me off his hands."

The American president's physique was frequently remarked on in England as one more example of his oddness. Some wag had suggested that the former rail-splitter mimicked the product of his labors.

"I'm telling you for your own good," Edmund insisted.

"Father is quite happy having you run the household and make Belfield shine. I wouldn't be surprised if he kept you busy ordering menus and counting the silver until you're too old to make a match."

Julia shook her head. "That's nonsense, Edmund. He wants the best for me. Every father wants to see his daughter married."

"Every father wants a successor. That's my job—to produce the proverbial 'heir and a spare.' Your job is to make his life comfortable."

"Edmund, that isn't nice," Julia reprimanded. She had been nursemaid too long to let a disrespectful comment pass unremarked. "I help Father run the household because I want to and because he needs me. Besides, I would much rather be useful than sit around sewing samplers."

"But why does he need you? Why doesn't he remarry? There are plenty of suitable women who could take Mother's place."

Julia shrugged, at a loss for an answer.

"I think he just finds a daughter easier to control than a wife," Edmund said. "Percy Beresford-Hope's mother died in childbirth, too, and now his maiden sister runs the family residence. She's thirty, well past courting. Even her brother admits she's looking a bit long in the tooth. You ought to marry before all the good men are taken, Julia. Pretty girls outnumber eligible bachelors, you know."

Julia was well aware of the newspaper reports on what some called the problem of "redundant women." There were simply too many women to men. Second and third sons inherited neither estates nor titles. As a consequence, many chose the army or a carefree bachelorhood on their small annuities. Loose women were universally condemned, but privately well appreciated when heirs weren't necessary, being cheaper and more pliable than wives. The prime minister himself had had a scandalous relationship with a certain Mrs. Cane, leading some punsters to wonder whether, in the sense of the Old Testament, the seventy-eight-year-old Palmerston was still *able*. Now the term "redundant" was being used to describe those gentlewomen for whom society had no use, and whose poor luck in the wedding lottery meant they never left the family hearth.

"You asked me about my friends at Eton," Edmund continued. "Tell me about the gentlemen you've met this past fall. Are there any possibilities?"

"Edmund, you sound just like Flora Bentley," Julia said. She found it hard to keep from smiling at his almost paternal concern. "You're getting to be a regular gossip. Next you'll be pointing out unmarried gentlemen at the opera."

"Julia, I mean it. You don't want to wait too long. You had your debut, what, four seasons ago? What happened to that fellow from Dorset who kept calling last spring? The one with the big ears."

"He was rather unimpressive. Everything he said sounded like a quote from a book he had read—and a dull one at that. Father was convinced that he was simply after my dowry. He shooed him off by saying that our stock was doing poorly. Besides, I would like to marry for love."

"Are there no men who might capture your fancy? Surely you've met someone who would be suitable. You know—a society type with a well-lined bank account and a belly that doesn't hang too far over the trousers. Presentable in public. Excels at bird calls, perhaps."

"Very funny, Edmund, but I've no intention of talking myself into marrying a man just to get it over and done with."

"Don't most women?"

"Edmund! You're much too young to be so cynical."

He laughed. "Well, of course I don't expect any young lady to have to do that with me. But what are we going to do with you? Surely you've seen someone you like."

Julia hesitated, "Well, there is an American whom I recently met. But you know how Father feels about anyone from the colonies."

"You mean he'd love them all to go to the devil?"

"More or less. He's never forgotten or forgiven George Washington's confiscation of the family property in Cambridge."

"You needn't tell me: 'Your great-grandfather escaped on a British man-of-war, with only the shirt on his back. Forced to abandon the graves of four generations, et cetera, et cetera.' Frankly, I'm tired of the tale. I say let Father go to the devil if he objects! The two of them would get along famously. So, tell me about your American chap. Not everyone from the States can be that bad. Don't forget Wellington: 'Being born in a stable doesn't make one a horse.'"

"Yes, but Wellington meant Ireland."

"The same must be true of America. Come now, what's he like?"

Julia looked out the window at the bare-branched trees of Regent's Park. She was silent for a few moments, thinking how to describe Baxter Sams. It was hard to explain what attracted her. His eyes came to mind, compelling, inquiring, inviting.

"He's from Virginia, studying at the Royal College of Surgeons," Julia said at last, giving up on any but the simplest description.

"Bravo, a Confederate! Father can't possibly object. He loves the scoundrels. I'll wager that he's ready to introduce Jeff Davis to Queen Victoria now that she's wearing black. We have a tacit agreement, Father and I. I send him the Eton cricket scores and he writes me about the latest Confederate victories. So far, both our teams are winning."

"I'm afraid being a Confederate isn't enough. I don't think Father would approve of any American."

"Which just goes to show you. Father wants the Confederates to win to satisfy his old grudge, but he wouldn't invite one to tea."

"Tea would be admissible. We even had Mr. Sams over a month or so ago, on business. But I don't think Father would be happy to see it go beyond that."

"Perhaps Sir Walter Birch will merely have to tolerate a wee bit of unhappiness, then," Edmund said with a wicked grin. "I understand it builds character—or at least that's what he said when he packed me off to Eton."

At that, their carriage pulled into the drive of Belfield Manor and Julia placed her hand affectionately over Edmund's.

"Thank you for the lovely gift. I'll treasure it."

"Use it, dear sister. You deserve someone who appreciates the person in that reflection. Father certainly doesn't."

"Edmund! It's Christmas!" Julia reiterated with exasperation.

"Okay, I promise to behave. Father and I get along better than before, anyway, now that I'm older. Like the lads at Eton, he seems impressed by a bit of height. We can talk about anything, so long as it's nothing of consequence."

Julia didn't bother to reprimand him again. She knew that growing taller had helped in the wider world, but at home their father was nearly as domineering as ever. Edmund had learned to show the proper respect, yet Father still required that his son keep a stiff upper lip in a world alien to his sensibilities. He would never qualify as a friend—someone in front of whom one might dare to appear weak. Perhaps most fathers didn't.

THIRTEEN

*A lady's imagination is very rapid; it jumps from admiration
to love, from love to matrimony, in a moment.*
—Jane Austen, *Pride and Prejudice*

They took their seats in one of the gilded boxes overlooking
the orchestra as the flickering gaslights dimmed. Swags of
black crêpe festooned the balcony of the Langham Concert Hall
in memory of Prince Albert. The audience ended their conversations in scattered whispers, and quiet fell as the maestro strode to
the podium. Dipping his wand and raising it with a flourish, the
German conductor brought magic out of the void. Where before
there was but a prolonged hush, violin and viola, oboe and flute,
harpsichord and harp swelled forth. Onstage, the imploring tenor
in the role of Orpheus sang as if reaching for the heart of every
woman in the audience. Julia closed her eyes and allowed the
melody to engulf her. She loved Von Gluck's *Orfeo ed Euridice*.

When the final strains of the second act had faded to thun-
derous applause, the house lights revealed Flora and Louise
Bentley in the gallery below, accompanied by two gentlemen
whom Julia had met on another occasion. Flora's lovely face
tipped up and she waived gaily at Julia and Edmund, who returned her greeting and made signs toward the foyer. When they
finally reached the packed reception area, Julia noted that Louise
was headed toward a drinking fountain in the rear, while her
companion, a vicar, followed close on her heels as if miming the
Greek lovers in the play.

"Julia, you haven't introduced me to your new beau," Flora

said after she and Julia exchanged greetings. "Such a heart-breaker!"

Edmund blushed but recovered quickly. "Auntie Flora, don't you know me? I realize you're quite a bit older than me, but surely your memory hasn't begun to fail already!"

Flora twinkled merrily up at him. "Now I remember. You are that impudent boy, Eddie. Has Eton finally taught you some manners?"

"The lads at Eton have taught me much, but I'm not sure it's manners."

"Doubtless you are learning all those beastly sports for which they are famed," she said. "Our brother, John, regularly returned with scrapes and contusions while he was at college. Between rounders and rugby, his face looked like a bruised pear. One Easter he showed up with a broken nose. I trust your parts are all intact? Or perhaps I should not inquire too closely."

Edmund blushed again. "I appreciate your concern, but I assure you that I can hold my own on the field," he countered, refusing to be bested.

"Which field would that be?" Flora asked with a disarming smile.

Julia followed her friend's repartee with a sense of having heard it before. Flora was irrepressible. Julia noticed that she had flounced the skirt of her taffeta dress to make sure it modestly covered her slippers. She always seemed most conscious of propriety when she planned to breach it. The period of official mourning for the prince consort must be wearing on Flora's high spirits. Opera was about as exciting as life got at the moment.

Julia pitied Flora's escort, Reginald somebody, who excused himself to purchase a punch for his flighty companion. Flora had a generous heart, but she was simply too lively for most English gentlemen. Julia didn't agree with her father's prediction that both sisters would be betrothed before the holidays were out.

She looked around for Louise and spied her near a tall window, talking with her escort. Louise had met Nathaniel White last fall, and seemed to have acquired a fresh enthusiasm for the Church of England in the process. He wasn't what Julia would call the romantic type—having a slight squint that suggested too much close reading—but Louise appeared happier than Julia had ever seen her.

Julia started to make her way over to the pair when she saw Mr. White lean closer. Louise was gazing up into his eyes, seemingly unaware of anyone else in the theater. She lifted her hand to his cheek. Julia's face flushed hot and she wheeled back to Flora and Edmund. Perhaps later would be a better time.

The gaslights dimmed. Intermission was coming to an end. "Let's make our way back to the box," Edmund said to his sister, a confident light in his eyes. He looked as if he had enjoyed crossing swords with the lovely—and older—Flora Bentley.

Julia and Edmund wound their way up the crowded stairs, through the landing that led to the boxes. Edmund spotted another student in his year at Eton and sent Julia on. She almost walked past a pale young man who stepped aside for her before she realized it was Henry Adams, Baxter's friend from Massachusetts.

"Good evening, Mr. Adams. Please forgive me, I almost didn't see you."

"Miss Birch, isn't it? You are forgiven without question. After all, we've met only once, and then briefly. At Foxwood last summer, wasn't it?"

"Yes, that's correct. I hope London is agreeing with you, Mr. Adams. I'm afraid it will be a rather long and somber season."

"Thank you for your concern. In fact, I'm rather celebrating tonight. I don't know if you follow the papers, but our two governments are at peace once more."

Henry's eyes sparkled with warmth, and she observed that he wasn't as serious, or perhaps as shy, as he had seemed the preceding summer.

"I read it just this morning. Lord Russell announced that the *Trent* affair has been resolved to England's satisfaction." Julia found herself increasingly drawn to stories of the American war in the *Times,* the *Standard,* and other periodicals that her father brought home from the newsagent.

"Yes. It looks as if we'll be in London for a while longer. As a result, my father has decided to take up more permanent lodgings."

"In what part of town, may I ask?"

"Right here. Actually, down this very street: number 5 Portland Place."

"That's across from All Souls, isn't it? My father rents a pew there."

"Does he? Then perhaps I may . . . I mean, we may see each other there sometime."

"Yes, I hope so," she said. "That is, you will if you bring props to keep your eyes open. Rector Eardley-Wilmot is a good man, but not an exciting one."

Henry laughed. "I've heard the same, but didn't know if I should repeat it." His eyes swept the landing, which was still emptying out.

"Langham Place is a lovely neighborhood," she said. "I'm glad you've found such pleasing accommodations and that you're able to stay on in London. Is it true, then, that we shall see the Confederate emissaries soon?"

"I suppose so, though that I am *not* celebrating," Henry replied with emphasis.

"Neither am I, Mr. Adams."

Henry smiled at her reply, opened his mouth to speak again, but then glanced down at the program in his hand, which he had squeezed until it fanned at either end.

Julia wondered when he had last seen Baxter. It had been a month since she had run into him at the Anti-Slavery Society and she wondered if Henry, his best friend in England, knew when he had sailed. Before she could ask, the lights dimmed again. She gave Henry a polite smile and bid him a prosperous New Year.

Julia took her chair in the box above the orchestra section, where Louise Bentley and Nathaniel White were seated, but she avoided looking their way, anxious not to intrude on another private moment.

Meeting Henry reminded her that she had been unable to answer Edmund's question as to why she thought Baxter a possible suitor. She had met the Virginian only three times. But she liked the way he looked her straight in the eye and talked about things that counted. He answered questions that touched upon his honor without flinching. He seemed less reserved than the Englishmen she knew, as if the layers of social convention in which people wrapped themselves were thinner. Baxter contradicted her image of Americans as aggressive boors. Perhaps the colonies weren't all she had been led to believe.

Yet it was Baxter's physical form that sprang to mind vividly now, in the darkness of the theater. His upright carriage, strong arms, warm handshake, and the ready smile that suggested he liked what he saw. It was alluring to be obviously admired. Very alluring.

Julia recalled the dark shadow of a beard under his smooth cheek, and she wondered again what it felt like. Did every woman have the impulse to touch the cheek of the suitor leaning toward her, as Louise had done? Would his shaved skin be rough, like the rasp of a cat's tongue, or smooth, like her brother's still innocent cheek? Julia closed her eyes, and for a brief moment allowed her imagination to roam across the Virginian's well-defined countenance. The theater felt warm even though it was the middle of January. Julia realized that her heart was pounding.

Surprised, she opened her eyes in time to see the plush curtain go up. Perhaps her complicated feelings for Baxter Sams were in fact something rather simple. Love, or, as the French said, *la passion.*

FOURTEEN

JANUARY 1862

An iron steamer has run the blockade at Savannah.
We now raise our wilted heads like flowers after a shower.
This drop of good news revives us.

—Mary Boykin Chesnut, *A Diary from Dixie*

The purser counted along with Baxter, each man checking the other's tally: twenty mango-wood chests of premium-grade Bihar opium, rolled into fist-size balls, encased in fine white muslin, and stamped with the ornate insignia of the British East India Company. Baxter opened each case to be sure that the forty balls inside, two rows deep, had not been disturbed. Each could be made into hundreds of opium pills or vials of morphine. They would bring priceless relief to men enduring lifesaving mutilation.

Baxter had witnessed amputations. Without four strong men to hold down the limbs of the wounded, and a fifth to handle the twelve-inch serrated saw, an amputation could not be executed on a conscious, unmedicated patient. Chloroform helped during the surgery, and opium pills afterward. Then all that the doctor had to worry about was sepsis, and the patient about *soldier's disease*—that stubborn narcotic addiction to which some amputees fell prey.

"Let's look at the second row down," Baxter said, pointing to the eighth chest they had opened. Sams and Sons' agreement with the captain was that they would randomly inspect the cargo to make sure that no one had pilfered it during the voyage. The captain himself would make good on anything that had gone missing en route to Nassau.

The purser carefully removed the top layer of opium balls, setting them on the oak deck. The Caribbean sun, beating down hotly, had evaporated all traces of the morning's swabbing. The deck was as clean as a table.

His leathery face reflecting two decades under a remorseless sun, the purser carefully broke the seal and unwrapped the first ball on the second layer. Wielding a thin-bladed knife as dexterously as any surgeon, he cored out the waxy sphere.

"'Tis good all the way through," he observed, and mashed the paste between his fingers. "It's an old trick, covering a ball of soap or tallow with a layer of opium. I've seen it plenty, but this here is genuine."

"Satisfied?" the captain asked. He stood to one side, arms folded.

The crossing from Southampton to Nassau had been rough. A hard gale lashed the ship all the way south, blowing the spume of the sea far into the air. Yards and masts were now encrusted with white salt, as if snow had fallen and failed to melt in the tropical sun. Nearly two weeks of thick weather and high seas had kept crew and officers on deck almost constantly, every man on board pulling his weight to keep the old tub afloat. The captain's eyes were red-rimmed from lack of sleep.

"Allow me to see that one, if you will," Baxter persisted, pointing to another ball deeper in the row.

The purser repeated the procedure, this time tasting the mash with a quick flick of his tongue. "She's the real article, all right. Nasty as day-old tea."

"Good. You can go ahead and seal the cases back up. It looks like the cargo is intact."

"I told ye there would be no problem," the captain said. "Me men know to keep their hands off the goods."

"Yes, well, I hope you can appreciate that I have to check."

"I would appreciate me bed more," the burly captain grumbled, rubbing his week-old beard with a callused hand.

"Beg pardon?" Baxter said.

"I said . . . if ye are satisfied, I'll be turning this matter over to the purser now." To the ship's officer repacking the opium, he snapped, "See to it. I want this cargo off-loaded before the day's out. We'll not be sitting on it in this port o' thieves."

"Aye, Captain," said the officer, knocking the last nail into the lid of the opened box.

"I've arranged to meet the captain of the *Rambling Rose* this morning," Baxter noted. "He'll send some men over for the cargo."

The captain merely nodded and took an abrupt leave. Baxter promised the purser that he would send the instructions for unloading before the noon hour, and made his own way down the battered gangplank, careful not to slip.

The capital port of the Bahamas seemed surreal after dim, icy London. Sunshine bounced from the sapphire sea onto puddles left in the streets by an overnight downpour. Between the brilliant light and the odd experience of walking again on a surface that wasn't rolling, Baxter felt slightly drunk. Now he merely needed to find Mary Mac's pub. The purser had told him to look for a pink two-story building with turquoise shutters next to the custom house. "Stands out like a whore at Sunday school," the sailor said.

"And there she is," Baxter muttered to himself. The insubstantial wooden building leaned against the stone government offices. Purplish bougainvillea and white jasmine ran riot across the front, climbing around the darkened doorway.

Baxter located an empty stool at the cool, shadowed bar.

"Good morning," he greeted the bartender, who was drying glasses with an old rag. "I'm here to meet Captain Ransom Harvey of the *Rambling Rose.* Can you point him out when he comes in?"

The publican cocked his head toward the end of the room, where a man sat studying a newspaper. "Yonder," he said simply, as if reluctant to waste more words so early in the day.

Baxter ordered coffee and approached the table.

A slender, neatly dressed man with a rakish mustache looked up from his reading. He pushed back his chair and stood briskly. "There you are. Mr. Sams? Excellent. You're spot on time."

"Captain Harvey," Baxter replied, shaking the proffered hand. The smaller man had a viselike grip.

"Indeed," he said with a sudden, white smile. "Welcome to Nassau. I trust you had smooth sailing?"

"Except when the swells tried to pitch me from my bunk, the ride was as gentle as a swing in my old bassinet."

"The Atlantic." Captain Harvey shook his head. "Never venture into it when it can be avoided. The Caribbean is like a bathtub in comparison . . . except for the occasional hurricane."

From the descriptions Baxter had read of hurricanes—which swept boats into the sea like leaves going down a storm drain—he wondered at Ransom Harvey's preference. In Baxter's experience, men fell into two groups: those who exaggerated perils, and those who treated risk like a plaything. Which was Harvey? If the efficient-looking officer had the skill to handle the fickle southern waters, it clearly didn't matter. He was the right man.

"Can you sail tonight?" the captain asked. "I'm expecting a steady wind. No moon—black as a kettle. Perfect sailing conditions. At ten knots, we'll be landed day after tomorrow." The captain smiled again, a brilliant gash in his tanned face. "You'll be able to order gravy and grits for breakfast." He had obviously brought more than one Southerner home to Dixie.

"I'll be ready when you are," Baxter replied. He would rather get the ordeal over with sooner than later.

The coffee arrived, and the two men plotted the final details. The captain would transfer the opium by noon. Baxter would present himself on deck at 1800 hours, and the ship would slip out of the harbor at 2200, well after dark. In addition to the medicine, the *Rambling Rose* would carry forty bolts of gray uniform cloth, two hundred Enfield rifles, and a crate of orthopedic devices for men who had lost limbs. London manufacturers made the best artificial legs.

"We've got a shipment of chloroform and quinine, too. 'Tis a regular mission of mercy," Captain Harvey noted with only a trace of irony.

His commission would undoubtedly add another brick to a small fortune at the Bank of England, it occurred to Baxter.

"Don't you worry about our weighing her down. I travel light. If you're greedy, the boat sags on the waterline. Better to make two quick trips past the devil than one slow one," the captain added with a jaunty air. "And now I had best make use of the morning to ready the sloop. You might want to get some sleep. It'll be a long night."

With a deep draught of his coffee, and another firm handshake, the captain left Baxter to nurse the remainder of the cooling pot.

The somnolence of the dusky pub seemed to deepen after the exit of the energetic sea captain. The only sounds were the occasional knock of the bartender placing a dried glass back on the shelf and the obscure chirp of a lone cricket that had failed to note the break of day. The glare from the open doorway threatened a hot, humid afternoon.

Baxter asked for a room upstairs, turned down the offer of female companionship at a nominal price, and trudged up the stairs with legs that felt weighted by iron braces. He sank onto the old bed, not bothering to remove any clothes except his shoes. The cleanliness of the mattress didn't bear thinking about.

Baxter doubted that he could sleep. The rough voyage to Nassau had left him exhausted, but the thought of crossing the path of the U.S. Navy pulled his nerves taut. Their bristling guns suddenly seemed as real as shark teeth. Up to this moment, he had felt as if he were standing in an endless queue. The arrangements had taken far longer than he expected. There had been numerous, frustrating delays, and he had sailed a month later than planned. Now, at last, he was at the head of the line, waiting to meet his fate.

Ransom Harvey seemed competent, Baxter thought, staring up at the moldering plaster of the ceiling. Brown water stains billowed around the rusty iron lamp that hung in the center of the yellowed expanse. Captain Harvey had pointed out the sea currents on a chart with the precision of an anatomist, showing the route they would follow that night and the detours they might make if the lookout caught sight of a Federal sail. Harvey had completed the run dozens of times. "Eminently reliable," the factor in London called the captain, who seemed as polished as a lieutenant of the Royal Navy. Baxter now turned over in his mind the possibility that Harvey might be trusted to get the cargo through without him. Baxter could see the sloop off that evening and be on the next cargo ship back to London. He wouldn't have to cross the watery line of blockade, twelve miles off the American coast.

No risk.

Except to the opium, every ball of which might save a dozen wounded men from shock and death. A case could go missing in the blink of an eye. Harvey only had to make a short stop at any of the coastal creeks that bled into the Atlantic.

Baxter closed his eyes with a weary sigh. He rolled onto his side and cradled his head in the crook of his arm, determined to get some rest. Harvey had warned that the trip across the Gulf Stream might be choppy. Baxter tried to relax. Pleasant thoughts, he would think pleasant thoughts. Grits for breakfast. Butter on biscuits.

She held the plate of biscuits for his inspection, leaning so close that he could sense the subtle warmth rising from her bosom. Julia Birch was wearing a green velvet dress that looked as soft as a pillow. "Why didn't you come back?" she asked him. Gold glinted in her hazel eyes.

"I tried, Julia, I just couldn't," Baxter struggled to say, but he was too sleepy.

"You were late for tea. We waited all day. Father said you had forgotten," she said with disappointment. Her thick brown hair was down this time. Curls swirled around her shoulders like the sea.

He reached out and took her in his arms. "I'm sorry, dearest. I won't be late next time." Lowering his head to find her mouth, Baxter closed his eyes. To his pleased surprise, she met his lips. He drew the curve of her waist closer, crushing the velvet with his fingers. Julia's skin smelled of flowers. He ran his free hand up the back of her neck. Her silky hair swallowed his fingers. Baxter pressed urgently against her. Julia sighed softly, yielding to his touch.

In a distant part of his brain, Baxter felt the temperature rise. It was too warm. The floor seemed to dip and sway. He opened his eyes onto a small, poorly furnished room that he didn't recognize. He couldn't tell if it faced east or west. The wallpaper was yellowed and peeling at the edges, and a hot square of sunshine beat across the back of his dark broadcloth coat. He was frying in it.

Nassau, he realized, awakening more fully. He was in Nassau. He was no longer on the ship out of London. Glancing toward the window, edged with fragrant white jasmine, Baxter saw that the sun had shifted. It appeared to be late afternoon. He closed his eyes again. Julia Birch had been in his dreams. She was returning his kiss. Baxter wanted to recapture the dream and hold her tight.

He started to fall back to sleep, but then sat up, swung his feet to the floor, and pressed his hands to his face to wake up. Dreams would have to wait. He had an appointment to keep on the dock. And real guns to face in the night.

FIFTEEN

*There was just a slight sound, like the quick snap of a
gun-hammer . . . then a shout from the deck of the unhappy
craft, and before a boat could be lowered she went down
all standing. This is what usually happens when an iron
steamer comes in contact with a wooden ship.*

—Captain James D. Bulloch, Confederate Agent,
The Secret Service of the Confederate States in Europe

"Mr. Adams, sir, welcome to Liverpool. Allow me to relieve you of your hat and coat."

Thomas Haines Dudley, U.S. consul in Liverpool, bustled to greet his guest. "There's a fearsome wind today. Chills you right through to your bones. You must be frozen. Come sit by the grate. Right here—get close to the fire." Dudley drew an armchair nearer to the stove for Charles.

The consul was a thin, cheerful, enterprising man with light-brown hair and a beard that was just starting to gray. He had sharply peaked eyebrows, a long face, and ears that stuck out like teacup handles, giving him an expression of alertness. He would have been perfectly homely but for his large, intelligent eyes. Charles found these qualities reassuring. He relied implicitly on Tom Dudley to be his eyes and ears in Liverpool, home to all the worst conspiracies in Britain against the Union cause. Like Adams, Dudley was an attorney. That, too, was comforting. He would spot evasions of the law.

"Please accept my hearty apologies for not meeting your train, Mr. Adams. I've been hard at it all morning to finish this report for you and Mr. Seward. I think I'm onto something."

"Splendid, Mr. Dudley. Why don't you tell me the gist of your report while I thaw out my fingers? I foolishly dropped my gloves getting off the train and have had to suffer for it."

Charles hated clumsiness, having been coached in deportment from the age of three—when the ladies of St. Petersburg made him king of the children's ball. Then he had worn white gloves, knitted from the silkiest cotton and buttoned at the wrist with real pearls. His mother couldn't afford more than two fashionable gowns, but her son dressed like a Russian prince with a coach-and-four on the river Neva. Sodden woolen gloves, reeking of damp sheep, were exactly what he deserved for carelessly dropping them now. He hung the offending pair over the iron grate to dry and briskly rubbed his cold, tingling hands.

Dudley was riffling through his papers, looking for a particular sheet. Charles waited patiently and then cleared his throat. "Mr. Dudley, I couldn't help noticing that our flag is not flying outside the consulate. You do realize that it is part of your duties to see that it is raised each morning?"

Charles didn't wish to begin the morning on a critical note, as Dudley was a political appointee of President Lincoln's, but he felt that the nation's full dignity must be maintained to the letter.

"Absolutely, sir. I'm afraid that it is being patched at present. We've had trouble with hooligans—Confederate sympathizers, I'm sure. This is the second time I've had to send it for mending. It will be flying by this afternoon."

"I see. Sentiment against us in Liverpool remains as strong as ever." It was a statement, not a question.

"I'm afraid so," Dudley said, "but I assure you that I'm doing everything in my power to check it. I gave a speech last week to the town merchants' association. Can't say they liked it—I got some cold looks, I can tell you—but I put them on notice that we will fight this thing to the end."

"Good work. Now, pray tell, what do you have?"

Dudley held up his penciled notes, thick enough for a small pamphlet. "Nothing in writing beyond my own scribbling, but I have it on the best authority that Miller and Sons are getting ready to launch a ship that is almost certainly destined for the Confederate navy. They're calling her the *Oreto*."

"What type of vessel?" Charles asked.

"She's a war steamer. No equipment yet, but she's being fashioned with gun ports. Would be the work of a day in the West Indies to fit her out with cannons."

"What makes you think she's Confederate?"

"The shipyard says she's intended for the Italian government. The vessel's supposedly bound for Palermo, and then for Jamaica. But I overheard some dockworkers laughing it up in a pub last week as a royal joke. More to the point, an Irish clerk over at the Miller shipyard—his sister lives in Boston—has given me to understand that this is merely a ruse."

Charles frowned. A war steamer would set a dangerous precedent. It would increase Britain's commitment to the Confederacy and give the South the start of a modern navy. "Did your source explain why?" he asked.

"Just what you would expect. The queen's Neutrality Proclamation forbids selling warships to a belligerent. So does the Foreign Enlistment Act. British law categorically prohibits fitting out or equipping vessels for use in foreign wars where the queen is neutral. So the shipbuilders are observing the legal niceties by pretending she's a merchantman. Any fool can tell from the construction that she's a man-o'-war. They'll turn her over to the Confederate agents only after clearing port—and so stay on the friendly side of the law."

Dudley shuffled through his notes, eyes intent. He was a Quaker who had drunk in abolitionism with his mother's milk.

Religious pacifism prevented him from taking up a gun himself, but he was doing his damnedest to keep weapons from getting to the Confederacy. He pulled out a sheet and read off the specifications. "She's got two funnels, three masts, and is bark-rigged. I counted eight portholes a side. Places for sixteen guns.

"By the way," Dudley added, looking up, "I checked with the Italian consul. He said he is unaware of his government ordering any such vessel."

Charles scrutinized the simple but precise drawing of the boat that Dudley had sketched. It had the power of both steam and sail. Arrows on the page indicated a retractable screw propeller that could be raised to minimize drag when winds were fair and lowered when the ship was becalmed or in a tight spot. The design was elegant—and lethal. Unarmed wooden merchant ships would be like mallards in a millpond. Charles felt a cold conviction settling in his bones. This ship would be gunning for the Union.

"I would like to see the vessel. Can we get a view from the wharf?"

"Yes, sir, we can at that. I've been watching them put the final touches on her for the last week. They're loading her with coal now. Gets my hackles up!"

Dudley spoke fervently, causing the rim of his ears to turn a delicate pink. Charles might have smiled at the incongruous images—fearsome dog with raised hackles, rose-handled teacups—if his mind had not been racing forward to the problem of proof. If there was nothing in writing, other than Dudley's own notes, how could he convince Lord Russell that the ship was an impostor? That it violated Britain's own laws and should be stopped?

Charles picked up his steaming gloves and turned them over. "These should be dry enough to use in a matter of minutes. May I prevail upon you for a cup of tea while we wait?"

"Of course, sir," Dudley said, springing to his feet. He lifted the tea cozy off a pot that Charles had noted upon entering the room and poured two cups, strong and dark. "Would you like milk and sugar, Mr. Adams?"

"Yes—in the English manner, thank you."

"Has London rubbed off on you, then, sir?"

"Long ago, I'm afraid, when my father was minister here. And my mother was a London-born American." Charles sipped the hot tea, invigorated by its sweet creaminess—one of the few vices he allowed himself. He could feel his mental faculties, dulled by the long trip, brightening. "Do you have any idea who's behind it? The ship, that is?" he asked the consul.

"I suspect a banking concern here in Liverpool called Fraser, Trenholm, and Company. They appear to be managing funds for some work over at Laird Brothers also—on the same quay as Miller and Sons."

"The Scottish shipbuilders?"

"The very ones," Dudley replied. "Right down the road from the Millers' shipyard—across the Mersey in Birkenhead. They're outfitting the Rebels, too—with nary a thought to the consequences. The Scots would take a commission from the Devil himself if he had ready cash and pocketed his tail. I'm just not sure who is behind Fraser and Trenholm. Investors in England appear to be bankrolling the venture. On the Confederate side, we're up against one J. D. Bulloch—Captain James Dunwoody Bulloch. Styles himself an innocent blockade-runner, if there is such a thing. But I'd be willing to bet—if I were a betting man, which I am not—that he's an out-and-out agent, or even a commissioned officer in the Confederate navy. He captained a ship that ran in a thousand pounds of Southern cotton not long ago. I hear he's from Georgia."

"Hmm . . . these feel dry," Charles said, pulling his wool gloves back on. "What do you say to a stroll along the dock?"

A freezing drizzle pressed down upon the day as the two men wound down the sloping streets sleek with rain to the vast granite wharves and piers that stretched for five miles on both sides of the river Mersey, leading to the Irish Sea. It was a busy scene— crews of the Royal Navy mingling with merchant mariners, stevedores, ironworkers, carpenters, and men of a dozen other trades. A half-painted trollop holding a makeup sponge cracked open a low window as they walked by, too late to make eye contact. Her suggestive words hung in the chilly air at their backs— "Ready for a romp, gents?" Charles quickened his pace. He would never get used to the brazenness of English prostitutes.

Near the entrance to Laird Brothers' shipyard, an enterprising tavern keeper had a small stand selling hard cider and Cornish pasties, hot from a brazier. "What ho, Mr. Dudley," the woman at the counter said cheerfully as the two Americans approached. "What brings you down to the quays this wet morning?"

"Good day, Mrs. Finnegan. How are you? Allow me to introduce my superior, Mr. Charles Francis Adams, minister to Great Britain. I'm giving him a tour of Liverpool commerce. Mr. Adams, this is Mrs. Bridie Finnegan, purveyor of the best pasties north of Cornwall and proprietress of the Cat and the Cage. But, Mrs. Finnegan, what brings you out in this weather?"

"Same old story. Another lad gone off at the last minute to make his fortune on the sea, leaving me to open shop. Can't hold on to them these days." She leaned forward with a confidential air, her heavy bosom straining against the counter. "I have to watch out for meself, make a quid where I can."

Mr. Dudley looked unobtrusively in either direction, then commented to Charles in a low voice, "Mrs. Finnegan has occasion to overhear conversations in her tavern. She's been very helpful to the Union."

"'Tis in my own interest. The town's practically empty. Your war is driving all the lads into shipbuilding or smuggling. The mills are shutting down. No cotton. I'll be happier seeing the Federals win and the whole mess coming to an end."

"So it's not that you fancy tweaking the nose of English aristocrats who dote on the Confederates, Mrs. Finnegan?" Mr. Dudley asked with a smile in his eyes.

"Oh, sure and there might be something in that also." The Irishwoman shrugged in amusement. "Not that I would be admitting to a fierce grudge or any such thing."

"You haven't seen the gentleman we spoke of last week around here today, have you?"

"If you turn around slow, you'll catch him now. He's with the gentleman what comes up regular from London to see the Lairds. But you didn't hear that from me," Mrs. Finnegan said, wrapping a meat-and-potato turnover that Charles had not requested and handing it to him. "Good day, gentlemen."

The Americans continued their walk toward Laird Brothers, past the two men standing outside the massive gates. The pair were so locked in conversation they did not look at passersby. Charles recognized one as Sir Walter Birch, an eminent, elegant Tory known in London for his cordiality toward Confederate envoys. The other man was unknown—a burly, well-dressed fellow of medium height who looked as if he had spent considerable time at sea. He had a handsome face, dark and deeply weathered, with heavy walrus sideburns that gave him a jowly, bulldog look.

"James Bulloch," Mr. Dudley remarked in a low voice once they were well past. "He's the one I told you about. I don't know the other chap. Do you?"

"I've seen him. He's Walter Birch—a friend to William Gregory and some of the others in Parliament who demand recognition for the Confederacy. I've heard that he has investments in shipbuilding, but I associate him with London, not Liverpool."

"Money from all over England pours through here. I don't doubt that there are substantial investors in London who've placed their bets on the Confederacy. Stands to reason," Dudley said.

The two men rounded a curve on the macadam road, passing

the front gates of W. C. Miller and Sons. Charles handed the warm pasty to Dudley, who ate it as they walked. At last they gained a high point where they could look back into the Miller shipyard. Dudley wiped the grease from his fingers on a folded handkerchief, then took a small pair of binoculars from his breast pocket and handed them to Charles. "There, the second one, that's the *Oreto*. Do you see her gunports?"

Charles examined the steamship. A war vessel, clearly. It was very like the new ships being used by the Royal Navy. A crew was painting a decorative red stripe on the black hull, while a cluster of officers on deck appeared to be consulting a document or blueprint. The boat was in the water and ready to sail, from what Charles could tell.

"Where there's one, there'll be others," he said, still peering through the lenses. "But if we have no proof, I don't see how I can register a protest with Lord Russell or even call for an investigation. We've got to have more details before approaching him."

Charles lowered the binoculars. "Do you think you could get the clerk you mentioned to make a sworn statement?"

"Not a chance. The man wouldn't have a job afterward. He told me only in the strictest confidence—to give us a heads-up."

"You said you overheard some dockworkers in the pub. Could we get affidavits from any of them?" Charles knew the suggestion wasn't much good, but he couldn't immediately grasp what method they could use to pin down evidence that would be convincing to Lord Russell. And it had to be very convincing. The foreign secretary had made it quite clear that all shipbuilders would be held innocent until proved guilty. Ships that sailed without any proven military purpose or direct connection with the Confederacy were entirely legal. If they acquired guns afterward, or were sold to different persons five minutes later, it was not the business of Her Majesty's government.

Dudley stroked his salt-and-pepper beard. He looked across the water at the *Oreto*. "No, not possible—at least I don't think so."

He turned to Charles, a gleam in his gray eyes. "Give me some time. I don't have much, but I've got some men who've been helping me. I think we can get better evidence, or at least more of it. I hesitate to be specific right now. Not all of them are what you would call gentlemen. Might be best if you didn't know the details—seeing as you have to look Russell straight in the eye. Is that all right?"

The American minister lifted the binoculars again and stared hard at the *Oreto*, with her black gunports and cocky red stripe. A similar steamship had brought down the empire of China in the first opium war. With only sixteen guns, the *Oreto* was at best a sixth-rate, certainly not a first-rate, warship, which would carry a hundred guns in the British navy. But against unarmed wooden merchantmen the iron-hulled *Oreto* would be plenty deadly.

Charles turned to the consul and handed him back the glasses. "Do whatever you can, but do it now and get everything on paper. I have a feeling that our nation's survival may depend upon it. More *Oreto*s and we'll be looking at a real Confederate navy, not the minnow fleet they've got now. We can't allow it to happen."

Charles's eyes were drawn back to the ship across the harbor. Not on my watch, he thought. Not this son of an Adams.

SIXTEEN

MARCH 1862

*A little girl came running to tell on her brother. "Oh Mamma,
Charlie is using bad language, curse words!" "What is it?"
"He says: 'Dam Yankees are here, prisoners.'" But Charlie
protested: "Well Mamma, is not that their name?
I never hear them called anything else."*

—Mary Boykin Chesnut, *A Diary from Dixie*

"It came while you were out, miss." The parlormaid handed a
battered envelope to Julia, who was untying her bonnet after
a brisk morning walk around St. James's Park. The lawns wore a
new coat of green, and the trees and shrubs of the formal gardens
had finally begun to bloom after the long winter, framing the
view to Buckingham Palace. Julia loved to look upon its façade
from the bridge that spanned the narrow lake meandering
through the park.

Victoria was the first monarch to live in the grand home. And
the royal standard fluttering in the breeze indicated that the wid-
owed queen was in residence now. The old royal seat of St. James's
Palace, built by Henry VIII, was shabby in comparison. The
new palace glowed in the light, as luminous as an ivory jewel box.
From the footbridge, Julia could just make out the changing of
the guard, like toy soldiers in the distance. In the cool, fresh-as-a-
brook morning air, old England seemed as young and vigorous as
spring itself.

"Thank you, Emily," Julia said. She dropped to the chair in

front of a cheery fire in the drawing room. Her father had gone to Liverpool again on business, but the servants kept the fire burning for his imminent return. Sir Walter wouldn't tolerate a cold room.

Julia blew on her freezing fingers and thoughtfully examined the envelope. The frank said Charleston, South Carolina. The letter must have run the blockade. It looked as though it had traveled in a dirty hull on a long and circuitous voyage twice around the Horn. Julia felt suddenly short of breath as she opened the seal.

My dear Julia, if I may,

The letter began in a handwriting she didn't recognize, but a voice she did.

I hope you will forgive me using your given name, but it comes often to my mind in these troubled days. I made it here safely after an anxious but uneventful voyage from Nassau. Apparently, I need not have worried. The cargo arrived intact, and I am grateful to say that the medicine has been forwarded to those who are in urgent need.

Otherwise, the news is grim. The Confederates have lost most of Tennessee, a state on our western borders. Federal reinforcements pour in without ceasing. Our forces haven't lost many battles—most are called a draw—but it seems that for every man the Northerners lose they have a replacement. We have none. It's rumored that as many as twelve thousand of our men were forced to surrender at Fort Donelson in Tennessee. I cannot fathom the numbers. My brother Robert escaped, thankfully—but just barely. He is now serving in a cavalry battalion under Colonel Nathan Forrest, and helped evacuate the town of Nashville.

Undoubtedly you will wonder at my sympathy for the Confederate losses. Every defeat strikes a blow at the hearts of those around me. Numbered among the thousands lost are a few whom we knew personally. Many have died. Even those who argued in favor of the Union before the war are struck dumb by the price that Lincoln is forcing the South to pay for its convictions. I still believe the Confederacy is in the wrong on the question of slavery, but it is nonetheless painful to see one's countrymen pummeled by a stronger force—and one that has profited from cotton just as long as the South.

The hatred here is intense. No one will speak the name "United States." It's always "Lincoln." Lincoln's mercenaries and Lincoln's warships. Everyone seems to blame the president, but not the people who elected him.

My mother spent the last week working at a Gunboat Fair. She and the other ladies are holding bazaars to raise money for ships. Everyone was greatly heartened by the performance this week of the CSS *Virginia*, a steam frigate that our navy has fitted out with iron above the waterline. She blasted several wooden warships on blockade outside the port of Newport News before being driven off by an iron-hulled oddity called the *Monitor*. In any case, the ladies here are much encouraged. My mother's association brought in over two thousand dollars. I don't know how many ships they will be able to buy with their money from peach pie and lemonade (coffee is unavailable), but their patriotism is at a white heat.

This brings me to my own predicament. Now that I've returned, there are many who say I should be engaged where my training as a surgeon can do some good. Qualified doctors are in shorter supply than qualified generals, in which the South is abundant. Vigilance committees pound the doors of those thought slacking. I received a warm welcome when I arrived with our shipment, but it has cooled in the past weeks. We expect a knock soon.

Julia felt a hollow space open up in her chest. Turning to the second sheet of the letter, she read swiftly, as if to overtake Baxter before he could act.

My parents are divided. Mother is frightened at the thought of yet another son at the front, but is mindful of all the mothers' sons who need medical attention. She wants me to volunteer. My father is opposed. He urges me to leave at once, before I'm conscripted. I feel conflicted and wonder if there is much difference between running medical supplies and operating a surgery at the front. But I still believe that this war had to come, and I am determined not to raise my hand, holding a gun or a scalpel, to defend the cause that has torn us apart. I honored my father's request to bring the supplies, and I will honor his request to return to England. It's painful to know that some will call me a coward. I hope not you.

Julia let out a sigh of relief, unaware that she had been holding her breath. She didn't care what anyone else believed. She didn't think he should serve either side. The idea of fighting for a binding compact among states was ridiculous. Europe had no such arrangements, nor need of them. Why should Baxter, whom she could picture in this very room, risk anything for such a cause? And to fight on the other side, the side of slavery, seemed terribly wrong.

She read on. Baxter reported that he would be on a ship to Nassau as soon as he helped his father conclude some business in Charleston. It was a complicated matter that might take a month or more to resolve. He regretted missing her at her uncle's countryseat in the early spring but hoped she might still receive him at Belfield Manor.

Baxter's final lines took her by surprise.

> There is a matter that I wish to discuss with you—and with your father, if you will permit me. The war has impressed me with the fragility of life. There are numberless widows and orphans here. Every night we bow our heads to pray for my brothers' safe return, frightened that the morrow will bring shattering news. I hope you will consider what I have to say, or at least allow me to say it, while opportunity exists.
>
> I am sincerely yours,
Baxter

Baxter. Not II. Baxter Sams, Esquire. Suddenly he was Baxter, and she was Julia. The use of a first name was halfway to a kiss on the lips. Very bold, hardly proper. Julia's heart raced. She wasn't sure if she should be affronted or delighted. Yet Baxter's expression of his feelings touched her own. Smiling unconsciously, she gazed over the familiar garden outside her window to the pale horizon beyond and decided upon delighted. It seemed that life beyond the home of her childhood was finally about to begin.

The heavy door to Belfield Manor closed with a distant thud. "Good day, sir," Julia could make out the butler saying, and Sir Walter Birch entered the room. A coachman followed, placing two burgundy valises on a sideboard.

"Welcome home, Father," Julia said, rising happily.

Walter smiled at the warm greeting. "Hello, my dear. How nice to see you waiting for me. Is everything well?"

"Very well, thank you, Father," Julia replied.

"You look particularly invigorated this morning. You've roses in your cheeks. Have you been out for a walk already?"

"Yes, St. James's is all abloom. I walked the whole length and back." Julia gave her father another smile as she retook her seat. The scroll of a climbing rose, just starting to leaf, framed the garden window behind her like lace.

Walter looked quizzically at his daughter. "Hmm, yes—well, that's very good, I'm sure. Walking strengthens the constitution."

"Did your trip go well, Father? I'm surprised to see you back from Liverpool so early in the day. Have they added an overnight train?"

"I actually got back last evening but decided to stay at the club. I had a late supper party. Mason and some of the Confederate purchasing agents were there. Quite intriguing."

"Really?" Julia asked, though she wasn't particularly interested in the answer. She turned back to the letter she was holding.

"I see you have a letter," Walter observed. "One of the Bentleys? Are they married yet—or are London's bachelors still quaking in their boots?"

Julia laughed. "Father, you must really stop picking on Louise and Flora. London's bachelors can more than hold their own, I assure you."

Walter raised one eyebrow ironically. "I doubt that. Lambs to the slaughter, I'm afraid." He remained standing.

Julia was conscious that her father was still awaiting an answer.

"The letter is from Baxter Sams. You remember him, I'm sure. The gentleman from Virginia who came for tea last fall."

"Yes, I do. But I recall that *he* came on business and *you* invited him for tea. Lady bountiful and all that. You must really stop being gracious to every beggar."

"Goodness, Father. Mr. Sams is hardly a beggar. I thought that you would want me to invite a business associate to stay for refreshment," Julia replied.

"Well, yes, normally that's true. But Mr. Sams isn't much of an associate. To be frank, I am not sure if he even supports his own country. Rather a coward, I would wager. I wasn't much impressed. Why is he writing to you?"

"I saw him later at . . . at an event I attended with Uncle Randolph. I suggested he write us when he arrived. I thought you would want to know if he made it through the blockade."

Walter shook his head in the negative. "I'm far too busy to wonder at the fortunes of every blockade-runner. I'm sure he has made a tidy sum for himself, but that is immaterial to me—as I assume it is to you."

"He impressed me as more than a blockade-runner," Julia replied cautiously. "I believe he is genuinely concerned about the suffering of the wounded."

"Perhaps. In any case, he's gone back to the Confederacy now. I hope you'll understand when I say that I expect you won't be responding to his letters." Walter spoke lightly, but there was a warning note in his voice.

Julia glanced down at the letter, then back at her father, her hazel eyes darkening to a deep green. She knew that he expected unwavering obedience. "As it so happens," she replied, choosing her words with care, "he says he will be returning to London. So I don't anticipate receiving any more letters."

Sir Walter looked sharply at his daughter. "There will be no sophistry in this house, Julia Birch. You know what I mean. I do not want you in contact with him whether he is making the rounds in London or mailing valentines from China. He is not suitable."

"Why do you say that?"

"I shouldn't have to explain. He's beneath you."

"My impression is that his family is a mercantile one, like ours. I believe his club is in Mayfair," Julia said.

Walter bristled at the implication. "I do not think of our family as mercantile. Edmund may go into Parliament someday. And I certainly do not appreciate being equated with former colonists dealing in pots and pans—or opium, as the case may be."

"So is it that he's a colonial, an American?" Julia struggled to sound reasonable and demure, as she knew he expected, but her father's prejudices offended her sense of fairness.

"Yes, because he is an American, and, more important, because he's a commoner. And, *most* important, because I say so. Really, Julia!" Walter shook his head. "I have enough to think about without this nonsense. You are under my guidance. I absolutely forbid you to see him."

Julia's face paled. She wanted to protest, but a lifetime of training stopped her. Instead, she folded Baxter's letter into thirds, one edge over the other, and placed it back in the envelope. Her motions were slow and deliberate.

"Do you understand me?" Walter demanded. His tone was sharp now.

"Yes, Father," Julia answered with her eyes downcast. "But I still don't see why," she said, quietly holding her ground.

"Julia. You know the answer. You know what the Americans did to this family. They robbed your grandfather, betrayed their king, and made off with an entire continent. Now the Union threatens Canada. And who knows if the Confederates will be any better, should they get their independence. When they aren't scoundrels, they're fools. I will *not* allow you to throw away your future by communicating with this man! It's scandalous enough that he writes you without my permission."

"But, Father," she said, looking up. "Surely he deserves some consideration as an individual, not just as an American. I don't understand how you can judge him without knowing him better."

Walter folded his arms. "You will simply have to trust my superior judgment. I have your best interests at heart."

Julia picked up the book that she had left next to her chair the day before and slipped the envelope between the pages. She glanced toward the window. Outside, a wind had sprung up, riffling the tender green shoots of spring, still susceptible to frost.

Her father encouraged conversation and even debate with his children about impersonal matters, but when it came to an order he expected his word to carry the power of commandment. Julia normally conceded without question. But polite acquiescence now felt like dry ash on her tongue. She stood up.

"If you will please excuse me," she replied with the only words she could find, "I need to see Cook about the menu for tonight."

SEVENTEEN

*Anxiety has become our normal condition, and I find a fellow
can dance in time on a tight rope as easily as on a floor.*

—Henry Adams to his brother Charles,
A Cycle of Adams Letters

The low light in the pub near the Birmingham railway station revealed two men hunched over evening brews. A late-spring rain pattered against the dark windowpanes, creating rivulets that reflected the candlelight in long yellow streaks.

"'But she doesn't *have* any thirty-two-pounders,' Edwards tells me, like he's speaking to a mental deficient," Dudley reported in a voice pitched below the murmur of surrounding voices. "Says there are no grounds whatsoever for detaining the ship under the Foreign Enlistment Act and that he's cleared her for sailing on the twenty-second of March."

"What about the documentation you showed him?" Charles asked, shifting on the hard seat. The urgent necessity of speaking to Dudley in person had drawn him up to Birmingham, the most convenient halfway point between Liverpool and London. It was a dreary town for dreary business. Sam Edwards, Liverpool's customs inspector, had refused to detain ships being built for the Confederacy, despite British law. "I thought you had four different witnesses."

"I had five! I told him we have five shipyard informants who swear the so-called *Oreto* is being built for the Rebels with the plan of fitting it out with arms in the West Indies. It's plain that the ship is intended for military use. I told him about her sixteen gunports, capable of accommodating at least six thirty-two-pounders in broadside. 'But the *Oreto* doesn't *have* any thirty-two-pounders,' he says."

"Do you know if he even read the documents?"

"Oh, he sifted through them while I was there. Kept me standing the whole time, and poked at my ten-page report like it was last week's leftovers. Said the evidence was all hearsay. That he couldn't understand why Lord Russell saw fit to forward the report to his attention when there was no legal testimony."

"Do you think he has some stake in the Confederate cause?" Charles asked. "Surely he realizes that he may be drawing Britain into the war."

"I don't know. I've heard that he speculates in cotton. Every bale that comes through the blockade is quadruple the normal price. So he may have a personal reason for backing the Confederacy. He says Miller and Sons swear they built the ship for the Kingdom of Naples and that's good enough for him."

Charles shifted again on the hard bench to ease a crick in his back. Was it possible that the *Oreto* really was bound for Italy? The Bourbon monarch had recently lost his kingdom when the flamboyant Giuseppe Garibaldi unified Italy under a single government, but would he order a gunboat? If he hoped to reverse his losses, he would have to fight on land. There would be little point to an oceangoing fleet. But the Confederacy's needs were altogether different. If they wanted to make a nation, they had to make a navy.

Dudley had fallen silent and was now looking into his dark porter, having touched hardly a drop. The lines in his thin face dragged downward more deeply than ever. Charles wished he could give the consul more specific instructions or help. Gathering evidence was a time-consuming, hit-or-miss proposition. It was also dangerous. Dudley and his agent spent late hours on the dark wharves and in riverside taverns hoping for a lucky break. He'd received several anonymous death threats to stay away from certain docks. There was absolutely nothing Charles could do to make the job safer. In fact, he must urge Dudley to go back out and try again.

"Mr. Dudley, you'll just have to keep at it. Your detective— Maguire, right?—see that he talks with any crew member coming off a blockade-runner. Hire another man if you need help up in Glasgow. You *must* get sworn affidavits so that the accusations cannot be dismissed. And please take care. Do you think anyone associates Maguire with you?"

"No. We meet only when absolutely necessary, and somewhere out of the way."

"Keep it that way, please. We can't afford to lose either of you," Charles said.

Dudley's mission was indeed critical. It might make the difference between the survival or the destruction of the United States. Charles felt perfectly useless. So far, he had had little power to stop Britain's supplying of the Confederacy. The *Oreto* and other gunships would swim down the Mersey while the American minister wore out his knees begging at Whitehall. Someone had to do it. He just wished, now more than ever, that it were someone more effective than he.

EIGHTEEN

An engaged woman is always more agreeable than a disengaged.
She is satisfied with herself. Her cares are over, and she feels that
she may exert all her powers of pleasing without suspicion.
All is safe with a lady engaged; no harm can be done.

—Jane Austen, *Mansfield Park*

"He refused to allow you to even receive letters from Mr. Sams?" Louise asked with sympathy.

"That and worse. Father said I am to have no contact with him at all. I can't even receive him when he comes to London." Julia pressed her hands into her lap to stop them from shaking.

Louise patted her friend's arm. They sat closely together on the sofa. "I'm sorry. I guess I'm lucky that it was so easy with Nathaniel. My parents might have wished for a smarter match, but no one can complain about a man of the cloth unless they want to risk their pew behind the pearly gates. Father was quite won over by Nathaniel asking for advice on how best to manage the parish finances. Even Flora, with her exasperating standards, calls him 'a dear pet.' John rolls his eyes, but I know he approves, too."

"You are indeed lucky," Julia said.

"Does it really matter so much? You've said you hardly know him," Louise pointed out.

"I suppose it shouldn't. But I would like to feel that I had some choice in the matter."

Julia recognized the reasonableness of Louise's observation. She had met Baxter only a few times. Yet he had intrigued her more on each occasion. In her experience, gentlemen usually became less interesting upon closer acquaintance, engrossed in their own affairs and happiest when airing their own opinions. The infrequency of her encounters with Baxter gave each a special piquancy in Julia's mind. Absence sharpened her desire to see him.

"Perhaps your father knows something about Baxter that you don't. Isn't he chummy with all the Confederates?"

"I don't think it's that. He knew everything he ever wanted to know about Baxter before he met him. Baxter is from America. That's all there is to it. My father can't abide the former colonies."

"Surely it's not merely prejudice. Perhaps he just doesn't like the thought of you moving across the ocean, if it came to that. No father wants his daughter so far away. I imagine that Virginia is hardly civilized. Slaves and all. Who knows—maybe even Indians?"

"I'm sure he wants only the best for me," Julia agreed. "I just don't share his opinion about what *is* best. Baxter Sams seems perfectly suitable. He's well-mannered, well-bred, and well-educated. He is a man of *purpose*." Julia spoke with increasing emphasis, building her argument.

"Surely you wouldn't consider allowing Mr. Sams to court without your father's approval?"

Julia paused. Her spirits sank again. "No. I suppose not," she said.

It was unthinkable to go against a parent's wishes. Every young woman knew that. If she wed anyone of whom her father disapproved, disinheritance could be expected. If she allowed Baxter to court her against her father's wishes, scandal might spoil all further chances of marriage.

"You'd have nothing of your own, even if he could support you," Louise cautioned. "A respectable woman can't enter marriage without some sort of dowry to fall back on. It would be simply dreadful—scrimping and saving from the household funds and having to beg for a new hat. You'd hate it."

"Yes, you're right," she said.

Julia had no idea how much Sir Walter planned to award her upon marriage, should she meet someone he found acceptable. Many fathers named a set amount, which would become common knowledge among eligible bachelors and careful parents. Her father hadn't yet done so, and Julia had begun to wonder when he would. She hoped her dowry would be near the fifteen thousand pounds that Louise and Flora stood to claim. Such a munificent sum would generate an annual interest of at least five hundred pounds, easily enough for spending money. Although a married woman had no legal right to call the earnings her own, most husbands granted their wives an allowance. A dowry gave a woman a certain moral authority even though she had no further legal identity. As the adage went, a husband and wife are one person, and that person is the husband.

"It's not just a matter of money. I would hate to lose my father's good opinion," Julia said. "He's taken care of me since my mother died."

It was indeed inconceivable to her that things could ever come to such a pass. An illicit correspondence was genuinely criminal in society's eyes, and hardly what her father deserved.

"You've taken care of him, too, I daresay," Louise observed. "No one manages a great house better than you—and at your age. I hope I do half so well—and I'll have only a small vicarage to think about."

"It comes of having the responsibility," Julia reassured Louise. "Necessity is the mother of invention, as they say—and as long as one has a mother there's no necessity. You'll grow into it . . . and be perfectly splendid." She felt her cheer partly restored by the reminder of Louise's approaching nuptials. It was helpful to think of something else. "Have you set the date for the ceremony?"

Louise had, and the two young women drank an entire pot of Darjeeling tea discussing the details. Louise planned to wear an ivory dress and carry a bouquet of irises and white roses. It was to be a simple affair, as befitted a vicar and his bride, and the couple would honeymoon in Brighton. Louise's mother had ordered an elaborate trousseau, including linens, bedding, and fifty new chemises, camisoles, nightdresses, and petticoats. Julia suggested menus for a first supper party at the vicarage, once they were properly settled. They pored over the recipes in *Mrs. Beeton's* cookbook and Louise took notes while striking off any items that she didn't think would suit Nathaniel's tastes. Lamb was out. And anything that called for capsicum. Too spicy.

The mood of the afternoon remained light, but when Louise excused herself to fetch a piece of trousseau embroidery, Julia's thoughts returned to her predicament. Her father was resolutely against the one man who seemed as if he might make a serious offer and for whom she had strong feelings. Louise had said what any friend of sense and breeding would say. Marriage was a contract one did not sign lightly. It was unimaginable to disobey one's parent on such an important matter, and hers was not the type of father to change his mind. He never did. As much as she hated to accept it, Louise was clearly right and Julia should take her advice.

But it stung. Her father was wrong about Baxter, Julia was convinced, distressed again at the injustice. His true character should matter. Her happiness ought to matter as well, and yet it didn't—not to her father, not even to her friend. It was as if she were merely a pawn, like Edmund at Eton, waiting to be moved to the square on the board that best suited her father's strategy.

She got to her feet, smoothed her wide silk skirt, and walked over to the sideboard to inspect her coiffure in a mirror hanging above the long, polished surface. A wayward curl had escaped the pins. She ducked to see her head better.

A somber young woman with rounded hazel eyes gazed back. Her lips were sealed and her expression strained. Julia studied the gloomy visage, which examined her in turn. "You're awfully tall for a pawn," she whispered.

NINETEEN

JUNE 1862

*[N]o one could be so simple as to believe that two armored
ships-of-war could be built publicly, under the eyes of
the Government, and go to sea like the* Alabama,
without active and incessant collusion.

—Henry Adams, *The Education of Henry Adams*

C harles paced back and forth across the length of the second-
floor study, his steps as measured and deliberate as those of
the guards in front of Buckingham Palace. Henry sat attentively
at his desk in the corner, ready to take notes. Dudley, down from
Liverpool for the day, stood up occasionally, as if to interrupt, and
then silently resumed his seat.

"No, Mr. Dudley, I don't agree," the minister suddenly pronounced, stopping in the middle of the room. "If we take the case
of the new Laird ship—the one they're calling the *290*—to the
Liverpool customs collector, he will simply rule it out of hand as
he did with the *Oreto,* now sailed for the Confederacy as the re-
named *Florida.* Edwards is a rogue—and probably on the Confederate payroll. All your painstaking work will be for naught.
We must go directly to Lord Russell."

The consul shot to his feet nervously and this time remained
standing. "You're right that he's a scoundrel, but our proof is
stronger this time. Maguire has documented the whole thing.
I don't see how Edwards can refuse to stop the warship. If you

go to Russell first, there will be a delay. I fear we'll miss the opportunity. The *290* is nearly ready."

"That may be, but Lord Russell alone has the power to force the admiralty and the customs officers to act. He can require the officers of the Crown to rule on the matter. We must to go to the top."

Dudley tried again. "Are you sure Lord Russell has any sympathy for our case?"

"To the contrary. We must assume that he has no sympathy whatsoever. His first and only concern is the interest of Great Britain. But we have to go to him nonetheless."

Charles turned to Henry, erect in his chair and ready with a pen. "Henry, take this down; we need a letter requesting an interview with the foreign secretary at his earliest convenience."

The minister began dictating the request to Earl Russell, and the only other sound in the room became the familiar scratch of quill against the heavy bond used for diplomatic correspondence. Dudley sat down again, his hands clasped tightly around his crossed knee.

Charles measured his words to balance restraint with insistence. He knew that whatever friends the Union had had in Parliament were fewer now and in hiding. He must take infinite care not to worsen relations while still putting maximum pressure on Russell.

The spring had been miserable. The Union had captured New Orleans, but the occupation wasn't going well and everyone knew it. Confronted with spittle, curses, and Confederate flags by the patriotic ladies of New Orleans, Union general Benjamin Butler had decreed that any female showing contempt for a blue-uniformed soldier would be arrested for prostitution.

British society recoiled at the insult and possible injury to genteel womanhood. The legation and the consulate were flooded with protests. Even ardent supporters of the Union protested. The novelist William Thackeray, normally a mild, good-humored supper guest, had trembled with indignation—his eyes actually filled with tears—at the coarse cruelty of Butler and Lincoln. The worst came when Prime Minister Palmerston sent Charles a stern note and declared in the House of Commons that he could hardly contemplate anyone belonging to the Anglo-Saxon race committing such a low deed. As a result, the British prime minister and the American minister were no longer on speaking terms—a damned awkward arrangement for a diplomat. Defense of Butler was worse than useless, of course. The legation simply had to batten down and weather the storm.

Butler's "woman order" had poisoned the Adamses' social relations as well. Though he rarely complained, Henry finally told Charles that he dreaded invitations to dinner, where he was typically made to hate himself and all other Americans. "It's hard not to think of one's countrymen as arrogant brutes when every one else does," he told his father.

Charles suffered no such pangs of self-doubt, but he nonetheless felt as sober as the presiding judge at a hanging. Joviality had fled the household. Charles must find a way to persuade the British to respect their own neutrality laws, even if they had lost all respect for the Lincoln administration.

Henry took down his father's final words, and then sanded the ink to dry them. "Is that all, then?" he inquired.

"Yes," Charles said. "Thank you, Henry." Turning to Thomas Dudley, he added, "You've done excellent work, Mr. Dudley, you and your Mr. Maguire. I don't know what we should do without you. This evidence will be invaluable."

Dudley nodded and shoved his hands into his pockets, apparently trying to contain his agitation. "I suppose I'll have to trust in the integrity and speed of Lord Russell," he said. "But I really don't trust him at all."

JOHN RUSSELL MOTIONED to his manservant to pour them a spot of Madeira. Charles had grown accustomed to the ritual of politeness, behind which he could still discern little of the English earl's true sentiment. The foreign secretary might as well have been making the American minister's acquaintance anew on each occasion. Though they met with some frequency, the two men remained strangers to each other's thoughts and Charles had shelved the hope that they might be allies in the cause of abolition. He now placed more faith in Russell's self-interested caution than in his goodwill.

"This case is like that of the *Oreto*, then?" Lord Russell inquired with a tone of mild interest.

"Precisely. It is exactly like the *Oreto*, now named the *Florida*, as you are aware. However this time we assume that Her Majesty's government will intervene vigorously to stop the ship, or at least to establish the fact that it is not intended for making war on the people of the United States." Charles felt the time had come to press harder.

"If it is a Confederate ship, as you claim, our government will certainly wish to detain it under the Foreign Enlistment Act. Last time the proof was rather thin, if I recall correctly. May I assume that the case has been more fully documented this time?"

Lord Russell perched the hand holding his sherry glass on his crossed knee. The slanting rays of afternoon sun caught and illuminated the amber liquid like a jewel.

Charles was painfully aware of the difference in strength between his own bloodied nation and that of the British Empire. Only law and public opinion restrained Russell and the other cabinet members from doing whatever they damn well pleased. That and a prudent regard for the safety of Canada, Charles recognized. Much as he deplored the empty rants of the New York papers, the minister had to admit that their threats had occasioned some useful queasiness on the eastern shores of the Atlantic.

"We now have nine affidavits. Two from my consul and his London detective, and three from citizens of Liverpool who testify to the true ownership and purpose of the vessel. We've also obtained sworn statements from four men enlisted to sail on the ship. They all confirm that the vessel is a cruiser that will fight for the South. There is absolutely no doubt that the 290 is a man-o'-war."

Charles Francis didn't know how Dudley had managed to induce the men to sign affidavits and didn't really want to know. He suspected that it had something to do with large quantities of dollars being converted into pounds sterling.

John Russell lifted his glass and twirled the Portuguese wine, observing the brilliant color given it by the sun. The summer warmth released the sherry's flowery aroma. Taking a small sip, the foreign secretary commented, "You must try this Madeira, Mr. Adams. I do not know a vintage that I have enjoyed more."

Charles held his glass by the delicate stem but declined to lift it. He met the English earl's eye. "Thank you, Lord Russell, but I do wish to know what approach you intend to take."

The earl looked thoughtfully at the ceiling. "Nine affidavits appear to me to be adequate reason to take this matter quite seriously indeed," he responded after a pause. "I understand that the Lords of the Treasury, who are in charge of the customs houses, do not share your opinion of the 290. But the admiralty, on the other hand, appears ready to entertain your suspicions, from what I gather." His lordship had clearly studied the matter, betraying a depth of interest otherwise cloaked by the contemplative manner.

Russell knitted his brow. "We need someone above the fray. I shall refer it to the queen's advocate, Sir John Harding. He's in a position to make a final determination. Once he does, this ministry can act accordingly." Russell looked directly at the American minister. "Will that answer your government's concern?"

Charles inclined his head to signal agreement. "We shall be very grateful for Sir John's prompt consideration of the matter." At last he took a sip from his glass. "You are quite right, Lord Russell. This is a delightful Madeira. May I inquire as to the merchant house from which you obtained it?"

❧✦❧

TWENTY

Our Navy does not look as it did in the last war. . . . Now our
ships do nothing but catch fishing schooners. The Alliance, *the*
Goudar, *the* Thomas Watson, *the* Bermuda, *the* Fingal,
the Amelia, *have all taken quantities of clothing, and military*
equipment of every description from here [to the Confederacy],
of which we have had notice beforehand. But I do not
see a sign of their capture in any quarter.

—Charles Francis Adams to Charles, Jr., in the
First Massachusetts cavalry, *A Cycle of Adams Letters*

The brief morning fog had lifted, revealing in the distance a
large citadel that shimmered above the calm water in the
summer sunshine. High walls came to the edge of the island.
Fort Sumter appeared to float at the entrance to the harbor,
where it stood guard over the merchant ships taking refuge inside. Patchy red brickwork showed where bombs lobbed from
the coast by General Beauregard's troops had exploded the preceding April, until a handful of Federal soldiers surrendered the
besieged fort two days later. The battery was now safely in Confederate hands, though two Union blockaders dipped and bobbed
just out of the reach of her sixty guns.

Baxter shoved a handful of Confederate dollars into the taciturn stevedore's fist as payment for hauling his two bags down to
the snug English steamer that would take him past Sumter and
on to Nassau that night. His baggage was considerably lighter on
this return voyage, and so was his mood. Once past the Union

blockade, it would be little more than two weeks before he was back in London.

The young doctor could hardly believe his good fortune. He was going to England with his father's blessing. He would not have to fight for or against the Confederacy. Unlike his friend Henry, Baxter had no special legacy or destiny tethering him to the country's fate, placing him in the glare of history's footlights. He embraced being one among millions. He hoped Robert and Jacob understood why he couldn't fight for their cause, yet whether his brothers did or did not, Baxter wouldn't have to raise a rifle to defend slavery.

But he was not merely leaving what he dreaded. He was also going toward that which pulled at his heart: the practice of medicine and, somewhat unnervingly, a woman who had taken to visiting his dreams at night in distinctly improper but immensely entertaining ways.

Baxter had some reason to hope that she thought about him, too, though more chastely. Julia hadn't indicated her interest directly, but she had invited him to visit her uncle's home and granted him a tantalizing liberty when they last met. For a heart-stopping moment, her warm hand had nested under his palm like a tame bird. He kissed it when they parted. Baxter sensed Julia was drawn to him despite her English reserve, and he was determined to bid for her love at the first opportunity.

Baxter turned to his father, who walked alongside him, intent on seeing his son off. William Sams looked tired. There were wrinkled bags under his eyes, as if he hadn't slept well for a long time, and his brown hair was shot with gray. Baxter noticed that his father moved stiffly in the mornings now. Would history offer William Sams any consolation for the loss of his sons, should it come to that—as it surely would offer Charles Francis Adams if the Union somehow prevailed? The South might win its independence, but the Sams family could never say their sons had died defending freedom. *God forbid it should come to that.*

"You don't have to leave before supper, do you?" Baxter asked, his voice warm with concern.

"I do, I'm afraid. Your mother will fret if I don't start right back. I don't want to give her anything else to worry about."

The men's eyes met. "They get through all the time, you know," Baxter reassured his father. "The *Aurora*'s a fast boat."

"It doesn't mean we won't worry. You'll send a letter as soon as you reach Nassau, right?"

"The moment we land."

Baxter was tempted to repeat the jibe that Lincoln's navy was blind in one eye and couldn't see out the other, but he knew that his father wouldn't laugh. It occurred to him to say that he felt shyer about encountering Julia Birch than he did about encountering a fully armed sloop of war, topsails flying, but he rejected that observation, too. Would his father remember how daunting it had felt to obtain a wife—to know who you wanted and not know if she felt the same? More important, his father's countenance suggested little scope for levity. Baxter longed to cheer him.

William Sams shifted his valise from one hand to the other, as if to delay the moment of parting. "You remembered the ring, didn't you?" he asked with a hint of his old smile. Deep wrinkles fanned out from his eyes as he squinted in the morning sun.

"Yes, sir. Got it right here," Baxter responded, patting the top pocket of his coat.

"Take good care of it till you get it on her hand. You won't find another like it."

By family tradition, the first son to wed offered his grandmother's engagement ring as a present. The slim gold band trapped a small, brilliantly cut emerald said to have come off a Spanish galleon more than a century ago.

"I wouldn't want any other, but don't jinx me!" Baxter said with a carefree laugh. "I don't know yet if she'll even have me."

"She'd be a dang blamed fool not to accept a man educated at the Royal College of Surgeons and heir to one-third of a fortune," William Sams observed pragmatically. Then his face opened into a wide grin. "Don't forget that I came home with an English lass once. Hog-tie her if you have to. Your mother needs company."

"Aye, aye, Captain," Baxter said, knocking off a crisp salute. "Hog-tying rope at the ready."

The salty breeze played with a dark curl on his son's forehead, and William smiled ruefully. "You get aboard lickety-split now. Wouldn't want to miss your boat."

The older man lowered his voice and added, "Better check to make sure the captain has laid by enough stores in case you have to wait out a patrol in one of the coves. Sometimes they have to hole up for weeks. Those blockade-runners tend to shave it close with supplies. You might want to hie out for the grocer's before sailing."

"Yes, sir," Baxter said. "I'll check right away."

The time had come to say goodbye. The two men embraced briefly, and William Sams turned to retrace his steps up the wooden dock. Baxter watched his father walk away, more conscious than he had ever been before that one chapter of his life was closing and a new one was opening. The war clouds were on the far horizon now, the future bright.

Baxter clambered onto the deck of the boat, holding on to the rigging in the absence of a gangplank. He would inquire about provisions and then head out for a last hot meal on shore.

THE CAPTAIN OF the *Aurora* counted upon the inky gleam of water and sky, hardly distinguishable from each other, to get them safely past the Federals that night. He also relied upon a quiet approach. The *Aurora* was one of the newer ships, equipped with sails as well as a propeller. The loud pistons of a steam engine could be heard distinctly over the quiet lap of the tide on a calm night, and the sails ensured stealth if not speed. Captain Howell would fire the engine only as a last resort. Silence was essential.

The USS *Pawnee* and the USS *Sabine* stood guard off the coast. Each had run out only a single anchor that it could have up within six and a half minutes. Massive lanterns lined the wooden frigates from stern to bowsprit, casting light for a considerable distance around the ships but making the water beyond seem even blacker. It was nearly midnight. On board, the night sentries watched for a break in the glimmer, for any dark shape moving over the surface. Contraband cotton fetched a handsome price in New York on account of the extreme shortage. Tobacco commanded an even handsomer one. Together, they would make a navy crew heroic, as well as wealthy in prize money. An ordinary seaman might fetch a thousand dollars for his share in a valuable cargo of confiscated contraband—a powerful incentive compared with a soldier's thirteen dollars a month on the front in Virginia. It sharpened the eyesight.

Baxter watched the experienced sailors of the *Aurora* work their sails to capture every wisp of the fitful land breeze. The winds blew offshore at night, favoring blockade-runners, and they were accustomed to milking the faint gusts until they filled the sheets. The steamer had the rhythm of a tightly run ship. Captain Howell gave commands infrequently, in a low rumble. The crew seemed to know their paces precisely.

Within the space of an hour, the *Aurora* glided silently alongside the opaque bulk of Fort Sumter, occupied by Confederate troops. A quarrel over cards could be heard through an open brick arch that was lit by the flicker and flare of a lantern somewhere inside.

"Give the signal," Captain Howell ordered quietly.

The young seaman at his side placed his hands on the gunwale, leaned out over the water, and gave a whistle in the dark that to Baxter's ears sounded like the trill of a warbler. The ship's boy waited, and then whistled again. A moment later, an echoing birdsong came from the fort.

Howell nodded to no one in particular. "Steady as she goes," he murmured, guiding the boat past the fort without a break in momentum.

The bright glow of the ship's lanterns illuminated the danger on the sea ahead. It was just a matter of steering around it. The blockade was undermanned, and a dark passage beckoned between the widely spaced frigates. The *Aurora's* captain had told Baxter that he would aim directly for it. There was a certain satisfaction in sailing under their noses, as he had many times, and a good story in it for a tavern audience in Nassau. The light winds also favored the straight route through the gauntlet. The long tack around the ships might be safer, but it was also slower, with the anxiety of prolonged exposure.

The *Aurora's* enterprising crew steeped their sails in chicory whenever they stopped long enough for an overhaul. The strong brew took the sheen off the canvas without weakening it. The ship looked mangy in the daytime, but at night its sheets reflected hardly any light in the black slick of the water.

"Handsomely now, handsomely," the captain whispered to his taut crew, waiting until the last possible moment before turning the wheel and allowing the mainsail to luff. The ship crept gradually upon the enemy. The distance narrowed steadily, until they could spot the forty-pound anchor chains, invisible from shore, reaching down into the deep. Baxter heard a gruff voice protest that it wasn't fair to fold before a fellow had a chance to win anything back, while another man snorted laughter. Sound carried eerily across the calm sea. Poker appeared to be the evening's entertainment for Confederates and Federals alike.

The watches on deck hadn't spotted the steamer, now moving at a steady clip past the danger in the night. She was at the midpoint, with one Federal warship a hundred yards off her port and the other at starboard.

But the *Aurora* wasn't the only vessel in deep shadow. The *Pawnee*'s launch had been lowered over the blind, windward side of the ship only moments before, carrying dispatches.

Their eyes dazzled by the brightly lit frigates to either side, both the crew of the *Aurora* and the midshipmen rowing the *Pawnee*'s launch saw only the towering warships. The two smaller vessels nearly collided before they spotted each other.

The two midshipmen in the launch called out at once, their young, clear voices pealing over the water. "Hey, what the . . . ship in the channel! *Pawnee! Pawnee!* Ship in the channel! At the ready! *Sabine!* Blockade-runners!" A warning gong sounded in response on the *Pawnee*. The Union sailors drew hard on their oars, clunking them loudly against the bronze oarlocks in their hurry. The dory spun on its heel to clear the line of fire.

"Damn!" cursed Captain Howell, standing near Baxter. "Propeller down. Let 'er rip! Passengers belowdecks!"

Steam that had been building in the boiler now found release. The engine roared to life, its loud throb bouncing off the high sides of the frigates. Sails quickly hauled, the *Aurora* shot forward as the screw gripped water. Her silvery wake turned frothy with the propeller's agitation.

On board the USS *Pawnee,* the closer of the frigates, the anchor was coming up with a loud clanking. Light from the lanterns winked off the brass buttons on the sailors' double-breasted uniforms. In a blur, Baxter saw a blue-coated marine raise his rifle over the side and take aim at the captain of the fleeing sloop. It happened too quickly to call out. Baxter shot forward, aiming for Howell's knees. The captain lurched sideways, one hand still on the wheel. The shot went wide and struck the deck. Howell straightened and gripped the helm. Baxter crouched behind a railing and twined his hand in a piece of rigging to keep from sliding. He had a sensation of cold, and his scalp tingled, as if each hair had lifted itself on end.

"Belowdecks, damn ye, I told you, belowdecks!" Howell bellowed furiously in a fine burst of ingratitude.

The crew of the USS *Sabine* were now pelting to stations, mastmen unfurling the sails. Gun crews on the starboard side furiously ran out the cannons. The sound of their commotion carried loudly. The anchors were coming up on both enemy vessels.

The steam sloop pulled past the bow of the USS *Pawnee*, heading for the sea, just in time to see the warship's broadside through a cloud of bilious white smoke punctured by orange flame. A twenty-eight-pound ball fell harmlessly in the wake, not five feet behind the sloop. The USS *Sabine* was farther to starboard, but it had bigger guns, with a longer range, and its crew took better aim. A cannonball flew straight over the deck, severing a piece of rope from the capstan. An eleven-inch shell grazed a man in the rigging. He cried out and pulled a wounded arm close to his body, but held on.

The big ships made way to sail. A light wind slowed their turning, as both had drifted to an awkward angle on their single anchorages. The *Aurora* passed swiftly out of the line of fire, making for the open ocean. With her momentum and head start, she was now freely outrunning them. The pitch black of the ocean ahead beckoned. Exhilarated by the *Aurora*'s daring and by the stiff wind in his face, Baxter could feel his luck holding.

Then one of the English crew spotted a *third* frigate arriving, apparently for a night rendezvous, and shouted to Captain Howell. Watches on the incoming warship, the USS *St. Lawrence* had heard the loud boom of the frigates' guns. The warship was now under full sail and moving at top speed to overtake the fleeing *Aurora*.

The smugglers' sloop turned sharply to starboard to evade the approaching vessel. A warning shot from the *St. Lawrence* whistled over the deck. "Heave to!" came the shouted order from an officer on the *St. Lawrence*. "Heave to *now*!"

Captain Howell of the *Aurora* declined to obey. "Scum-faced arseholes!" he shouted to the wind. "I'll be sunk first."

The sloop continued hard right, sailing a diagonal course away from the onrushing *St. Lawrence,* exposing its flank to a broadside.

If she can just make it into the dark, Baxter thought. He leaned unconsciously toward the bow, willing the boat to greater speed. *Go, goddamn it!* Baxter's mind felt amazingly sharp and focused. Every detail of the looming *St. Lawrence* stood out sharply, from its billowing sails to the impassive mien of the blue-robed maiden carved on the bow. But underneath his mental calm Baxter could feel his blood racing pell-mell to the mad pounding of the *Aurora*'s engine.

A shell whistled past his ear, just missing him. Before Baxter could register relief, it hit the forward boiler. A geyser of steam exploded into the air with a deafening hiss. A warm gust of mist bathed Baxter's face. The engine cut out a moment later, and the *Aurora* slowed to a gentle drift on the tide.

In the nightmarish hour that followed, he yielded his papers to the *St. Lawrence*'s first lieutenant, who took one look at Baxter's well-tailored civilian clothes and separated him from the British crew—despite his protestations of English citizenship. He then endured a rough search of his person for weapons, fashioned a makeshift bandage for the arm of the wounded sailor, retrieved his smallest satchel, and said goodbye to Captain Howell under the glare of the suspicious Federal prize crew. Salt water in the bottom of the *Sabine*'s heaving launch sloshed over his leather boots.

"You're in luck, mate," a cheerful midshipman informed him, while the crew pulled on the oars in the direction of the anchored warship. "Usually we has to keep bastards like you under hatches for weeks. Can't go running up to New York every time we pick up a goddamned blockade-runner. But the *St. Lawrence* is our replacement. Providence must like you, 'cause we sail on the next tide. You'll go straight to prison."

Shortly thereafter, propped between crates in the damp hold far below the top decks of the USS *Sabine,* Baxter felt his breast pocket. A small hard lump at the bottom, like a bit of gravel, reassured him that he still had the only possession he cared about. When his eyes had grown accustomed to the deep gloom, Baxter carefully scanned his wood-hulled jail. Barrels of ship's stores crowded the space. Two other prisoners were asleep on a wooden pallet near the stern. The air of the ship below the waterline was as cold and stale as a tomb. Shafts of light through a narrow crack in the floorboards above fell dimly on a barrel of nails carelessly left open. Baxter crawled toward the cask.

Wedging himself between two barrels to counteract the roll of the ship, he wrapped a handkerchief around a four-inch nail to protect his hands from the rusted iron. Slowly, using his new tool, he prised the low heel off his left boot, careful not to bend the cobbler's tacks that fastened the heel to the sole. Fingers growing numb with cold, he then dug at the leather-covered block of wood with the sharp tool.

A small cavity gradually took shape on the underside of the heel, where it butted up against the shoe. As day broke outside, Baxter finally wedged his grandmother's ring into the snug depression, fitted the heel back to the sole, and struck down squarely until the boot was a seamless whole again. He pulled it back on his icy foot and listened to the thud of men walking above his head.

The ship was waking up. From the sound of it, she was making ready for the voyage to New York. Baxter reached into the small sack of provisions the guard had tossed him before bolting the hatch and took a bite of moldy ship's biscuit. There was nothing further to do but wait.

TWENTY-ONE

JULY 1862

The Trent *business coming first destroyed all our country visits,*
for people have given up inviting us on the just supposition
that we wouldn't care to go into society now. . . . I might
just as well be anywhere as here, except that I can't leave
the parent bird thus afloat on the raging tide.

—Henry Adams to Charles, Jr., at the front,
A Cycle of Adams Letters

Julia studied the thin crowd at the elegant home of Lord John
Russell. The women were mostly middle-aged and dowdy,
the men pompous and bored. A quartet of elderly men playing
whist seemed to be having the liveliest time of anyone. Julia
thought that she must be the youngest person present—by a century or so. Several of the guests looked as if they stayed alive out
of a sense of duty alone. It was sure to be the last party of the season, now that summer had begun in earnest. The air in London
was atrocious in July. Most of the more fashionable and energetic
residents had already retired to the country.

Then she spotted Henry Adams, the son of the American
minister, apparently studying the crowd much as she was. He was
lodged in a corner, pinching the stem of a glass of wine as if holding a noxious flower. Their eyes met at almost the same moment.
Julia gave a small wave and stood to greet Henry as he circled the
room. "Mr. Adams, how good to see you here."

"Miss Birch, the pleasure is all mine!" Henry replied enthusiastically. He blushed, then stammered, "I see that you are not yet in the country—that is, you've not left London."

The poor man must be desperate, Julia thought. Nothing else would account for the pathetic observation. But she smiled nonetheless. It would be a delight to have company at such a boring affair. She hadn't seen him since the opera months back.

"I little thought to see you here," Julia said. "Most everyone has left for the summer."

"We expect to leave soon as well," Henry replied, "but business detained us. And we never turn down an invitation to one of the earl's suppers."

"Because of the renown of his table?" Julia asked mischievously.

Henry's face froze in a mask of politeness, but when Julia crooked one eyebrow he broke into a grin. It was well known that Little Johnny Russell lived off the small allowance that his older brother gave him. A former prime minister and now foreign secretary, the earl was nonetheless only a third son, with no income of his own. Compared with other lords, Russell entertained on a meager scale.

"Honestly, we would rather dine at the prime minister's, whose Saturday Reviews at Cambridge House were a marvel and whose wine"—Henry raised his glass and looked askance at the contents—"was at least drinkable. I've never seen such an elegant buffet as Lady Palmerston presents. But I'm afraid that members of our legation are no longer welcome there."

"Why is that, if I may ask?"

"You probably already know if you've read anything about General Benjamin Butler of the Union Army."

"You mean Beast Butler?"

Henry winced. "Yes."

"That's what I've heard my father's associates call him ever since the 'woman order' controversy. I hope I've not offended you."

"No, you haven't, but I'm afraid I've become tediously sensitive to slight. The past two months have convinced me that the art of diplomacy is to endure casual insults and terrible food with good manners."

"Surely it isn't that bad," Julia said with a smile.

"Worse. Most slights are purely unintentional, compounding one's sense of insignificance. The last time we dined at Lord Palmerston's his footman introduced me from the foyer as 'Mr. Handrew Hadams!' When I quietly corrected him, the good man merely stated more loudly, 'Mr. Hanthony Hadams.' I whispered my name again, but then he came out with 'Mr. Halexander Hadams,' whereupon I gave up. I've thought of myself as Halexander ever since."

Julia laughed. She hadn't expected such a mordant sense of humor.

"But surely that is not the reason you're no longer attending the Saturday Reviews?" she asked.

"No, it's rather more serious. Lord Palmerston's outrage at Butler's actions in New Orleans prompted him to dash off a most undiplomatic note to the legation, expressing his personal outrage. Tiberius Palmerston appears ready to throw us to the lions. My father cannot afford to tolerate such an insult in his precarious position, nor can he afford to demand an apology. He believes the nation's dignity now requires him to keep his distance if he is to maintain his personal reputation. Cold reserve is our only card."

Henry spoke impersonally, but she sensed that the situation must be difficult for him as well. It was awkward to represent an unfashionable cause, especially if one was a foreigner with few friends at hand. From what she had read, Lincoln hadn't won a single important battle. Nothing had been accomplished but killing and more killing. Voices in Parliament called louder than ever for Britain to recognize the Confederacy, break the naval blockade, and force the brawling parties to their senses. Practically everyone reviled the North's violent invasion of Dixie. Conservatives like her father saw the war as poetic justice for the folly of democracy, which England wisely rejected for itself. Henry must feel an outcast.

"I say," Julia said, tactfully shifting the conversation away from the painful subject of politics, "I'm famished and there's nothing to do at this party except eat. Would you care to join me at the buffet—even if it's not a horn of plenty? I'm afraid it would look frightfully indelicate to be first in line all by myself." Julia made a pretend-sad face and widened her eyes hopefully.

Henry laughed at the cheerful pantomime and gave Julia his arm, patently grateful for the request. Servants placed a variety of foods on their plates, and then delivered them to one of the small tables out on the expansive terrace, where Julia and Henry took their seats. Orange and red papier-mâché lanterns from Paris threw a festive ruddiness over the darkening grounds. They discussed the opera in London and a botanical exhibition recently mounted at Kew Gardens. Henry recounted a visit with Sydney Smith, the writer who, upon seeing a society matron's violet turban, had commented, "Now I know the meaning of grotesque," and a country party where the affable host, nearly as wide as he was high, invited his guests to a game of leapfrog on the lawn. He told Julia of small triumphs, like translating a waiter's "'Amhandheggsir?" for his bewildered father at breakfast, and about bitter sorrows like the dark day that the elderly Duchess of Somerset—"a terrible vision in castanets"—had compelled him to perform for her guests a Highland fling with the daughter of the Turkish ambassador. He shared his fear that he was ill-suited to modern politics, based so much on appeal to the crowd, and that he might end up as nothing more than a schoolteacher—a man employed to tell lies to small boys. Julia laughed at his stories and felt confirmed in her guess that the attentive young American was starved for conversation. Neither of them noticed the vinegary tang of the wine.

"And have you heard from our mutual friend, Mr. Sams?" Julia eventually inquired over coffee.

"No," Henry replied. "He decided to return to the South several months ago. He's beyond the blockade now, I assume."

Julia hesitated, and then commented, "Yes, I'm aware that he decided to go back. I saw him at a meeting of the Anti-Slavery Society before he left. He told me that he intended to return to London, though, after . . . after helping his father." She thought it best not to mention the matter of medical supplies.

"Perhaps he will, but that depends at least partly on the U.S. Navy. They've tightened up the blockade, you know. It's much harder to get through."

"Is it?" Julia asked.

The London papers routinely dismissed the blockade as ineffective whenever they weren't complaining about the "cotton famine." It hadn't occurred to Julia that the two might be related, and that the closing of textile mills throughout Lancashire indicated the success of the Union blockade.

"Yes. Of course, some ships still get through—no point in denying that—but our navy has much better control of the Southern coast now that we're in possession of New Orleans and Norfolk. We feel confident that the blockade will be almost entirely effective quite soon," Henry said. "The only danger now, I'm afraid, comes from those naval powers that might consider trying to break the blockade—not merely evade it."

"Do you mean England?" Julia asked.

"England or France—though we believe that Napoleon III will follow Great Britain's lead, in this case."

"You've no fear of the Confederates themselves breaking the blockade, then?"

"No. They don't have the navy to take on our warships. Their suppliers endeavor to slip past our blockaders, or their commerce raiders try to pick off our wooden merchantmen, but they don't have the firepower to attack a man-o'-war directly. Fortunately, there's no contest there."

Julia looked down at her plate and absently brushed away a piece of black smut that had drifted down out of the London sky. Outdoor dining was a mixed blessing in the crowded, smoky city. She wondered where Baxter Sams was, although her father's opposition meant that she wouldn't see him regardless of which side of the blockade he was stranded on.

"I say, I sincerely hope you won't take my remarks amiss," Henry said with a note of concern in his voice. "It's just what one reads in the papers—members of Parliament clamoring for the Royal Navy to intervene, and all. The queen herself gives us no pause. We assume Great Britain's neutrality will hold, at least for a while yet."

Julia didn't notice the approach of an older man until he spoke. "Henry, please pardon me. May I interrupt you for a moment?" he asked with a genteel accent that seemed neither British nor American but a soft, cultured blend of the two.

Henry laid aside his napkin and stood. "Father, of course. But may I first present Miss Julia Birch? Miss Birch, this is my father, Mr. Charles Francis Adams."

Julia rose, and Charles bowed courteously.

"It's a pleasure to meet you, Mr. Adams. Your son has rescued me from hunger and boredom. If not for him, I might have starved—or fallen asleep under a potted palm."

"I'm delighted to see that he is making himself of use, Miss Birch, though I think it's likely you who rescued him, for which I thank you."

Charles smiled at the young woman, obviously charmed by her aplomb and self-effacing humor.

"Your mother is feeling somewhat under the weather, Henry,"

Charles said, turning to his son. "I think I ought to take her back to the legation. I hate to tear you away. Would you like to stay and catch a hansom cab later?"

"Is Mother all right?" Henry asked with concern.

"Yes, I think it's just the season—the summer air in London. She's complaining of the assault on her eyes and nose. I'm sure that the holiday in Scotland will give her relief and restore all our spirits."

"But aren't you expecting Mr. Dudley later this evening?" Henry asked. "Don't you need me for that?"

"Yes, umm . . . well, I believe I can manage," Charles said.

Henry turned to Julia with regret. "Miss Birch, my father is too good to insist upon my accompanying him, but I really should. An extra pair of ears is sometimes vital in our calling. Will you forgive me?"

"Of course, Mr. Adams. I think I may have to go, anyway. Here is my father now. Sir Walter Birch," Julia said. She gave a small nod toward the tall, elegantly dressed figure approaching their table from across the terrace.

"Julia. There you are," Walter said. "I've been looking for you a good half hour."

"I've been right here, Father. Have you been introduced to the Adamses yet? This is Mr. Charles Francis Adams and his son Henry. Mr. Adams is the minister."

Walter looked blankly at the younger Adams, as if he were a valet offering a hand towel, and then at Charles, whom he addressed. "I haven't had the pleasure, I'm sure," Walter said with the barest hint of a bow. "A minister? May I ask from which country you are accredited?"

Charles stiffened. The expression in his steely blue eyes hardened slightly. "The United States of America, of course. But perhaps you are not invited to court often."

"Of course, please forgive me. Come to think of it, I do believe I've seen your name bandied about in the *Standard*." Walter's elite Etonian accent was more pronounced than usual. "Please tell me, how many states are there now in the United States?"

"Thirty-four since the admission of Kansas," Charles replied.

"Really?" Walter queried disingenuously. "But I thought that some have gone out. Subtract eleven, right? Doesn't that make twenty-three? I thought that's what the present war is all about."

"The war is about preserving the Union, yes. But it was precipitated by the question of slavery—as you are undoubtedly aware."

Walter assumed a puzzled expression and placed a finger to his chin. "You will have to pardon my ignorance. I had understood your president—Mr. Lincoln, right?—to say that he intended no harm to the practice of slavery in the Old South. A former workingman like him must appreciate the pennies that slavery contributes to the U.S. Treasury. After all, human bondage is the foundation of your republic's prosperity, isn't it, despite the claim that all men are created equal? But perhaps I read his position wrongly."

"You read it quite correctly, Sir Wilbert," Charles replied.

Walter started visibly at the incorrect name.

"Oh, pardon me," Charles continued smoothly, "Sir Walter, is it? Yes, you are quite right that President Lincoln has never demanded the abolition of slavery in the existing Southern states. Instead, our party has taken a position against the extension of slavery into our newer territories. But, well before this war began, the president questioned whether the nation could continue half slave and half free. I believe the war has proven him right. Its resolution, many of us hope, will eliminate the fundamental problem at the heart of the conflict. Indeed, I am convinced that this war will topple the institution of slavery."

Charles interrupted his own speech with a small bow. "But I mustn't bore you with arcane details that cannot possibly interest those whose ken doesn't extend beyond the Irish Sea. It seems my wife has taken ill. Will you please excuse us?"

Charles nodded now at Walter, mirrored by Henry, who turned to say goodbye to Julia. Her smile felt frozen on her face, and she knew that it no longer reached her eyes.

"Good evening, Miss Birch," Henry said. "It was a pleasure to see you. I do hope you enjoy your summer in the country." He looked at her with an especially kind expression that made her wonder if he had intuited how difficult her father could be.

Julia dropped into a curtsey and lowered her gaze. "Thank you again for your company, Mr. Adams."

Henry and his father left, walking toward the lit doorway.

When the American minister and his son were safely out of hearing, Julia turned abruptly in a rustle of silk. "Father, that was mortifying," she said in a low voice. "What possessed you to speak to Mr. Adams in those terms? You know very well who he is. You told me yourself. Must you put your animosity on display in public?"

"Where else should I display it, my dear? The curio cabinet? Besides, those Adamses are tougher than you think. They've been annoying the rest of the world for the better part of a hundred years. They're used to a little annoyance in return. I'd heard that the minister is only a pale copy of his famous father, however, and I see what they mean. An ineffectual squeaker compared with Old Man Eloquent. Still, it wouldn't do to underestimate him. Quite the iceberg, that one."

Walter tipped his square chin back and chuckled. "Oh, but it will be fun to see him melt!" He gave Julia a wink and added, with a malicious gleam in his eyes, "Keep your eyes on the papers and look for news of the Laird shipyard, my dear. Too bad your grandfather isn't here to read them. They say that revenge is best served cold, and I believe that might be true."

Julia accepted her father's arm as he turned to leave. But it wasn't Charles Francis Adams whom she thought of as cold just then. What purpose did it serve to nurse the old grudge, generation after generation? When did hatred come to an end? And was it really necessary to shame Mr. Adams? Good for him that he refused to be shamed.

In fact, Adams was someone to admire, Julia thought, recalling his dignified but spirited rebuttal. At the moment, she didn't admire her father at all.

TWENTY-TWO

England's power of absorbing truth was small.

—Henry Adams, *The Education of Henry Adams*

Thomas Haines Dudley ducked his head as he stepped quickly through the doorway into the study, as if dodging the low beams of an English tavern. Charles immediately put down his book and rose to greet the consul. Henry set aside a letter he was writing but remained seated at his worktable, a fresh quill at the ready.

"Mr. Dudley. Thank you for coming down. I trust the train trip wasn't too onerous. No drunks, I hope."

On the minister's advice, Dudley had taken to riding second class in order to avoid meeting anyone who might recognize him. Up and down the coast between the docks of Glasgow and Liverpool, Dudley was on guard for anyone following. As his superior, Charles took comfort in the knowledge that the consul had some experience in subterfuge. More than a decade earlier, Dudley had penetrated the South disguised as a slave trader, hunting down a free black family who had been deported below the Mason-Dixon Line under the Fugitive Slave Act, which compensated judges five dollars for ruling in favor of a Negro who purported to be free, and ten dollars for giving him to any Southerner claiming ownership. Dudley tracked the falsely convicted family all the way to South Carolina, where he paid one thousand dollars to get them back. Now he paid for information, but he was still on the trail of slavers.

"Not too bad this time, Mr. Adams. Not too bad. I would have come earlier, but I had to check on a lead in the city. I meant to be here by supper."

"That's all right, Dudley. We were dining at Lord Russell's anyway. We got back only an hour ago."

"Damn!" exclaimed Dudley, throwing his hands up and looking skyward in frustration.

"Why, what's the problem?" asked Charles, alarmed.

"If only I had arrived sooner! You could've spoken to Lord Russell this evening. Is there any chance of going back?"

Charles glanced swiftly at the floor clock in the corner. "No, it's eleven. Everyone will have gone home. Lord Russell keeps to an early hour—especially midweek. But why?" he asked.

Dudley spoke rapidly. "I heard a rumor up in Liverpool that our case before Sir John Harding has been derailed. I couldn't get anything more specific—just some snide allusions—so I decided to follow up with my detective in London. I telegraphed him when I sent word to you. This afternoon, just before I arrived, he trailed Sir John's valet to St. Thomas's Asylum for the Insane. The man's been committed!"

"Who? The valet?"

"No! Sir John Harding—the queen's counsel—the one who's supposed to be ruling on our case. The 290 sails at any moment, and the damned royal advocate has gone balmy. What's worse, it looks like he's taken all our affidavits and documents with him. The valet let slip to our man over beer that Sir John is suffering from delusions. Packed all his papers in a strongbox and insisted on taking them to the asylum. Says they'll clear his name of treason or some such fool thing. Won't part with a scrap."

"Who knows this?" Charles asked.

"Apparently, only the family so far. They've tried to keep it quiet."

"We've got to get to Lord Russell immediately. I'll send word first thing in the morning." Charles glanced over at Henry, who was already taking a clean sheet of diplomatic bond from his desk drawer.

"I hope and pray that's soon enough," Dudley said.

"I cannot take the risk of waking Lord Russell. It would be most irregular, and we need to keep in his good graces."

The consul sank down onto an armchair next to the cold hearth. His thin shoulders caved forward. He had never looked so discouraged. "The ship could sail tomorrow," he warned. "The foreign secretary will have to telegraph the customs collector in Liverpool if he wants to seize the vessel before it's too late. It might be too late even now."

"What makes you think the 290 is sailing that soon?"

Dudley looked up wearily. "I thought I had told you. A couple of my informants—the ones who enlisted for the voyage—said they were ordered to report to the ship today, July 28."

"Then we'll have to get you back into position in Liverpool in case I can persuade Russell to act swiftly. Edwards might otherwise claim that he learned too late what London wanted. A ship can cast off its moorings in a matter of minutes, but it will be hard for the customs agent to play dumb if you're camped on his doorstep. I hate to ask, Mr. Dudley," Charles continued, "but could I prevail upon you to take the night train back to Liverpool? I'll request a meeting with Lord Russell over breakfast. I can telegraph you the results in an instant."

"Of course. No question, Mr. Adams. We've got to try," Dudley replied. He straightened despite his obvious fatigue. "Would it be possible for your housekeeper to set me up with some coffee or a flagon of tea for the trip?"

"Katie should be awake. She never turns in until all her charges are down for the night, no matter how many times I tell her not to wait up."

Charles reached for the embroidered bellpull that sounded in the kitchen.

The Irish housekeeper knocked once and entered the room. Not a pin out of place in her bun, Charles noticed. Regardless of the hour, he had never seen her unprepared. He supposed she went to bed fully dressed and arose bathed.

"Kathleen, could you please prepare a hamper for Mr. Dudley right away? Something to eat and some hot drinks? He has to catch the first train back to Liverpool."

"I'll have it for him in a trice. I know just the thing. Come along, Mr. Dudley, if you please. We'll have you home and dry before you know it."

Dudley nodded briefly to Henry and shook hands with Charles, who clapped him on the back in encouragement. The consul struggled to smile in return, failed, and then strode from the room, ducking as he left.

TWENTY-THREE

Dr. Gibbes says the faces of the dead on the battlefield have grown as black as charcoal, and they shine in the sun. Now this horrible vision of the dead on the battlefield haunts me.

—Mary Boykin Chesnut, *A Diary from Dixie*

Baxter stood patiently in the long line that snaked across the prison yard at Fort Lafayette. It was either be patient or go mad. The humidity made him feel as if he were being stewed over a low flame. Most of the men bore it stoically and avoided moving around more than they had to. Baxter could feel rivulets of perspiration running down the curve of his spine. When he glanced at the pavement, drops of sweat from his face splashed in star shapes onto the hot surface. It seemed to take forever to reach the rough plank table where other prisoners were dishing out the noon meal.

Dinner was the most important event in a prisoner's day. Breakfast was hardly more than a biscuit, accompanied by coffee that tasted of foul water and burned chicory. Supper was a thin soup of corn or cabbage with a piece of bread and maybe some underdone potatoes. But at midday dinner the prisoners got a large chunk of fat pork with a ladle of beans. They were allowed to collect their rations in the yard, where they could catch a whiff of the fresh sea breeze that came up the Narrows into the Port of New York. Warden Wood, a hard man, allowed the prisoners only two hours of exercise in the courtyard each day—one hour in the morning, one in the evening. Noon rations brought a third prized glimpse of the open sky. Every man looked forward to dinner, if he wasn't too sick or downcast to care about anything.

Baxter held the battered tin plate issued the day he arrived. When he first glimpsed Fort Lafayette from the prison launch, he felt that he was back at Fort Sumter, which was built of the same red brick, with arched batteries for mounted guns. A thick mist obscured the base of the fortress. Situated on a rock a quarter mile off the tip of Staten Island, with massive, thirty-foot walls to the edge of terra firma, the army base appeared to float at the entrance to New York Harbor.

Once inside the fort, the young doctor was searched and his name copied into the roll book. He was allowed to keep the clothes on his back and the boots on his feet. He also managed to hang on to his copy of *Gray's Anatomy*, a blank notebook, and two pens. These items, plus his tin dish and a three-tined fork, were now the extent of his material wealth. Everything else had been confiscated. For the first time in his life, he was penniless. He ate what he was given and went where he was told. The prison guards controlled everything but his thoughts.

"So, anyone know what's on the menu today?" Devereaux Council asked, squinting against the dazzling sun. The wiry New Orleans native was a six-month veteran of Fort Lafayette, transferred there from the Tombs, the Manhattan jail that housed the first privateers to be captured. Council was a purser. Shackled to his captain and the chief officer of the blockade-runner *Lizzie Davis*, he had been paraded in chains through the Bowery district.

"Oh, I expect it's stuffed pheasant, Dev," Baxter replied gamely. He lifted his nose and took a deep sniff, as if drawing in the beguiling aroma of sage, onions, and crispy skin.

"I heard tell it's goose, with red huckleberry sauce," Virgil Sweetwood said. "And butter peas. Butter peas with salt and extra butter." The Georgian licked his lips, tasting the savory legumes already.

Recalling favorite dishes was their way of inuring themselves to the prison grub, of staking a claim to the future and all the good things they would eat in it. The other prisoners just ignored them, but it mattered little. The undaunted trio had elaborated the noontime fiction ever since discovering that they shared a mutual hankering for boiled peanuts.

"Not this time of year," Council contradicted. "The butter peas are done played out. Vines have gone stringy. Nope, they're serving pole beans. That's a bona fide summer crop. My mama used to grow them out back a' the house. Now the Yanks must be stealing them."

"I don't know," Baxter said, steering the conversation to a safer subject. He had heard Devereaux cry out for his mother, deep in his sleep. It must be torture to know one's home was under occupation. "Seems to me I heard they're serving bay shrimps, those little ones, along with lettuce cooled on ice in the blockhouse."

"Wait a cotton-picking minute," Council said. "You're not s'posed to mention ice. It's against the rules of engagement. Damned inhumane, mentioning ice at a time like this. Criminy, Sams, do I really gotta tell you?" The blockade-runner shook his head in disgust.

"I do apologize," Baxter said at once. "I have no excuse but a parboiled brain—my own, that is. I intended to say that I thought I smelled fresh buckwheat cakes. Buckwheat cakes with cider sauce."

Cider sauce. That one got them thinking. The taste of anything sweet was a distant memory.

A quiet argument at the head of the line suddenly grew louder. Baxter could make out a few phrases above the shouts that rang off the walls of the yard. "That's damn unfair!" one man yelled. Prisoners along the line craned their necks to get a better view of the commotion.

"What's that about?" Sweetwood wondered aloud.

A man standing next to the plank table suddenly shot out his hand and grabbed one of the servers by the collar.

"Damn you, you weasel! You'll get your rations. Gimme mine!"

The ominous cock of a sentry's shotgun caused the prisoners to pull their heads back into line like so many quail. Whispers raced down the queue, finally catching up to Baxter and his cellmates.

"They've cut the rations. No meat," they heard from a hard-faced man in front of them. "No meat," he repeated with a glare.

The angry man at the plank table let go of the server, who fixed him with a deadly look and deliberately poured only half a ladle into the plate. The prisoner said nothing more, but took the tin without looking down and stalked away.

When Baxter finally got his own rations, he saw with relief that there was meat after all, just less than usual. Instead of a big chunk on the side, small bits of fat and flesh swam in the brown beans.

Sweetwood, Council, and Baxter took their plates back to the cell they shared with thirty or so other men. The twenty-by-thirty-foot room had previously been a battery. The army had since removed the guns, bricked up the archways that faced the sea, and placed bars on the windows and locks on the doors. Instead of acrid gunpowder, the space now reeked of armpits, dirty feet, unwashed hair, slop buckets, and the intestinal ruminations of men who ate beans every day for dinner. The men called it the Bastille, mocking the marquis of revolutionary fame for whom it was named. Despite Lafayette's idealism, the Bastille had come to America.

The prisoners sat on the floor with their mess kits, since there was no furniture other than a few beds. By common consent, no one sat on the bunks during the day in order to avoid fights. In the evening they took turns. Sunday and Tuesday were Baxter's nights to share a plank and horsehair mattress with Council and a few dozen bedbugs. Otherwise it was a woolen blanket on the stone floor with the other prisoners and an occasional rat.

The men ate slowly. Baxter concentrated on each juicy bean until he broke the skin of the last one. His messmates licked the thick broth off their plates freely. Baxter had suggested that it was better than their dirty fingers, though he nonetheless felt shamefaced to lick his own plate the first time. Hunger soon accustomed him to it.

Council and Sweetwood had heard the story of Joseph Lister's medical theories more than once. Baxter speculated that if cleanliness could heal sick men it might keep well men alive. A typhoid epidemic had carried off dozens of prisoners at Fort Lafayette the preceding fall. Every man up to the warden feared a repeat, or a deadly outbreak of smallpox or dysentery.

Baxter in turn had listened to countless tales of hunting rabbits in Georgia and privateering off Louisiana. Council had crewed for one of the private warships licensed to capture Northern merchants. Letters of marque signed by Jeff Davis allowed them to sell their prizes lawfully in Southern ports.

"Did ya hear what they said about the meat?" asked a freckle-faced teenager from across the cell, his blue eyes round.

"Nope," said Sweetwood.

"A guard told one of the cooks that the Yanks are riled 'cause we get better grub than their soldiers. They say the Blues have to eat their beans plain, so we can, too."

"This is nigger food. That's all I gotta say," drawled a tall man who had been captured in an open boat off Cape Hatteras running whiskey to thirsty Confederates. He was a Mississippian. Prison gossip said that he had a pile of gold stashed away in Havana, in the keeping of a pretty mistress.

"Not where I come from," Council said. "Nigras in Louisiana eat meat. They get plenty a' corn and greens, too."

Baxter wondered how much Devereaux Council had seen of Louisiana, but he said nothing.

"Now your Mississippi nigras, they're scrawny. Mississippi is backward, that's a fact," Council continued, warming to the subject. "If it weren't for Mississippi and South Carolina and all them fire-eaters, we wouldn't be in this mess nohow. Pigheaded and backward, that's plain to see."

Baxter gave Council a kick with his boot, as if adjusting his position. When Council started to protest, Baxter met his eyes with a warning look that said quite plainly, "Shut up, stupid."

"Ain't tomorrow mail day?" Sweetwood asked loudly. "I was just wondrin'. Seems like it oughta be."

The Mississippi whiskey-runner shrugged and said he didn't know. It didn't matter to him. Baxter wondered if the rumors were true, and if the man's mistress could read or write well enough to send letters. If not, mail day would seem pretty unremarkable.

"I think so," said the freckled teenager. "Seems like it's been two weeks."

Baxter knew precisely how long it had been since the last mail call: thirteen and a half days. Tomorrow morning the prisoners would have their fortnightly opportunity to send or receive letters from home. Baxter expected one from his mother and father, who wrote faithfully. They would pass on the news from Jacob and Robert. Baxter didn't dare to expect any other letters.

He had postponed writing to Julia until he was sure that he wouldn't qualify for the prisoner exchange. Only enlisted men were eligible. Confederate privateers and blockade-runners, considered the lowest of the low, were not. When Devereaux Council was transferred to Fort Lafayette, he told Baxter, they weren't even allowed in the yard with the other prisoners. Council hadn't seen the sun for three months, except through a barred window. "They charged me with piracy," he recalled. "And we had our privateering license and everything, damn it."

When Baxter finally put pen to paper, he did so with bleak fortitude. It wasn't hard to tell the story of his capture, but it wasn't fair to leave it at that. He must free Julia of any expectation. He should have known better than to say anything to begin with.

> The matter to which I alluded in my last letter from Virginia must be postponed for the foreseeable future.

He wrote stiffly, to mask the despair he felt in the pit of his stomach.

> I hope you will forgive me for having written so precipitously. I see no end to my confinement, except in the resolution of the war itself. You must plan your future accordingly, if you will forgive my presumption in saying so. Please rest assured, however, that no matter how long the conflict rages, I will remain faithfully yours, Baxter.

The letter had gone out two weeks earlier. He anticipated no reply, feeling that he might as well have placed the note in a bottle and cast it over the walls into the turgid riptide of the Narrows. He had been a damned, inconsiderate fool to reach for Julia Birch. No American could call his future his own, at least for now.

"Pick up your cards, Sams."

"Hmm?" Baxter asked, suddenly realizing that Virgil Sweetwood had been talking to him.

Unlike Council, Sweetwood wasn't easily riled. But there was one thing he wouldn't tolerate for a minute, and that was inattention at cards. "I said pick up your hand—if'n you're gunna play. Lordy, you're as slow as molasses in January. I ain't got all afternoon."

"Course you don't have all afternoon," Council said, grinning. "More like a year, I reckon."

Sweetwood merely glared over his hand at the thin riposte.

While Baxter had endeavored to save one medical book, Virgil had hung on to a worn poker deck, from which they all derived infinitely more enjoyment. Baxter reached for his cards, wondering how they would have kept their sanity without them. He studied the hand dealt him.

"I'll take two," he said, discarding a ten of diamonds and a two of clubs. "And give me a better hand next time."

"Can't pin it on the cards, my friend," Sweetwood observed. "You gotta play 'em right."

"I'm trying," Baxter replied. He crossed his long legs in front of him on the grimy floor. "Believe me, I'm trying."

TWENTY-FOUR

SEPTEMBER 1862

*The indraught into the burning ship's holds and cabins,
added every moment new fury to the flames, and now they could
be heard roaring like the fires of a hundred furnaces, in full
blast. . . . By the light of this flambeau upon the lonely and silent
sea, lighted of the passions of bad men who should have been our
brothers, the* Sumter, *having aroused herself from her dream of
vengeance, and run up her boats, moved forward on her course.*

—Admiral Raphael Semmes, *Memoirs of Service Afloat
During the War Between the States*

Reading the dispatch from the American consul in Portugal, Charles could only shake his head in dismay. They had done every last thing they could.

The morning after Dudley's late-night visit, the legation messenger returned with the news that Lord Russell had caught the first train out of London en route to his home in the country. He would be in transit all day. It would be nearly twenty-four hours before they could even get a message to him.

The *290* slipped out of the Laird dock that afternoon and anchored in the broad stream of the Mersey under pretense of a trial run. With her masts of yellow pine, her copper-bottomed hull, and her shiny steel rigging, she was as pretty as a duckling. A sprightly celebration for invited guests was held on board. Ladies' laughter and the merry strains of a fiddle carried out over the water to the wharves. Back on shore, the Liverpool customs inspector rejected Dudley's final plea to detain the man-o'-war; there was no evidence to justify such an act. The day after, on July 30, the *290* anchored off Holyhead on the coast of Wales. An informant sent word that the ship was taking on gunpowder from a tugboat. Charles telegraphed yet another urgent request to Lord Russell.

The suspense was hideous, but the next day, the very last day of the month, the foreign secretary finally relented and sent a direct command to the customs collector: Seize the *290*. She was in violation of the Foreign Enlistment Act.

But it was too late. The *290* had vanished in the mists off Wales. They learned later that her captain sneaked around the stormy top of Ireland and bolted for a remote cove on the Azores. There the crew took on the cannons that Bulloch had sent ahead. One marine league off the coast, just outside Portugal's jurisdiction, the crew of the *290* hauled down the Union Jack and raised the Confederate Stars and Bars. The CSS *Alabama* was ready to fight for her country.

The letter Charles was now holding spelled out what British collusion had cost the Union since that day. The CSS *Alabama* found its first victims in early September, in the whaling grounds of the mid-Atlantic. Circling the Azores like a shark, the *Alabama* picked off one New England whaler after another. Creeping up under a U.S. flag, the Confederate naval vessel struck the Stars and Stripes and hoisted her true colors only when she got within cannon range. A blast or two across the bow quickly convinced the unarmed whalers to surrender.

Adhering strictly to notions of honor among gentlemen, the Confederate captain allowed the crews to put to shore in their own launches. Once on land, they reported that the gallant Southerner appeared to revel in turning their ships into pyres. The great barrels of whale oil, fueling noxious black clouds that roiled over the Azores, kept the ships' timbers burning even when adrift upon the water. The *Ocmulgee,* the *Starlight,* the

Ocean Rover, the *Alert,* the *Weather Gauge,* and the *Elijah Dunbar* were no more.

Dudley suspected that Laird Brothers in Liverpool had received a tip from a friend high up that they passed on to James Bulloch—"Sail tonight," or some such warning. With a young man's rush to judgment, Henry blamed Earl Russell for doing his best to damage the Union out of pure spite. Charles himself didn't know if Sir John Harding's sudden bout of madness was a true conspiracy or simply a comedy of errors, but he certainly held the British responsible for allowing the warship to sail.

All three men had been plunged into anxiety at what damage the 290 might wreak. They need wonder no longer.

The American minister laid the dispatch on the desk in front of him. He smoothed the paper with his clean palm until it was almost flat. He then turned it over and drew his thumbnail slowly across the back to erase the fold mark. The sheet looked almost new when Charles finally placed it in his file of recent letters, corners squared with the others underneath. It was as tidy as he could make it—in inverse proportion to the messy events.

Charles stared out at the tall spire of All Souls Church across the street. He knew two of the captains on the ships that had sunk. One had spoken at John Quincy's funeral. Charles had failed them both—failed them all. He had not done enough or been persuasive enough. A bleak hopelessness welled up in him. Parry, feint, strike. The duel against the British went on and on. Back home, the fields were soaked with the blood of more than a hundred thousand dead, many of them killed with bullets manufactured in England. If he didn't keep up his guard, the war would allow Britain to accomplish what it had failed to do in 1776 and 1812. And he would bear the responsibility.

A firm knock sounded at the door, breaking his troubled reverie. Abby put her head around the jamb, holding the edge of the door with her small, strong hand. Her dark hair was parted in the middle and swept up into a simple bun at the back of her head, a style she had worn since they were a young married couple living in Boston, just embarking on the life that had eventually led to London. She never seemed to change or grow older, at least in ways that mattered. "Charles, aren't you coming to breakfast? You need to eat."

"Later, Abby, later," he replied soberly. He had little appetite.

"Dear, you know I hate to press, but you really must take some nourishment. It's nearly ten o'clock. Brooks and Mary have already left the table." Abby's expression was mild, but there was a stubborn light in her eyes. Charles recognized that it was futile to argue. This was one fight he would not win, and the thought oddly cheered him. He wished all his battles could be with Abby. She was right, anyway. It wasn't prudent to miss breakfast.

"All right, I'll join you. I've finished here. Nothing more to be done anyway."

Abby's face relaxed into a smile, despite Charles's gloomy statement. "Emma has made your favorite scones. I'm sure they'll make you feel better," she said, as if reading his mind. Which she probably had.

Henry looked up when his parents entered the breakfast room, arm in arm. "Good morning, Father," he said.

"Henry. Are you still breakfasting? I thought you would have gone out for your walk long ago," Charles said.

"I was delayed getting home last night. It seems all the hansom cabdrivers decided to go on holiday at once. I was ready to paste a stamp on my forehead and go by post when one of them finally appeared."

Charles was reminded of the letter he had just received and gave Henry a vague nod.

"Fine, Henry, that's fine," he replied, and took his seat. He made a mental note to show Henry the dispatch after breakfast.

Abby passed her husband a platter of scones studded with currants.

"No newspaper?" Charles asked.

"I haven't asked Katie to send it in yet," Abby replied. "I prefer to read it after pouring the tea. Shall I ask now?"

"Of course," Charles said, his tone more clipped than he intended. "I don't see what tea has to do with it."

"Why, Charles, a cup of tea improves everything, and especially your disposition in the morning. But I'll get the *Times* at once, if you prefer."

"You know I do," Charles muttered under his breath. The papers were his lifeline across the Atlantic. Cyrus Field kept saying it was possible to lay a telegraph cable across the vast sea, but until that happened Charles depended on the *Times,* the *Morning Post,* and the other broadsides of Fleet Street. He scanned them avidly for victories and with trepidation for losses.

Kathleen brought the paper up promptly. Charles was careful not to rest the grimy newsprint against the green morning cloth.

And then there it was—again. Bull Run! Charles stared in disbelief at the headline: "Another Disastrous Federal Defeat at Bull Run." He scanned the publication date at the top of the page with an awful sense of déjà vu. It was indeed September 1862, not August 1861.

The two massive armies had wheeled upon each other after weeks of bloody, inconclusive campaigning in the muck and mire leading to Richmond. Suffering incalculable casualties, General George McClellan failed to take the Confederate capital. Falling back, more than one hundred thousand men faced off again across the meandering creek of Bull Run, which was barely a trickle in the thirst of August. A brook so runty and reedy that it was a wonder anyone had thought to name it. The men and horses must have stamped it out of existence.

General Stonewall Jackson had outflanked the Union troops under John Pope, capturing the heavily stocked U.S. supply depot at Manassas, with its treasure of guns and ammunition. Federal soldiers withstood the withering artillery fire this time, but were eventually forced back to the capital. Fifteen thousand

Northerners had been killed or wounded or had gone missing, while tons of supplies had again fallen into enemy hands. Nine thousand Southerners paid for the victory with their lives. Twenty-four thousand men eliminated in the scope of a few days.

The *Times* special correspondent disparaged the vicious, fratricidal bloodshed, reminding readers that it all went back to the election of an "obscure, harmless, and happy lawyer from a small country town." If it hadn't been for Abraham Lincoln, the correspondent mused, the conflict over slavery might well "have been pent up within peaceful limits." Not that Lincoln was malicious. He was a model of "honesty and simplicity," the writer admitted.

Damning, hateful praise, Charles thought angrily. In other words, fools rush in where angels fear to tread.

Charles felt a sharp, unaccustomed swell of pride in the president. Lincoln hadn't faltered or flagged despite defeats, doubts, and the public contempt of all those who were sure they knew better. The president wasn't polished. People laughed at his backwoods phrases—but they repeated them. "I hate an interruptious fellow," Charles had heard an English aristocrat quote with genuine amusement.

Charles himself had doubted that Lincoln was up to the job. Now, after months of his own vain striving, he doubted that anyone else could have persevered as well. The simple rail-splitter was made of iron. "Keep a-peggin'," Lincoln told his generals.

But the blood that was on his hands—on all their hands—was a terrible price to pay. "I tremble for my country when I realize that God is just and that his justice will not sleep forever." Charles's own father had drilled those words into him—words penned by Grandfather's most bitter rival and oldest friend. Jefferson would have looked with horror on all that Charles could see, but he would not have been surprised.

And his namesake was in the thick of it. Abby had given

Charles seven children. His son thought that should be more than enough offspring. But the young man on the front in Virginia couldn't appreciate that the loss of any child was like severing a limb. An amputee didn't miss his leg any less because he had another. One still felt the phantom pains. Charles had known this since Arthur, then the youngest of the boys, perished at age five of a sudden illness. Charles still awoke some mornings with an ache to twine his fingers in the child's bright, shiny curls and hear the hiccuping laugh he made when rolling on the floor with his brothers—or, even better, to brush a crumb off his cheek, lift him onto the swing in the garden, or explain a new word. Do something—anything—for him. But time moved forward with every tick. Charles and Abby couldn't stop their children from making their own choices, regardless of the consequences. He sometimes wondered when they would receive the telegram from the War Department. He and Abby fell asleep each night grateful that it hadn't yet come.

"What is it?" Henry asked.

Charles started and looked at his son as if seeing him for the first time that morning. Then he realized that he was gripping the butter knife so tightly that his knuckles stood out white. He blinked twice, quite slowly, and replied, "I'm sorry, Henry. Just some bad war news. Another defeat at Bull Run."

Charles folded the newspaper and passed it to Henry. He then reached for the butter plate with deliberate calm. "I think we should be prepared to see the Confederacy's bonds rise again on the London market—and its stock go up in Parliament," he commented.

"It won't be the first time," Henry replied with aplomb, playing his father's parlor game of tranquil dignity.

"It also won't be the last," Charles said, the strain in his voice apparent only to those who knew him best.

TWENTY-FIVE

Another man showed me some wonderfully ingenious things
he had made while prisoner. He said they were issued rations for
a week, but he always devoured his in three days. He could
not resist doing so. Then he had the gnawing agony of
those inevitable four days remaining.

—Mary Boykin Chesnut, *A Diary from Dixie*

Julia stepped lightly out of the hansom cab while the driver
held the horses still. It felt good to be back in the city after
the months away. She had decided to come on the spur of the
moment, having received Flora Bentley's letter about Louise's
delicate condition. Julia was delighted for her friend and, since
Louise could no longer be seen in public, had returned to London to call.

There was no need to telegraph the servants at Belfield
Manor to make ready for her arrival. The housekeeper and the
butler ran things so well that Julia felt perfectly confident that
she could turn up at 2:00 P.M. and order a formal supper party for
fourteen guests at seven. As it was, they would need to fetch only
a light tea for her.

The front entry was quiet, but she could make out the faraway
sounds of the housekeeper instructing a chambermaid. The scent
of beeswax hovered in the air from the morning polishing. A silver salver held a few cards from visitors who had called, including
Captain James D. Bulloch of the Confederacy and her father's
solicitor in Liverpool. A stack of letters perched on the mantel-

piece indicated that the postal carrier had just stopped by with the second delivery of the day.

Julia riffled through the pile. Most of her friends knew that she was staying in the country and wouldn't write. The majority of letters were for Sir Walter, including a thin envelope with Edmund's handwriting on the front. She was glad to see that her brother had written so soon after the start of the new term at Eton. He had become increasingly thoughtful. He was growing up.

There were only two pieces of mail for her. One was a gilt-edged invitation to tea from Lady Catherine Forsythe. Its gold leaf reflected the sunny afternoon light like a wedding band. The other was an odd, dirty envelope bearing the insignia "Fort Lafayette, New York," along with the muddy waffle of a footprint across the back. The letter appeared to have been dropped, perhaps more than once.

She opened the foreign envelope, curious, and drew out the letter. Black ink looped in tight, dense rows across a single page. The writer appeared to be trying to save paper.

My dear Julia, it began.

Julia's hand trembled unconsciously as her eyes raced across the page. Baxter had been caught in the blockade off Charleston. He was being held at Fort Lafayette, with no hope of release before the end of the war. He wished her the best for the future and asked her to pardon his earlier forwardness. He would remain *faithfully yours.*

The room whirled for the barest instant, and Julia reached out to the hall table to steady herself. Where in New York was Fort Lafayette? Were the Northern prison camps like the Southern ones? The *Times* special correspondent had reported horrific conditions. She seemed to recall one camp where thousands had died of typhus and dysentery. The prisoners had little food and only unclean water. The camps were yet another scandal of the American war.

Julia laid the letter on the table. She looked at the firm shapes made by the Virginian's hand and traced her finger over the signature at the bottom. *Baxter.*

The sharp clack of heels on the floor disturbed her reverie and Julia raised her head.

"Oh, miss! We wasn't expectin' you," the parlormaid said, clearly startled.

Julia heard her own voice reply with a practiced serenity that sounded as imperturbable as Queen Victoria—and that completely belied her inner tumult.

"Good afternoon, Emily. I decided to come home only yesterday. Could you please tell Mrs. Worthy that I've arrived?"

"Yes, miss," Emily replied with a bob.

The parlormaid was only fourteen to Julia's twenty-two years. Emily had come to them the year before through Randolph Barclay's charity work. It had taken six months to put a dimple in her thin face, and now a small frown was raising a pucker on her forehead. The girl stood twisting the handle of a feather duster, as if hesitant to leave.

"What is it, Emily?" Julia asked impatiently, unsure how long she could maintain a façade of calm.

"Just that, miss, I was supposed to place the mail on Sir Walter's desk. I only left it there for a moment, I did. Mrs. Worthy was calling me."

"That's fine, Emily. I can do it myself."

"Yes, miss, but, I, but. . . ." Emily stumbled over her words. A scarlet flush was working its way in paw prints up her white throat.

"What is it, Emily? What's the matter?"

"It's just that Mrs. Worthy asked me, specifically asked me at Sir Walter's request, to make sure that the mail goes to him first every day."

"I'm sure it's all right, Emily. I'll put his letters on the desk right now. You're not to worry."

"But, miss, you see, he wants *all* the letters. He wants

them . . . well, first." Emily looked down at her shoes. The blush had now reached the roots of her fair locks. The part in her hair was like a pink exclamation point.

Julia stared at the girl, who was practically twirling the duster in her agitation. Motes floated in the sunbeams of the quiet hall.

"Emily," she said with mild sternness after a tense pause, "please look at me."

When the girl looked up, Julia handed her the pile of letters, minus one.

"This is the day's mail. This is all the mail that came. You do understand, right?"

Emily lifted her eyes to her mistress, who was clearly holding one envelope aside. The girl ignored the hand holding the solitary letter and looked straight at Julia instead, her eyes wide and deliberately ignorant.

"Yes, miss, that's all the mail. I'll put it on the master's desk now."

"Thank you, Emily," Julia said.

The parlormaid curtseyed again and disappeared through the doors into Sir Walter's private study.

Her father was censoring her mail. Emily might as well have printed it on her plain, honest forehead. The poor girl was caught in the middle, afraid to lose her position. It was all that stood between her and the poorhouse. Julia opened the drawstrings of her reticule and slid Baxter's letter into a satin side pocket.

Turning to the wide, marble staircase, she quickly mounted the steps to her suite of rooms on the second floor, heart racing. Inside, she threw her traveling cloak across a chair, dropped her handbag onto the writing desk, and sat down on the bed. She covered her face with her hands.

Baxter had disappeared into some awful place. He mightn't have enough food, she thought in horror. And what about a warm coat? The coming fall evenings would be frosty. Julia shuddered to think of what she'd heard about overcrowding. And didn't the Northerners and Southerners hate each other? What if a brutal jailor was tempted to take out his bitterness on Baxter? What if they had whips? They *must* be armed.

Julia felt again as if she might faint, and she sank to the soft coverlet.

A gentle knock sounded at the door. "Yes?" she called, without moving.

"Begging your pardon, miss. I thought you might take some tea after your long journey."

Emily held a tray with a teapot and a plate of ginger biscuits. She had obviously gone right to the kitchen after placing the mail in the study. The girl looked at her with worried concern.

Julia sat up slowly, pushing through the whirl of lightheadedness.

"Let me 'elp you, miss," Emily said, placing the tray on a bedside table. Plumping the large pillows, she guided Julia backward to rest. "It must be the trip."

"Yes. It was a long train ride."

Emily poured a steaming cup of tea, added sugar and cream, and held the saucer while Julia settled herself.

At last she took the cup, blew on it, and took a sip. The brew was hot, but refreshing. She felt the weakness pass. And then, looking into Emily's young, kind face, she remembered the order that her father must have given the servants. She thought carefully about what to say next.

"Emily, dear, thank you for your thoughtfulness. I . . . I understand that Mrs. Worthy wants to make sure that my father receives the mail promptly. Of course, he has many urgent matters of business to attend to. Can you say how long you have been handling the mail thusly?"

Emily glanced down at her shoes again. "Yes, miss. 'Tis been a few months."

It must have been around the time of Baxter's first letter, before she left for the country. Julia wondered how many other letters she might have missed, and what the servants' gossip had been. The mistress normally attended to matters of running the household. Julia had often been the first to see the post, separating tradesmen's bills from her father's more important correspondence. The servants must think Sir Walter no longer trusted her. Julia's cheeks burned at the thought. All trace of faintness vanished, replaced by anger.

"I see. Well, thank you for thinking of the tea. It has positively revived me." Julia gave Emily a reassuring smile and nodded her head in dismissal.

When the girl had gone, Julia rose quickly, went to her writing desk, and took out a sheet of stationery. Sir Walter was likely to be home soon. She would have to write fast. Anxiety for Baxter blurred with fury toward her father, sharpening both emotions. The words came in a rush that she did not bother to check.

Dear Baxter,

I just received your letter of last August, though it is now nearly October. I might never have received it at all but for a fortuitous coincidence of timing that I cannot explain at present. I am deeply distressed to hear your news, and wish there were something that I, or my family, could do to be of assistance. Above all, however, I wish you to know that my prayers are with you in your ordeal. I, too, remain faithfully yours.

Fondly,
Julia

P.S. In future I would find it most convenient if you wrote to me in care of my friend, Miss Flora Bentley, of Brockton Manor, Mayfair.

Julia folded the brief note into a crisp rectangle, and then hesitated, conscious that her heart was beating wildly. Reaching into her handbag, she drew out the enameled mirror that Edmund had given her at Christmas.

The looking glass reflected an expression so agitated that Julia hardly recognized it as her own. The mirror also revealed a stray curl that had worked its way out of the pins at the back of her neck. Taking up a pair of scissors, Julia cut the lock of hair, twined it into a circle around her finger, and dropped the strand into an envelope along with the letter. She would put it in the mail herself, on the way to see Flora and Louise in the morning. She hoped her friends' love of romantic intrigue wouldn't fail her now.

TWENTY-SIX

❧

OCTOBER 1862

*Things are a little out of joint. The Queen secludes herself
and does not get over her grief. . . . The operatives are getting
poorer and poorer, and yet there is so much capital in the city that
interest is at two and one-half per cent. The country really seems
to be rolling in wealth, and yet there are miserable beggars
in rags assailing you at every corner.*

—Charles Francis Adams to Charles, Jr.,
A Cycle of Adams Letters

Charles handed his top hat and overcoat to the cloakroom attendant at the Reform Club, the gentleman's establishment on Pall Mall. "I am afraid these got rather wet on the way in, Dougal. You may wish to shake them out before putting them on the rack."

"Of course, Mr. Adams. Don't you worry, sir. I'll have them dry before you leave. 'Tis a mess out there, isn't it, sir? Mr. Bright came in looking like he'd fallen in the Thames."

"Mr. Bright's here already, then?"

"Yes, sir. Came in not half an hour past."

"Thank you, Dougal. I'll pick up my things after lunch. If you can make them serviceable by then, I shall be most grateful."

"Certainly, Mr. Adams," the valet said, handing him a much thumbed wooden token.

Charles took the stairs to the library at an easy pace; his step was lighter than it had been in months. Walking into a British gentleman's club was an altogether different thing now that Lincoln had finally made the war a fight for freedom and to rectify "history's greatest crime," as John Bright put it. The president's recent Emancipation Proclamation finally allowed the legation to say that the war was indeed about slavery. The press still carped noon and night, but Charles had caught some friendly glances across the foyer at the symphony two evenings earlier, and a cabdriver in Hyde Park had bent Henry's ear with enthusiasm for Lincoln's measure. "The workingman's behind you, young fellow—don't give up!" he told a grateful Henry, who shared the story like winnings from a long shot at the track. The mood was finally starting to change, the balance tipping.

In the spacious library, a haze of aromatic cigar smoke mimicked the thick clouds outdoors and drifted in broad curlicues above the heads of club members, who were reading, talking, or dozing in heavy armchairs scattered about the spacious, oak-paneled room. A twosome was playing chess next to a tall window. The men were sunk in identical postures of concentration, like elderly twins, each with an arm folded across his chest and a hand propping his chin. Low murmurs of conversation punctuated with occasional bursts of laughter hummed above the crackle of a fire at the end of the hall. Large paintings in lavishly carved frames imparted color to the room.

As his eyes adjusted to the masculine gloom of the rainy October afternoon, Charles spotted John Bright sitting in a well-stuffed armchair under one of the stronger gaslights. He held the *Times* in one hand and a paper knife in the other, as if preparing to butcher the day's news. Bright looked up at Charles's approach and immediately set the newspaper down.

"Charles. Excellent! Good to see you. Beastly day, isn't it?"

John Bright stood to shake the American minister's hand, moving with brisk energy despite his imposing girth.

"Indeed, John. Let's hope it doesn't portend a torrential winter."

"If my name were Noah, I'd be hunting up animals in twos. It's positively biblical out there," Bright said. He turned his face toward the streaming windows that looked out onto the broad boulevard. "I suppose we shall have to trust to Providence that Whitehall isn't swept down the Thames. Though that might not be such a bad thing, eh?"

Charles smiled warmly at his bluff Quaker friend. John Bright was well known for colorful rants against his countrymen, whom he routinely dismissed as a nation of bullies who ought to meet their maker immediately. Of course, Bright would have said the same about Spaniards, Frenchmen, Austrians, Swedes, and Russians, whom he held in no higher regard. God had washed away the entire human race once before without discernibly cleansing its morals. Never couching his opinions of anybody, Bright would have been a nightmare as a diplomat. His sweeping hyperbole gave Charles a deep, vicarious pleasure.

Bright was also the legation's staunchest defender in Parliament. From nearly the moment of their arrival, Charles had relied on the reformer's wise counsel. He was one of the few Englishmen who had taken the full measure of the war's significance and understood the stakes for liberty.

"But how would your club sustain itself, John, if Whitehall were to disappear?"

"True, true," Bright said, his large, spaniel eyes taking in the assembly of gentlemen in various poses of leisure around the room. "What one must suffer for the convenience of a first-rate supper. But here," he said, gesturing toward the chair beside him, "do sit down. Have a brandy before you catch your death of cold."

Charles settled comfortably and took the warmed snifter offered by a waiter.

"So tell me how you and your colleagues are getting along with the business of running England these days."

"Most of the scoundrels are off to their country homes, bedeviling the poor fox and geese."

"Why aren't you out in the country, then?"

"I find it a bore and a chore. Mary's out there now with the children—all eight. A man can't get to the breakfast table without tripping over one of them. They're like puppies."

Charles nodded acknowledgment. When he and Abby had had all seven at home, the house in Quincy seemed ready to burst at the seams—with children in the parlor, on the porch, under the tables. Now, with only Henry, Mary, and Brooks, their London residence sometimes felt half empty. Fortunately, Louisa and John Quincy II were safe in the North, but he wondered frequently about Charles, Jr. In the last letter to his mother, he described an artillery shell that barely cleared his head, traveled thirty yards, and took off the legs of three infantrymen. The conspicuous cavalry, high on their mounts, drew fire as lanterns drew moths.

"I'll go for the weekend to please my wife," Bright continued, spreading his hands to register his resignation to marital duty. "But for now I'm enjoying the peace and quiet. Not to mention, I can follow the news better from London."

Charles leaned forward. "And what is the news? Your note said that you had some information from the Russian ambassador."

"Yes, well . . ." Bright hesitated conspiratorially, glancing around the room. The only member within earshot appeared to have dozed off in his chair, his ample jowls cushioning his chin. Bright leaned forward. He lowered his rich tone to the dim hum of the club.

"It appears that the Russians are refusing to be party to a joint agreement to recognize the Confederacy. Certain members of Palmerston's cabinet have apparently approached both France and Russia—and perhaps Austria and Prussia—to solicit a European pact. They want mediation on the basis of separation. If the North refuses to negotiate, the Europeans as a bloc will recognize the South. They think it would be impossible for the U.S. to retaliate against them all. Safety in numbers, you know."

Charles took a sip of his brandy, controlling the frown that he could feel gathering. If Europe acted in concert, the Union was done for—that much was clear. But this kind of threat had loomed from the beginning.

"How is this any different from all the other rumors we've heard over the past year and a half?" he asked.

"In that it's not merely a rumor," Bright replied with a shrug. "I have it on the highest authority."

"Is that why the cabinet meeting's been called for October twenty-third?"

"It's certainly earlier than usual," Bright observed. "Palmerston and Russell normally wait until more members are in from the country."

"That would explain why Lord Lyons hasn't yet returned to Washington from his vacation," Charles said, thinking of his last conversation with the British representative to the Federal government. "When I saw the minister a couple of weeks ago, he said that he planned to sail back to the States on the eleventh. Yet he's still here. Do you think the cabinet intends to send him with an ultimatum for Lincoln and Seward?"

"That would be my guess," Bright replied.

"Will the cabinet go ahead without agreement from the Russians?"

"The Russians? Oh, good God, yes. They were probably solicited only at the request of Victoria. You know how she likes to keep the other royal families informed. I think that Pam and Johnny really care only about the French, and maybe the Austrians, though of course they'd like as many countries on board as possible."

"If they're serious about intervening this time, Gladstone's recent speech at Newcastle would make more sense," Charles observed.

He had otherwise tried and failed to understand the strategy behind the chancellor of the exchequer's speech earlier that month. William Gladstone, number two in the government next to Prime Minister Palmerston, had traveled nearly to the Scottish border to deliver a political address at Newcastle upon Tyne. The event came hard upon the heels of the Emancipation Proclamation, which President Lincoln had announced after the battle at Antietam Creek, another slaughter at which Charles, Jr.'s, battalion had come under heavy shelling. The proclamation declared all slaves in the Confederacy free as of the New Year, three months away. Rebels would forfeit their property unless they surrendered by December 31. Britain's skeptical press had scorned the proclamation as nothing but a last, desperate ploy to improve world opinion. Lincoln's measure would result in servile insurrection, they charged, and condemn the South to the bloody path followed by Haiti—blacks murdering their masters until the rivers ran red. The *Times* called the proclamation "absurd, impracticable, and impossible." The paper also pointed out that it pertained only to territory over which the Union had absolutely no control.

And then, at Newcastle, William Gladstone told a throng of admirers who lined the bunting-draped streets and choked the town hall that the South had made an army, a navy, and a nation. The independence of the Confederacy was "a certainty," he'd predicted, and the time had come to lay down arms.

"Absolutely," Bright said. "Most intemperate—unless it was a prelude to recognition. You know that Gladstone has to be in on anything that Pam and Johnny are cooking up. They would never fail to consult the exchequer, since he has to bankroll their misadventures."

"But why now?" Charles asked, bewildered by the perverse timing. "I would have thought the proclamation would clarify the larger purpose of the war for them. Surely this administration doesn't want to ally itself with slavery, now that it's obvious the war will help bring it to an end?"

Bright shifted in his chair, the stiff leather creaking under his bulk. "I don't think the proclamation has really taken hold in their imagination yet—except for the risks it might bring. They're dull-witted boys over at the Ministry. Russell is also under tremendous pressure to break the blockade, you know, and get Lancashire back on its feet. Conditions for the operatives are dreadful. Close to starving, some of them."

Charles felt a chilly foreboding. Seward had been lecturing him to be sterner with Russell about "deliberately and wickedly" abetting the South. Russell, meanwhile, appeared to be growing more resolute about confronting Seward with the futility of further resistance to disunion. Each man was the ram on his ship of state. A disastrous, splintering collision could well be inevitable—and Britain had the more seaworthy vessel.

"What do you suggest?" Charles asked Bright candidly. He trusted the feisty member of Parliament more than any other man in Britain.

"Other than capturing Richmond?" Bright asked with an ironic smile.

"Other than capturing Richmond," Charles echoed, with a heavy heart. The repeated failure to take the Confederate capital was a suppurating wound. The spring offensive, launched with such confidence, had dragged into summer and fizzled out in the fall. Tens of thousands had died on both sides. His son risked life and limb every day, and the intelligence that he sent from the battlefield was rarely good. Charles knew that Abby spent many sleepless nights staring into the quiet dark.

"You need to strike a solid blow, and soon. I'm afraid that it may already be too late. It's hard to see how anything less than a major victory will stem the sentiment against the Union in Parliament—even with the Emancipation Proclamation. In the short run, Lincoln's new policy may even do more harm than good," Bright warned.

"That's obvious," Charles said, restraining his tight grip on the brandy glass. "But surely Russell is open to an appeal of some sort."

Bright pursed his full lips, considering. "Perhaps you ought to ask for an interview prior to the cabinet meeting on the twenty-third," he said at last. "You do have an effect, you know. It's that old Adams tenacity. Makes them stop and think. They've seen your kind before."

Charles appreciated the reference. He wanted more than anything to believe that Bright was right—that his own unyielding conviction in the rightness of their cause made a difference. Realism stopped him from getting his hopes up, however. The Liverpool docks were as active as ever. Dudley had written that Laird Brothers had installed gaslights in their shipyards to allow work to go on into the night. The firm appeared to be building two more cruisers for the Confederacy, ironclad steamships now tipped with steel rams to puncture and sink wooden vessels. Warships powerful enough to challenge the navy, sweep the Potomac, and take the battle directly to Washington, if launched.

"Perhaps you're right. I'll write to the foreign secretary to request an appointment. I'll have to think carefully about what to say when we meet, though. It's delicate. I don't want to sound aggressive, but I do want Russell to understand that the United States shall resolutely resist any coalition arrayed against it—no matter how many countries are involved. We'll fight to the bloody end, come what may. We shall never give in."

"Oh, I doubt you'll have to think too hard about how to put that across," Bright replied with an amused gleam in his shrewd eyes. "Stubbornness positively radiates from the Adamses."

"Yes, we've been told that before," Charles said with a smile meant to suggest more confidence than he actually felt.

Stubbornness might not be enough. Should the British and the French unleash their armadas against the United States, the country would go down regardless.

———

CHARLES WALKED THE long way home from the club on Pall Mall to clear his head. It took him through neighborhoods that he sometimes liked to walk with Brooks, who was still innocent enough to enjoy the zoo at Regent's Park. The sky had finally lightened and a thin mist had replaced the lashing rainstorm of the morning, with wisps of fog gently blurring the edges of the buildings and obscuring the topmost branches of the trees in St. James's Park.

London had been a market town since Roman times, and Charles sought forgetfulness in the bustling atmosphere of her streets. It gave him satisfaction to navigate his way, confident of arriving back at the legation regardless of his starting point. When he was a child in London, he wouldn't have been able to say if Greenwich was north or south of the Thames. The city had been a gigantic blur in which only a few familiar streets stood out. Now he could chart his way from Kensington to Bloomsbury without a wrong turn and direct a hansom to the Royal Observatory across the river if necessary.

Charles had followed his father's career from the age of two, first to Moscow, next to Paris and London, and finally to Washington. Quincy was the navigational reference point for the rest of the universe, but he didn't need to be there to feel oriented. Wherever he was, he was home. Being anonymous—rather than known to barber, barman, and bailiff—concerned him not at all, with his wanderer's temperament and his foreign upbringing. Charles knew that it was different for the children, who had done all their growing up in Massachusetts. It was particularly hard on Henry, who was well past the diversions of childhood but was not yet anchored by marriage or a profession. It had been difficult to make friends in Britain—surrounded by diplomats, politicians, and cautious functionaries who, as Henry put it, were never smart and seldom young—but his middle son also suffered from not being in contact with the world that defined and recognized him. A woman would help, Charles thought. It wasn't completely out of the question. His own father had found love in England years earlier, marrying the shy, pretty daughter of the American consul.

Wooden stalls lined the street fronting St. James's Park, where a black-and-white Jersey cow nibbled the lush grass and a dairy-maid was selling milk to nannies whose young charges ambled on the green. Awnings drawn against the morning's rain were rolled up now, dripping from their scrolled edges, while merchants called out their wares. At one booth, two women quarreled over the price of cabbage. Charles noted that several stalls had the first apples of the season. A pyramid of knobby green Bramleys put Charles in mind of a proper New England pie, and he wondered if Abby could teach Emma how to make one.

That was one aspect of living abroad that did unsettle him at times: the difficulty of finding food prepared in the ways to which one was accustomed. He could remember his mother's frustration with cooks who clung stubbornly to local traditions, convinced that anything else was bizarre and unnatural. And so in Russia they drank their tea with jam instead of sugar. In France, they dined on eggs for supper instead of breakfast. Now Emma would probably insist on putting a brown-sugar crumble on top of the apples, which might be good but not what he had in mind. Charles wanted to break the crisp, slightly salty crust of a cinnamon-flecked American apple pie. Instead, he would probably have to make do with a lumpy English streusel.

A flash of cherry red caught Charles's eye. A tall, bony merchant was lining up a row of colorful wooden dolls on a table brimming with toys, woolen scarves, India-rubber boots, and other mismatched wares. Charles stopped and stared. He had had one of those dolls in Russia when he was a boy.

He picked up the closest doll. The lacquered face on the smooth surface stared up with innocent blandness. She had a yellow peasant scarf, vivid as an oriole, which was drawn up in a bow under the chin. A scalloped white apron with yellow roses covered her brilliant red dress. Charles twisted the two halves of the doll in opposite directions against the squeak of fresh birch wood. It came apart, revealing another doll nestled inside. He opened the next and the next, until six dolls, each smaller than the one preceding it, stood in a row. The tiniest was smaller than an acorn. Each had a different-colored head scarf and apron, but the same shiny black eyes and pink cheeks.

"They're *matryoshkas,* aren't they?" Charles asked the merchant, the word rising like a bubble out of the deep pool of memory.

"Oh, I wouldn't know that now, sir. They're just Russian nesting dolls to me. But I do know they're awfully pretty. Would you like one? Or perhaps two? I can make you a fair bargain."

Charles carefully selected the most finely painted of the dolls. He would tell Abby the story of his childhood collection in Moscow. She would enjoy lining up the roses on the painted aprons, fitting each doll into the nest made for it by a larger one, just as he had as a boy.

Charles strolled back along Oxford Street to the American legation with the wrapped package under his arm, enjoying the fresh, rain-swept air. He had considered buying a second set for Mary but decided that she would think it beneath her, now turned sixteen, to play with dolls.

That left the playing to him and Abby. Charles smiled to himself. Mary was too young to understand that people were like *matryoshkas.* Underneath the sedate surface of his fifty-five years was the passionate young man who had courted Abby at an age considered unseemly by both of their families. Within that shell was the lonely boy who had played with dolls in remote postings and tagged along behind his industrious father through the courts of Europe. Each was intact, each still inside.

"They're so perfect!" Abby exclaimed as she opened the

cheerful dolls in their bed that night, spreading them in a row across her lap.

Charles had wrestled with his correspondence late into the evening, anxious about John Bright's forewarnings. Now he rested against the pillow, content to watch his wife sealing and unsealing the Russian toys. Her hair was down for the night. Silver strands glistened in the candlelight, intertwined with the raven tresses of her youth. The peach fuzz of Abby's flannel nightgown mimicked the soft texture of her skin. She looked up at him with a carefree smile.

"I want more!" she said, tugging playfully at the solid ends of the smallest doll.

"You would. You just love teeny, tiny things," Charles teased, pinching the air with his fingers in a fussy imitation of her gesture. Abby adored miniature tea sets, Chinese bird's-nest boxes, dollhouses—anything petite.

"You do, too, and you know it," she replied with spirit. "I've seen the way you lock each tiny drawer of that rolltop desk. You're as fussy as a hen."

"Wait a minute, you're the hen," Charles said, scooting deeper under the covers onto his stomach and reaching an arm over Abby's warm lap. "I'm the rooster."

One of the *matryoshkas* rolled off the bed and bounced lightly on the wooden floor. "You'll break them," Abby complained, picking the dolls up off the coverlet and placing them on her nightstand. Her husband didn't bother to defend himself. His eyes were already closed. Abby ran her fingers gently through the graying tufts of his once full head of hair. Then she leaned over him and blew out the candle. Charles had fallen asleep.

He dreamed of the old house in Quincy.

It was dark, and he kept bumping into chairs and tables as he walked from room to room looking for Grandfather. He called out, but there was no answer. Charles made his way to the kitchen at the back of the house, feeling for obstacles with his hands and trying not to trip. Surely Cook must be somewhere about. But the kitchen was dark.

He turned into a room he had never seen before, though he felt no surprise at its existence. He supposed it had always been there. It was larger than the drawing room, but the floor was sloped, sagging deeply at one end. He felt his way cautiously, pushing down on the floorboards to test for give. The foundation appeared to be slipping.

Moonbeams through a set of tall windows revealed a massive bookcase at the far side of the room. He approached it, though he could see that the shelves were tilted on an outward slant. It occurred to him that the case might come down on top of him.

The books were part of Grandfather's library—worn volumes bound in rich Spanish leather. John Adams loved his books, writing in the margins and returning again and again to parts he found intriguing. Novels and poetry mingled with works of law and philosophy like bohemians at a supper party.

One shelf held the books from Grandfather's revolutionary days— Tom Paine, Thomas Jefferson, Alexander Hamilton, James Madison, and Noah Webster, among others. Grandfather knew them all.

Charles carefully slid Webster's grammar off the slanted shelf. He remembered Grandfather teaching him how to spell "center" from it. One arm draped across his grandson's narrow shoulders, John Adams had pointed with bent finger to the American spelling—"er" instead of "re." Grandfather thought Webster went too far in rejecting common usage, but he admired the schoolteacher's attempt to create a new, plainer style of English for the democratic republic. "You must write it just this way, Charlie," Grandfather said, tapping the word twice. "It shows you were born of men bold enough to tweak the nose of King George."

Now the pages were blank. Charles squinted in the dim light, but there were no ABCs to see. He flipped through the book quickly. The familiar words had disappeared, wiped from the page.

Just then, a loud noise startled him and he dropped the old reader, flinching away from the expected blow of the bookcase. But it remained standing.

The walls of the room glowed with a stronger light now, and Charles looked around, searching for the source of the illumination. It seemed to be coming from somewhere higher in the house. He noticed a staircase at the side of the room. It must lead to the bedrooms above.

The walls grew brighter as he climbed the steps, like a summer sun rising behind the fields. Then he felt the pulsating heat.

From somewhere upstairs an old man cried out in terror. "Help! Fire! Help!"

Charles broke into a run, taking the narrow risers two at a time. Grandfather had become amazingly weak in the last few years. He couldn't possibly get out by himself. He'd be trapped.

"Grandfather! Grandfather! I'm coming!" Charles called, climbing the steep stairs as fast as he could.

He saw the smoke now. It filled his throat and he began coughing. He had nearly reached the top when a rotted step gave way under his foot. The staircase was wobbling, lurching, breaking away from the wall. With a metallic screech, the nails tore loose. Charles grabbed instinctively for the banister, but it swung outward into the room, and he caught at the air to avoid falling with it.

"Help, Charles! Help!" Grandfather yelled, terrified.

And then a barrier of fire materialized at the top of the stairs, as red and furious as the Devil himself. Flames licked eagerly at the ceiling, fanning out toward Charles. Billows of black smoke framed the landing.

Charles coughed and coughed. His throat closed convulsively. He struggled to call to his grandfather but choked on the words.

"Charles! Take a drink," Abby said, shaking her husband by the shoulder, "Charles. Here."

The minister woke in a fit of coughing. He gasped and sat bolt upright. A fleck of goose down had lodged in his throat. He took the glass that Abby offered.

"I had an awful dream," he finally said, when the ferocious tickle had subsided. "There was a fire. Grandfather was trapped in the old house. I couldn't get to him."

A piercing panic filled Charles again at the thought, and he felt a sweat break out on his forehead. John Adams had passed away decades earlier. But the voice in Charles's dream was horribly real and unmistakably Grandfather's. He couldn't shake the appalling conviction that he had failed to save the old man, so precious to them all.

Abby took the glass from him and placed it on the table. She pulled Charles down next to her under the covers. "Come, Charlie," she said, using the name reserved for tender moments. "It's okay. Go back to sleep."

Charles wrapped his arms around his wife. His blood was still pounding, as if he really had run upstairs. He relaxed with an effort, calming his mind and waiting for the thumping to diminish. Slowly, the dream faded away. The safe, peaceful room in London became real again as Charles pressed Abby close. His heartbeat refused to settle down, though, and he gradually realized that Abby's familiar softness was making his heart beat fast for a different reason.

Charles reached down to trace his fingers lightly across his wife's breast through the warm cloth of her nightdress. He waited, and then slowly, with a timing known only to the two of them, repeated the intimate question that had led to their seven children. She had never yet told him no. Abby stirred in his arms, straightened against him, and sleepily raised her chin. Charles shut his eyes against the anxieties of the day and the terrors of the night, and pressed his lips softly against Abby's. He forgot Quincy and London. Only he and Abby existed. He would tire of her when he tired of eating, Charles realized. Then, with absorption in nothing but the moment, he lost himself gratefully in his loving wife.

TWENTY-SEVEN

The men from the country had often not passed through the ordinary diseases of child life, and no sooner were they brought together in camps, than measles and other children's diseases showed themselves, and spread rapidly. The malarial influences of the rivers, too, produced a most depressing effect upon men brought from higher regions, and more healthy surroundings. Violent remittent, intermittent and low typhoid fevers invaded the camps, and many died.

—Dr. John H. Brinton,
Personal Memoirs of John Brinton: Civil War Surgeon

Baxter pulled on his boots. They were the only part of his clothing that still fit well. The prisoners were now down to half rations—a small portion of beans at midday, a crust of bread in the morning and at night. His frame had gone from strapping to what could at best be called skinny. Devereaux Council called it downright pitiful.

"You look near as bad as me," Baxter's garrulous cellmate proclaimed. Council ran a hand over the stringy beard he had grown at Fort Lafayette.

"Yeah, Dev, but at least he didn't start out pug ugly," Virgil Sweetwood chimed in.

Baxter laughed. Despite his scarecrow appearance and the choppy haircuts that Council gave him with a bowie knife, despite the worn trousers that he belted more tightly each month, Baxter felt surprisingly well. Hunger bit at the edge of consciousness continuously, but not bad enough to make him desperate. He found that he could live on much less than he would have thought possible.

He studied *Gray's Anatomy* every morning, recommitting the bones, muscles, and sinews of the body to memory. The path-breaking book had come out during his first year as a medical student, and now Baxter marveled at how he had rushed through it, chanting lists under his breath between lectures and forcing his brain to absorb the dry information. It had been a chore. Now he lingered over the intricate plates as if meditating on panels from the Sistine Chapel, with each illustration revealing the wonder of God's creation. Study passed the time. Limiting himself to a page a day, Baxter calculated that he could last at least a year before going stark raving mad. That should be time enough for someone to win the war.

Other prisoners had taken to consulting him about their physical complaints and fears. At such moments, Baxter nearly forgot the life going on outside. He had a full practice.

"Who you callin' ugly?" Council demanded.

"No one. You called yourself ugly," Sweetwood reminded the New Orleans privateer. "I'm just being agreeable."

"Well, at least I don't hail from a former penal colony," Council retorted.

"Hey now," Baxter soothed. "There's no call for that. Right now we all hail from a penal colony."

"In that case, I nominate you guv'ner," Council said, taking the opportunity to turn onto a more cheerful path. He was a man you couldn't get down. Testy sometimes, but fundamentally cheerful. Virgil Sweetwood, who was from a small town in Georgia, had a good heart but was taciturn in comparison.

"No thank you," Baxter replied. "Town doctor is good enough for me."

Council drew his head backward with a sudden jerk. "Pee-yew! What in the Sam Hill is that smell? Take it outside, for

Christ's sake!" he called out across the room. "You're gunna make me puke my breakfast before I get a chance to eat it."

The pungent, membrane-burning odor of rank raw sewage swelled like a sulfur cloud in the close confines of the cell. Most of the men were quiet in anticipation of roll call and rations, but now groans and angry objections rose in a ragged chorus.

"Hey, I don't think he's doing too well," one man said, offering an explanation. He was leaning over a prisoner still huddled on the floor against a wall, trying to stay warm under a single army blanket. "I think he's lost it."

Baxter stood and crossed the small space. Other prisoners shuffled to let him through.

The Virginian hunched on his heels beside the stricken man, who was moaning softly with tightly closed eyes.

"Isn't this the new guy? Longman or something?" Baxter asked.

"Name's Lonigan. Just came off a sloop from Cuba trying to shoot the blockade," a cellmate answered. It was the tall whiskey-runner from Mississippi, Jack King.

"How long has he been in the Bastille?"

"Dunno. Three days, maybe."

Baxter felt the man's sweaty forehead, and then his pulse. Lonigan stirred briefly, sending a fresh wave of the hot, churning scent into the close air. A guard opened the door to allow the men outside and a scramble to be first ensued.

The young doctor looked up into King's gaunt face. "Can you tell the guard we've got a man in here who's ill? He needs to be in the infirmary."

King nodded silently and followed the others out.

Baxter turned to Council and Sweetwood, who were waiting.

"I hate like heck to do this, but I've got to take a look. Give me a hand?"

Council rolled his eyes but shrugged assent. Sweetwood got down on a ragged knee. "What ya fixin' to do?" he asked.

"I need to see what kind of mess he's making."

Baxter unbuttoned the man's pants, and Sweetwood helped pull the sodden breeches over Lonigan's trembling white legs. The sick man resisted briefly, grasping pitifully at his waistband, and then lost consciousness.

The back of his legs were smeared brown with watery feces. Blood and pus stained the graying long johns that the sailor wore under his trousers for warmth.

Trying to breathe as little as possible, Baxter asked Council to slip the blanket under Lonigan as they wrestled the fouled pants all the way off.

"We might as well git him comfortable," Council said, holding his nose. "That looks pretty bad."

The three men managed to roll the wet, soiled clothing into a heap and bundle the shivering prisoner in his blanket by the time two guards came into the cell.

"What's going on?" the taller of the guards asked in a metallic New York twang. He looked young, probably not much more than fifteen, and was carrying a rifle. "We heard some guy shit himself." He took a sharp step backward at the stench. "Whoa! Guess that's gotta be true."

"This man is sick. He needs to be admitted to the infirmary immediately," Baxter said with an unmistakable tone of authority.

"Sorry, Johnny," the New Yorker said, using the nickname the guards called all of the Rebels. "I can get you a bucket, but the infirmary is full. They can't take every guy who gets the runs."

"This isn't just diarrhea. He's got a fever, and he's bleeding."

"So his stomach's upset. Tell him to lay off the rich foods."

The guard snickered and glanced sideways at his companion to see if he was laughing, too.

The other guard was an older man with only one arm, probably invalided from the Army of the Potomac. It was known around the fort that the blockade-runner from Virginia was a London-educated physician. The guard looked stone-faced at Baxter. "He's bleeding, you say?"

"Yes," said Baxter. "And he's just up from Cuba. I think he might have tropical dysentery."

"Dysentery?" asked the younger guard.

"Bloody flux."

The two guards looked down at the unlucky Confederate. A dead man, probably.

"Better get him out of here then, or the whole cell's gunna come down with it," the older guard said. He nodded at Baxter and Sweetwood. "You two. Take him up to the infirmary. Council, is it? You get a bucket. Swab this place twice. Get hot water from the kitchen." At that, the Federal soldiers left the cell and the prisoners to their work.

Breakfast and the morning exercise period had passed by the time Baxter and Sweetwood got back to the battery, in which only a residual whiff of feces remained. The Union doctor had probed Baxter's knowledge of tropical dysentery at some length, interested to learn how British hospitals were handling the disease in India. Dysentery had decimated Federal prisoners on Confederate soil, but the North's frigid winters had kept the worst forms of the disease at bay. Baxter told the Union medic all he could remember from lectures. For good measure, he threw in Lister's theories about clean healing. Before leaving the infirmary, Baxter and Sweetwood soaped their hands twice.

"I'd say I got the shitty end of the stick," Council commented with a wry grin upon their return. "But at least I didn't miss breakfast."

Sweetwood merely took out his card deck. "Anybody for poker?"

"Ah, come on. You don't think I'm low enough to eat without ya?" Council asked. He reached behind him for two small rolls that he had carried on his tin plate. "They let me have these. Sorry I couldn't fetch you any of that delicious Lincoln coffee. I only had the one cup."

Baxter restrained the urge to snatch up the bread, and instead allowed Sweetwood to pick first. The Georgian took the nearest roll, pointedly not examining the two for a difference in size. Baxter took the hard bread and tore off a small piece to make the meal last longer. He resisted the temptation to jam it into his mouth all at once.

"Ain't today mail day?" Sweetwood asked. The Georgian generally didn't receive letters from his illiterate parents, but a sister who lived in the next town over helped his mother send an occasional note. Each word was a puff of country air, he said.

"Sure is," Council replied. He had taken up Sweetwood's worn poker deck and was carefully cutting the cards, sliding one half of the deck into the other. The men had agreed to stop shuffling in order to preserve the stiffness of the paper. Council started dealing while Baxter and Sweetwood finished their skimpy meal.

"Nope, deal me out," Baxter said, shaking his head. "I haven't read *Gray's* yet."

"Jeez, Baxter. We can't play with two. Ain't you got enough book learnin' already?" Council asked.

Council had developed a high opinion of Baxter's medical knowledge after the Virginian reset his dislocated shoulder. The shoulder had been weak ever since he'd taken a bad fall out of the ship's rigging during a storm in the Gulf. It now had a tendency to go out, and a shoving match in the prison yard had helped it along. Baxter popped the shoulder right back in and fixed him up with a sling. Council swore he hadn't felt a twinge, Baxter was that good—like slipping pie into the oven.

"It's my morning routine," Baxter replied.

Council nodded at the justice of this excuse. They all understood the importance of establishing a pattern to give a man a sense of control. Some prisoners didn't attempt one. Those were the inmates who slept most of the day and fretted during the night, the ones whose world made a little less sense every day.

"Hey. Deal me in. I'll play," Jack King said. The gruff Mississippian was sitting with his back to the wall a short distance away.

Council looked at King suspiciously, drawing the deck an inch closer to his chest.

"Let him play, Dev," Baxter said in a low voice. "He got the guards."

"All right," Council called to Jack King. "Until Baxter here is done with his book. He's our regular partner."

"I know that. Christ, I seen you playing every day for six months. You think I'm a fuckin' idiot?" King scooted into the small circle, folding up his long legs. He picked up the hand that Council had dealt onto the stone floor.

Baxter finished the last morsel of dry bread and opened his book. He was in the section on female anatomy. The reproductive system bloomed on the page before him, leggy Fallopian tubes and fertile ovaries stemming like lilies from the womb. Unbidden, the thought of the flowery apparatus tucked under Julia Birch came to mind.

The prisoner felt his groin stiffen in response. He shifted the book higher on his lap and turned the page. No better. It was a diagram of the chest and the mammary glands. The breasts sloped down in two soft curves. Baxter closed his eyes and silently began reviewing the twenty-six bones of the foot. He flexed each toe in his boots as he counted. It occurred to him with clinical detachment, and a certain amusement, that his southern section was still in rebellion and definitely in fighting trim. Baxter was grateful for the sanctity of the cranium and the breadth of the book.

"Male call," he heard a voice sound out. Baxter blinked his eyes wider, distracted from the anatomy lesson. The meaning snapped into focus. *Mail call.*

A prisoner assigned to postal duty read out the names, flipping letters like playing cards in the direction of those lucky enough to receive something. "Sams," he called. "Ya gotta pair of deuces."

Baxter took up the precious envelopes that fell just short of his boots. His mother and Julia. Without the slightest sense of disloyalty to the maternal line, Baxter shoved the letter from Richmond between the back pages of the medical book.

He hesitated before opening the envelope from London. That she had written at all was astounding. What young woman in high society would think twice about a man stuck in a foreign jail? Baxter thought he was reconciled to never seeing her again, but the letter flushed an ember of hope from some chamber of his heart that Gray had neglected in his diagrams.

Baxter glanced down at his right boot, where he had stashed his grandmother's ring. The Charleston shoemaker's work held firm. Apparently the boots were worth the considerable price he had paid. The ring was still safe. Maybe it would bring him luck.

He opened the envelope. Julia's graceful, determined handwriting swept across the page. It was a short note, yet it told Baxter all that he needed to know.

She had signed it "Julia."

Julia!

What a beautiful word! Baxter had feared that she would find his use of her first name jarring, but the worry now evaporated as if it had never been. She wrote that she remained faithfully his. Baxter wasn't sure exactly what that meant, but his tiny flame of hope burst with a fiery brilliance. She might wait. She *would* wait, he thought. Longing and relief flooded him. He couldn't believe she had written. In the filthy, hopeless hellhole of Fort Lafayette there was something to live for.

A shadow in the corner of the envelope caught Baxter's eye, and he opened it wider. A soft wisp of curl lay nestled at the bottom. Julia had sent a lock of her hair. Baxter reached in a finger and touched the precious strand, afraid to disturb its beguiling shape.

"What in the heck did you get? A Federal pardon?" Council asked, with a glance over the cards at his friend. Baxter was staring into the envelope with the smile of an imbecile.

He blushed a healthy red. "Huh? Oh, just something from a friend in London." Baxter closed the envelope.

"Must be somethin' pretty special. You look like the cat that ate the canary."

"Yes, um, well, I guess it is like a pardon. A pardon, or a promise of sorts," Baxter replied. "Only from someone much prettier than Abe Lincoln."

"Well, that wouldn't be too hard. Man's as homely as they come."

Council looked as if he was thinking about pressing Baxter further, but Baxter ignored his cellmate and began ripping a sheet of paper from his blank notebook. From a battered top pocket he took out a pencil.

My dearest Julia, he wrote. *I hope this letter reaches you in fine health. My own is quite good, and my spirits are restored by the note from you that I received today. To a man in prison, there is nothing more precious or more heartening than to know that there is someone outside who thinks of him fondly.*

Baxter looked at the words and remembered the first time— the only time—that he had danced with Julia. She had said something about not judging people as "types." He rolled the piece of paper into a ball, and then tore out another. He would not write to her of prisoners in general but of himself.

My dearest Julia, he began again. *Your letter makes me feel like a new man. To know that you think of me fondly gives me heart in this dark place.*

Prisoners were allowed no more than one page, so he put as much as he could into the short space, leaving no margins. Devereaux Council and Virgil Sweetwood came alive under his pen, as did the prisoners with whom he had shared his budding medical knowledge. He told her about *Gray's Anatomy* (the parts one could mention decently), and concluded with the news of poor Lonigan. He asked her to give his best regards to Henry Adams, should she cross paths with his old friend, and to the Bentley sisters. He did not tell her of the half rations or of the guards' indifference.

Baxter hesitated to sign off. He wanted nothing more than to declare his affections, but he had so little to offer her under the circumstances that mention of the future would be grossly unfair. At last, he wrote:

> The moments we had together in England remain my happiest memories. I hope we will spend more time together once this terrible war is at a close. The lock you sent of your beautiful hair allows me to hope that you feel the same. I will treasure it.
>
> > Faithfully yours,
> > Baxter

Council, Sweetwood, and King played poker steadily, slapping down discards and talking quietly among themselves. The trio ignored the young doctor hunched over his writing. Every man had times when he escaped from the Bastille into his mind, even if it was only while sleeping. The moment commanded universal respect.

Council was particularly quiet, though he stirred from time to time on the hard floor. Just before midday, the wiry sailor drew a ten and a queen of hearts for a straight flush. King folded in disgust, and Sweetwood packed the cards away in his faded shirt pocket. Council triumphantly took a pinch of tobacco from each man as his winnings. No one smoked the rare commodity, but it made for solid-gold currency.

When the doors to the cells swung open for the second time

that day, Baxter, Council, and Sweetwood took their usual places in the line strung across the exercise yard of Fort Lafayette. Council made a show of drawing in the clean salt air with pleasure.

"Well," he said with a cocky smile, turning to Baxter, who had finally emerged from his daze. "What do you suppose is on the menu for dinner?"

"Roast beef," Baxter said, picking up from the day before, his voice ringing with new certainty. "And I do believe I smell fresh horseradish."

TWENTY-EIGHT

*I think we must allow the President to spend his second batch
of 600,000 men before we can hope that he and
his democracy will listen to reason.*

—Lord Russell to Lord Palmerston, *Palmerston Papers*

"No, thank you," Charles replied to the butler's offer of a seat in the anteroom to Lord Russell's chambers. "I prefer to stand."

A clerk sat quietly copying documents at a desk just outside the open door, but otherwise Charles was alone. He removed his top hat and smoothed the lapels of his immaculate frock coat to make sure they were straight. A quick glance in the gold-leaf mirror above the coal fireplace showed that his hair was still neatly combed back off his balding forehead. The mirror reflected an oil portrait of the queen behind him. Charles turned to study the familiar likeness as he waited.

The door to John Russell's office opened with the soft hush of fine wood gliding over even finer carpet. Charles heard the earl bidding someone good day, and Baron de Brunnow, the Russian ambassador, stepped out from the door that closed behind him.

"Minister Adams. It is good to see you," the ambassador said with surprise, extending his large hand. Brunnow's English was inflected with French and Russian accents, like hints of vanilla and cinnamon in a plain shortbread. He wore a bright-purple cravat. The flamboyant, dark-bearded man reminded Charles of courtiers to whom he had bowed as a child. The impression never failed to evoke a faint nostalgia. Charles had seen the Russian at Whitehall only a month earlier.

"We meet again, Ambassador, and in the same place."

"And perhaps for the same reason? Are you seeing our friend about British overtures to the Confederate States again?"

"I'm not at liberty to say, but you may be assured that such matters are always foremost in my government's concerns."

The Russian ambassador leaned forward and took Charles by the elbow, steering him out of sight of the open door through which the clerk could be seen writing.

"I think that you should not worry too much, my friend. At the bottom of its hard heart the English government would like your country to break into two republics. Then you would counterbalance each other and leave her with a free hand. But the British are also very cautious. They don't want to advance too far in front of Europe. Trust the English to know their interests. I don't trust them otherwise, mind you, but I do trust them to know their interests. In this case they will adhere firmly to the policy of neutrality. Don't ask how I know, but I am certain of it."

Charles had not intended to ask how Brunnow knew, since that would violate an unwritten diplomatic rule. Nevertheless, he was curious.

"I wish we could have your faith, Ambassador, but I am afraid that public statements made by certain members of the cabinet give us pause."

"Certain members of the cabinet sometimes speak out of turn," Brunnow said. He cocked his head to one side. "You recall that just last week the minister of war reminded the British public that offers of mediation won't be received by a conclave of philosophers. He warned that Britain might come to blows with the North without procuring one single cotton boll for the mills."

"There are voices of reason," Charles agreed. "I believe that Sir George Cornewall Lewis knows the butcher's bill would be high. Even so, perhaps Gladstone wanted to see how the public would react to a change of policy favoring the Rebels. Testing the waters before taking the plunge."

"That may be. But I know for a fact that Monsieur Gladstone doesn't yet have the votes in the cabinet. I believe they are rather split. Prime Minister Palmerston has been capricious in his opinions, and now seems to be waiting for a more propitious moment, such as the defeat of the Republicans in your next election, or a decisive blow on the battlefield. But Russell has also been warned that England will not have the Russians behind her if she insists on mediation between the North and South."

"Warned by you, I take it?"

"Now it is I who am not at liberty to answer a direct question. But may I remind you that I've told you before, the British won't waver in their neutrality, not without Europe behind them? I was correct then, and I am correct now."

"Yes, you were quite right on that occasion. But I have information of another nature that excites my concern as well, which I am not free to disclose. Perhaps at some future point I will be able to put you in possession of evidence that could change your judgment. You might call it 'ironclad.'"

Brunnow's brown eyes brimmed with intelligence. He obviously knew about the warships being built by the Lairds. "Ah yes, well, that is another matter. But for now I say to you, don't worry too much."

Just then the door to Lord Russell's office opened, and the foreign secretary's assistant invited Charles to enter. The Russian ambassador shook Charles's hand and bid him good day.

"Mr. Adams. How do you do? Please have a seat. How may I help you?"

The fastidious earl indicated the small sitting area next to the fire, where two chairs were drawn on either side of a Dublin Chippendale table carved with scallop shells and lion's-paw feet. As usual, the fanciful Irish style outshone its staid English cousin. Charles wondered if the earl had brought it back from his idiosyncratic travels beyond the Irish Pale.

"Thank you for seeing me, Lord Russell. As I indicated in my note, I was hoping to hear from your lordship as to when Lord Lyons will be returning to Washington to take up his post."

"Ah, I see. Well, I am pleased to tell you that our minister will sail on the *Scotia* in two days. We had some matters to clear up in the cabinet, but we've finished for now." Lord Russell settled lightly in his chair, as if the most important subject under consideration had been concluded.

"Excellent," Charles replied with a gracious nod. "We hope that you are prepared to let him stay for a good long while this time. My government would like to see Lord Lyons remain in Washington indefinitely. He is a worthy representative of Her Majesty's government."

"I thank you for that compliment on Lord Lyons's behalf. You can be sure I shall convey it to the prime minister."

John Russell gave the polite diplomatic rejoinder with the practiced ease of someone who never had to review the formula. His keen eyes flicked over at the jeweled clock under glass on the mantelpiece to check the time, no doubt he hoped unobtrusively.

"As for myself, I am obliged to confess that I have been wondering lately if I myself might be returning to Washington soon," Charles said, with a rueful laugh and an air of wonder manufactured especially for the occasion. "It's driven me to ponder the state of my carpetbags and trunks, should I have to leave soon."

Lord Russell shot Charles a piercing look, though otherwise he did not stir a muscle or betray surprise.

"Why might that be? Is Mrs. Adams well? I hope the fresher air of fall is agreeing with her."

"Yes, she is quite well, thank you. Much better, in fact."

Charles paused, as if hesitating to mouth the words that he in fact fully planned to say. "But I follow the *Times* and the other London papers closely, as you might expect. If I trusted the opinions expressed in them—especially after the delivery of a certain speech in Newcastle earlier this month—I would have concluded that my mission was at an end. But, of course, I preferred to wait and see whether the speech should be considered authoritative or not."

A slight pink flush showed around Russell's collar, and the earl shifted ever so slightly in his elegant armchair. "I take it you mean Mr. Gladstone's address a few weeks ago?" John Russell asked in a mild tone. "I am afraid he was much misunderstood. Of course, Mr. Gladstone is entitled to his opinion as an individual. He has them on all matters of the day, as might be expected."

Russell reached forward to take a sip of the sherry that had been placed on the table between the two men. Charles lifted his sherry, too, and waited.

"I wouldn't presume to disavow anything Mr. Gladstone says on his own behalf, but you needn't infer from his speech that Her Majesty's government has any intention of changing its policy at this time," Russell continued. "Not at all. It's merely the fashion for public men to air their views."

"I certainly do not expect a disavowal, from either you or Mr. Gladstone," Charles replied. He sensed that somehow the calculus of the conversation had shifted. Russell appeared on the defensive for once. Charles decided the moment had come to press the point, and he began the speech he had thought through earlier in the day. "I wouldn't expect Mr. Gladstone to remain silent on the great issues of the day. However, I cannot sufficiently express my regret at the deleterious consequences of such statements made in a public forum. His remarks are certain to be published by every newspaper in the United States, strengthening the rebellion in the South and inflaming hostility toward Britain in the North. I'm afraid most Americans will read it as the official position of Her Majesty's government."

Russell now looked decidedly uncomfortable. He slipped a finger inside his stiff collar, loosening it slightly. The trim, wary earl reminded Charles of a fox sniffing at a trap. "Yes, well, it's most unfortunate." The foreign secretary nodded gravely, as if in complete agreement with Charles but unwilling still to see the matter as anything more than a regrettable slip of the tongue.

"It's worse than unfortunate, I'm afraid," Charles replied with a mild tone and a stern expression. "It seems to me that the goodwill I enjoyed when I arrived a year ago last spring has declined steadily. Speeches like that at Newcastle upon Tyne have a tendency to confirm unfavorable popular opinion toward the United States."

"That may be," Lord Russell conceded with obvious reluctance. "Public sentiment is much divided on the subject."

"Not just divided, I think you will agree."

"Well, it does seem that aristocratic opinion is gathering against the United States. But I wager that most workingmen sympathize with the Union even now, when supplies of cotton are down and they must wait for work."

"I think you're right, Lord Russell, but I hope you will not take offense at the observation that workingmen cannot vote, and that one or two more speeches by Mr. Gladstone could easily damage the remaining feeling of friendship toward my country among those classes that do. I wouldn't think of impugning the exchequer's intentions, but the effect of his speech was certainly to undermine the spirit of neutrality."

Russell picked up his sherry and drank as if it were a draught of medicine. Then he looked Charles straight in the eye. "Yes, well, I must admit that there are some in the cabinet who feel that Mr. Gladstone was a bit presumptuous in his statements. We do regret that he made them."

"Then may I be assured that it is still the government's intention to adhere to the policy of neutrality?"

"For the time being, yes. Of course, I cannot say what might happen from month to month in the future. Circumstances do change," Russell said, gesturing with his free hand as if to suggest the unpredictable vagaries of fortune. "But, yes, at present it is Her Majesty's policy to let the struggle come to an end without the slightest interference."

Charles nodded, his face impassive, and set his own glass back on the table. Apparently, Russell did not reckon sixteen-gun warships and military supplies as interference—but at least it wasn't outright recognition of the Confederacy as a nation, from which there could be no recovery.

"Thank you, Lord Russell. That will be satisfactory to us."

The foreign secretary and the American minister both stood, anticipating each other's moves like chess masters, and Charles took his leave.

Walking back to the legation, Charles replayed the meeting in his mind. He was relieved that he could write William Seward that the British did not propose to recognize the Confederacy or attempt mediation, at least for the time being.

But he struggled to make sense of Russell's mood. The man seemed almost embarrassed. Was it Gladstone's gaffe? Had the exchequer really spoken out of turn? Which had embarrassed Lord Russell more—that England might be seen to support Southern slavery or that Gladstone had exposed the plan prematurely?

Charles heaved a sigh, realizing only then that he was scarcely breathing. The minister drew in a lungful of cold fall air and let it out in a long, deliberate exhalation. It looked as if they would be staying through Christmas again.

TWENTY-NINE

※※※

DECEMBER 1862

*Parliament will bring society, and this I dread. The son
of the American Minister is likely to meet with precious little
favorable criticism in London society in these days,
and, after all, I'm very little of a society man.*

—Henry Adams to his brother Charles,
A Cycle of Adams Letters

Julia gave her card to the starched housekeeper who answered the door at the legation. "I hope Mr. Adams is receiving callers this morning."

"I believe so, Miss Birch," the woman responded in a Dublin accent, showing her to an empty parlor.

Julia rose nervously when Henry entered the room. A spontaneous smile lit his face. "Miss Birch. What a pleasure to see you. It's been too long."

"Thank you, Mr. Adams. I do hope I am not calling at an inopportune moment." It had taken all her nerve to come this far. If he was busy, she doubted that she would try again.

"Not at all. You've relieved me of an obligation to a ghastly pile of dull copying. It had me on the verge of tears. Moses couldn't have been more grateful at the parting of the Red Sea."

Julia smiled with relief at Henry's comic hyperbole. "You're still acting as your father's secretary, then?"

"I am, indeed, though I am sure he could find someone far more competent. I suppose this is the definition of nepotism."

Henry gestured to the satinwood settee. "Please don't stand on my account. I've asked Kathleen to bring us some tea. I hope you can stay for it."

"Thank you. I would be delighted," Julia replied, taking her seat. "I'm sure that's not true, though, about nepotism. Your father is very lucky to have such a faithful and trusted assistant. These must be very trying times for all of you."

Henry's eyes were warm. "Thank you, Miss Birch," he said simply. "They truly are."

The housekeeper entered the room balancing a full tray. Julia observed that she had brought not only tea but also scones, finger sandwiches, and a small chocolate cake. Perhaps she thought Julia was staying for the winter.

"Would you like me to pour, sir?" the housekeeper asked.

"Please allow me, if you will," Julia said.

Henry nodded, and the housekeeper left the room.

"I'm afraid I can't stay long," Julia said, once they both had tea in their cups. "My father's public posture on the Confederacy makes it awkward for me to be seen at the legation. But I've come for your advice on a matter of what may be of mutual concern."

"Of course," Henry said at once, leaning forward. "Tell me how I may help."

Julia took a deep breath and let out the question that was pent up inside. "Are you aware that Baxter Sams is a prisoner in New York? Apparently he was caught trying to return to England."

"Yes, I know," Henry replied, his expression suddenly opaque, as if a shade had been drawn. "We had a letter from his father."

"I don't understand why Mr. Sams is being detained. I know that he . . . he brought contraband on his voyage into Southern waters, but surely it was an innocent act to return to England for medical school."

"The blockade goes both ways, Miss Birch," Henry said. "He was on a vessel that was taking cotton out of the South. Everyone on board is considered guilty, whether cook, captain, or passenger."

"Even those who have no connection to the shipment?"

"Even those. Anyone crossing the line of blockade, in fact."

"Are you sure?" Julia asked.

"I am quite sure."

Julia paused and stirred her tea. The room fell silent. In fact the whole house seemed quiet, as if lying in wait. She wondered if their concern about Baxter was truly mutual. Henry seemed stiff and even—inexplicably—distant. Perhaps he felt betrayed by Baxter. It wouldn't be unreasonable, she admitted to herself, but still, Baxter was Henry's friend.

"Aren't the prisoner of war camps terribly dangerous?" Julia persisted. "Isn't there some way to get him out?"

"Of course they are dangerous," Henry answered, now with a hint of anger. "I told him it was dangerous. I'm afraid he will have to suffer the consequences."

Julia looked down at her cup, untouched, not seeing that she had forgotten to add cream to her tea. "Is there no hope, then?" she asked. "Must he really stay for the duration of the war?"

"I'm sorry, but there is little that can be done," Henry said. "We are all in for the duration."

The young American must have intuited her dismay, because he then added more gently, "But Baxter is lucky to have you make inquiries on his behalf. It seems all England loves a rebel, so long as he isn't Irish." Henry let out half a laugh, though it failed to hide a certain regret in his eyes.

"Oh, Baxter didn't ask me to make inquiries," she said, falling into first-name usage unconsciously. "He seems resigned. He's made a place for himself as a doctor of sorts to the other prisoners. But he did ask me to give you his regards."

"Thank you for conveying them," Henry replied. He hesitated, and then added, "I have to say that sounds just like him.

He used to keep a rope under his bed at Cambridge in case one of us got home past curfew. I'll never forget the time he hauled me up and hid me in his room until daybreak." Henry looked out the window, as if seeing a scene from long ago. "I miss him."

Julia lowered her eyes. "I do, too." And then it occurred to her that Henry might be disappointed in her as well. His initial welcome had been unmistakably eager. Perhaps he hoped she had called out of interest in him, not Baxter. Her heart sank. She should go.

Henry cleared his throat, and she looked up. He wasn't smiling, but his eyes were kind and he had a resolute air.

"Well, I suppose that the class of '58 ought to stick together—if we can do so without committing treason. I hesitate to mention it, but there is one possibility that Baxter might be able to find a way out."

"Really?" Julia asked with surprise. "But how?"

"Baxter's mother was born in London," Henry began.

Julia's eyes widened with understanding.

"Only American blockade-runners are seized. It's illegal to imprison citizens of another country, which is why the navy typically confiscates smugglers' cargoes while letting the men themselves go. If Baxter can prove he is English—or part English—then he may have a basis for arguing for release as a British citizen."

"How can he do that?"

"I'm really not sure if it can be done, but I suppose one would start with the parish record. His mother was born somewhere in the parish of St. Paul's. Baxter's father mentioned it in a letter he had written to the legation. Her birth might have been recorded there."

"I could try to get proof of that," Julia said. "The dean of St. Paul's was a friend of my mother's. I'm sure he would help. Would that be enough?"

"I think not. It would be a first step, but it would help if you could get a high official to weigh in. Someone who would suggest that the British government or a member of Parliament takes an interest in Baxter's situation. Surely one of your father's friends might intervene?"

Julia flushed. She had anticipated this question, but it was still awkward to answer. She tilted her chin and said, "That's an impossibility, I'm afraid. My father can't know about this. He would just as soon see every American rot in jail."

"I see. Hmm." Henry frowned. He looked out the window again in deliberation, and drummed his fingers on one knee. The room fell quiet again.

"Is there any chance your father might be able to do something?" Julia asked, putting into words the question with which she had first approached the legation. She twisted the ring on her right hand. "I realize that my father's attitude toward the war would give the minister little call to want to help me, but I would be very grateful."

The image of her father's attempt last summer to snub the American minister came unbidden to mind. It had been such an embarrassing end to a pleasant evening. Julia didn't see how the minister could possibly ever overlook it, though she fervently hoped he might. She realized that a tingling blush had started up her neck and covered it with a gloved hand.

Henry didn't answer. Then he smiled. "Remember when my father called him Sir Wilbert?" Henry's eyes sparkled with the familiar good humor that had been missing from his demeanor.

Julia's awkwardness fell away in a rush. She laughed heartily, unable to stop for a good minute. Henry burst into laughter as well.

"Oh, I could have kissed him then," Henry said. "The Chief is such a hard-boiled old egg at such moments!"

Julia took a handkerchief out of her bag and wiped her eyes. "He was brilliant," she said. "Twice as clever as Father."

"I tell you what," Henry said. "You work on St. Paul's and I will speak with the Chief—my father, that is. He's been known to have a romantic streak under that cool exterior."

Julia's cheeks went rosy at the implication, but her voice was steady. "Thank you, Henry, if I may call you that. You are a true friend to Baxter and to me."

It was Henry's turn to flush with pleasure. "I don't have many friends here," he admitted. "I hope my father can see his way clear to help."

"HENRY, HOW CAN you ask that?" Charles inquired with mounting exasperation. He was still knotting the elaborate bow tie over his high, stiff collar. He and Abby were due at a party near Piccadilly Square in an hour.

Looping one end of the silk over the other, Charles added, "You know how Washington feels about the blockade. If it weren't for people like Baxter, this war would have been over last year."

"I realize that, Father. I've copied enough affidavits on the subject. But Baxter is a friend."

"Politics and friendship are a poor combination, as you are well aware."

Charles didn't have to name all the friendships their family had seen destroyed by politics. Thomas Jefferson was the most famous, but the list was long. The abolitionist Charles Sumner, whom Henry once worshipped like a god, added his name in the months before the war, vying with Charles for influence in the Republican Party and the post in England. *A friend in power was a friend lost.*

"Baxter didn't make a political choice, or at least he didn't intend to. He's a doctor. I know he felt a responsibility to the suffering."

The minister didn't respond. He had almost mastered the slippery bit of reluctant silk. Abby wouldn't let him out of the house until the corners passed muster. He concentrated on his image in the mirror.

"The doctors in the field treat the wounded regardless of which side they're on," Henry continued. "Hasn't our own Charles told us that? Think of the men we'd have lost if it weren't for the Confederate surgeries."

"Yes, and then they send our soldiers to prisoner-of-war camps."

Charles caught Henry's image behind him in the full-length mirror. Henry's hair was dark brown, and he had the smooth complexion of youth. Charles's hair was gray now, and his skin worn by the years. He looked like a faded daguerreotype next to his vibrantly youthful son. But they had the same oval face and intense eyes. They were versions of a man at different points in his life, now young and idealistic, now tired and pragmatic, arguing their respective points of view. Heart and head locked in the eternal struggle. Charles felt a pang of mortality. Life passed so swiftly.

"Shouldn't a man on a mission of mercy be treated with mercy?" Henry argued.

Charles returned his attention to the recalcitrant tie. "That's not how the courts see it, and with good cause. The blockade-runners endanger the very existence of the country."

"Baxter is not a blockade-runner. He *ran* the blockade, but only once and not for profit. Surely that's a relevant distinction."

Charles merely gave the ends of the bow a tug, pulling it tight. He picked up a brush lying on Abby's vanity and attacked his hair with it. Henry had run out of convincing arguments along that line. They both knew it.

"Then you might want to consider the source of the request," Henry said.

"Julia Birch? The daughter of that impossible man? I would just as soon clamp *him* in Fort Lafayette," Charles said, turning to face Henry. "You know he's in cahoots with James Bulloch. I saw the two together outside Laird Brothers myself. Dudley has witnesses who swear that he's a source of financing for the Confederacy. The devil can take him and his daughter, as far as I'm concerned. Birch is the materialization of the principle of evil."

"Julia said that he would not want to help Baxter. Perhaps that's why we should."

"What do you mean? Surely her father approves of Confederates?"

"She says he would be happy to have all Americans rot in prison."

"Hmm. That's a bit odd, though not necessarily surprising. The Tories have long memories." Charles placed the brush back on the vanity, ready for Abby's inspection.

"I think she and Baxter may be in love."

"I see."

Charles sat down on the bench next to his wife's dressing table, mulling over the pros and cons. He liked Baxter. The first time that Henry brought the young Southerner down to Quincy from Harvard, they sat through the night discussing James Fenimore Cooper. Baxter found the Mohicans infinitely more sympathetic than the pioneers, including the cantankerous Hawkeye, whose popular appeal he couldn't remotely fathom. The articulate guest conveyed an easygoing charm, and even his most assertive statements were phrased to avoid offense. But Charles sensed depth under the courtly manners; Baxter seemed to think about things. It was a quality prized in Quincy, yet too often absent in Washington and other points south.

But liking wasn't enough. Baxter was an adult. He had made his choice knowing full well the possible consequences, and he would have to live with them.

The minister turned the argument around in his mind and looked at the other side. Walter Birch had conspired with the Confederates to split the United States. He was at the center of a large and influential group of peers who hammered unceasingly on Parliament to recognize the South. Any day now, they might have their way, with devastating consequences not only for the United States but also for four million Negroes in bondage. Meanwhile, Sir Walter was also helping to finance Confederate shipbuilding, including the rams that could penetrate Federal defenses and bring fire and rain to Washington, Philadelphia, New York, and Boston. The man clearly needed a distraction. And maybe his daughter deserved a chance to marry the man she loved, even if he was an American. "I really don't know that a letter from me would carry much weight," Charles told Henry.

Henry caught at the implication. "It would help, I think. Miss Birch intends to obtain proof of the English citizenship of Baxter's mother. A letter from you to the responsible official in New York could suggest that the army cooperate for the greater good of Anglo-American friendship."

Charles closed his eyes wearily, and then opened them with a resigned expression. As a father, he understood Walter's parental caution. As head of the American legation, he could see some advantage in helping Baxter Sams, the enemy of his enemy.

"All right, then, Henry. It's not by the book, but what in this war is?"

"Thank you, Father. I don't believe you'll regret it."

Henry smiled into the mirror, meeting Charles's clear-blue eyes. His father returned the smile. Youth and heart had won the battle. Charles didn't really mind.

THIRTY

*Dr. Gibbs is a bird of ill omen. Today he tells me eight of our men
have died at the Charlottesville Hospital. It seems sickness is
more redoubtable in an army than the enemy's guns.*

—Mary Boykin Chesnut, *A Diary from Dixie*

"Damn! Shoo!" Baxter said, waving at the seagull that had
alighted on the ledge of the open window and lowered its
beak for a drink. Startled, the bird knocked over the water with
its long white tail feathers as it darted away, but Baxter caught
the dripping glass before it could roll onto the stone floor and
break.

Water was at a premium in Fort Lafayette. Cut off from the
mainland, the men depended mostly upon rain that collected in
the island cistern. Bits of debris from the drainpipes and the ancient basin settled to the bottom of any cup of water. The prisoners mostly didn't notice it, preferring coffee. No one wanted to
see the water before it was flavored and darkened.

But Lonigan and Council needed clear, clean water. Both
were severely dehydrated from diarrhea. Blood and fluid loss
meant either could go into a fatal shock. Baxter and Virgil
Sweetwood had been promoted to hospital orderlies to look after
them, but that was a euphemism for quarantine. The warden
didn't want anyone else in the cells coming down with the disease
to which these four men had been exposed. Under the crowded
conditions, it might easily sweep the prison.

Council fell sick a day and a half after they took Lonigan to the infirmary. Baxter and he were sharing a bunk, and Baxter could feel through his blanket that Council was hot. He kept turning, waking Baxter every hour or two. Irritated, Baxter finally tried to rouse Council. Then he realized that his friend was sick.

The next days were a blur. Baxter and Sweetwood moved into the quarantine room of the infirmary along with their patients. They helped each other through the days and nights of holding the unsteady men over slop buckets and cleaning up when they couldn't get to one fast enough. Despite the chill winter drafts, they kept the window open to let fresh air into the fetid sickroom.

The only good that came out of the ordeal was better rations. The guard who brought their noontime meals made sure the orderlies had a chunk of pork or beef with their beans. Warden's orders. But while they felt less hungry, they felt more anxious and washed their cold hands until they were raw.

"Sweetwood. Can you get me some water?" Baxter asked, holding out the glass. Lonigan had taken a turn for the worse that morning and was now holding tightly to Baxter's hand. It was as if all the strength in the man's body was concentrated in the attempt to hold on. Baxter's fingers had grown numb, but he dared not remove them. With his free hand he kept trying to get more water past Lonigan's cracked lips. He hoped the prisoner would yet rally. He had seen sicker men do so.

"Sure. Gimme a minute." Sweetwood dipped the jug into a barrel of water and brought out the brimming container. He took the glass from Baxter and placed a bit of cheesecloth over the top before pouring water through the makeshift filter.

"Thanks," Baxter said. He lifted the water to his patient. "Lonigan, drink this. You have to. Come on now."

But the blockade-runner just seamed his mouth more tightly and refused. For a moment he opened his eyes and stared intently at Baxter as if to ask a question, but then closed them again in exhaustion. His skin was gray, and the blades of his cheekbones, too prominent for such a young person, threw shadows across his face.

Baxter looked up at Sweetwood. The Georgian shook his head silently and resumed his seat at Council's bedside.

"Feel his forehead," Baxter said, nodding in Council's direction. "Please."

From his right hand Sweetwood unwrapped the strip of old sheet that he used to keep warm, leaned over, and placed his bare palm on Devereaux's pale brow. During the past week Sweetwood had learned to tell the difference between warm and fevered. Fever gave off a slight charge, like static electricity underneath the skin.

"Looks like he's shet of the chills fer now."

"Good. See if you can get him to take some more water."

Sweetwood put a glass to Council's mouth. "Dev. Hey, Dev. Take a drink."

The sailor appeared to be dozing, but he took the water in lapping gulps without opening his eyes. Sweetwood refilled the glass. Council drained it halfway.

The Georgian put the glass on the night table and took out his poker deck. He laid out the cards in a game of solitaire. Baxter shifted *Gray's Anatomy* onto his lap with his free hand.

There was nothing to do but wait. Lonigan appeared nearly spent. He had nothing more inside him to expel, other than the water, but at least he was now resting more easily. Council seemed tougher, and came out of his delirium every now and again to complain about the scratchy blankets. Baxter took it as proof of innate contrariness, the type that tended to keep death at a distance. The night before, Council had swallowed some beef broth without ill effect.

Baxter found that he couldn't concentrate on *Gray's* that morning. On the second floor of the old fort, the infirmary had a small window that looked out on New York Harbor. In the weak winter sunshine, Baxter could make out what he thought must be the tip of Manhattan on a distant shore, from which boats sailed to and fro, leaving crosshatches on the water. It was months since he had seen life outside the prison, and the window now was like a magical book of moving pictures, though limited to sky, water, ships, and birds.

He had stayed at his uncle's home in Philadelphia many times on his way to and from Boston, but had never made it to New York. Now he was there. What a pity he couldn't see the theaters or the busy streets. Baxter remembered Henry talking about Jenny Lind, the Swedish Nightingale, on Broadway. "I've never heard anyone hold a note so pure and true," he'd said.

The thought of Henry led to Julia. Baxter opened *Gray's* to the section on female anatomy, where he kept her letters as a bit of whimsy. The thin sheets were shoved close to the binding so they wouldn't drop out. Baxter reread the first one. He had never before seen an example of her handwriting and now could have plucked it from a file box containing hundreds of others.

At times that letter seemed to speak volumes. When he read "fondly," he heard "love." When he read, "I wish I could help," he saw "we will find a way." But when he awoke at night in the cold dark of the sickroom, beset by torturous doubts, the letter seemed to be little more than a thoughtful note to an acquaintance who had fallen victim to misfortune: sympathetic but formulaic. Her subsequent letters had been equally kind—and seemed increasingly affectionate—but part of him was afraid to hope.

And yet he couldn't stand to let the feeling go. The hope that she returned his love was like New York through the window. Dry land. As Baxter studied the precious parchment pressed flat by the weight of *Gray's Anatomy,* he wondered again whether mere pity for his plight kept her writing or if she felt something more than friendship. And why had she asked him to send letters in care of the Bentley twins? Was she ashamed to correspond with a man in prison? She probably ought to be.

Baxter suddenly realized that the pressure on his fingers had slackened moments earlier. He looked down at Lonigan and, aghast, immediately recognized the bloodless cheeks and waxy lips he had seen in London hospitals when making rounds. Baxter laid two fingers across the carotid artery, searching for the pulse. Nothing. He pressed more deeply, but it was like palpating a piece of meat. No movement, no life, just a sickening stillness in the tissue. The blockade-runner was gone.

Baxter cursed silently. He felt furious—at the war, at Lincoln, at his own impotence. He hadn't even made a good nurse. Far from healing the sick, he wasn't even able to provide a drink of clean water. What a waste.

Nauseated with regret, Baxter released himself from the sailor's grip and tucked the dry, slack hand under the thin cover, taking care to cover the unfeeling fingers against the prison's dank cold. "Sweetwood," he hissed sharply.

The Georgian looked up from his game of solitaire. Council lay sleeping behind him, his cadaverous face as washed-out as the pillow.

"We'd better get the guard."

THIRTY-ONE

FEBRUARY 1863

*The anti-slavery feeling has been astonishingly revived by
the President's proclamation and the kindly disposition
by the supplies furnished to Lancashire. It is however to be noted
that all this manifestation comes from the working and
middle classes. The malevolence of the aristocracy
continues just as strong as ever.*

—Charles Francis Adams to Charles, Jr., at the front,
A Cycle of Adams Letters

"What do you mean they're for sale?" Charles asked Dudley.
"The Lairds are giving out that Bulloch has decided to
sell the ironclad rams. The customs collector at Liverpool—you
remember Edwards—told me that Captain Bulloch is calling it
quits. Apparently, he told Edwards himself that it just wasn't
worth the bother anymore. Didn't think the Foreign Ministry
would allow the vessels to clear the Mersey."

"Calling it quits?" Henry asked dubiously. "Is that likely?"

The three Americans had arranged their seats in a semicircle
around the fireplace in the office of the legation. Dudley was
perched on the edge of his, eager to impart the latest news. And
anxious about it. He tapped his long fingers against the base of
the chair.

"I don't know. I'm suspicious of anything that Bulloch does—
especially anything he does publicly. But apparently there have

been some buyers down at the Birkenhead yard, looking around. Edwards said he thought they were French."

Charles sat back, his hands in front of him with the fingertips touching, as if holding an invisible sphere. He wished he had a crystal ball. Dudley's early intelligence on the two newest vessels had been frightening: warships clad in steel five inches thick, with iron rams that extended seven feet beyond the bow. The plans revealed a watertight compartment running the length of the hull. Filled with seawater during action, it lowered the vessel four feet, allowing the ram to hit enemy ships deep in the belly. The projection would cut a hole the size of a coffin in the side of any wooden vessel that suffered a direct hit.

Charles could easily picture the heaving ocean pouring through a splintered hull—the icy inrush of dark, bitter brine, sloshing round the ankles and dragging at the knees until the vessel lost balance and the men were sucked into the sea. It sickened him.

"It's conceivable that Bulloch would let the vessels go," Charles said finally. "The underwater rams make the ships more blatantly warlike than anything else that he has commissioned. Lord Russell might be forced to act."

"I just can't believe Bulloch would give up," Henry protested. "After all these months? When he's so close?"

"He is a very pragmatic man," Dudley demurred. "We've seen that before. He'll take the money and buy something else. He's still got boats going up in Glasgow, and at Miller and Sons in Liverpool. I've registered protests about the new steamer *Georgiana*, but Edwards will probably let her sail. Just like the *Florida* and the *Alabama*. The commerce raiders are easier for the Rebels to get through customs than the bigger warships."

"Pick your poison," Charles said, allowing his mind to range freely. "Terrible though they are, commerce raiders are less damaging than ironclad rams designed to break the Union blockade. We can better afford to sacrifice our commercial fleet than our navy."

"Surely you don't believe this rumor, Father?" Henry asked. "It's got to be a ruse."

"It might, and it might not." Charles turned to Dudley. The consul's beard was almost entirely gray now. Dudley looked considerably older than he did just a year ago, but perhaps they all did, Charles thought. "I know you'll keep a sharp eye on everything that happens at Birkenhead," he said. "Please make sure to let me know if this rumored sale goes any further. I would be especially curious to see who buys the vessels, if they're indeed sold."

"Of course," Dudley said. "I'll telegraph immediately." The consul turned to his other news. He handed Charles an ill-printed leaflet, smeared across the bottom with cheap ink.

"I brought along the resolution passed last week at Manchester's Free Trade Hall. The crowd was tremendous. The hall was completely full. Two thousand more stood outside. That makes fifty-six public resolutions since last December."

Charles looked at the leaflet, then handed it to his son. Henry read the statement endorsing the Emancipation Proclamation.

"How did they react to President Lincoln's greeting?" the minister asked.

"With cheers. They stamped their feet and yelled so loudly, I thought they might break a window."

"Were there many references to the arrival of the *George Griswold*?" The humanitarian relief ship from the United States had tied up at Liverpool only the week before, on February 11, laden with thirteen thousand barrels of flour and hundreds of cases of bacon, corn, and rice. Churches and civic groups across the North had collected food for textile workers in Lancashire who had been put out of work by the war. Porters and stevedores at the British dock refused to accept wages for unloading the provisions. The railways shipped them onward to the manufacturing towns for free.

"Heavens, yes! Nearly every speaker praised the Union for its generosity. The point was made again and again. The nation that's freed the slaves stands by England's workingmen. I can't imagine the connection could have been any clearer."

"Thank God *The New York Times* was useful for once," Henry added. "Its reports about the famine really stirred public sympathy. John Stuart Mill—you know him, Father, the curious-looking economist with the shy manner—he told me the same when I sounded him out last week at the duke of Argyll's party."

Henry had summarized the newspaper articles for his father back in November. They were the first glimmer of a more productive attitude by the American press. The relief movement spread spontaneously afterward. In December, believing that the movement could only help their cause with the British public, Charles had encouraged Seward to support it however he could.

"I'm curious," Charles said, leaning intently toward Dudley. "I'm curious if you think that the crowd in Manchester was impressed more by the *Griswold*'s food cargo or by the Emancipation Proclamation."

"No question," Dudley answered. "I think the last speaker summed it up best. He pointed out that the workingmen declared their support for the proclamation well before there was even talk of relief."

Dudley dug into his vest pocket. "Here," he said, dredging up a scrap of newsprint. "I'll read it to you. The paper carried the speeches the next day. Let's see . . . Ernest Jones—he's the Chartist leader, the one in favor of universal manhood suffrage, you recall—he said, 'Ere one pound's worth of food was shipped or collected, the voice of the working men of England went forth in a cry of sympathy to the North, and for ratification of the principles of liberty.'"

Dudley looked up. "I think that answers your question."

Charles leaned back in the armchair and brought his fingertips together again. "You know, the tide may be turning at last. Lord Russell is a long-standing advocate of abolition. He's going to have more public support now for acting on it. Or at least he'll have a better answer for those who insist on intervention in support of the South."

Dudley and Henry exchanged wary glances. "I'm sorry that I can't share your optimism about the earl," Dudley admitted, speaking for what was obviously Henry's point of view as well. "From my few observations, he puts the Jesuits to shame in the matter of duplicity. But you're the one who has to keep on friendly terms with him."

Henry glanced at the grandfather clock in the corner. "Father," he said, "I trust you remember our next appointment."

Charles looked up out of his reverie. "Yes, of course. Miss Birch. Is there anything more?" he asked Dudley.

"No, sir. Thank you for your time."

"Thank *you*, Mr. Dudley. Once again your presence in Liverpool has proven to be of incalculable benefit to our country."

The consul ducked his head in modest acceptance of the compliment and took his leave.

"Now, remind me again," Charles said to Henry after the door shut. "What is it you want me to do?" The minister felt a prick of irritation. He had not been entirely comfortable helping Baxter Sams.

"Just see her. I believe she wants to thank you for the letter you wrote."

"You mean the letter *you* wrote," Charles corrected his son.

"All right, then, the letter you signed."

Charles reached over and rang the bell that sounded downstairs in the kitchen. Kathleen could show their next guest to the drawing room.

Julia Birch entered with a swish of silk. She was wearing a yellow moiré frock that contrasted brilliantly with her lustrous dark hair. Charles and Henry stood, while Charles held out his hand to the stately young woman.

"Mr. Adams, thank you for receiving me. Good morning, Henry," she added with a gentle nod.

Noting the difference in address, Charles wondered about his son's feelings for the Englishwoman. There was magic in a petticoat to a man of Henry's age. It would be natural to want to help such a creature, even if a friend had claimed her first and even if the gesture wasn't prudent.

"Please have a seat, Miss Birch," he said crisply, and gestured toward the chair evacuated by Dudley. "How may I help you?"

"You already have, Mr. Adams. I would like to thank you personally for intervening on behalf of Mr. Sams."

"You're very welcome, though I am not sure how much use it will be. The best the legation can do is suggest leniency in consideration of Anglo-American relations. Much will depend on who reads the letter. Do you have the corroborating documents?"

"I do. It took much longer than I expected. The dean of St. Paul's was in the country before the season opened. Then the holidays intervened. I received the letter of confirmation only yesterday."

"May I see it?" Charles asked.

Julia passed him the envelope.

Charles took out the letter, unconsciously smoothing the bent page as he read. Muriel Baxter had been born in a small lane off Fleet Street. It was an area of town inhabited mostly by shopkeepers and tradesmen. Charles noted that the month was January 1815, right at the end of America's second war with Britain. He and his mother had made a frightening journey from Moscow that month to join his father following the negotiations in Belgium. The cold in the coach had been so bitter that it froze their provisions.

"Hmm . . . yes. Well, this looks in order, but as I said, much will depend on the interpretation given this information by officials in New York. Do you have a solicitor there? Or someone who could at least hand-deliver the documents?"

The young woman shook her head. "I'm afraid not." She looked down at the satin-brocade purse in her lap, and then up at

Charles. "My father has connections in the South, but they are of no use to me, nor can I ask for his help in this matter. I shall have to trust to the Royal Mail. Henry has given me the address to which the information should be sent."

Charles glanced at Henry, who nodded agreement. Both men knew it was extremely unlikely that anyone in New York would care. Those who went into the Bastille came out feetfirst or in a formal prisoner exchange. But Charles could see from the determined look in Henry's eyes that he didn't want to be the one to disappoint Miss Birch or rob Baxter of his slender chance of release. It surprised him that Henry was so tenderhearted. He himself had not been, not at that age.

In fact, in retrospect he'd been a rather callous young man. Charles believed that once you'd made your bed you must lie in it, so when life's disappointments and mistakes had worn down his older brother, George, more than thirty years earlier, Charles had been angry. George Washington Adams never knew when to stop drinking, flirting, or gambling. He had the intellect of a Harvard graduate and the judgment of a spoiled child. George exhibited every natural gift except self-discipline, to the point where it seemed he'd modeled his life on Grandfather's gloomy prognostication that every generation needed at least one spectacular failure in order to check family pride and turn society's envy into pity. Some good came even from the worst evil, the old man had observed. He, too, had had an alcoholic son, whose antics had kept the whole house averting their eyes during Grandfather's declining years.

Charles had determined early not to be one of those failures. He'd lost touch with his brother, and when George went missing over the side of a steamship in 1829, Charles wasn't surprised to find among his debts and other papers a will providing for Eliza Dolph and her child. Had George truly cared for the pretty chambermaid whose reputation he'd blighted for the rest of her lifetime? Charles implemented the bequest but, in his mind, scorned the man who hadn't lived up to his parents' high hopes. George's inadequacies made him feel self-righteous. Charles wasn't the one to disappoint John Quincy. Charles had married well, gone into politics, and published books—done any number of things to burnish the family name.

His response shamed him now. He couldn't think of a more abominable form of vanity than to hold himself above and apart from his feckless brother. He should have found some way to help George, or at least loved him better, despite his failings.

Charles's sympathy for Julia Birch and Baxter Sams deepened. They had turned onto difficult, perilous paths—motivated by love and loyalty. Henry was right to help them. He was a better man at twenty-five than Charles had been.

"There is no one who can deliver it for you?" the minister asked again, searching Julia's face. "A brother or an uncle, perhaps? I really do believe an appeal would be most successful if made in person."

"No, there isn't," Julia replied, her expression resolute. "But I feel I must try."

"Then I wish you the best of luck," Charles said. He genuinely did.

THIRTY-TWO

A son is a son till he takes him a wife,
a daughter is a daughter all of her life.

—Irish proverb

Julia found an empty seat in the new reading room at the British Museum. Windows circling the base of the high dome sent shafts of warm sunlight into the vast space, glancing off gold leaf and snowy plaster. She took out the letter that Flora Bentley had received from Baxter the day before. Louise was scandalized at the secretive arrangement, but Flora had pronounced it "terribly romantic."

"There's a reason why people go mad and throw themselves off bridges in novels," Louise had said, her arms crossed over her rounded abdomen. "It's because the heroine makes some silly choice that no one in her right mind would consider."

"Oh, pooh," Flora said. "You're just being stodgy." Turning to Julia she added, "Don't listen to Louise. Becoming a wife has had a most alarming effect. Sometimes I don't know if I'm talking to my sister or my mother."

Louise crossed her eyes at her twin, and Flora laughed.

But as Julia left some time later, Louise cautioned her nevertheless. "Do be careful, Julia. I know I sound stodgy, but I worry," she said, as she walked Julia to the door, arm in arm, out of Flora's hearing. "Why keep up this correspondence? Your father will never allow you to marry Mr. Sams. And there's a war on. It's dangerous. Your reputation is at stake, and that means your entire future, you know."

Julia now pushed Louise's lecture from her mind as she unfolded Baxter's letter in the anonymity of the library. It was the fifth she had received. The other four were hidden in a hatbox from Miss Meredith's millinery shop.

My dearest Julia, it began. As on other occasions, Julia was immediately beguiled by Baxter's voice. She felt that he was there, whispering in her ear with his bourbon accent.

There had been an outbreak of scurvy at Fort Lafayette. Julia intuited that he had helped in the diagnosis. It went on:

I noticed that a number of the prisoners were listless, and two officers from South Carolina complained of loose teeth and painful gums. The doctor finally convinced the warden to bring in some vegetables. Now we have all the raw onions we can stomach. They also brought vinegar, which works surprisingly well. The worst cases are out of the infirmary, though they weren't happy to give up their cots.

Julia felt a thrill of pride. A doctor was at least as close to God as Louise's pastor—and of more immediate use, she thought.

The camp surgeon had kept Baxter on as a hospital steward, which meant that he could look out at the harbor all he wanted. Julia squinted up at one of the skylights in the dome. It showed an opaque square of pale blue. What would it be like to have only one window onto the world?

Virgil Sweetwood had qualified at last for a prisoner exchange. They were becoming rarer, so the Georgian was lucky. Devereaux Council sulked for a week, but then made friends with a young sailor who also hailed from New Orleans. Their tireless yarns of life on the water put Baxter right to sleep at night, if he wasn't in the infirmary with a prisoner too sick to be left alone.

Julia read the narrative carefully, alive to any implication that Baxter himself wasn't well. A previous letter told her that Council was out of danger, which meant that Baxter was, too. News of the scurvy outbreak now informed her that the prisoners hadn't had fresh vegetables or fruit in nearly nine months.

I reread your letters every day, the missive concluded. *They are worn thin, but your handwriting remains distinctively you. They brighten every hour.*

Love,
Baxter

Baxter had first written that simple, fateful word in the third letter she received. He made no mention of plans after the war, yet Julia felt the word summed up the feelings that had been slowly taking root in her heart and mind. She hadn't used it in return. It bespoke a commitment that she wouldn't make without her father's approval. Instead, she prayed that after Baxter's release, after his return to London, her father would come around. She would find a way to change his mind, perhaps with Edmund's help. But she nonetheless looked for "love" at the end of each letter, and it stopped her breath every time.

The clock at the end of the reading room tolled the hour in a clear, resonant tone. Julia took out a clean sheet of paper. She hadn't told Baxter of her efforts to win his release, because she was unsure if the pieces would fall into place. Now she had genuine hope. She had mailed the documents to New York just two days earlier. *Mr. Charles Francis Adams was particularly helpful,* she wrote now.

It was nearly five o'clock when Julia finally placed her letter in one of the new red pillboxes that had sprouted on London street corners to collect the post. She quickened her step in the approaching darkness and hailed a hansom cab on Bedford Square. Her father usually arrived home by seven. He looked forward to supper on the table and to his daughter's attentive company. She would be there.

———

"HE'S IN THE drawing room, miss," the butler said, taking Julia's cloak when she came through the rear entrance to Belfield Manor.

"Thank you, Mr. Thomas. Would you please tell Mrs. Worthy that I would like supper served early tonight? If she can manage it within half an hour, I would be grateful."

Julia wondered what had brought her father home early. She hoped he wasn't feeling ill. She opened the door to the drawing room quietly, in case he was resting in front of the fire. But Sir Walter was standing at the drapes covering the windows that looked onto Pembroke Lane. He held the ball-fringed border of the heavy fabric in one hand, and Julia had the instant impression that he was spying, looking for something or someone coming down the street. His posture was taut and rigid.

"Good evening, Father," she said. "I didn't expect you home so early. I'm afraid Mrs. Worthy won't have supper ready for another half hour." Julia dropped her bag onto a small carved chair and crossed the room to kiss her father on the cheek.

Walter spun on his heel and put out his hand. "Stop."

Julia came to a halt, and then took an instinctive half step backward. Her father's face was distorted with emotion. His right eyebrow was drawn up sharp as a lightning bolt, and his eyes flashed black, brilliant rage.

"I've been waiting for you this past hour. You've been in correspondence with that American. Don't lie to me. I know you have."

"What do you mean?" Julia asked.

"What do I mean? You know very well what I mean. That . . . that Bastard Sam, or whatever his damn name is!"

Julia didn't answer, shocked at the profanity, and her heart started a drum roll in her chest. She felt suddenly out of air, unable to catch a breath.

"I saw the dean of St. Paul's today. You didn't think of that, did you? I ran into him at Boodle's, having lunch. He asked me if the letter clarifying the citizenship of Baxter Sams had been helpful. He said you were trying to get the man released from Federal custody." Walter's face took on a purplish hue. "I looked bloody ridiculous! What in the world are you up to?" he demanded, fixing Julia with his eyes, daring her to move an inch.

"I wanted to help. He was caught last summer in the blockade."

"Last summer? You've known about this since last summer? Have you been writing him, then?"

"Yes, I have," Julia answered, tilting her chin.

Walter drew his breath in sharply, and Julia could see that the brevity of her response had merely increased his anger. She had never dared to disobey him, and now she hadn't given him even an apology or an explanation.

"I told you explicitly that you were to accept no further correspondence from that man," Walter said. "I told you in no uncertain terms, and yet you've deliberately defied and deceived me. You are a wicked, foolish girl!"

"Why is writing such a crime?" Julia responded, her voice rising. "I believe there is freedom of speech in England."

"Freedom of speech? There is also freedom to starve. Plenty of it. I'll cut you off without a shilling if you persist. You don't know what it's like to be penniless. Your grandfather could have told you, when the Americans robbed him of everything he owned. How dare you insult our family's name by corresponding with that . . . that scoundrel." Sir Walter spat out the word.

"He's not a scoundrel. He's a physician and a good man. He deserves our help," Julia answered. She faced him without a flinch, but her fists were trembling. She had never seen her father so angry. Primitive force shimmered under the aristocratic façade.

"A good man? A good man?" Her father's face darkened further, and a broad vein pulsed in his forehead. "He's an American.

I will neither have my daughter in bed with a damned Yankee nor a shilling of my money going to his defense. And I will *not* have you brook my authority!"

Walter's composure dissolved. Crossing the room in what seemed two steps, he snatched Julia's rose-colored reticule off the chair. "Is this where you're keeping his letters?"

Julia reached out and caught hold of the fabric. "Give me my bag, please."

"I bought and paid for this bag," Walter declared. "Everything in this house belongs to me."

Julia tightened her hold on the purse. "I would like it back," she repeated.

Walter ripped the brocade from his daughter's fingers. The silken drawstring gave way. A mirror and a comb fell out. He shoved his hand into the reticule. Hearing the crackle of paper in a side pocket, he pulled out the letter and opened it. He glanced down at the signature.

"Love, Baxter," he read aloud. Walter looked up in anger and disgust. "My God," he said. "What exactly have you done? What makes him feel entitled to *this*?"

Walter looked hard at his daughter, then turned and without another word crumpled the letter and tossed it onto the gray lumps of coal in the fireplace. A tongue of orange flame leaped out of the ash and licked the edge of the page. With a sibilant *poof,* the paper caught fire and a burst of warmth filled the room.

"If I ever hear of you writing to Sams again, or any other man of whom I do not approve, I will send you to the country permanently. Good luck finding a suitor there," he said.

He slung the purse onto a chair and took his seat by the hearth, apparently calmed by seeing the letter burn. "For now, you will go to your room," he said, and picked up a half-empty glass of whiskey.

Julia didn't move for a long moment. She saw only two choices, scream or be silent, and she dared not lose control in the face of her father's temper. So she mutely gathered up the spilled items off the floor, placed them in the damaged handbag, and left the room, closing the door behind her.

In the brightly lit hall, Julia examined the torn reticule with shaking hands. Her nerves hummed as if she anticipated a blow. Edmund's mirror was cracked. The satin pocket on the inside of the bag was torn along one seam, drooping like a wilted petal. She looked around her numbly. This hallway was her father's. The table, the polished candlesticks, the vase of roses, and the Turkish carpet were her father's. The chandelier belonged to her father, as did the oil paintings on the wall. None of it was hers.

In a state of shock, Julia started up the stairs. At the top, she halted. The reality she hadn't wanted to see confronted her now. Edmund was right. Her father didn't care if she ever married. She was too useful, like a sturdy valise or a talented cook. She was his possession. He owned everything in the house. He'd said so. He would give it away when he chose to, or not at all, and she could let him control her or she could resist. He now wanted to shame her, as he had tried to humiliate Mr. Adams, but Adams had refused to be shamed.

Flooded with a sudden and overwhelming conviction, Julia turned left at the landing. It was as if her body knew what to do, even if her thoughts and emotions were too disordered to tell right from wrong, prudence from folly. Legs and feet showed a steady purpose. She followed them down the hall to Edmund's suite, where she closed the door behind her. She lit the small lamp on the bureau and turned it low so that the glow wouldn't be seen from the hall.

She stood still for a moment, drew a deep breath, and then opened the doors to the wardrobe. She looked on the top shelf, where she had told Emily to place the trousers Edmund outgrew the year before, when he finally sprouted past her. A pair of gray flannels caught her eye. Julia shook them out and held up the trousers to gauge their size. She opened the bottom drawer and slipped out a high-collared white shirt. A matching waistcoat and suit jacket hung on pegs at the back of the capacious closet. Hatboxes sat on top of the wardrobe.

Julia took a complete suit of clothes and went to her bedroom. Her father was wrong. He didn't own everything at Belfield Manor. He didn't own her.

THIRTY-THREE

MARCH 1863

*[T]he excessively friendly relations which appeared to exist
between Russia and the United States made me
suspicious of any proposition coming from St. Petersburg.*

—Captain James D. Bulloch, Confederate Agent,
The Secret Service of the Confederate States in Europe

Albert Edward, the prince of Wales and earl of Chester, had yielded to his mother's demands and married. It was known that she blamed him for weakening his poor father's constitution over the actress in Ireland. Prince Albert was indeed distressed by his son's youthful fling, but no one except Queen Victoria seriously thought that it had contributed to his death from typhoid, and she was unbalanced by grief. The queen now spent most of her time at remote Balmoral Castle, stirring only to arrange her heir's wedding to the safely pious daughter of the king of Denmark.

From the pew where he and Abby sat in the rear of the great church, Charles noted that the affable twenty-one-year-old prince seemed utterly undiminished by the capitulation. Edward smiled happily after the ceremony and escorted his new wife down the aisle to the congratulations of those who had gathered to see the marriage of their future king. The diplomatic corps and their families were among the last to exit. Coaches waited to take guests to the palace reception, where prince and princess would be fêted with all the delicacies of vineyard and farmyard.

Charles spotted Russian Ambassador Brunnow in the throng at the reception. His chest was a minefield of jeweled medallions and crosses, and he wore a stunning gold cravat. The ambassador caught Charles's eye, smiled broadly, and made his way over. Baron de Brunnow bowed deeply to Mrs. Adams and inquired after the health of her children.

Aware that Charles hoped to have a word with the ambassador, Abby gave him a warm smile and a short answer. She excused herself to greet an acquaintance.

"You may have heard that the Russian admiralty is in the market for some new ships, Minister Adams," Brunnow remarked pleasantly, sipping champagne brought by a liveried servant. "We have our eyes on two new ironclad rams being built in Liverpool. Apparently they are for sale."

"I had heard," Charles replied, "though I wondered if it was merely rumor."

The chief of the American legation didn't mention that he had also caught a rumor that the United States Navy was thinking of making an offer, too. Charles wished they would keep him informed of their plans but despaired of cooperation between navy and state. The left hand of Lincoln's administration never knew what the right hand was doing. Brunnow apparently got more information from his Russian admirals than Charles did from Washington.

"The Lairds make the finest war vessels. I wish our own shipyards could compete. They used to, when Peter Alekseyevich was at the helm. But the day will come again, God willing. Until then, we must buy," Brunnow said with a philosophical air.

The Russian ambassador glanced round the milling crowd and added in a confidential tone, "We think that the transfer of the ships from the Atlantic to the Baltic may also be of use to our friends."

Charles nodded. "I'm certain that my government would look with appreciation on the purchase. As you know, we've raised our concern about these particular vessels with Lord Russell repeatedly."

Despite his speculations to Henry and Dudley, Charles still feared that the ships were headed for the Confederacy. Bulloch hadn't been seen in Liverpool in a month, but that meant little. He was an implacable, cunning opponent who would stop at nothing. A boilermaker recently swore in an affidavit that he had seen the Confederate captain giving directions to the foreman for the two new vessels, called the *294* and the *295* by the shipyard. Dudley had also taken a statement from Clarence Yonge, the consul's spy on board the *Alabama*. Yonge swore that both the *294* and the *295* were being built as Confederate warships.

"We've met in Lord Russell's chambers more than once, but I've noticed that your conversations with him do not make you very happy," Brunnow said.

"A diplomat's life isn't always a happy one," Charles replied, taking a canapé offered by a waiter. "But we eat well."

The jovial Russian laughed. He accepted a square of melba toast heaped with black caviar and minced egg.

"Lord Russell asserts that his hands are tied by British law," Charles continued in a more serious tone. "He seems to consider the escape of the CSS *Alabama* and *Florida* a misfortune, but no one's fault. 'I can't go beyond the law,' he has told me any number of times."

"It seems a poor law that cannot prevent such a mockery of the British Crown's Neutrality Proclamation," Brunnow said.

"I agree. And I assure you that we appreciate Russian support in these difficult times."

"Your president and our tsar are like cousins," Brunnow said. He took another square of toast and caviar from a passing waiter. "Alexander Nikolaevich freed the serfs in 1861, just as your war started. Now no man is the property of another. The tsar is a great reformer, like Lincoln. The world is changing. You see, the tsar wants you to win your war. Our admiralty plans to send the navy on a goodwill visit to New York this fall. That should make clear whose side Russia is on. Perhaps the Laird Rams will be in our fleet."

Charles contemplated the image of the ironclad rams sailing up the Hudson under the Russian flag. It would be better than the Stars and Bars of the Confederacy.

"You know that I spent my childhood in Moscow?" Charles asked.

"*Da,*" Brunnow replied.

"My father told me that he enjoyed his conversations with Alexander I, your tsar's grandfather. He considered him a real friend to America."

"Russia and America have always been friends."

Charles didn't think it politic to repeat the criticisms of Russian autocracy that his father also sprinkled liberally in his reminiscences. Instead, he replied, "I would like you to know that in my family we have an especially good feeling about the name Alexander."

"Thank you," Brunnow said with a small bow. "May I say that we Russians have a good feeling about the name Adams?"

At that moment, Abby returned on the arm of an elegant middle-aged man with wavy dark hair that brushed his collar like Lord Byron's. He wore an eager, anticipatory smile.

"Charles . . . Your Excellency . . . may I present Randolph Barclay? Mr. Barclay is a leading figure in the Union and Emancipation Society."

"Mr. Barclay. What a pleasure to meet you," Charles replied, shaking the Englishman's hand with genuine appreciation. "Mrs. Adams told me about your fine speech last week. I wish I could have heard it."

Abby frequently sat in the ladies' section at the London meetings of the society, which had organized numerous public gatherings around the country since the first of January. Enthusiastic audiences cheered speakers who read Lincoln's proclamation aloud. The English were considerably more excited about abolition than the majority of Americans, from whom it was exacting a higher price. Nevertheless, Lincoln had finally fired the passion of English liberals. John Stuart Mill, Harriet Martineau, and John Cairnes, all stalwart defenders of liberty, stood in the leadership of the Union and Emancipation Society.

"Mrs. Adams is too kind. I merely paraphrased what many others have said better. Palmerston's government is guilty of the grossest violation of Her Majesty's neutrality," Mr. Barclay replied.

Charles shook his head. "If I may say so, it is you who are too modest. Your speech was inspired."

Ambassador Brunnow interrupted. "If you will forgive me, it is I who am too hungry. Mr. Adams, perhaps you will allow me to escort Mrs. Adams to the table?"

Charles smiled. "Of course, Baron. I would be very grateful. We shall follow shortly."

Abby took the Russian's arm and left in the same direction from which she had brought Randolph Barclay. She had an unerring sense of timing, Charles noted. If she hadn't been a diplomat's wife, Abby would have made a nimble stage manager.

Randolph Barclay leaned avidly into his point. "The shipbuilding interests are making a travesty of our neutrality."

"I couldn't agree more, though I do understand that the Foreign Ministry can't hold itself above the law. Lord Russell has been most courteous. I believe he would act more forcefully if he could."

"Perhaps. Old Johnny used to be a firebrand on abolition. But power corrupts, you know."

Charles avoided agreeing with Barclay, conscious that any criticism of the foreign secretary made outside the four walls of the legation could easily worm its way back to Westminster, no matter how well-intentioned one's listener might be. "We were especially grateful for your references to the Laird Rams in your speech," Charles said instead. "We remain extremely concerned about them."

"I think you should be concerned. Everyone knows that the Scots are up to their red eyebrows in the Confederate conspiracy. John Laird likes to pretend otherwise, but the British public won't be fooled. That's why our government's behavior is so reprehensible, so truly reprehensible."

"We have proof that the rams were originally commissioned by the Confederacy," Charles noted, "but as you may be aware the Lairds recently declared that the unfinished ships are up for sale. So now we have to see to whom ownership will be transferred."

"That is the question. Watch carefully. I doubt the Confederate agents or their English accomplices will give up easily. They're stubborn men. A bogus ownership transfer is easy enough to arrange."

Randolph Barclay paused, and a strange, uncomfortable expression passed over his handsome face that Charles did not know how to interpret. Guilt? Dismay?

"I probably shouldn't say this," Barclay said after a moment's hesitation, "but my brother-in-law is one of Laird's backers. Walter Birch is a bulldog when he's got something between his teeth."

Charles raised an eyebrow at the family connection, but said simply, "I'm aware of the Confederates' persistence, Mr. Barclay, and I thank you for your words of warning. You can be sure that we're watching quite closely."

A chime sounded the call to be seated. The pianist on a raised dais began playing Henry Purcell's *Sweeter than Roses*. Crystal vases of tulips, narcissus, and hyacinths on the banquet tables testified that the musical selection for the prince's March wedding was apt.

"It looks as though we ought to find our places," Randolph

observed. "Your wife must be wondering what has become of you."

"Yes, and again, thank you for your stirring speech at the Union and Emancipation Society," Charles said.

Randolph shook the minister's hand warmly. "It's the least I can do. Some Londoners may not yet agree, but I'm certain that history will prove your Mr. Lincoln right."

~~~~~

THIRTY-FOUR

April 1863

*Eliza made her desperate retreat across the river just in the dusk
of twilight. The gray mist of evening, rising slowly
from the river, enveloped her as she disappeared up the bank.*

—Harriet Beecher Stowe, *Uncle Tom's Cabin*

The first shorebirds had appeared the evening before, when Julia took a turn on deck just before sunset. The experienced matron to whom she had attached herself early in the voyage told her to look for seaweed, but she hadn't spotted any. Instead, it was a flock of brown and black geese squawking overhead that alerted her to the approach of land after many long days at sea.

Two weeks earlier, her father had wanted Julia to attend the wedding of the prince of Wales with him. It was the first truly festive public event since Prince Albert's death a year and a half earlier. Julia complained of a spring sniffle and steadfastly maintained that she couldn't be seen with a red nose.

She looked well to him, Walter commented, but did not persist. He seemed to believe that she would resume the role of contented housekeeper if given a little time. But once her father's carriage had left for the wedding, Julia twisted her grandmother's ruby ring off her finger. Underneath, the skin was red and chafed.

She moved quickly, for fear that she would lose her resolve. She set the ring beside a sealed note telling her father that she would write when she reached her destination. She had posted a letter to Edmund the night before, explaining her mission and asking him to look out for their father. She hoped he would understand.

Her uncle had. In fact, he had given her the loan that made flight possible.

"For what do you need it?" he asked. "Surely your father has given you funds."

"He gives me a monthly allowance," she answered evasively, "but I won't come into funds of my own until I marry."

"But isn't your allowance sufficient for the time being, my dear? Your father is quite wealthy."

"My father and I have developed some grave differences," she told him directly. "I'm not sure how long I can live under his roof."

Randolph's brow wrinkled with worried surprise. "You may take over my house in the country if you like," he offered.

"Thank you, but I can't. At least not right now. But I beg you not to say anything to Father. Promise me that you won't."

"Of course not, but please, Julia, don't do anything rash."

Julia couldn't make that promise because she had something very rash in mind, indeed. Instead, she asked, "Just tell me, Uncle, if I were to marry a man of whom *you* would approve—a person of integrity and substance—might you consider granting me a small dowry? Just something so that I could hold my head up?"

Randolph questioned her closely about the unnamed gentleman's suitability, but in the end he agreed to the unusual proposition. Julia knew without being told that her uncle hated to see the daughter of his dead sister, the only woman to whom he had ever been close, under the thumb of Sir Walter Birch.

On the day of the prince of Wales's wedding, the largest, most important event in London's social calendar, Julia told Mrs. Worthy that she was going out for some fresh air. It was true. She couldn't breathe any longer at Belfield Manor.

A trunk with Edmund's clothes and a few simple dresses was

awaiting her at a bustling inn near Waterloo Station. She had engaged the room in her deceased granduncle's name and sent the trunk on ahead.

When she got to the inn that morning, Julia took a key from the front desk for the declared purpose of setting her uncle's rooms to rights. The rest was easy. She'd left through the smoky tavern a new man. The hotel key was handed off to the barkeep, who called a porter to carry her trunk. Julia had no idea when she had become so brazen. Walking with a long, confident stride— her stature of use, for once—she simply pretended to be Edmund. The patrons who gave her admiring glances when she walked into the hotel ignored her when she left. She was invisible. Gone on the train to Southampton port as neatly as a hat trick.

Since only the Confederacy was under blockade, purchasing a ticket for a regular steamship crossing to New York had been a simple matter. Commercial traffic to and from America remained brisk, with war providing its usual incentive to profits. On board, Julia tried to use as few words as possible when answering the white-liveried steward who asked which cabin she had booked.

"Second class. Portside. Number 442."

She spoke gruffly, lowering her voice to what she hoped was a manly timbre. It sounded unconvincing to her ears, but the steward just heaved her trunk onto a trolley and crooked his head aft in the direction of a long corridor.

Julia had planned every move carefully, choosing a small interior cabin that would provide privacy and excite no attention. The servants in second class would be far too busy carrying out slops and exchanging bed linens on the crowded ship to trouble themselves over the identity of an undemanding passenger.

Julia followed the steward, maintaining the long stride that had taken her from Waterloo Station to the docks at Southampton. He finally stopped and took out a set of keys. He tried one, and then another. Overcoming her self-consciousness for a moment, Julia saw him clearly for the first time. His collar was loose on his thin, lightly freckled neck. She realized that he was just a boy. Probably not even sixteen, Edmund's age.

The inexperienced steward tried a third key. This time he jammed it into the lock, turned the key hard one way and then the next. He mumbled an apology and hoisted down the bag he had been carrying on his shoulder. The young man flushed, looked more closely at the ring of keys in his hand, and then glanced up at Julia.

"I'm sorry, sir," he said with obvious embarrassment. He wore an expression that seemed almost fearful. "If you'll wait, I'll find the head steward. He has the master keys. I'm really very sorry for the trouble. I'm new." The boy looked around the empty corridor in a mild panic, as if hoping to conjure up a settee for the inconvenienced passenger.

Julia instinctively leaned forward to reassure him, but quickly drew back. "It's no trouble," she said. "No trouble at all," she added in a lower tone. "Let me see those."

The steward handed her the ring. Julia sorted through the keys and selected one that looked especially worn. She slipped it into the lock, which turned easily.

"How did you know?" the steward asked, his eyes wide.

"It's seen the most use," Julia said, thinking of the brass key ring that Mrs. Worthy kept in the pantry of Belfield Manor.

"Thank you, sir," the young man said. He looked at her closely for half a moment, as if puzzling over something, then gestured for her to enter in front of him. He pushed the trunk into the room and lifted it onto the narrow bunk. "Should I summon one of the chambermaids to help you unpack, sir?"

"No, that will be all."

Julia shoved a hand into her pocket and drew out a shilling.

The steward glanced down at the coin she proffered, and then looked up with an expression that still seemed quizzical. "Thank you, sir."

When he left, Julia turned the lock on the door and then slid the bolt that ensured complete privacy. It was hot in the small cabin, but she felt wonderfully relieved to be alone. She immediately took off Edmund's hat and let down her pinned hair, running her fingers through the damp tresses. Then she opened the trunk, shook out the first gown, and began hanging. As she placed the last dress in the cabin's small locker, Julia noticed her right hand—slim and elegant, still gloved in white. A glove set with pearl buttons.

For a moment, she stopped breathing. The steward had noticed the feminine gloves. What if he told someone? No, she thought quickly, he was a novice; he wouldn't know what to make of it. Overwhelmed by his duties. Someone she would probably never see again.

Julia sat down on the bunk, her knees suddenly weak. No one else was likely to realize that the slender young man who boarded under the name of Julian Birch had exchanged places with a tall dark-haired woman named Julia. Yet if she was caught in the lie, the ship's owners would certainly return her to her guardian's custody, with apologies for causing him any distress. She would have to be very, very careful to avoid the curious eyes of the newest steward. How could she have been so stupid as to overlook that detail?

To her relief, she did not see him again on the passenger ship during the course of the fortnight. The end of each uneventful day on board the crowded liner brought another reprieve. Now, from the deck of the steamship, the gold-and-pink sunrise was becoming more glorious by the moment. As Julia watched, the hazy shoreline grew distinct and she could see trees toward which the shorebirds seemed to be wheeling. Her great-grandparents had fled from America during its first civil war, the revolution in the colonies. It was hard to believe the place was real, and half its citizens under siege. Yet Julia felt no fear, only a sharp exhilaration. The horizon seemed hers, like a birthright.

A clean spring breeze carried the earthy scent of the approaching landmass. Julia gripped the damp railing of the deck and faced the wind with mounting excitement. Somewhere out there, very close, was Baxter Sams. She would find him.

THIRTY-FIVE

*Yesterday we went to the Capitol grounds to see our returned
prisoners. . . . Oh, these men were so forlorn, so dried up, so
shrunken. There was such a strange look in the eyes of some;
others were so restless and wild looking; others again had placidly
vacant faces, as if they had been dead to the world for years.*

—Mary Boykin Chesnut, *A Diary from Dixie*

With Sweetwood gone, they didn't talk about the menu anymore. Council's new friend from Louisiana, Billy Ray Wallace, was a poor boy who had gone to sea early. He'd never eaten much beyond navy beans and sea biscuits.

"Billy Ray," Council said as they stood in line, "you ain't still working that knot?"

"Oh, I got it. I'm just making it better," Wallace piped in a youthful voice. Wallace had his towhead down, playing with a short stretch of the dirty rope they'd filched one day on garbage detail. It provided him and Council with endless diversion, comparing fancy nautical knots they knew.

"Well, don't shilly-shally, now. It's my turn," Council said. He flexed and straightened his fingers at his sides, like a man flicking water. He grimaced twice in rapid succession, a nervous tic left over from the forced march toward death that Lonigan had finished and he'd escaped. Council turned to Baxter. The doctor was looking up at the span of sky framed by the walls of the fort.

"Whatcha looking at?" Council asked. He scratched his thin backside. "Dang fleas, they done used me up."

"Just the seagulls . . . Look!" Baxter exclaimed, suddenly pointing west. "Do you see that one? I think he's got a fish."

Council searched the sky.

"Missed him. Too bad he didn't drop it. The only fresh fish we get are outta Tennessee," Council complained, using the prison slang for new inmates.

"That bird's probably just as hungry as we are," Baxter replied, still squinting up at the sky. "And he's got no one to feed him."

"Well, we don't neither, from what I can see," Council said. "Damn, this line is slow. Why are there allus a hundred men in front of us? Why can't we be first just once?"

Baxter looked down the irregular line of filthy, unshaved prisoners. The server at the soup cauldron was standing with his arms crossed, talking to a guard. Baxter guessed the pot was empty and the man was waiting for another from the kitchen. Forward motion had ground to a halt.

Fear suddenly swept over Baxter like a cold wash. What if that was all they had? What if the kitchen had run out? Would they have to wait until supper for the next round of rations? Baxter didn't think he could make it through the hunger.

He closed his eyes and looked back up at the sky, forcing his jangled nerves to relax by concentrating on the seagulls. The lack of food and the cramped, dirty quarters preyed on their spirits. Warden Wood had cut the prisoners' exercise time in half a few months earlier, and though he had placed the blame on overcrowding, the men considered his action to be one more example of spite toward secessionists. They were now allowed into the yard for only half an hour, twice a day. Panic and paranoia came easily, surfacing like a venomous cottonmouth in the marsh.

Roast beef and horseradish no longer came to mind. They were too exotic and unreal. Instead, Baxter pictured his old life in Virginia when he had fed his horse on oats, jealous now of the plump, cakelike grains. He would give almost anything for just a bowl of porridge. Thick and filling oatmeal seemed like nature's best gift.

When released, Virgil Sweetwood had bequeathed his heavy uniform coat to Baxter, who now pulled the gray wool tighter against the spring breeze. Any wind seemed chilly now, thin as he was. The sun was struggling to burn through the leaden clouds overhead. It was the same sky as that above London, the same sun shining down, Baxter told himself. He remembered Julia Birch sitting on the window seat at Belfield Manor. The image pushed the hunger from his mind, even if he couldn't entirely ignore the pitiless churning in his belly.

She's probably reading one of her books, he thought. She probably has a stack so high it could break a man's foot if it fell on him. She could build a bridge to China with those books. She could make a stair to heaven. A slight smile came to his lips at the images and then died away.

The warden had withdrawn mail privileges, too. The prisoners weren't allowed to send or receive letters any longer. Federal policy.

The wave of anxiety washed over him again. Had Julia written him? What if she thought he was ignoring her letters? Or that he had died? He had no way of holding on to her now, not even with chicken scratch on paper.

He ran his hand over his hair to brush away the morbid thoughts. "Brace up," he told himself, "be a man. Think of something else."

"Hey, Dev," he said, turning to his friend. "Tell me about the time you got caught in that hurricane off Santo Domingo. How many days did you get whipped about? I've forgotten."

A rare smile broke across Council's hollow face. He took a deep breath, just as the line began to inch forward again.

"Well, it was so bad that the captain made us strap him to the wheel," he started in. "I wasn't too worried 'cause I figure if you're born to hang, you won't drown. But I can tell you it was pretty lively for a while. You see, just when you think you're past a *hurricano*, and the waves have dropped from sixty feet down to maybe forty, it'll . . ."

Jostling up ahead interrupted his tale.

"Hey, he's flanking!" Baxter heard someone yell.

An angry murmur broke out and the line instinctively lurched forward. The guards didn't worry about catching prisoners trying to double back for seconds. The inmates were far more jealous of the camp's food than the sentries were. Council craned his neck to see who was trying to get away with it this time. Baxter, a good eight inches taller, peered over his head.

In the line of prisoners coming back with their rations, Baxter spotted Jack King gripping his tin plate with both hands. The tall Mississippian was wearing a grim, determined expression. He appeared not to hear the irate accusations flying at his back.

"Dammit!" Council spat with disgust. "We're fuckin' low on beans already. Flanking! That's vile."

Council, close to the ground at five feet five and as ornery as ever, ducked low and stuck out his foot like a board as King walked by, staring straight ahead.

The former whiskey smuggler didn't see it coming and fell flat out. The tin plate hit the pavement with a ping, and his beans and gravy spilled onto the ground. The plate continued rolling on its side, turning juicy cartwheels across the yard.

King jumped up, quick as a snake, and swung a hard fist at Baxter. Baxter threw up a hand to block his face and caught the brutal blow on his wrist. He heard, more than felt, the crack.

Council threw himself onto King's back. The Mississippi ruffian shrugged off the scrawny sailor with a single powerful twist and grabbed Baxter's collar. He closed ten fingers around the doctor's throat and squeezed down.

The viselike fingers dug into Baxter's flesh, depressing his trachea. He kicked out at King but missed the shin he was aiming for. His throat burned. The deadly pressure lifted Baxter onto his toes. He kicked wildly and missed again. His head pounded with the force of pent-up blood. He couldn't breathe. How had King retained so much strength? Baxter wrenched his head to the side, until King's fingers pulled slightly apart and he was able to gulp a breath, but King bore down again, digging deeper into Baxter's neck.

The Mississippian leaned into his face. Baxter felt King's hot, rancid breath. "You fucking weasel. You stinking razorback!" he hissed. "I'll teach you to rat on me. You been agin' me from the start. Think you're so damned smart. Talk so fancy." King tightened his iron grip until Baxter could hear a rattling wheeze. Was that his windpipe?

Fighting panic and sucking air, Baxter resisted the primal instinct to pull away. Instead, he caught hold of King's homespun coat and jerked the man closer into his own body, and thrust his knee sharply upward into King's groin. The pressure on Baxter's neck ceased and the Mississippian sagged downward in agony just as two guards caught him at the elbow. A third stood off to one side with a shotgun leveled at King's head. He cocked the gun with a loud, sharp click that brought all commotion to a standstill.

"Well, well. It looks like you're in the market for some new jewelry," the guard wheezed. "Guess you're gunna get some new chains."

The man gestured with his gun in the direction of the cells. "Gentlemen," he said to the other guards, "could you please drag this man's pitiful Rebel ass back to the holding cell? We got ourselves a job." The guard then stepped forward and pointed his gun skyward. He kicked King viciously in the shin, landing the blow that Baxter had failed to. "And I don't like extra work, Johnny. I got plenty to do already."

THE SURGEON WRAPPED Baxter's broken wrist with a skilled hand. "That should do you," he said, tucking under and pinning the end of the bandage. "But don't try to swim to Staten Island, you hear?"

"I'll bear that in mind," Baxter said.

"Sorry there's nothing I can do about your throat. Those bruises will heal in a few days, though. You'll be able to swallow better."

Baxter nodded. "That water burned like moonshine." He inspected his wrist. "That's as fine a job as any I saw in London. Nice work."

"Thank you. I never had much book learning, but I got plenty of practice before I took that slug to the knee at Shiloh. I can't complain, though. The Reb who did it may have saved my life. Lafayette isn't such a bad rock to watch the war from."

Baxter raised an eyebrow.

"Maybe not from your point of view," the doctor admitted. "But it's better than a lot of places they coulda sent me. A couple hundred men at Lafayette is nothing compared to the ten thousand Rebs they've got down at Camp Delaware. I've heard more die in prison than on the battlefield, if you'll pardon my saying so."

Baxter tried to imagine being penned up with ten thousand half-starved men. He couldn't. Lice, fleas, and bedbugs would be the least of one's worries. Smallpox, dysentery, and typhoid would take out hundreds under such crowded conditions. Death might be welcome. On the battlefield, the suffering was at least over quickly.

The surgeon's eyes suddenly crinkled in merriment. "A friend wrote me that there's more life *on* the POWs than in them!" With that he slapped his knee and guffawed so hard that he had to wipe his eyes.

"Sorry about that," he said finally. "Gallows humor. Ya gotta laugh sometimes. I guess it's pretty hard to keep down the bugs in the larger camps."

"It's pretty hard here, too."

"Yeah, well, I'm right sorry to say it's not likely to get much better. Secretary of War Stanton now says he'll cut off prisoner exchanges if Jeff Davis doesn't back down. Davis says he's going to hang any white Union officer caught leading black troops, and sell off any enlisted men. Apparently they've already auctioned one Negro POW in Texas. I can tell you the newspapers had a field day. His folks are pillars of the community in Massachusetts."

"But how will the prisons cope? Don't they count on the exchanges to make room for new people?" Baxter asked. "There isn't enough food and water to go around already."

"I don't know. We'll be swamped, that's for sure. And it looks like the Confederate Congress is going to back Davis. They're still hopping mad about the Emancipation Proclamation."

The surgeon grew thoughtful and began rolling up the cloth left over from setting Baxter's bone. "You know, it's too bad you're in here. A London-trained medical man like you changing bedsheets and emptying chamber pots. Taking a beating from an uneducated hooligan. Seems a shame."

"Perhaps you would like to share that opinion with the warden," Baxter said, keeping his voice light.

"You're pretty dang scrawny, too, and I think there's something wrong with your eyes. Have you noticed them itching? Seems like you're blinking an awful lot."

"They don't itch, but they have been giving me some trouble in the mornings. My tear ducts seem to be working overtime. I assume it's the dust."

"Well, whatever it is, prison doesn't agree with you much." The medic paused. "You know we need trained surgeons. We need 'em bad."

"What do you mean?"

"We need surgeons on the lines. You wouldn't have to fire any bullets, just dig 'em out."

Baxter looked at the Union medic, whose graying hair and

kindly expression reminded him of his father. It was tempting to think of him that way—to believe they were both part of some larger fraternity, as medical men or as Americans. But he couldn't anymore. The man was a Yankee, which made him a damn Yankee. And Baxter was a Southerner, a Johnny Reb. Prison had taught him that. Every day inside widened the gap. Hell, he'd even inherited the uniform. He'd be strung from a tree before he defected to the Union.

Baxter shook his head. "I'm afraid that would require taking the oath."

"What, too proud to 'swallow the yellow dog'? Others have done it."

"I know. But I won't."

"You could take the noncombatant's oath. They wouldn't put a gun in your hands."

Baxter looked down at his bandaged wrist, avoiding the man's eyes. He didn't trust his own resolution. He knew there were extra rations in the back closet. Prisoners who were starting to fade were given food to replenish their strength, so they could go back into the cells and starve some more. Baxter had spoon-fed them himself. Would the cupboard open if he said yes? Would they fatten him up to send him out onto the lines?

A traitorous hunger roared up in his stomach at the thought. Just a biscuit would be fine—or two, or ten.

In the ensuing silence, the faint hum of a harmonica drifted through the open window. Someone in the cells below was playing "Swanee River."

Far, far away, Baxter thought, supplying the lyrics in his mind. His mother liked to play it on the piano. The world suddenly seemed as sad and weary as the song suggested, and he took up the melody quietly, whistling through his teeth.

"I think it's riskier in here than it is out there," the surgeon said. "And I know the food's a damn sight better in the army."

"Anything's got to be better," Baxter agreed. Then he shook

his head. "I know you want to help, but my brothers are on the other side. I won't swear allegiance to people who are trying to kill them."

"That's mighty noble, but I don't think that Jack King is going to be so gentle next time. He's the type to hang on to a grudge, I suspect."

"I plan to keep out of his way."

"How you'll do that in a twenty-foot cell is beyond me—but all right," the surgeon said with a shrug. "It's your funeral. You'll have to tough it out. Seems a pity, though. You Rebs are as stubborn as mules."

Were Southerners really as stubborn as mules, or did they just have a death wish? Baxter asked himself silently. It seemed he had become as contrary as Jeff Davis. No wonder there was a war on.

THIRTY-SIX

MAY 1863

They are discussing in Congress the question of retaliation of
ill usage upon our prisoners of war. . . . If the rebels will feed our
prisoners on turtle-soup, theirs should be fed the same.
If they give them a pint of meal a day, theirs
should have no more, man for man.

—Henry Adams to his brother Charles,
A Cycle of Adams Letters

Julia lifted the hem of her hoop skirt off the littered pavement
and climbed the short flight to the prisoner-exchange section
of the War Department. The temporary office was crammed into
a first-floor, front-facing tenement on Orchard Street. At that
same moment, a woman in bright, cheap finery exited the front
door with a flirtatious backward laugh and sallied down the narrow stairs toward the street. Julia stepped aside, conscious that it
was more perilous to descend than to climb. The lower-class girl
didn't notice the courtesy, however, and merely smiled as she
swept past. "Hallo there," she called cheerily without stopping, as
though they were acquainted. Julia didn't have time to return the
greeting before the girl was swallowed by a bustling crowd of
peddlers and pedestrians.

The social equality between strangers in New York City had
surprised Julia from the first. No one seemed reluctant to address
those who in England would have been recognized as their bet-
ters. Even the laundress who delivered clean towels at the hotel

made small talk like a neighbor. Once, when Julia absently ignored a question, the woman bristled, as if the Englishwoman was putting on airs. Julia took care next time to pay closer mind and avoid giving offense. It felt strange to trip over routine social cues.

Not as strange, however, as walking into the office concerned with Southern prisoners of war, Julia reflected as she looked around her. She had traveled thousands of miles in order to arrive at this one spot. The office was dim and deserted, disconcertingly unprepossessing.

The only occupant was a middle-aged officer slouched over a counter strewn with papers. He glanced up at her without interest. The collar of his blue uniform was buttoned tightly, pushing the creased skin of his neck toward his heavy jaw. The sweltering humidity of summer had raised small beads along his receding hairline, like a row of piping, although the day had scarcely begun.

"Yeah?" he said as she approached.

"Good day, Officer," Julia said. "I'm here to inquire about the release of a British prisoner at Fort Lafayette."

A flicker of suspicion crossed his brow and then died of apparent boredom. The man shook his head. "We don't keep British prisoners in Lafayette, miss. They're held over at the Tombs. You better check there."

"I'm aware of that, sir, but it appears that a British citizen has been mistaken for an American. He's being held at the wrong facility."

The suspicious look flared up again. "I don't know what you're talking about, but there are no English prisoners at Fort Lafayette, miss. Anyone out there is a Reb. Ain't a shadow of a doubt."

"Yes, I know that is the policy, but this appears to be a case of mistaken nationality. The papers that prove the matter were sent here from London."

The man's eyes narrowed to a slit. "You his sister or something?"

"No, I'm a friend," Julia answered, her heart giving a thump at the direct inquiry. She hadn't thought about how to explain the connection. She hadn't anticipated being asked such a personal question. It wasn't done at home. Julia felt the start of a flush in her face; she believed that what she was doing was right, but she also knew that it was wrong—or at least most people would think so. Guilt had a way of sneaking up when her guard was down.

"Hmm. Well, the Rebs have a whole *lot* of English friends from what I hear." He tore off the edge of a piece of paper on the counter and picked up his pencil. "What's this one's name?"

"H. Baxter Sams," Julia said, leaning forward slightly to watch him write. "There's an *s* on the end," she added.

"It sure doesn't sound English. And what kind of first name is Baxter? Sounds to me like he's right out of Dixie. Raised on cornpone and collard greens, I'll bet."

He turned with the piece of paper and sauntered through a door behind the counter. "Wait there," the officer ordered over his shoulder before closing the door.

Julia took a seat across from the counter. Dust collected on the unswept floor in wispy nests under a long line of empty chairs. The release of prisoners apparently didn't occasion much foot traffic, and the homely room looked like the front office of a desolate warehouse that dealt in dry goods, rather than the imposing gates to Hades she had imagined.

The door to the street opened and a young lieutenant walked in, his Federal uniform crisp despite the moist heat. The man looked startled to see Julia, but then gave her a brash, appraising smile once his eyes registered the deserted counter. He tipped his blue hat.

Julia cast her eyes quickly downward with what she hoped was the universal sign of unavailability. No gentleman openly greeted a lady until she gave him leave, and she had certainly not done so. Just then the door behind the counter opened and the desk officer reappeared. He nodded silently at the young lieutenant, who took a last, undisguised gander at Julia before slipping into the interior office.

The officer brought forward a thick, well-used ledger book. "We don't have any record of that, miss."

"I'm sorry," Julia said, stepping quickly back to the counter. "A record of what, precisely?"

"A record of correspondence," the officer snapped, as if tired of explaining the obvious. "We haven't received any letters or petitions concerning that name."

"But I sent the packet of documents from London nearly two months ago. It should have arrived well before now."

"That may be so, but it ain't here. We don't have it."

"It has to be here," Julia insisted with rising alarm. "There was a note from a London barrister explaining the problem, along with a birth document from St. Paul's Cathedral in London. Mr. Charles Francis Adams sent a letter as well."

"I don't know who that is, but I do know that we have nothing for this fellow." The soldier pointed a stubby finger at the scrap on which he had written Baxter's name.

"Mr. Adams is the American minister to the Court of St. James's. Surely you're familiar with him," Julia stated. She could hear her voice rising.

"Minister to St. James's? You mean the Brits?" The stocky officer snorted with disgust. "Well, I guess somebody's got to walk that picket. Poor sap. Must be frustrating, watching John Bull fatten himself at our expense, unable to do anything about it."

"Mr. Adams is the son of John Quincy Adams, your sixth president," Julia retorted with disdain, stung at the insult. "I assume you know *his* name, at least."

The soldier flashed her a resentful glance. "Yeah, I know that name, but I don't know this one." He crumpled the piece of paper.

"I apologize," she said quickly, fear dousing her anger. "It's just that I've come such a long way."

She took a deep breath and put on as pleasant a face as she could manage. "Could you . . . could you please look again? Perhaps someone else in your office has the documents. Really, they must be here. I'm certain of it."

The soldier looked at her hard for an instant, and then sighed as if bored anew. He flattened out the scrap and placed it like a bookmark in the ledger before shutting the heavy tome. "Yeah, well, I'll ask around. You can check back in a few days if you want. But don't get your hopes up."

His warning was unnecessary. Julia walked back out into the noisy crush of the bustling street, painfully aware that her entire plan might be ruined. She had no copies of the documents she had sent, and it would take months to recover them if she had to return to England. Her uncle's money wouldn't last. The chance to free Baxter Sams might be lost altogether. In fact, he might be gone already, one more casualty of the endless war.

She squeezed her eyes hard against the hot tears welling up. Determined not to lose control, she balled her gloved right hand and turned in the direction of her hotel, but suddenly found herself in a whirl of street urchins. They looked like ragpickers. One of the taller, more heavily muscled boys stared straight at Julia for a moment, close enough to touch her and apparently arrested by something in her appearance. It reminded Julia that she was an easy and obvious target, so she gripped her handbag firmly under her arm, reined in her emotions more sternly, stood tall, and pushed through the crowd toward her hotel.

She would track down the packet, no matter what it took. The alternatives were unthinkable.

———

JULIA WAITED FOUR days before returning, anxious not to further alienate the resentful officer at the front desk, but the man was gone, his place taken by the young officer who had stared at her so boldly the first time. He wrote down Baxter's name with exaggerated care, placed the piece of paper in a file, and asked if she was hitched. Julia wasn't sure what the phrase meant, but his tone suggested that the inquiry was improper, if not insulting to a gentlewoman.

She asked to see a superior officer at once, and he emerged from the back office with all the joy of a man roused from a Sunday nap. They started over. When the documents were finally located after two weeks of patient visits, she was informed that only the British Consulate could make representations on behalf of British citizens. She returned the following week with the consul, only to be told that such representations must be made in Washington.

It was a month before the consulate could part with a staff member to go to the capital. They were only now headed south on a train. The cars were crowded with jostling, blue-uniformed soldiers who appeared to outnumber civilian passengers. Most carried rifles and sabers, and some had pistols strapped to their waists.

At the front of the train, an older, apparently seasoned officer sat on an overturned barrel. He was sleeping with his head tilted back against the doorway and his mouth slightly open. A purplish knot of scrambled flesh covered the spot where his ear should have been. For the first time, Julia felt the hot breath of the war. She wondered how many of the men before her eyes would survive the season. They were all ages. Some looked as if they should be in schoolrooms, others running farms.

The temperature climbed with every town they passed, mercury and train heading in opposite directions. The humidity was outrageous. Julia could hardly imagine why anyone would choose to live under such sweltering conditions. The tulle on the high neck of her dress scratched as if ants were filing in and out, and her shirtwaist felt as if the laundress had forgotten to iron out the steam. The junior consul sat across from her. He was a portly, dark-haired young man whose cheeks shone with dewy perspiration. He pretended to be engrossed in *The New York Times*, but she could feel his sidelong glances. She kept trying to read *Wuthering Heights*, one more tragic romance sent by Louise, who still hoped to divert Julia from the path of doom. Nonetheless, it was something to take her mind off her worries.

Without warning, the train began to slow and Julia saw that they were heading onto a side spur to allow yet another southbound train to pass. It was the fourth time that morning. From what she could spy from her window, all the other trains were equally crammed with bluecoats, which made it hard to fathom why their journey South should be so much more urgent than that of the train she was on. Weren't all the soldiers going to the same place?

The junior consul put down his newspaper, apparently glad for an excuse to stop reading. "I can't imagine why we are pulling off again," Mr. Braithwaite said, as if guessing her thoughts.

"It is inexplicable," Julia agreed.

"Like so much about America," Braithwaite said with a philosophical shrug. "It's hard to believe this nation was ever part of the British Empire. We're lucky to have separated from them. Such disorder. I can tell you, it's taken some getting used to."

"How long have you been here, if I may ask?"

"Nearly three years. I expect to be recalled to London in the fall. I'm hoping that my next posting will be somewhere a bit more civilized. Or at least cooler."

"It's very good of you to make this trip to Washington with me at the height of summer," Julia said with sincere gratitude. "To be honest, I had not anticipated that it would take so long to resolve this matter or that it would require visiting the capital."

"The American government seems to make up the rules as it

goes along. It was much better before the war, of course. Now we resign ourselves to mostly futile gestures, trying to defend the rights of our citizens. We've quite a few Englishmen stranded behind the blockade in the South, and any number of others whose property has been seized from merchant ships as contraband."

"Futile gestures? Why futile?" Julia asked. The sense of alarm that she often found herself battling flared again. "Surely the government listens to your representations?"

"Yes, of course, but they don't always agree, even with one another. We find ourselves running higgledy-piggledy from one government department to another, each afraid to make a controversial ruling first. The bureaucracy has become enormous and is completely disorganized."

Julia's eyes grew wide, and her distress was so apparent that the junior consul added, "Of course, we believe that the case involving Mr. Sams should be fairly straightforward. After all, we already have the approval of Mr. Adams in London, which should help a great deal. His name carries weight."

"I should hope so," said Julia, looking down. Her nerves had been so strained by the weeks of uncertainty that she didn't trust herself to say more. The silence between them stretched into minutes. Julia hardly noticed.

"I say, are you related to Mr. Sams?" her companion finally blurted out, vulgar curiosity obviously getting the better of his manners.

Julia stiffened and looked up. "I'm a friend of the family. As you are surely aware, they are unable to travel freely themselves, considering the war. They, too, are stranded behind the blockade."

"And you're here alone? In the States?" Braithwaite's eyes revealed an unseemly voyeurism.

"I'm here with my family's permission. My brother would

normally accompany me, but he is unable to travel at the moment and the situation is rather urgent, as you are aware."

Julia was uncomfortably conscious of the lie, or, at least, dissimulation. Her brother might have approved—had she asked him—but her father never would. She looked Braithwaite straight in the eye, however. She needed his help, and it was indeed poor breeding on his part to ask such a personal question. The three years away from England showed.

It was the junior consul who averted his eyes this time, pretending to find an article of engrossing interest in his newspaper. After a moment, the train jerked to life again and began backing onto the main track. Braithwaite glanced up with a tight smile. "Yes, well, I sincerely hope we are able to help him. I shall do everything in my power. One trusts it's enough."

With that he gave her a correct, rather superior nod, as if what she'd said had confirmed some latent suspicion, and returned to his paper. Julia took the occasion to look out the window at the passing scene. Somewhere in the far distance, smoke from a fire smudged the skyline. Both she and Braithwaite deserved to be rebuked for impropriety, Julia thought, although she wasn't sure who deserved it more.

THIRTY-SEVEN

JULY 1863

We got into Alexandria by two o'clock and went into camp on a cold, windy hillside. We were under orders to join our brigade at Manassas, but when we got to Alexandria we found Manassas in the possession of the enemy and we did not care to report to them. . . . Our road lay along in sight of Mt. Vernon and was a picture of desolation—the inhabitants few, primitive and ignorant, houses deserted and going to ruin, fences down, plantations overgrown, and everything indicating a decaying country finally ruined by war.

—Charles Francis Adams, Jr., to his father,
A Cycle of Adams Letters

"Charles says he is thinking of asking for a Negro regiment," Abby told her husband, looking up from the letter she was reading over tea. The kitchen maid had just whisked the breakfast crumbs from the table, but left behind a basket of scones, a jar of clotted cream, and a bowl of fresh strawberries. "He says it right here in his letter."

"Yes, I know, Abby," Charles replied. He set down his copy of the *Standard,* the opposition newspaper. Disraeli had neatly minced the Whigs into hash in Parliament again. "Charles wrote me, too."

"Do you think that's wise?"

"I'm not sure it's wise, but he thinks it must be done. The

freedmen should be given the chance to fight for their own people—or the whole war doesn't make sense. The most basic human right is the right to self-defense. The first Negro soldiers have performed bravely and with discipline."

Abby glared at him as if the war had been all his idea. "But won't that expose him to further danger? Hasn't Jeff Davis said they will hang any white officer caught leading colored troops? Surely you will advise him against it?" Abby's tone was sharp and stung like a wasp.

Charles reached across the table and placed his hand over hers. He felt at a loss for words. It was hard for a mother to accept that a grown son should be left to his own devices. From the letters he had received, it appeared that only God's grace or sheer dumb luck would preserve their boy. In his last engagement at Aldie's Gap in the Blue Ridge Mountains, Charles's cavalry regiment had lost thirty-two out of fifty-seven men—nine killed, twelve wounded, and eleven missing, probably captured. The young captain wrote his father that nearly every order he received contradicted the one before it, exposing the men to fresh danger. It seemed they could not possibly prevail in view of what Charles, Jr., called "the blunders and humbug of this war, the folly, treachery, incompetence, and lying!!!"

Death surrounded their son, who had had two horses shot and killed from under him. How could the minister reassure his wife that the future would be any less dangerous, when even those on the front line didn't think the Union could win?

"I can't tell him what to do, Abby. It's his choice," he pleaded now in a soft tone, in the hope that she might see reason. "But he's a good soldier, and a careful one. He's made it this far. I don't think he will take any risks that aren't essential."

Abby didn't speak, but quietly wiped away the tear rolling down her cheek.

Charles stood up and went around the table. He placed his arm around his wife's shoulders. "Don't cry, dearest. Our boy will be fine. Really he will," Charles whispered into her ear, hoping that he hadn't told a lie. He squeezed her to his chest.

Abby leaned her head against him and then seemed to steel herself. She tilted her head backward, looked up with a weak smile, and said, "At least he's kept his sense of humor. He says his trousers are so ragged from sitting in the saddle and so covered with grease that they would fry well."

Charles laughed, relieved at Abby's bravery. "It sounds like he's learned something about cooking. The army can't be all bad."

With a knock on the door, Kathleen entered the breakfast room carrying the unmistakable envelope of a telegram. "This just arrived, Mr. Adams."

Abby and Charles looked at each other with instantaneous alarm. He could read in her wide eyes the fear that leaped to his own mind.

"Thank you, Katie," he said, thinking few things were more vile than superstition. Of course it wouldn't be about Charles merely because they had been speaking of him. Nonetheless he grasped at the flap of the envelope with shaking hands. It tore, nicking his index finger with a paper cut, and he tried again, ripping the envelope with needless haste.

Charles scanned the lines quickly. His eyes lit up and a grin broke out on his face.

"What is it?" Abby demanded. Her eyes were still wide, but with the start of hope now rather than fear.

"A minor miracle, that's what it is," Charles said. "And on the Fourth of July, too. I can't believe they've done it!"

"Who? Who's done what?"

"Grant's taken Vicksburg, the Confederate fort on the Mississippi. The entire army under Pemberton was forced to surrender. Thirty thousand prisoners! But that's not all. General Meade turned back a Southern attack on Pennsylvania. Somewhere called Gettysburg. We took heavy casualties, but the Confederates were routed. Two major victories in the same day!"

Charles sat down abruptly in his chair. He couldn't stop smiling, and he reached over and squeezed Abby's hand on impulse. He felt happier and more intensely alive than he had in months. Euphoria spread like drink through his veins.

"Routed? Does this mean the war's over? Will the South surrender?"

"I don't know, Abby. Probably not. Or not yet. But it does mean there's real hope. And the British will recognize that the South is not the entity they take her for. Jeff Davis has *not* made a nation. William Gladstone will eat his words yet!"

"You said heavy casualties. Isn't Charles in Pennsylvania? Under Meade's command?" Abby's questions poured forth in a gush. She seemed unaffected by the joy that the telegram had produced in her husband.

"I don't know. I don't know the answers to any of those questions," he freely admitted. Charles's eyes glistened with enthusiasm. "But don't you see that there's a real possibility now that the Union will survive? We're winning! We can look Russell and Palmerston and Gladstone in the face with pride. The Union stands!"

"Pride? Pride?" Abby spat the word. "I care nothing for pride. I want to know if there is hope for our *son*." She covered her face with her hands and shook her head. "I know I should care about the others. But it's gone on too long. All I can think about is Charles and what may happen to him. Too many have died . . . I can't help it." Abby stood and fled the room with a sob. The door swung twice on its hinges and closed behind her.

Rooted to the spot in surprise, Charles looked after Abby and then at the table. The house was quiet and sunny and clean. The remains of an ample breakfast sat on the morning cloth. What was his son seeing at this moment? Charles wondered. Not scones and strawberries. The dead?

Charles, Jr., had recently written about a Rebel he'd ridden past. The man lay flat on his back on the grass, motionless and staring open-eyed, with one hand raised straight above his head as if he were asking a question in class—though his question had apparently been answered in the negative. Charles described the man as tall, slim, and athletic, with fine features and long, light hair that flowed from his high forehead in heavy waves. He was a "magnificent-looking 'secesh,'" Charles wrote. Magnificent, that is, until one saw the red mass of his lower belly and the stained trousers.

What kind of man had the boy from Quincy become, who could describe a mutilated victim of the war with no more apparent feeling than a professional butcher sizing up a dead hog? And what kind of person had the minister become, who could speak to a grieving, worried mother about the pride of winning? What had the war done to their humanity? What more would the war do before it was over? Charles looked again at the paper in his hand.

But there was hope. Real hope for the first time in more than two years—laid out in the cold type of a telegram—and that felt good.

Muffled sounds penetrated the quiet of the breakfast room. Footsteps on parquet indicated that Henry, who hadn't heard the news, was finally coming to breakfast. Charles stood up with the telegram in his fist and joy in his heart.

THIRTY-EIGHT

AUGUST 1863

*"My strength is quite failing me," I said in a soliloquy. "I feel
I cannot go much further. Shall I be an outcast again this night?
While the rain descends so, must I lay my head on the cold,
drenched ground? I fear I cannot do otherwise: for who will
receive me? . . . In all likelihood, though, I should die before
morning. And why cannot I reconcile myself to the prospect of
death? Why do I struggle to retain a valueless life? Because I
know, or believe, Mr. Rochester is living."*

—Charlotte Brontë, *Jane Eyre*

It had been the loneliest summer of Julia's life. The trip to
Washington had been a victory, though a humbling one. During their extended stay in the chaotic capital, Mr. Braithwaite had
made a strong argument to the overburdened War Department
and managed to get the State Department to intervene based on
Minister Adams's letter. Baxter Sams would be released to British
custody. Yet the weeks had been awkward, even painful. Braithwaite was perfectly correct in his public behavior, but whenever
they weren't in some office with an American official he exuded
doubt about her respectability. The junior consul wouldn't quite
look her in the eye—except for the time that he had had too much
wine with supper and suggested that she join him in the snug of
the hotel's barroom for a cordial. The conclusions he drew from
her admittedly unorthodox circumstances made Julia feel tawdry.
Sheer will kept her going when she was at her most discouraged

and humiliated. Upon returning to New York, she used her dwin-
dling funds to hire a chaperone for company whenever she went
out. Kathleen Busby was a pleasant woman of middle years whose
ample bosom rested at her waistline. Since then, impertinent
questions and looks had mostly ceased.

Mrs. Busby stood at her side now as Edward Archibald, the
senior consul, waited with Julia on the bare dock at Fort Hamilton.

"Ah, that must be them now. Excellent. I do say, when these
birdcages pop open they're generally spot on time," the consul
said, nodding in the direction of the island. "We should make the
afternoon mail packet back to the city."

Julia stared out across the Narrows, shielding her eyes with a
hand drawn up in salute. The noontime sun scattered dazzling
beads of light across the water. Then she saw what he meant. In
the bob of the waves, a rowboat was pulling away from the
prison, closing the silvery gap between Fort Lafayette and Staten
Island. There were three men—two in blue, one in gray. The
oarsman was rowing against the powerful tidal current with the
easy rhythm of a sailor, as if placing one foot in front of the other
on a paved surface. The launch drew nearer, and she could make
out their faces. The Confederate was an older man wearing a
blindfold; the man sitting opposite him cradled a rifle. Neither
was Baxter Sams. He wasn't in the boat.

Julia's heart sank. She could hardly believe her wretched luck.
After all her travails in Washington, they had won the release of
the wrong man. The long road had come to another dead end.

Julia hadn't had a letter from Baxter since leaving England.
Flora Bentley wrote her that they'd received nothing. Julia fretted
that something dreadful had happened until someone in Washington mentioned that prisoners were no longer allowed mail:
Union policy. But now, after all these months, her efforts were in
vain once again. A case of mistaken identity. "Sams is a power-
fully common name down South," a Federal clerk snapped when

Julia had pressed him to find the paperwork. "I got twenty if I got one."

The rowboat from Fort Lafayette butted up against the far end of the pier. Julia wound the drawstrings of her handbag, knotting and unknotting them around her fingers as the guard with the rifle poked from behind at the bearded, blindfolded man. The stooped prisoner labored up the rope ladder, missed the top rung, and for a moment dangled perilously above the watery green void. Then he grasped a metal stanchion and hauled his torso flat onto the pier. After a moment, he crawled forward, pushed himself to his knees, and stood up unsteadily, while his armed companion clambered up behind and threw a small sack onto the dock. Once both men gained the pier, the boat turned and began pulling back toward the island. The jailor handed the parcel to the prisoner and they started down the pier.

Julia had met Baxter on only three occasions, more than a year and a half earlier. But she knew with certainty that the frail-looking, emaciated prisoner in the blindfold and the ragged uniform was not the civilian doctor for whom she had defied her father and braved the Atlantic. As he approached, she could see that his clothing was dirty and frayed and his cheekbones pushed out sharply over a full, dark beard. He looked like an engraving from the Potato Famine of '46.

Would they send the poor man back to prison once she revealed their mistake? And what of Baxter? She didn't know if she could afford to start her search anew. Would she have to return to Belfield Manor disgraced as well as empty-handed?

"Are you the consul?" the guard from the launch asked.

"Yes, my good man, I certainly am. I take it this prisoner is Baxter Sams?"

"I'm not your good man," the stocky, acne-scarred guard retorted. "But this here is one Baxter Sams. I'm supposed to release him to your custody. The paperwork says he's a British citizen. Is that true or just another damned Rebel lie?"

The consul ignored the insult. "Do you have anything for me to sign?" he asked crisply. "We're intending to catch the mail packet."

"Sure do. Can't pick up a rock around here without signing something." The jailor looked at Julia and Mrs. Busby. "Will you excuse us, ladies?" He jerked his head in the direction of an administrative building. "This way," he told the consul.

"I beg your pardon," the prisoner said in a husky baritone. "As you see, I'm somewhat incapacitated, but I can still vouch for myself. H. Baxter Sams. May I inquire as to your name, sir?" The prisoner blindly put out his thin hand.

Julia gasped, disbelieving. The Southern voice and manner were unmistakable. She looked closer and saw that the man had Baxter's high forehead, and at short range it was now apparent that he was actually quite young. She could hardly accept that this filthy ruin was truly Baxter Sams. Facing him after months of no communication—so altered, so diminished—Julia felt paralyzed. Perhaps she had made a terrible mistake. Perhaps even he would feel so. His feelings may have changed as much as his outward appearance. The reunion that she had imagined and the reality that faced her were so different.

The consul grasped Baxter's hand with both of his and gave it a gentle shake. "Mr. Sams. At last! It's a pleasure to meet you, sir. We've been working on your case for nearly four months. I'm Edward Archibald, Her Majesty's consul in New York."

"Thank you, Mr. Archibald. I'm deeply grateful. I presume you've been in contact with my father and mother?"

"No. I'm afraid that it's been increasingly difficult to send letters through—ah, well, through the normal channels," the consul said lamely, alluding to the convoluted procedures for getting mail around the blockade, but also apparently unsure whether to acknowledge the unusual basis for Baxter's English citizenship. He looked over at Julia, as if querying her silence. She averted her gaze.

"Tell you what," the guard interrupted. "Why don't you two swap lies later? I've got better things to do. Sams, you set down over there while I sign you over to the Brits."

The consul bristled at the man's insolence, but apparently thought better of arguing with a surly jailor and turned instead to Julia and her companion. "Please excuse us then, if you will. I'll be right back. Mrs. Busby, will you kindly show Mr. Sams to the bench?"

Mrs. Busby hooked her arm through Baxter's. "You poor dear! Right over here. Watch your step now. That's it."

Julia mutely followed the pair as Mrs. Busby steered Baxter to a bench under the shade of a leafy sycamore, where he felt for the seat before taking it and then placed the sack that seemed to contain a few possessions at his feet. With every awkward moment that passed, it became harder to know what to say. She was stunned. Despite all that she had read in the newspapers, all that she had gleaned from his letters, she had had no idea that the ordeal had been this bad.

Mrs. Busby clucked sympathetically at him. "Are you all right?" She sat down next to Baxter. "Whatever happened to your poor eyes?"

"It's kind of you to ask, ma'am. It's just an inflammation that keeps acting up. The surgeon advised me to protect my eyes from dirt and bright light. It's awfully inconvenient, though. I do apologize if I leaned on you a'tall."

His Southern accent had deepened during the time in prison, Julia noticed.

"Can you still see?" Mrs. Busby asked.

"Yes, it's not affected my sight—at least I don't believe so. I'm hoping to obtain an eyewash as soon as I have my liberty. That should cure it. That and a few good meals."

"Well, now, that's fine news. But do you mean to tell me that you couldn't get the medicine you needed at Fort Lafayette?"

As Mrs. Busby had told Julia any number of times, her husband was a Democrat and a fierce critic of the administration. She stood ready to believe any tale of prisoner neglect. Lincoln had botched the whole secession crisis, as far as she was concerned.

"No, ma'am. They reserve the supplies for the front. Those fellows need it more than we do, for the most part."

So he wasn't blind. Julia was caught in such a whirlwind of emotions that she wasn't even sure how she should feel—though she was relieved for him. What difference had it made to Jane Eyre when she finally found Mr. Rochester? Would she, Julia, have been as selfless?

Mrs. Busby looked over at Julia. "Miss Birch. Have you nothing to say? Heavens to Betsy, I've rarely seen you so quiet."

Baxter, who until then seemed literally bent with weariness, straightened. "To whom are you speaking?"

"Why, to Miss Birch. Your sponsor."

Baxter reached up and pushed off the blindfold. He blinked hard in the bright light and peered as if looking through heavy fog. Then his eyes widened in shock.

"Julia!"

He spoke her name with hushed fervency. "How can it be? I thought Father . . . But it was you. How . . . ?"

Julia looked into his eyes. They were reddened and sore, but they shone with a passion unlike any she had ever seen.

"Is it really you?" she asked, afraid to believe, afraid of the gulf between them. She was ashamed for thinking it, but he looked like a tramp from the worst part of London. Her heart clenched with pity.

Mrs. Busby turned from one young person to the other, sighed in what was either consternation or understanding, and rose to walk down to the pier.

"In the flesh. What's left of it," Baxter answered in a stronger voice. He spread his arms to reveal his gaunt frame. "But, dear

God, what in the world are *you* doing at Fort Lafayette? I can hardly believe you aren't a mirage. A posy on a battlefield."

He stood and reached out his hand to draw her to the bench. "Sit . . . please," he said. "I don't trust my legs. The world's turned upside down."

Julia looked at his hand, remembering her bewilderment of the previous year, now compounded a thousandfold. Should a lady take a gentleman's hand? Was she a lady anymore? Was this ragged prisoner a gentleman?

Her father didn't think so. His angry letter had made that clear. *A man who turns his back on his country has no honor; a woman who turns her back on her family has no virtue.* The enormity of the risks she had taken—that Baxter might not be waiting for her, that he might not be right for her, that she might be ostracized forever—suddenly overwhelmed her. The Southerner was so changed.

Baxter sat down shakily and shifted his rough knapsack away from his feet.

"Please, join me."

Julia folded her hands and sat. Her face was pale.

"Tell me how you came here. Is your uncle with you? Or your father?"

"No." She paused, determined that he should know the truth at once. So many had looked askance at her since she arrived in America—and he might be as troubled by her conduct as she was by his appearance. "I came alone."

"You came *alone?*" he asked, his eyes now squinting against the bright light, then widening, afraid to miss anything.

"I was concerned that you might not make it. I thought I could help."

The simple statement appeared to leave him speechless. "You left your family behind to help me?" he finally asked, his words cracking with amazement. "I can't believe that you would do such a thing . . . you, the picture of decorum . . . to save my life." His voice quieted again, almost to a whisper, as if he were talking to himself, or perhaps to a phantom, not someone completely real. "Whatever were you thinking?"

Then, without explanation, Baxter looked around wildly and began tugging on his dusty boot. He swayed slightly but caught his balance by placing his foot across his knee. "Please, turn away!" he implored her. With a jerk, he pulled the boot off and then began knocking the heel against the pavement.

"Baxter! What in the world?" Julia cried in alarm. The stress of imprisonment and the surprise of seeing her had obviously been too much. "Please . . ."

"Never get too close to a prisoner who hasn't had his shoe off in a month," he said with a broad, unexpected smile.

She placed a hand on his sleeve to calm him. The fabric was stiff with dirt. "What are you doing?"

"Don't you worry. This should"—Baxter rapped the boot again, loosening the heel. He glanced at the ground, finishing his sentence—"make things right." Leaning over, he put down the boot and picked up the knapsack, which Julia now recognized as a square of rough sailcloth tied in a knot. He undid the packet, revealing a large, dusty book and a battered mess kit. Grabbing the shoe again and laying it across the books, he began prizing the scuffed heel away from the sole with an old fork.

Panicked, Julia glanced down at the waterline where Mrs. Busby was pretending to watch the boat traffic. She might know how to calm him. His behavior was so bizarre.

"There!" Baxter cried, dropping the shoe and allowing the book to slide unheeded to the ground.

He held up some tiny object. And then, as he rubbed it clean with a corner of his shirt, Julia realized it was a ring. A ring with a green stone. Baxter held it up to the sun, closed his hand over it, and turned to her.

"Julia Birch, there is something I've been wanting to ask you ever since you stepped on my toe two years ago," he said with a light in his eyes. Confidence had returned to his voice, the lilt of which she had imagined so many times while reading and rereading his letters.

But then he hesitated. His eyes blazed with confusion, hurt, then sudden understanding, and he looked at her with an intense expression that she found unreadable.

He glanced down, grimaced, and shifted his unshod foot under the bench to hide the brown, rotted sock. The limp boot lay flat and broken on the ground now, a cobbler's reject. Loose letters spilled from the old book. "You didn't say hello all that time," he finally observed after a long pause. His voice was even quieter than when he'd first said her name. "You watched while I crawled onto the dock, bellyfirst, like a dog. And then you said nothing. Nothing at all. I know I must look pretty awful. I know my clothes are a sight. But why didn't you speak until that lady asked you?"

Julia flushed. "I'm sorry," she said, still at a loss, not knowing what terrible emotion might seize him next. "I . . . I wasn't sure it was you."

"Well, it's me." He looked away, silent.

In the extended, painful moments that followed, the distant sounds of boat traffic and birds suggested a fullness to life elsewhere that excluded those on the bleached and barren prison dock. Julia had no idea what he was thinking. What had he intended to ask her? Surely the ring meant something. Her eyes darted to the letters spilling from the book on the ground, and she realized that they were the ones she had written from London.

"Why didn't you just send someone?" Baxter asked, his voice harsh. "You wouldn't have had to see this. I don't need your damn pity, you know." He shook his head as if clearing cobwebs. "Please forgive me," he began again, but coolly. "I shouldn't have said that. You don't deserve it, not after all your trouble. It's just that I was about to make a grave error. This is a lot to take in. I beg your apology."

"An error? I see," Julia said, finally comprehending his change of mood and why he had stopped short at completing his question.

He must have thought of marrying her until the full meaning of her statement caught up with him—until he realized her disgrace. What else could account for the ring he had hidden and the letters he'd saved? Was he ashamed for himself, or for her? Scandalized at the way she had thrown herself at him, traveling halfway around the world alone and exposed? *A woman who turns her back on her family has no virtue.* Once compromised, a woman's reputation was irretrievable. Julia had known this all her life. It was *fact*, like the boiling point of water or the sinking of the Spanish Armada. He must feel that her character was as soiled as his tattered garments—and more permanently stained.

Julia felt a slow, searing burn rise up in her throat. She wouldn't inquire what Baxter had wanted to ask. It hardly mattered.

"Thank you for helping me," Baxter said with a ghost of his old smile. "I don't know how I can repay you. My family and I are deeply in your debt."

Prison hadn't completely dimmed the Virginia polish. Apparently the elegant gentleman she had met in London was still under there.

"You're welcome," Julia replied, but her brevity was an unspoken rebuke.

She stood, drawing herself to her full, dignified height. The wind off the water whipped her hair across her face, but she hardly felt it. Her uncle would give her a home, even if her father didn't welcome her back. And she would never again be under his control, like the poultry man's daughter. But Sir Walter had been right about one thing: America had absolutely nothing to offer.

"I believe I shall fetch Mrs. Busby," Julia said. She enunciated the phrase as carefully as a diction lesson, the words a polite and meaningless formulation. "Mr. Archibald should be nearly finished. You'll soon be free to go."

Clear at last in her mind, Julia turned to the wharf and away from the man who, until then, had been the object of all her hopes and striving. She would be on the first ship back to England.

"Wait," she heard Baxter call out hoarsely behind her, and then more loudly, "Wait a minute, please."

She stopped and gazed back over her shoulder.

Baxter was standing tall, his shoulders thrown back, his eyes insistent. He hesitated a moment, but then crossed the short distance that separated them and brushed the curls back from her face.

"If I don't ask this now, I'll regret it for the rest of my life," he said in a voice that was both stern and tender. "My dignity is all that I have left, but it's not worth the one thing I really care about. I know that in Mayfair my appearance would make dogs bark and the police turn around. I'd be arrested for vagrancy or thrown in the workhouse. But regardless of how I look, Julia, you have to hear me out."

Julia fixed Baxter with a glare. She knew it was irrational and unfair—she really had been dismayed at his appearance—but how dare he accuse her of such prejudice? She had crossed the sea for him!

"Could you do that, for at least a moment? Just forget your pity and your damned British snobbery?" he persisted.

Julia whirled to face him squarely. "Pity? Snobbery?" She strode to the bench, snatched up the ruined boot, and shook it at him. "Do you really think that I care about *this* . . . or whether your clothes are clean after a year in prison? Or what I look like to the people in this mad country? If I were in thrall to appearances, would I be waiting outside a prison in New York? Or have left my family to help you? I love you, damn it." She threw the boot aside and sat down on the bench, arms folded in anger and frustration.

Baxter gaped with surprise, then burst into a brilliant smile. "My God," he said with a laugh of pure joy. "I should have known—but you never said so."

The Virginian pinched the emerald ring between his thumb and forefinger, took a deep breath, and lowered a knee onto the pavement. "In that case, Miss Birch," he said as he looked up into her face, "will you marry me? Provided I bathe first?"

Julia felt giddy and breathless. He was every bit the Baxter whose courage in pursuing what mattered had drawn her three thousand miles. And, contrary to all logic, he still respected her. He'd come through the torment bruised but not broken, with even his sense of humor intact. Star-crossed lovers needn't go mad or perish tragically. Half of English literature could go in the dustbin.

Julia leaned forward to touch Baxter's cheek. His skin was cool with the salty breeze. There was no sandpaper stubble, no cat's tongue roughness, only a soft, long beard. She stroked the side of his face and cupped his chin in her hand. Baxter closed his eyes and inclined his head, nestling into her palm. The masculine cut of his jaw underneath the dark whiskers sent an unfamiliar tingle racing from her toes to her throat. Her heart was pounding. She would never give him up, no matter what.

"I can hardly believe . . ."

Baxter opened his eyes, straightened his head, and gazed at her intently, demanding an answer to his question. She met his look with a whisper of a smile, and then a dazzling one.

"Yes. Of course I will. Yes."

THIRTY-NINE

SEPTEMBER 1863

*I wanted to hug the army of the Potomac. I wanted to get
the whole of the army of Vicksburg drunk at my expense. . . .
It was on Sunday morning as I came down to breakfast
that I saw a telegram from the Department
announcing the fall of Vicksburg.*

—Henry Adams to his brother Charles, in Virginia,
A Cycle of Adams Letters

Charles thought that Vicksburg and Gettysburg would turn the tide. Grant had split the Confederacy like a melon, cutting off supplies and reinforcements from the west. Meade had magnificently foiled Lee's attempt to take the war home to the North. The news of both battles had broken upon the legation like a brass bugle of deliverance. The British would *have* to see that the Union would prevail.

But apparently they did not.

After news of the Northern victories in mid-July, Charles and Thomas Dudley unleashed a flood of new affidavits attesting to the true purpose of the Laird Rams and insisting that the foreign secretary impound them. Now, at the opening of September, the ironclad warships were anchored in the heavily trafficked Mersey Channel undergoing a final outfitting. One of them, the *294*, had just completed sea trials and was poised to sail. Dudley reported that its ram glistened in the water at the Liverpool christening like an unsheathed sword. James Bulloch, the Confederate purchasing agent and spy, had been in the crowd, surrounded by Scottish bodyguards. There wasn't a sliver of doubt that Britain, in its persistent malignity toward the Union, had colluded with the Confederacy to make war upon the North. The release of the Laird Rams—the most deadly, formidable naval vessels ever built—constituted but the latest and gravest act. As Charles had written to Lord Russell in July, using the strongest possible prose short of insult, "All the appliances of British skill to the arts of destruction appear to have been resorted to for the purpose of doing injury to the people of the United States."

What more could he have said? "This is war"? Since then, two tense months had passed, during which Charles and Dudley had striven to compile every last shred of evidence. Lord Russell had now sent what seemed to be his final answer.

No. The foreign secretary would not intervene.

Charles studied the photograph of the *294* that Dudley had secretly made and given him a couple of days earlier. The Confederates needed no more than a month to arm the ironclad before it could attack Washington from the Potomac, or New York from the Hudson. He felt as if he were holding a picture of the end. It exhausted him.

The door to the drawing room opened. Henry looked in. His hair was tousled, as if he had been outdoors in a breeze. He was carrying a letter.

"Father? Mr. Dudley has arrived. Are you ready for him?"

Charles looked at his son. He didn't know what he would have done without Henry. The minister resisted favoring any of his children and would never knowingly have expressed a preference among them. His eldest sons, John Quincy II and Charles Francis, Jr., had accomplished much: one as a wartime aide to the governor of Massachusetts, the other as a decorated cavalry officer. Henry's only service, which no one outside the family would ever know, had been to help his father—copying documents, enduring dull parties where the good and great ignored him, patiently listening to Charles's worried musings late into the night. Now, when all was lost, when the prospect for poor America was so dark, Charles loved Henry more than ever.

"Yes, I am. Please show Dudley in. You'll join us, of course, won't you?"

"Couldn't tear me away, Chief," Henry answered with a smile. He smoothed his hair with a hand, pulled the bell cord to signal Kathleen, and then handed Charles the missive. "You'll want to read this later on," he said, taking his usual seat at the writing table. "Baxter's been released. He's in New York—engaged to Miss Birch."

Charles's spirits lifted for a moment to know that some good had come of his efforts. He thought of when he had met Abby and their own engagement years earlier. And then of their boy, Charles, Jr.—fighting in Virginia. He numbly laid the letter on the table. None of it had been enough to end the war.

The Liverpool consul strode into the drawing room. "Good to see you, Mr. Adams. I trust you and Mrs. Adams had a pleasant holiday?" He shook the minister's hand.

"It's kind of you to ask, Mr. Dudley. Under the circumstances it would be hard to qualify any trip within Britain as pleasant, though we celebrated our thirty-fourth wedding anniversary and Mrs. Adams found considerable relief from the congestion of London, thank you."

"I'm glad to hear it. I know she has suffered terribly from the summer air."

"Indeed. And how was your trip down from Liverpool? I do appreciate your coming."

"Fine, sir, just fine. Train right on time. I'm sorry I couldn't get here earlier. I was up in Glasgow having another look at the vessel in the Thompson shipyard. As I told you last month, it's a copy of the Laird Rams. Didn't get your message till I got back."

Dudley finished his statement with an air of hurry, apparently conscious that the minister had something more on his mind than the latest update on British perfidy. The telegram Charles had sent was terse, even cryptic.

"Yes, well, I wanted to inform you in person, Dudley. I didn't want to send this the usual way."

He picked up a copy of the letter that he had written to Lord Russell three days earlier and handed it to Dudley.

The consul took the sheet of elegant bond, inscribed with Henry's careful penmanship, and scanned the letter, stopping to read aloud the phrases that leaped from the page: *It is impossible that any nation retaining a proper degree of self-respect could tamely submit . . . I have no idea that Great Britain would do so for a moment . . . I prefer to desist from communicating to your lordship lest I should contribute to aggravate difficulties already far too serious . . . I transmit by the present steamer a copy of your note for the consideration of my government. . . .*

Dudley looked up with a look of puzzlement. "What does this mean?"

"Russell has turned down our request. His reply means it's over. We have at most a month left in England."

"Why a month?"

"It's an average. I've noticed that's about the time it takes for a dispatch to reach Washington by steamship and for the government's reply to get back to London. My final instructions should be here within thirty days or so. And I assure you that nothing could induce me to stay here one hour after duty ceases to demand it."

"So that's what you were doing this morning, Father?" Henry asked. "Calculating averages? Was that why you asked for the year's correspondence?"

"Yes," Charles answered simply.

"So you think President Lincoln will recall you to Washington?" Dudley asked.

"I think he has no choice. Lord Russell has refused to act on the evidence that's available."

"Isn't it possible that he might yet stop the ships?"

"I don't think so," Charles said. "Despite the rumors that whip through London, Russell's letter made it frightfully clear that he won't stay the Lairds' hand. He says that the lawyers have concluded the case is nothing but hearsay."

"Hearsay!" Dudley exploded. He glowered at Charles, as if speaking to Russell directly. "My God, we've seen it with our own eyes! Tell the men who've watched their ships go down in flames that the British construction program is only hearsay!"

"The Lairds apparently maintain that Monsieur Bravay is the rams' legal owner," Charles replied. "The Frenchman now claims to be buying the ships instead of Bulloch."

"But it doesn't matter who the legal owner is. They'll turn the rams over to Bulloch as soon as they've cleared the coastline. I saw him on the dock the day the *294* hit the water, for Christ's sake." Dudley's face flushed red and he ran his fingers roughly through his hair, causing it to stand on end.

"Yes, but Bulloch's been supremely clever. The paperwork supports his case down to the last rivet," Charles pointed out.

"It's all false!"

"I'm perfectly aware of that, Thomas. Perfectly aware—as anyone not determined to avoid the truth would be. That's what accounts for my letter to Russell." Charles rose from his chair. "May I?" he asked the consul, reaching for the copy.

Dudley handed the letter back.

The minister read the carefully chosen words at the heart of the missive: *"It would be superfluous in me to point out to your lordship that this means war."*

I'll meet you and raise you, Charles thought. It was his highest card, the one he had been holding in reserve and had hoped never, ever to play. War.

A profound gloom settled instantly upon the room as each man contemplated the implications. Of course there was no honorable or realistic alternative but war. The British had left the

Union no choice. Lincoln's government would be forced to act in self-defense, and it was ready to do so.

Charles spoke again, voicing the mental calculations being made by his son and by the consul. "Seward told me after the *Alexandra* case in July that he was ready to bombard British ports to destroy blockade-runners. Including Liverpool, if need be. I didn't tell Lord Russell about Seward's threat, for fear of pushing the Foreign Ministry over the edge into belligerence. But I'm afraid the latest developments mean the British are going to learn their mistake the hard way. Once they launch the rams, there will be no turning back. Today's *Morning Post* suggested that the Foreign Ministry still might stop the ships, but it's the rumors we've heard before."

The minister sighed heavily and began to pace the room. He went on, as if rationalizing the grave decision. "This rebellion has been kept alive by the British from the very first day. If it hadn't been for hundreds of English steamers running munitions and supplies, Confederate troops would be fighting without a stitch on their backs or a bullet in their guns. . . .

"Not to mention the commerce raiders!" he continued, his volume rising. "The Confederates have run their Financial Department, their Commissary Department, their Ordnance Department, and their Naval Department from the shores of the British Isles. The Crown's neutrality is an absolute travesty—and Russell knows it. His lordship is entirely complicit!"

Henry and Dudley listened without responding. Charles had never voiced his opinion of British policy so openly or so forcefully. The minister spoke as if he were delivering the closing argument in a long, bruising, contentious trial. He paced the length of the room with a troubled expression, looking less tired and more angry with every step.

"And now it's come to this. Let's face it, the war on the seas is being conducted and carried out against us by Englishmen. That's the bald truth. Russell and Palmerston deceive themselves if they think we will permit matters to go any further than they have already. We have to act and, believe me, no one in the diplomatic community will be surprised. Now is the time. Before it's too late."

Charles put a hand over his chin. His side whiskers had gone white during the two and a half years they'd spent in England. He stopped walking for a moment, eyebrows cocked, head angled to one side, thinking through the logistics.

"They'll defeat us on the ocean, I'm afraid. We can expect that. The British navy is far superior to ours. But at least we're situated better than we were in 1812, when we had only seventeen armed ships to their thousand. Seventeen, if you can imagine! Lincoln's commissioned nearly everything afloat. We're up to almost four hundred now, I believe. At least we've had some time to prepare."

The minister furrowed his brow. "Of course, they'll do the most damage on the seacoast. The smaller ports will be destroyed. I don't think Boston and New York will be under attack—at least not at first. The British will target the more vulnerable towns. Perhaps Nantucket. And Providence. Or they'll burn Portland again. Of course, they might try to torch the White House as they did in 1812, but I think it's more likely that they'll let the Confederates take care of that with their new ironclad rams. Washington is only lightly defended. The Rebels will sweep the Potomac. Britain, though, Britain will hit New England."

He resumed his anguished pacing. "We'll have the advantage on land, of course. They'll never beat us on our own soil. Never! Lincoln will probably march troops into Canada. He ought to. We should be able to capture some provinces there. That will give them something to think about."

Charles stopped dead. He looked at Dudley and then at Henry, without really seeing them. "But the lives lost!" he groaned. He shook his head and clenched his hands into fists.

"There's no way to calculate what both sides will lose in the way of lives, or treasure, or damage to ship and shore. A two-front war will certainly finish the Union. Anglo-American friendship will be a dead letter. Slavery will go on as before. What *can* Lord Russell be thinking? Is he insane?"

Charles's grandfather had negotiated the Treaty of Paris of 1783. His father had signed the Treaty of Ghent in 1814. In what continental city would the next truce with the British be forged? What fragment of the United States would be left to ratify it? His mind ranged over the scope of the coming hostilities and how they might end. The terms were what mattered now.

He doubted that he would be asked to help. He had failed in the most important mission of his life, though he didn't know how it could have ended any differently. He had staved off the collision as long as any man could—perhaps too long.

Dudley, clearly unnerved by the minister's distress, stood and began pacing, too. Charles had never before betrayed anything but calm. Rays of Indian summer poured hotly through the swagged drapes, and the air was thick, as if gathering for a thunderstorm. Dudley walked to a side window and placed his two palms on the sash.

"Would you mind if I let in a breeze, sir?"

"No, of course not," Charles said, waving a hand absently.

Dudley lifted the window, letting in the muffled sounds of the street below along with the air. The rumble of a passing carriage filled the room. The Liverpool consul looked out, apparently arrested by the sight of the vehicle. The rumbling stopped.

"Mr. Adams. It looks like one of the queen's messengers."

"What did you say, Mr. Dudley?" Charles asked, turning around.

"I believe there's a queen's messenger at the door. The coach bears her insignia."

Charles strode rapidly to the window and looked down. The courier had disappeared under the portico. The bell rang downstairs and, moments later, a knock sounded on the door of the office.

"Mr. Adams?" Kathleen said. "There's a letter for you from, well, you know who. That man."

"Thank you, Katie."

Charles took the envelope from the housekeeper and looked at Henry and Dudley. He paused, fearful of what was inside. The last letter he had sent to Lord Russell had virtually declared a state of war between their countries. The nation's fate might be sealed inside this slim envelope.

"Open it, Father. It's better to know," Henry said. "Then we can pack."

Charles broke the red wax seal.

Russell was brief. His lordship wished to inform the minister that Her Majesty's government was still actively considering the matter of the rams. An effort to detain them could be foreseen. The earl signed off in the flowery language that diplomats used to mask the reality that one country had the power to swat another like a fly: *I have the honor to be, with the highest consideration, sir, your most obedient, humble servant,* etc., etc.

The letter was cautious and vague, but in Victorian England, what wasn't said was as important as what was.

Charles inhaled sharply, as if someone had jerked him back from a precipice by the scruff of his neck just as his feet slipped at the edge. He looked up from the letter, conscious that his fingers were trembling. "I don't believe it," he said. "I just don't believe it."

"What does he say, Father?"

Charles looked at his son, a slow smile dawning across his face.

"Lord Russell sends his compliments with typical British economy, Henry, but I believe the old man has decided to stop the rams!" Charles laughed out loud, and waved the paper overhead with the glee of a boy. "We've done it!"

"My God! Stop the rams? Congratulations, Mr. Adams! Well done! Well done!" Dudley said. The consul gripped Charles's hand and the two men shook passionately, reluctant to stop, half hanging on to each other.

"Congratulations to you, Mr. Dudley. Your fine work made it possible."

"Thank you, sir, thank you," Dudley replied, his ears rimmed coral with pleasure.

Charles turned to his son, who had risen from his desk. He saw Henry anew. The boy's face had grown fuller during their trial, his gaze steadier. His chin was firmly set, and the beard under the skin colored his cheeks evenly now, no longer the patchwork of youth. It struck Charles that Henry had matured into a serious man in the two years abroad, finally unafraid of what others thought. He wondered if his other sons had aged as much. What did they look like now? The years had been bitter, but at last they were worth it. England would not fight the Union, and she would stop aiding the South.

"Congratulations, Father. Your letter must have finally awoken the cabinet. They can't want a fight. What purpose could it serve?"

"I believe you're right, Henry."

"Russell blinked first," Henry said with conviction. "You've saved us a war, Father. You may have saved the Union."

"I don't know about that, Henry. The Sphinx is more easily interpreted than John Russell. The Divine Being alone could have softened his stone heart. But whatever the cause, it means we will be staying more than a month. With the foreign secretary finally seeing reason, we could be here for the duration. At least your mother and I will be."

An unspoken question hung in the air.

Charles knew that if Henry stayed, he would forfeit any chance whatsoever of heroism. He would command no regiment and the war would end without him. No one would know his name, the name that weighed on every Adams child yearning to slay Goliath and save the world.

They were entering an entirely new phase in America's charged, tangled, all-important relationship with Britain. Henry's optimism and faith gave Charles courage every single day, and the minister hoped that his son would choose to see their mission through, rather than enlist in Lincoln's army. He needed Henry, but he wouldn't ask again.

The younger Adams met his father's eyes. Henry's flinty intelligence, so clear in his shining expression, reminded Charles of the portrait of John Quincy in their library back home in Massachusetts. The two men were of a kind, the lineal heirs of Lexington and Concord.

"Don't worry, Chief," Henry replied with the wry grin that made Charles's heart sing. "Lord knows misery needs company."

AUTHOR'S NOTE

This story is based on the lives of the Adamses, as recorded in their memoirs and wartime correspondence. Thomas Haines Dudley, James D. Bulloch, Samuel Edwards, John Bright, Baron de Brunnow, and, of course, Lord John Russell are all real historical figures. The quotes at the start of each chapter are genuine, and the events described are drawn as faithfully as fiction permits from memoirs, newspaper reports, and historical accounts.

Julia Birch and H. Baxter Sams are entirely fictional, although the character of Baxter is based loosely on Henry Adams's Southern classmates at Harvard, including General Robert E. Lee's second son, William Henry Fitzhugh "Rooney" Lee. Julia's and Baxter's adventures are my creation, aided by accounts of the American Civil War. Among the best are the letters of Charles Francis; Charles Francis, Jr.; and Henry Adams as collected in *A Cycle of Adams Letters*. The other invaluable source, and a masterpiece of American literature, is *The Education of Henry Adams*, written by the man himself. The Adamses tell their own story with immediacy and verve, and I wish to acknowledge that I have borrowed many of their phrases and observations.

Abraham Lincoln, the Great Emancipator, was assassinated in 1865. Alexander II of Russia, liberator of the serfs, was assassinated in 1881. Both leaders had endured numerous death threats. The legacy of each man was a strengthened national commitment to human freedom and dignity. Lincoln, especially, gave what at Gettysburg he called "the last full measure of devotion." Today, a statue of Abraham Lincoln stands in Parliament Square, across from Westminster Abbey.

Great Britain's prime minister Henry John Temple, 3rd Viscount Palmerston, also died in 1865, and Lord John Russell became the new leader of Parliament. After the Civil War, Charles Francis Adams helped negotiate a settlement between the United States and the United Kingdom in 1872 for the damages resulting from British shipbuilding. England agreed to pay $15 million to settle the so-called Alabama claims.

In 1925, more than fifty years after the events depicted in this novel, Stanford University professor Ephraim Adams, a founder of the Hoover Institution on War, Revolution, and Peace, obtained access to the previously closed papers of Russell, Palmerston, and Gladstone. From these he discovered, contrary to all that Charles Francis or Henry Adams ever knew, that the British government had decided to detain the Laird Rams just prior to receiving Minister Adams's final war threat, and not as a consequence of it. However, this does not diminish Adams's record of service or the critical role that his determined diplomacy played in stopping the warships, keeping Britain neutral, and preserving the Union.

James D. Bulloch was the uncle of President Theodore Roosevelt, who was a child during the Civil War. Teddy visited "Uncle Jimmie" in England in the 1880s, where he persuaded the older man to write his memoir. Bulloch never sought, or received, a pardon for his role as a Confederate agent. He died in Liverpool, laid to rest under the epitaph "An American by birth, an Englishman by choice."

The same year that England settled the Alabama claims, Parliament passed a ballot act allowing for the secret vote. By 1885, Britain had nearly universal male suffrage, fifteen years after the U.S. Constitution's Fifteenth Amendment granted suffrage to adult men of all races—at least in principle. In 1870, Britain passed the Married Women's Property Act, which allowed women to own their own property, and in 1882 granted them a legal identity separate from that of their husbands. In 1918 and 1920, respectively, women in Great Britain and America won the ballot. Not until 1964 and 1965, however, did civil rights legislation in the U.S. provide for the full enforcement, at last, of the constitutional protections concerning race purchased at such great price in the Civil War.

The Adamses had many children whose spirit of public service has burned bright for more than two centuries, through every uncertain trial. In the Iraq War after the attacks of September 11, 2001, the first American naval officer to give his life was a twenty-seven-year-old Californian on a special joint assignment with the Royal Navy. Related to two presidents, and buried under two flags, his name was Thomas Mullen Adams.

ACKNOWLEDGMENTS

I wish to acknowledge friends and family in Ireland and America who supported or advised me while I was writing this novel, including Richard Aldous, Myra Burton, Maurice Bric, Betsy Crimmins, Paula Harvey, Amy Hoffman, Sue Kirk, Joyce Lane, Clive Lee, Michael Morse, Paul Ross, and Clare and Desmond O'Halloran. Literary agent Jodie Rhodes gave me invaluable editorial advice and the confidence to push on. The staff at iUniverse were unfailingly encouraging, especially Kathryn Robyn and Mandy Sparks. Marc Selverstone of the University of Virginia helped me at a critical juncture, and Michele Rubin of Writers House saved the day—cheered on by Brianne Johnson. Caitlin Alexander of Random House has been every writer's dream of an editor. I would also like to thank Leon and Joyce Nower, friends and mentors for forty years, whom I can never thank enough. My mother, Joanne Davis, shared a love of books that inspires me to the present. While we lived abroad, my teenage daughter, Victoria Shelby, made many insightful observations on the nature of romance, and my son, Gregory, acted as my right-hand man in our adventures across Europe. My husband, Daniel Hoffman, is my finest critic and my best friend.

PHOTO: BETSY CRIMMINS

ELIZABETH COBBS HOFFMAN, Ph.D., is a winner of the Allan Nevins Prize for literary distinction in the writing of history. She holds the Dwight Stanford Chair in American foreign relations at San Diego State University and is the author of *All You Need Is Love: The Peace Corps and the Spirit of the 1960s*, among other books of history. Dr. Hoffman is a native Californian, a graduate of Stanford University, a political commentator, a mother, and an expert pie maker. She wrote *Broken Promises* while teaching in Dublin, Ireland, on a Fulbright grant. This is her first novel.

www.elizabethcobbshoffman.com